Edgewood Village

BY LINDA KOENIG

Edgewood Village

Dedicated to my mom, the first goddess I ever knew and the one who believed I could do anything.

Dedicated to the goddesses; AP, CH, CN, BW, NT for your friendships and being a beautiful muse for my imagination.

Dedicated to all the goddesses in my life. You have filled my crown and I am fortunate beyond measure because of you.

"I would rather walk with a friend in the dark
than alone in the light."

—Helen Keller

Edgewood Village

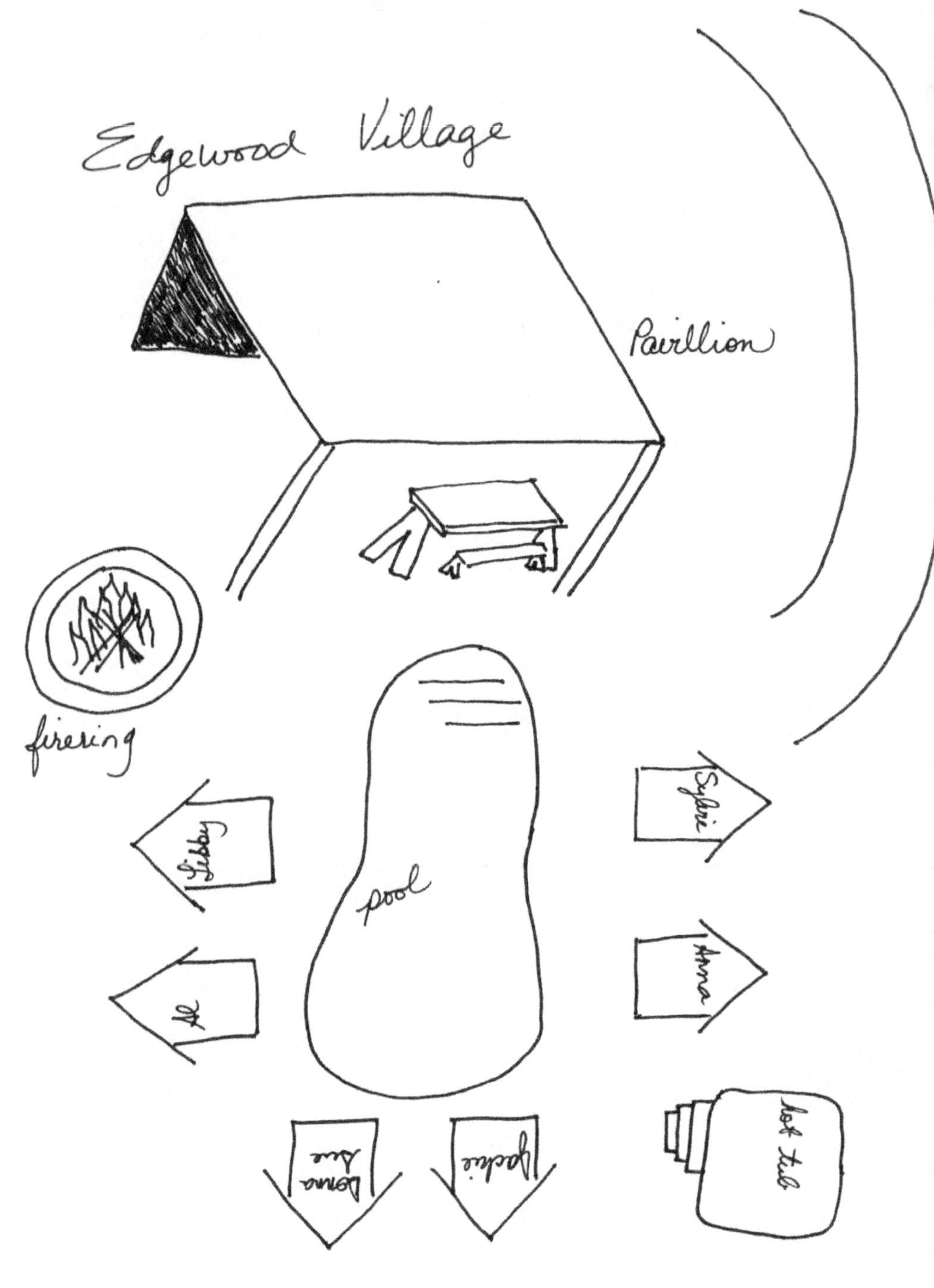

Anna Perry: Goddess of Maternal Love, the nucleus of devoted friends. A career educator, Anna made a home with Tony Perry on beautiful Edgewood Avenue in historic Columbia. They shared a love for the old home and worked together to restore it to its original glory. Anna and Tony raised two beautiful daughters; Ellie and Mia. Anna is intuitive, thoughtful, intelligent, creative, a steel magnolia.

Sylvie Russell: Goddess of Passion and the bold orator. Sicilian-bred; Sylvie worked as an advocate for those with marginalized voices. Married to the love of her life and soul mate Chip Russell, they have three sons; Alex, Danny, and David. Sylvie loves big, talks loud, adores food, celebrates all holidays, and cannot abide being told to calm down.

Al (Aunella LeVisa) Schmitt: Goddess of protection and guardian to all. Al married Mack Schmitt, 15 years her senior and they raised two children; Nathan and Marie. A career educator for 33 years, Al loved teaching, mentoring, and caring for students. Outdoorsy, strong, and a worrier, Al is happiest when doing things for others. Her devotion to friends and family knows no bounds.

Jackie (Galloway) Algorotti: Goddess of fun and good times. Jackie's natural beauty and fun-loving spirit make her the life of every party, even if it wasn't a party to begin with. Jackie has two children; Seb and Charlotte with her ex-husband Sebastian Galloway and married Logan Algorotti two days before her 50th birthday. Her signature laugh and face-splitting grin are memorable to all who meet her.

Donna Sue Bryant: The Intrepid Goddess. Self-reliant and assured, Donna Sue enjoyed a successful career in property management with her life partner, Ron Lake. A tall, slender blond with piercing blue eyes made men and women take notice-no matter what her age or theirs. Donna Sue is intelligent, planful, poised, confident.

Libby Stevenson: The Goddess of love. Leaving her childhood sweetheart in the small town where she grew up, she set out to find an exciting life full of love and adventure. Working many different jobs over the years, Libby is best at seeing the good in everyone she meets. Libby is smart, beautiful, sensitive, indecisive.

Mia Perry: Goddess in training. Anna's youngest daughter and the landlord of Edgewood Village. Mia is independent, strong-willed, and a wonderful gardener and businesswoman. Beautiful but guarded, Mia learns about love and loss with the help of the goddesses.

Sylvie

What a day. No one should ever have to endure such a day. Sylvie looked out the limo window at the scenery sliding by. It should be dark out, low clouds that barely skim the earth. There should be rain dripping, falling, pooling, sinking. The air should be heavy, weighted. But no. The sunshine, clear sky, daffodils, and blooming magnolia trees seemed an insult to her senses. The beautiful day was obscene and grotesque. Her son Alex, reached across the seat and patted her knee while his wife Meredith wore her usual pinched expression. Sylvie gave him a watery smile. Her son Danny and his girlfriend/wife looked out uncomfortable, unable to face the stark grief ravaging Sylvie's face. David, her youngest son, was unafraid to face his mom's grief but didn't have a clue how to help console her.

The limo came to a gradual stop and doors began opening. Once outside the car, the brilliance of the day made some wince while others remarked on the beauty of it before they could pull the words back. Sylvie walked with her sons up the gentle rise to the tent that had been erected. She saw the shiny box. Chip. Chip was in the box and she would never again see him on this earth. She felt her side vision tunnel gray until the only thing she could see was the box. She could hear someone talking but couldn't understand the words. Her blood began to pound loudly in her ears, drowning out all sound. She thought about Chip and how the sickness had racked his body and made him so weak he couldn't hold his head up for a sip of the precious coffee he had drunk all day. She thought of how he fought and struggled for each breath. No one should ever suffer that. Not Chip. Chip with his sideways grin and lank of red-brown hair that fell over his forehead until he swung it back. Chip with his easy-going attitude and a kind word for everyone. Chip who could bring Sylvie down from a fiery tirade leveled at a politician, neighbor or even one of their children who dared contradict the ideals that she was so sure of. Even her dearest friends would feel the need to appeal to Chip when they found themselves crossways with her. Chip who fed the squirrels, sang to his dogs, and always left a 25% tip for servers. Chip dying. Chip in that goddamned box.

She thought back to how they had met. It took some doing, but she had finally convinced her parents to let her move into an apartment close to campus. Being the youngest in a family of seven and considering they were a very close, tight-knit Sicilian family, it was difficult for her parents to understand or accept her desire to live anywhere but the family home. In the old country, it was typical and even expected to have two and three generations living together. Sylvie knew that no matter how loud the discussions got, by next Sunday's dinner all would be forgiven. All Buono. She and her two roommates had a ball buying used furniture and setting their potted plants in the windows. They were intrigued by the two guys in the next apartment. Try as they may, they couldn't seem to do more than pass each other at the door of the apartment building. All three girls were interested in knowing more about them. One, Luke, was very tall with dark hair and a booming laugh. Sylvie couldn't help but wonder where his people came from. He could be a cousin with his olive skin and big personality. The other roommate was Americano and much quieter, Chip. His reddish-brown hair always needed cutting but he had a crooked smile that made Sylvie think of him long after he was out of sight. After several weeks of frustration, Sylvie decided to take things into her own hands. Finding the breaker box, she flipped the switch to the kitchen and waited until she heard the two guys in the hall. Opening the door to the apartment as if she was surprised to find them there, she explained that she was having trouble with the toaster oven. Luke smiled and said, "You need Chip for that job. He's the handy one. The only thing I know how to fix is a sandwich," and disappeared into the apartment across the hall. Sylvie was suddenly nervous and found herself laughing too much while Chip looked around the kitchen flipping the light switch off and on. When nothing happened, he asked where the breaker box was and Sylvie play-acted like she didn't know what that was but if it was the gray panel in the hallway then right this way. It took only a second for Chip to flip the breaker on and the lights in the kitchen and the toaster oven came to life. Sylvie laughed again and offered to share the meal she was reheating with him to thank him for saving the day. Chip accepted and they enjoyed the Pasta alla Norma and cannoli fresh from her momma's kitchen. Years later when Chip teased her that it was her mother's cooking that brought them together Sylvie admitted to flipping the breaker switch. It never took much to make them reach for each other and the fond memory of that first encounter was more than enough reason to forget the rest of the day and take each other to bed. In the aftermath of their lovemaking, Chip twisted around so he could see Sylvie's beautiful face and with his crooked grin, he confessed that he had known all along about her ruse to get him into her apartment.

Back in the present and forgetting that she wasn't alone, Sylvie let out a moan. It was long and low and full of pain. Alex put his arm around her and Danny leaned in to look at his mother's face. Both men could see their mother but they could also feel her shrinking into herself, pulling farther away from them even as she sat in a chair closely spaced to their own. Sylvie let out another long, low moan that drew the attention of the minister and all that were crowded around the burial tent.

"Mom, are you alright? Do you need something?" whispered Alex as his wife shifted her weight feeling her three-inch heels sinking into the ground.

"Mom?" repeated Danny.

"See if she wants some water, she may need a drink of water," he whispered.

Suddenly, violently, Sylvie wrenched her hand from her son's grasp. She jumped from her chair and looked around the tent with wild eyes. Alex and Danny stood up immediately, trying to placate Sylvie into sitting down. She whirled on them.

"Mom, are you alright?" repeated Alex.

"NO! I am not alright! I do not need water or a tissue! I need my husband!" Sylvie's voice was strident and broken. Her sons, not knowing what to do, continued to pull at her, not so gently insisting she sit down.

Sylvie shook their hands from her and took a small step away. She whirled on the crowd. Her voice, though cracked, was firm and gained momentum as she spoke.

"We shouldn't be here! Chip shouldn't be here! This is not what we planned. This is not what we wanted. We wanted to buy an RV and travel around the United States. Not Europe! No. He wouldn't consent to a trip to Spain or Germany. But Idaho! South Carolina! We were going there. I've always hated camping but he showed me the inside of a deluxe RV and we agreed. We had plans, goddamn it!"

Sylvie drew a ragged breath and continued, "We never agreed to this. We were going to take restaurant trips and festival trips and museum trips and possibly visit our children. We agreed to redo the kitchen and not get any more dogs. We just got started and now he's gone."

Alex again tried taking his mother's hand as his wife grimaced at the spectacle Sylvie was making.

"Mom, please. You're making people uncomfortable," Alex murmured.

Sylvie seemed to reel back as if Alex had slapped her.

"I'm making you uncomfortable?" her voice rose to yet a higher volume and pitch. "I'm making people uncomfortable?" she was yelling now. Her hands gestured wildly as they did when her passions rose. "Well too damn bad! I'm uncomfortable! My husband is dead and these people are about to shovel dirt over all that is left of him! That is making me so fucking uncomfortable that I can hardly breathe!" A tiny bit of spittle had worked up around Sylvie's mouth. She began to grab her hair with both hands as she continued. "It's fucking uncomfortable watching the man you love, the only man you've ever loved wither, suffer, until he has all but disappeared! Do you know how uncomfortable that is?" Sylvie's dark hair was wild now that her hands had been in it. Her dark eyes flashed and her face was flushed. Any makeup she had applied was smeared and misshapen.

"It's so unbelievably uncomfortable that you lay awake at night wishing he would die so you don't have to watch him suffer and hating yourself for it! That's uncomfortable! You say I'm making you uncomfortable? Then you can leave. You can all leave. I'm sorry I've made you uncomfortable." Sylvie turned away from her sons, and the crowd under the tent. She held herself, breathing heavily. The minister turned to the crowd and said, "This concludes our graveside service. You are welcome to join the family inside the community room for a light lunch provided by the lady's auxiliary."

The large crowd made of family and friends turned away, feeling uncertain about what to do or how to help Sylvie. Alex's wife gave a single jerk of her chin to indicate he was to follow her. He glanced once at his mom who stood with her back to him huffing and puffing as if she'd just run a half marathon. Danny touched Sylvie's back and then backed away to follow the others. David stayed an extra beat hoping his mom would turn around and be suddenly over the terrible spasm of grief and madness. He wanted her to but when she didn't, he too turned and walked across the cemetery lawn, pausing to glance back once.

Sylvie was unaware of the crowd leaving or how long she stood staring at the shiny box and the hole in the ground. She wondered if there was a limit of tears a person could cry or if it was in an infinite amount that had started flowing when she sat down in the god-forsaken tent and hadn't stopped. She acknowledged a feeling of exhaustion and a definite crick in her neck. Lifting her head for the first time she looked ahead of her at the wooden box. Slowly turning around, she looked back at the empty chairs. Empty except for the four in the middle. In them sat four of her best friends; Anna, Al, Donna Sue, and Libby.

"Is it okay if we come hug you?" asked Anna in a shaky voice. It was obvious the four friends had been crying as they waited for their oldest friend to turn back to them.

"Are you going to smack shit out of us like you did Alex?" asked Al in an attempt at levity.

Sylvie didn't speak but made a small motion that translated yes to her dearest friends, affectionately known as the goddesses by everyone who knew them. They got up slowly and made their way around the chairs until they circled Sylvie in an unending hug. More and more and more tears were shed.

Finally, and by one accord, the ladies stepped back a half step. Sylvie looked at each of them and opened her mouth to speak. Before she could get a word out Anna murmured, "Don't even think about saying you're sorry."

"And if you even think about saying you're ashamed of your behavior or your language I swear I will kick you right in the throat," said Al. None of the ladies batted an eye at such an outlandish threat as it was Al's favorite and was given out freely to anyone; friend, stranger, or relative that caused grief to someone Al cared for.

"No one shushes a goddess, we don't shush," added Libby.

Donna Sue said, "Gals, it's times like this we could sure use a shot of tequila. It's a shame none of us thought to bring it."

"Tequila at a funeral?" mused Libby, at 60 she was the youngest of the friends.

Just then their attention was drawn to a car that had pulled up crooked in a place where there shouldn't be a car. They watched as the door swung open and a mop of gold and graying curls appeared. Jackie Algorotti lifted a hand to wave and then began making her trek across the graves.

Arriving at the tent, and talking already, the circle opened and let in the newest arrival who was slightly winded and clutching an oversized handbag.

"Oh my God, Sylvie! I am so sorry about Chip! I was in D.C. with Charlotte and I got here just as fast as I could. I just didn't think he'd… I thought we had more time. My sweet friend! I know your heart is broken and it sounds like you may have lost a little of your mind as well. I ran into that wife of Alex's at the front of the community room and she mentioned you may have dropped your basket during the graveside service. Of course, I told her to go fuck herself and ran right back to my car to get up here to you as fast as I could," gushed Jackie, the final member of the goddess group.

Sylvie allowed Jackie to embrace her and the two friends cried all over. Slowly Jackie straightened up and held Sylvie at arm's length.

"It's times like this when a good shot of Patron helps you get a grip." With that, she reached into her bag and pulled out a small square-bottomed bottle with an oversized cork.

"We are delivered!" said Anna.

"We need to sit down if we're fixing to get delivered," said Donna Sue.

"These men may not be very happy with us if they can't finish up," murmured Libby. "Hey guys, why don't you go grab some coffee? We're going to be a minute," she said with her lovely smile to the men standing to the side patiently waiting to finish the job they had started.

The six friends rearranged the chairs to make a circle. Jackie opened the bottle of tequila. She lifted it and said in a solemn voice,

"To Chip Russell! The best butterscotch Rice Krispy treat maker in the world!" After an amen from the group and a healthy gulp, she passed the bottle to Al. Al raised the bottle and said,

"To Chip! The best cribbage player in the history of the game! Fifteen-two!" She took a drink and passed it on to Donna Sue.

Donna Sue raised the bottle and said, "To Chip! The master prankster—I'll keep an eye open for your next trick!'"

The friends continued to pass the tequila and toast Chip until it was empty. Sylvie looked at her friends one at a time sitting around the circle. The lines on their faces and the streaks of silver in their hair were testimony to the rich lives they had lived. She opened her mouth to speak and instead of words a small hiccup came out.

"Thank you for not shushing me earlier. Thank you for not making me keep all that toxic waste inside. I felt like I was going to explode if I had to sit there for one more second. Thank you for saying Chip's name out loud and sitting out here with him. I'll have to shovel a bunch of horse manure to make it right with the kids. And I know I'll have to do penance with the church ladies for my foul language and my less than decorous behavior." After a heavy sigh, Sylvie continued, "And somehow I'll have to try and get used to life without that goofy man. I sure don't know how I'm going to do that." Sixty-eight was simply not old age, certainly not dying old age. She thought of her dear friend Anna, who lost her Tony almost ten years earlier. She had a strong faith in God, but she felt she was being tested sorely.

"There's no right or wrong here Chicca. This is uncharted water you're navigating but you're not alone in the boat," said Jackie.

"And no one shushes us!" added Anna.

"Don't worry about the church ladies or your kids. They are all grownups and if they can't take a funeral, forget'em," said Donna Sue.

"We'll talk about Chip all day long. Hell, we'll talk TO Chip and see if he'll reveal his secret recipe for those Rice Krispy treats," said Libby.

"We're here. You're not alone. We've got you," assured Al.

Sylvie remembered another time when her friends had saved her from drowning. Literally. It was years ago, Donna Sue had taken the women and kids to Ron Lake's house at Lake of the Ozarks for a few days during the summer. The men were all working so they left them at home and were having a ball watching the kids cannonball and dive like playful otters. Sylvie was intensely proud of her Sicilian heritage and it was somewhat ironic that her people came from an island as she was deathly afraid of the water and rarely went near it. When she did venture in, she would go no further than her knees. The friends suspected a traumatic water event when she was a child, but they never knew for sure the source of her fear. Danny, Sylvie's middle son, and Nathan Schmitt were twelve and so were able to take the blue paddle boat into the cove. They convinced their moms to get in the rear-facing seats and the boys would take them for a 'boat ride'. Sylvie was apprehensive but seeing the excited faces of the boys made her grab an orange life vest and walk to the end of the dock. "As long as you don't go too fast and spill my drink," she said. "And I DON'T, under any circumstances, get my hair wet."

The goddesses had created their own cocktail; iced tea-quila, which was iced tea with a healthy shot of tequila and fresh lime. Sylvie had had more than one already and was feeling brave with her fresh drink in hand. Al stepped into the small boat first holding Sylvie's drink while she stepped off the dock. It was clear immediately that two boys and two goddesses exceeded the weight limit for the small plastic boat. Water began spilling in the back filling the foot space. Sylvie could feel black panic clawing its way up her throat as her feet got wet. "Get me out! Get me out! Get me out!"

she screamed trying to lift her feet out of the water and watching with growing alarm as the water continued to pour into the back. The two boys were pumping the foot pedals furiously and Sylvie continued to shriek, clutching Al's arm. Al volunteered to jump out and lighten the boat but Sylvie couldn't let go and refused to listen to Al's reassurances. She was sure the whole thing would sink to the bottom and she would be helplessly stranded in the water. Suddenly Sylvie became aware of other slicked hair heads in the water. Donna Sue, Jackie, and Anna had abandoned their sun-bathing rafts and jumped in to help get the boat ashore. They kicked at the back of the boat to help the two frantic boys and in a few minutes, the boat bumped bottom. Everyone took a breath as the two frightened boys jumped out of the boat and turned to stare at their mothers.

Libby met them in the shallows and helped Sylvie step out of the boat. Al handed her the drink she had held onto throughout the six-minute ordeal. "It's okay Chicca. We got you. We weren't going to let that boat sink with you in it," Libby said. Chagrined by the commotion and never afraid to laugh at herself, Sylvie calmly said, "Well at least we didn't spill my drink." She was thankful to her friends for saving her then. And now.

The ladies stood as one. Jackie shoved the empty tequila bottle back into her bag. Sylvie pressed her hand to the shiny box and said a few quiet words that were just for Chip. Then she called to the workers sitting 30 feet away, "He's all yours fellas. I wish you could have known him. He was one of the good guys." She turned to her friends and reached out a hand to the nearest one to catch herself from losing her balance.

"I'm afraid we're going to need a sober ride home," said Sylvie.

"I'll text David," suggested Anna. "He owes me a sober ride."

"Me too," said Donna Sue.

"Me three," said Jackie.

"I get the point. My youngest is still trying to find himself," said Sylvie.

"If he can't find himself, I wish he'd find Taxi Terry. That boy does not know when to say when. And if he even mentions the fact that we need a ride I swear…" said Al.

"You'll kick him in the throat! We know!" the others finished.

Arm in arm in arm in arm in arm in arm the goddesses moved somewhat unsteadily away from the tent towards the community room where a few cars remained.

Anna

Anna stood in the middle of the room. Dust motes drifted through the morning sun. She listened to the profound silence of the house. The house. It was so much more than the sum of its parts. She could look back like it was yesterday and see the day Tony brought her here for the first time.

The two-story brick stood like a stately matron at the end of one of the oldest streets in town. Tony was so excited he could hardly contain himself and babbled as they parked in front and walked up the broken concrete walk to the front door.

"I know how much you love this part of town with these old houses. Now keep in mind, she's rough-it's the only way we could afford something in this neighborhood. The floors need to be redone, the kitchen needs to be gutted and we'll need to add a bathroom upstairs but it has great bones and I can do a lot of the work myself," gushed Tony. "It is a little bit crazy how this house seems to have dropped into our laps. I was doing some insurance business with this guy Carmicheal. We started talking about the property and he said he'd like to sell it but was having a hard time letting it go. When I said I'd like to make an offer I didn't know if he would even consider it but then he seemed relieved. It was amazing how easy it was- it was like it was meant to happen."

Anna trailed Tony into the living room with its original fireplace and mahogany mantle. She noticed everything; the stained glass at the landing of the double staircase lent an ethereal light to the short space. As he continued into the kitchen, Anna paused and looked up the stairs. With a sharp intake of breath, she registered a young woman standing on the landing with her hand on the railing. Before Anna could utter a sound for Tony the woman was no longer there, only dust motes drifting slowly in the strange-colored light. With a pounding heart, Anna shook herself and quickly caught up with Tony in the space that was the kitchen. Before she could get the words out, the condition of the kitchen killed whatever thoughts she had. The space was tiny, depressingly so. There was hardly any cabinet space and only one countertop. The stove, the only appliance visible, wasn't quite an antique but was definitely obsolete. The sink faced the wall and was small and grubby. One look at Anna's face and Tony began in earnest.

"Now don't worry about this. I can take out that wall that divides the kitchen from the mudroom and open this up. It will double the size of the room as well as the storage and countertop space. We'll move the sink under that window so you can look out at the yard. By the time I'm done with this, it will be a show stopper." Anna was having a difficult to impossible time imagining the kitchen in the grand way Tony was describing. She thought it best to not say anything and just kept her feet moving. She followed him through an archway into a dining room space. She knew it was a big IF for Tony to redo the kitchen but realized the space off of it would be perfect for her grandmother's dining room table and her beautiful dishes.

"I think you're going to like this room," said Tony as he crossed a threshold into a room that was made completely of windows on the south side of the house. The afternoon light filled the space and for the first time, Anna began to feel Tony's excitement. What a perfect room! No matter the season this room would be suffused with light. She wanted to stay in the sunroom for a few minutes and just take it in but Tony was on the move.

"Come on, I want to show you upstairs!" he exclaimed as he grabbed Anna's hand and pulled her towards the staircase. For a brief second, Anna remembered seeing something or someone standing on the landing but as Tony noisily climbed the first steps, she convinced herself it must have been a trick of the beautiful light from the stained glass window. She wondered about the history of the old house and who had insisted on adding the beautiful panes of stained glass. She hurried behind Tony and peeked into four small bedrooms that opened from the central hall. "These are small rooms but I figured we could take two and make a master suite and that leaves two for kid's rooms," gushed Tony. "Two is enough, isn't it? If it's not I'll build more!" he said and grabbed Anna around the waist and swung her around in the hall. His excitement was contagious and Anna threw her head back and laughed with the man she loved.

Meeting Tony during her undergrad years had rocked her world. More precisely, it rocked her Chicago parents' world. He was from a small rural town. His dad ran a seed and feed store and his mom sold eggs out of their kitchen. To say the two sets of parents had little in common to discuss at the bridal brunch was, to say the least. Anna had never met anyone like Tony. His big, outgoing personality was impossible to ignore. He never met a stranger and had friends in six counties. Most importantly, he adored Anna with a love that was so powerful it made it hard for her to breathe at times. He called her 'My Anna' and she knew she would spend the rest of her life with him.

They closed the deal on the house with a little help from Anna's dad-something Tony wasn't happy about at all. He wanted to be completely self-sufficient and he especially wanted to show Anna's family that an insurance agent can provide as well as a banker. Tony was always aware that he wasn't the high society husband Anna's parents had hoped she would marry. It made him work that much harder to show them that he could give her the life she deserved.

As soon as the house was theirs, Tony set in right away on an unending list of improvements. The first job was the kitchen and Anna was sure it would be the end of their, up to then, brief marriage. After tearing out the wall to the mudroom and demolishing what did exist in the space, he discovered the wiring was not up to code and would require a professional electrician and a huge check to begin putting the room back together. In the meantime, they lived out of a blue cooler and cooked most of their meals on the tiny cement patio off the kitchen. One night as they grilled small steaks for their evening meal he said, "I'm sorry about this. I didn't think it would be this hard. I promised you a fantastic home and I can't even finish the first job I started. This is not how I thought this would go. Look at us-we're basically camping out-and I promised I would never take you camping."

Anna wrapped her arms around Tony's middle and hugged him tightly. "That's okay. I'd rather camp out with you than dine in with anyone else," she assured him. "I like it back here. It's like our own little oasis. Those beautiful oak trees are our protection from the neighbors and the lilacs smell so nice and sometimes I see a rabbit hopping around. I'll probably want to cook out here even after you finish my gourmet kitchen," she said.

Tony turned to Anna and kissed her thoroughly. "I love you so much, Anna. When I finish the kitchen and the floors and the bedroom…" Anna began to laugh at the long list. "I'm going to build you a deck that's beyond your wildest imagination!"

"Yeah?" asked Anna.

"For sure! Let's eat so I can carry you up to bed," Tony laughed as he grabbed the tongs and scooped up their dinner.

They'd been in the house for eight months before the kitchen was completed and it was stunning! Even Anna's parents and sisters exclaimed over the lovely finished product. Tony had outdone himself by building custom cabinets and having quartz countertops installed. The new stove was a five-burner gas range beauty with an elaborate hood that managed to look old and new all at the same time. The relocated kitchen sink was deep and wide with an old-fashioned-looking faucet that had multiple functions. The wall dividing the mudroom from the kitchen was gone and the original door leading out of the mudroom now opened to the small patio where they had done most of their cooking in the time the kitchen work was being done. The room was perfect and Anna couldn't have been more satisfied. She looked forward to a time when she could invite family and friends in for cozy dinners. Unfortunately, the rest of the house remained in rough shape as Tony had thrown himself into the kitchen work every extra hour he had.

She encouraged him to give her tasks to help with the house. He gave her a hand sander and showed her how to lightly go across the treads of the stairs so the hardwoods could be restained and sealed. Anna, equipped with a dust mask, went to work on the top stair. The work was mindless as she listened to the droning of the sander and watched the dust swirl around her. She soon realized she had made it to the landing and sat back on the bottom step and looked up at the stained glass, marveling again at how beautiful it was and wondering who decided to add it to the window. Lost in thought about someone else toiling on the house the way she and Tony were doing now, she got the distinct feeling that someone was behind her. She could hear Tony banging around on the main floor and since they were the only two in the house the hair on her arms and the back of her neck stood up as if electrified. Slowly, Anna turned to her right and looked over her shoulder at the top of the stairs. She let out a shriek and leaped up from the step. The same young woman she had thought she'd seen on the landing was standing at the top of the stairs just a few steps from Anna. Anna backed up one step and hurtled down the lower flight of stairs shrieking and calling Tony's name. Tony met her in the kitchen and held her while he tried to ascertain if she had hurt herself somehow with the hand sander.

"There's someone upstairs! I saw her! She was standing at the top of the stairs looking at me," rushed Anna as she held on to Tony.

"Anna, calm down. There's no one here but you and I," he assured her.

"I saw her! She was right there not four steps from me," continued Anna.

"Okay, easy. I'll go look," said Tony and he gave Anna a quick hug.

"No, I don't want you to go," said Anna.

"I'll be okay, you wait here," he said and quickly went to the bottom of the stairs. He called out, "Hello?" then gave Anna a quick look and went up. Anna could hear his heavy boots walking through all the rooms upstairs before he returned.

"Nobody there," he said. "I checked every room."

"But Tony! I saw her!" asserted Anna rather wildly.

"You saw something and I'm sorry it scared you. It was probably the dust from the floor and the light from that stained-glass playing tricks on you. You're okay. I've got you My Anna," he assured her and pulled her in for a tight, long hug. Anna loved the feel of Tony's strong arms around her but her heart was still pounding and she knew her eyes had not tricked her. She was trying to decide if she should mention seeing the woman before, the first time they walked through the house but Tony was suggesting they head downtown for a much-needed coffee break at The Chez. Looking back over her shoulder, Anna could only see the bottom step of the staircase and there was no one there. She followed Tony out of the house and tried to forget the fright of seeing someone in their house.

Over the next days and weeks, Anna had a hard time shaking the feeling that someone else was in the house. She wished there was someone she could talk to about it but it was clear that someone wasn't Tony. She didn't like that he didn't believe her and had joked about it several days later to their friend, Matt, a contractor, who had been a big help to Tony in the kitchen and had come to see the finished room.

"I'll bet Anna's pretty excited about having the kitchen done! You did a fantastic job, man!" said Matt.

"Yeah, she's pretty pleased but now she's seeing ghosts!" he laughed. "She nearly broke her neck getting down the stairs recently. She said she turned around and saw someone standing there," Tony told Matt. Matt looked at Anna.

"What did the person look like?" he asked.

"Oh, I don't really know. It was probably the light and the dust," laughed Anna, feeling embarrassed by the unwanted attention. Matt looked at her with an intense look before he turned and followed Tony to inspect his next project area. Before leaving that night, Matt brought his empty plate to the kitchen where Anna was cleaning up. He cleared his throat and said nervously, "Uh, I don't want to scare you or freak you out or anything…"

"Matt, what are you talking about? You're not scaring me," laughed Anna as she loaded his dishes in the dishwasher and wiped the counters.

"No, it's just that I've done a lot of work on these old houses and sometimes that disturbs…you know" Matt's voice stammered but his look was direct.

"Disturbs what?" asked Anna.

"Like I said, I don't want to freak you out but sometimes the guys get funny feelings and they see things when they're working on these old properties," he continued.

"Matt! What are you talking about?" asked Anna.

"Don't make me say it because I don't really know what they are. I just know if you say you saw something or someone then you probably did," he finished.

"Are you talking ghosts? Do you think I saw a ghost?" laughed Anna. Matt looked embarrassed but kept his eyes on her.

"I'm saying, it wasn't your eyes playing tricks on you or your imagination. Look, I'm no good at explaining this but there is a place downtown where some of my homeowners have gone, to find out…more information. You might pop in there sometime and see if they can shed any light on your situation," said Matt. "It's called SoulShine." With that Matt said good night and went out the backdoor. Anna continued wiping down the gleaming countertops and mulled over what Matt had been trying to tell her. Thinking back to what the woman looked like it amazed Anna at the amount of detail she could recall. She had worn a high-necked, long-sleeved blouse. A high-waisted skirt or, she guessed, it could be slacks. She was young. She had a big up-do. Now Anna was feeling a little freaked out just acknowledging how clearly she had seen the woman. She shook her head to clear the images, wiped her hands on the towel, and turned out the light. She thought about what Matt had said about a place that may be able to shed some light on her 'situation.' Maybe she would check it out but it was unlikely.

The next day, Anna arranged to meet Tony at the coffee shop downtown. She dropped off a bill at the city building and ran another errand and still had close to an hour to kill. She decided to do some window shopping and people-watching, some of her favorite activities. She strolled down Ninth street with all of its shops, coffee places, and eateries. She noticed a newly 'reclaimed' alley and decided to explore it. Passing the pretentious sushi place she noticed a small art gallery that looked interesting. As she turned to the door of the gallery she noticed an offset door to the left of it. SoulShine was written in beautiful script. She felt her heart jump when she recognized the name and looked inside curiously. Finding the shop didn't surprise Anna, the fact that she found herself opening the door and walking down the three short steps did.

"Welcome!" came a cheerful voice before Anna could see the speaker from behind a counter stacked with crystals and beads. "Wow! You are very bright!" said the same voice.

"Excuse me?" said Anna uncertainly. "Very bright?"

"Hi, I'm Libby. Welcome to SoulShine!" said a woman who now moved into view. She was beautiful with blond hair in loose curls and sparkling green eyes. "Yes, you are extremely bright. Do you get a lot off of people? Their thoughts, feelings, maybe lucky guesses that turn out right?" she asked Anna.

"Uh, yes I guess I do. But bright? What do you mean by that?" Anna asked, feeling more and more uncertain about her decision to enter the shop.

"Your aura is extremely bright. You are open to messages that don't usually come to others, you know? Some people don't have any shine but you are positively glowing. What's your name?" asked Libby.

"I'm Anna. I've always been lucky if that's what you mean." It was true that she had always had uncanny hunches, lucky guesses, and intuitions that turned out right more times than not. Tony called her his 'Anna luck charm'.

Libby smiled knowingly and asked, "Lavendar's not here now-Wednesdays are his teaching days. Is there something I can help you with?"

Anna tried to frame her thoughts before opening her mouth. She was still thinking about Libby's description of her 'aura' and didn't want to come off sounding like a kook. She had no idea how to interpret the Lavendar remark. "My husband and I recently bought a new house-an old house actually" she rushed to add. "I'm sure it was just a weird trick of the light or something, but I think I may have seen something and I don't know what it was or how to explain it. My husband assured me I didn't and then our friend Matt suggested I stop in here…"

Libby laughed and said, "Come on over, let's talk." Anna followed Libby to a book-lined corner of the small shop that smelled faintly of incense. They sat at two wrought iron chairs around a small round table. "Tell me about the house," began Libby. "When was it built? What part of town are you in? Are you remodeling anything?"

"We're on Edgewood a few blocks north of downtown. I'm not sure exactly when the house was built but my husband thinks in the early 1900s. It's beautiful! The original wood trim is amazing and it has a sunroom that I love. It's the kind of house I always wanted to live in." Anna wondered if she sounded overly privileged or snooty to the other woman but Libby was nonplussed and continued to look at Anna with warmth and an inviting energy that was easy to talk to. "The first time I went in the house before we even signed the papers, I saw or thought I saw someone on the landing. I kind of forgot about it. My husband is a huge skeptic of things that he can't understand or explain so I knew better than to ask him if he had experienced anything. Then recently, I was working on the staircase and I felt someone standing behind me and when I looked, she was there again! It was the same person I saw that first day," Anna was shocked and a little embarrassed at how fast she was talking.

Libby didn't seem to find her retelling of events surprising and spoke to Anna in a calm voice, never breaking eye contact. "Edgewood is one of the oldest streets in Columbia. Many of the town's founding fathers were men of means and built grand homes in the style of Chicago or St. Louis in that area. We've talked to several families from that part of town who have started a remodeling project and experienced some strange things. It's understandable really," she said.

"Understandable? I'm not sure I follow. What did I see? And why would remodeling the house have anything to do with… whatever it was?" stammered Anna.

"A lot of times, those old homes, particularly the brick ones, have a lot of energy or supernatural activity in them. When you tear things up or change rooms around, sometimes they get disturbed and that's when a lot of people become aware that they are sharing their house with someone else," finished Libby.

"Someone else? Do you mean a ghost? You didn't say ghost but that's what you're saying? My house is haunted?" Anna's voice began to rise at the end of her thoughts.

"Haunted has such a negative association," began Libby. "The first thing you need to do is find out about the history of your exact location." Before she could say more Anna jumped up from her seat checking her watch.

"I have to meet my husband. Thanks for … your time," she stammered, backing toward the door. Libby stood and watched her go with the same small knowing smile still on her lovely face.

"Bye Anna," she said.

Anna met Tony at the door to The Chez. He laughed as she distractedly bumped into him. "Hey, I thought I was late. What's up, you look…" Tony paused looking for the right word. "Bothered," he said.

"I'm fine. I just lost track of time and then I had to hurry to get here," explained Anna.

"Cool. What did you find to look at? I hope you didn't find a shoe store down here," teased Tony.

"No shoes," said Anna. "I did discover an art gallery in the alley." She didn't mention that she hadn't gone inside.

"Awesome, but I hope you didn't buy anything. Our budget barely allows for occasional lattes at this point much less some pricey squiggle of paint someone decided was art," laughed Tony as he ushered Anna inside the coffee shop.

Over coffee, Tony told Anna about the new insurance business he was writing. Things were picking up and going well considering he had decided to leave the agency he had been working for to open his own office. It was a risk but he loved the idea of being his own boss and setting his own hours. He was a hard worker and Anna knew he would put in the time and sweat equity needed to be a success. With that said, he often started his day at The Chez and very much liked setting the hours better suited to him. He seemed much happier this way so Anna was supportive. In a lull in the conversation of Tony's office and Anna's new position as principal of an elementary school, Anna asked, "What do you know about our house?"

"What do you mean? Why are you asking?" asked Tony.

"I'm just curious. I know we bought it from the Carmichaels but how long did they live there? Who owned it before them? When exactly was it built?" Anna's questions tumbled out in one breath.

Tony laughed. "Why this sudden interest in all those details?"

"I'm just curious. All the work we're doing on the house makes me wonder about who built it and who else has loved it enough to work on it as we do," said Anna.

Tony looked at Anna with a funny look. "You can find out all that stuff at the local courthouse but honestly, when are you going to have time to go in there and dig around in a bunch of old records? You're never home from school before 6 and government buildings don't have weekend hours," he said. The time Anna devoted to her job as an elementary school principal was one of the few things they regularly disagreed about. Tony maintained the hours she spent at school, not counting attending every school function, were not commensurate with the compensation she received. Anna didn't disagree but tried to help him understand the time she devoted to school was simply what the job required. She hadn't gone into public education to get rich. It was a rubbing point between them and she tried to steer clear of discussions about her work schedule. She let the conversation die and they finished their coffees and headed home.

Pulling into the driveway, Anna could hardly believe this beautiful grand house was their home. "That's weird," said Tony. "Why did you leave a light on upstairs?"

"I didn't," replied Anna, glancing up at the second story. The small east bedroom had a light shining from the window.

"Huh, you must've left something on unless your ghost friend can turn on the lights," said Tony as he parked the car in the small single-car garage. Anna didn't respond but thought about the vision she'd seen on the stairs.

"You're right. I must have left a reading light on," she said knowing two things. First; she hadn't left anything on when she left the house and second, there was no furniture in that room so she couldn't imagine where the light was coming from. She made sure she went upstairs ahead of Tony feeling more curious than afraid. Her conversation with the woman in the shop returned to her. Haunted. She said the house was haunted. Anna did not know how she felt about that but she knew she was an intelligent person who would approach this 'development' like any other she had encountered in her adult life. She would find out as much as she could about the house and its origins and then she'd find out all she could about 'supernatural energy'. If it needed debunking, information was her friend. If she couldn't debunk it then she'd figure that out later. Gaining the top step, Anna paused for a second then rounded the door of the small bedroom. The empty room would one day be a nursery when the time came and Anna was ready. They had put a few boxes of building materials and extra gallons of paint inside the door to keep them out of the way as they worked their way through the old house. Anna was unaware that a work light on a stand Tony had used on his late-night sessions in the kitchen had been stowed away in the corner of the small bedroom. It was the source of the light they had seen from the driveway.

Anna went into the room and switched the light off. She joined Tony in their bedroom and he asked if she had turned out 'her 'light. Assuring him she had, she promised herself some time to collect information. She wondered again about her sightings and now the light. She did an internal check on her thoughts and feelings about the possibility of a ghost being in the house. She decided her curiosity was stronger than her initial fear. What was the woman's name at the shop? These were the thoughts in Anna's head as she drifted to sleep.

When Anna stepped through the door at SoulShine she heard musical bells she hadn't noticed before. She looked around the shop in wonder. It was beautifully appointed with rich tapestries and rugs. Beautiful art made of stones and wood was strategically placed around the small space. She was impressed and at ease which was surprising. It wasn't that Anna made a habit of visiting shops like this-actually she avoided them for one main reason. Patchouli. She had a sensitive nose and certain scents could bring on a massive headache. Patchouli was the absolute worst and the reason she wouldn't enter candle shops or frequent some bookstores. She appreciated the understated loveliness of the store. It seemed more cozy than cliche and the absence of cloying scents was a welcome relief. Almost immediately Anna heard her name and turned back to the door to see the same woman she had 'visited' with previously. She had a small watering can in her hand and was tending the beautiful flowering plants that were growing in colorful pots in the front window.

"Anna! How nice to see you again," said Libby.

"Hi, thanks…" said Anna.

"Libby," said the woman.

"Right! Nice to see you again too," said Anna.

"What can I help you with today? asked Libby.

"I'm not exactly sure," said Anna. "I've been thinking about what we talked about the last time and I guess I need a little guidance."

"Of course," said Libby. "I have some wonderful reads on spiritual guidance or I can put you in contact with Lavendar if you're looking for more of a psychic coach."

Anna was alarmed at the nature of Libby's suggestions and had a strong sense to turn and go back the way she had come. She interrupted Libby, "No, no. I don't mean spiritual guidance. I don't even know what that is. I mean guidance on how to find out information about my house. You suggested it when we talked before and I am just not sure how to go about it."

"Oh, sure! Silly me! Come on over," laughed Libby. Anna was relieved at Libby's light-hearted reaction. She would have definitely been out the door, never to return if Libby had acted like Anna's request was beneath her level of service. They sat again around the small round table and Libby fished around in a woven basket on a built-in shelf. Unsure of what she was looking for Anna was relieved when she pulled out an ordinary yellow legal pad and pen.

"Okay, we just need to do a deed search for your address. Those records are free to the public and will tell us about the land before the house was built and who built it and of course, what year. After that, we'll find out as much as we can about who lived there. Then, any major changes that have been done and who the owners have been up until you bought it. Piece of cake," said Libby as she quickly wrote the steps down, neatly numbered.

Anna was taken aback. She was always careful with stereotyping people. She felt that as a public educator, she was held to a high standard in the way she treated people, especially strangers. She prided herself on always giving people a chance to prove themselves. But seeing how Libby dressed in embroidered gauzy dresses and wore the kind of shoes made from recycled material and that she worked in a 'spiritual' shop had led Anna to a predetermined decision about the kind of person she was. This organized and informed list of how to access the information she wanted was surprising. Anna was ashamed of her thoughts.

Libby gave her a wink and tilted her head to one side. "Don't be surprised. I didn't always work here. I worked in a law office for a while so I know my way around the records routine."

Again, Anna was surprised and embarrassed by her short thinking about the other woman. Libby was tearing off the legal sheet to hand to Anna. "Let me know if you need any help. I love looking into this kind of thing. I think it's fascinating looking at the old records. It's like a little window back in time. Sometimes you find out some really helpful information related to whatever activity you have going on and sometimes it's just your standard built by, sold to, etc and the mystery remains unanswered. Either way, it's great. I think the more information you have, the better," said Libby.

Anna had to shake her head. This woman was such a paradox. Her exterior and open manner were casual hippie but the interior was a mind that loved information and organization-just as she did. She took a breath and said, "I hope you don't think I'm totally lame but I'm not even sure how to go about finding this information."

Libby smiled and said, "You want some help?"

The two agreed to meet at 4:30 the following Wednesday. The shop closed early on Wednesday, Lavendar's day to lead his reincarnation group. Anna strategically planned to leave school well ahead of her normal stopping time as the county building closed at five pm. Libby seemed to know everyone at the security checks and many of the people down in the archive room. They started with the plat maps as they were the easiest to obtain and their time was limited. Libby showed her how to select the correct volume based on city and year. The heavy tome gave Anna goosebumps as they carried it back to a bar-height table and opened the heavy cover. Glancing at Libby, she could tell she too was feeling excited about what they may discover inside the book.

"First we look for the part of town that is west of Providence Road and south of Broadway. Then we can zoom in on plats until we find your address." With very little effort and owing to Libby's comfort level with the resources, they discovered the land was originally bought by Dr. Edwin Somner in 1911. He contracted with the Hayward Brothers Builders to build the original house and it was completed in 1915. Anna was thrilled to see the drawings and read the handwritten entries about the origin of the house. As she studied the building plan, she noticed that the house was perfectly square, and the sunroom on the south side that she enjoyed so much wasn't part of the original floor plan. Obviously, it was added later. Gaining this much information was thrilling and Anna copied it all down to use as her jumping-off place for further research. The two ladies gathered their things and headed for the stairs. Libby was just as excited at what they had uncovered. "So, we need to find out as much as we can about Doc Somner and when he sold it, and who added the sunroom. None of that is hard, we'll just…" She stopped mid-sentence as they reached Anna's car on the street. "Oh, sorry! I just get so carried away," she added.

Anna looked at Libby and smiled. "It's okay," she said. "I appreciate your enthusiasm and I could use the help. I've never done this kind of thing before and I've only lived in Missouri for a few years so it's not like I grew up knowing the history of Columbia. I'd love your help." Anna was surprised at how much she meant it. After she met Tony, it never occurred to her that they would return to Illinois where her parents and sisters lived. The friends she had made in grad school were dispersed all around the United States. She had colleagues that had become friends but many had young families and not a lot of time to socialize. Anna felt the absence of friends, especially female friends. Libby was so friendly and Anna enjoyed her company. It was fun to share the excitement of discovering the house's history with someone.

They agreed to meet Sunday afternoon at The Chez and compare notes on their research into Dr. Somner and decide what direction to take next. When Sunday arrived, Tony offered to drive Anna to The Chez for her meet-up with Libby. Anna had mentioned meeting Libby and explained how she had helped her discover who built the house but not where they had met. Tony would not listen to talk of 'energy' or paranormal anything. To him, it was all stuff and nonsense. Anna was surprised when he parked instead of just letting her out. When she looked at him, he said casually, "I'm just going to pop in for a latte to go. I'll be back to get you in an hour or so."

Libby was at the table in the window and there was no getting around introducing the two-a fact that Anna realized was Tony's plan all along. She made the introductions wondering what Tony was thinking of Libby's tie-dyed dress. Libby was her natural self and luckily didn't mention anything about why she was helping Anna. Tony got his latte and gave them a wave and was gone. Anna couldn't wait to tell Libby what she had discovered and was anxious to hear if she had found out anything more.

"So, Dr. Somner trained at the University of Missouri and then went to Thailand for a few years. He returned to Columbia in 1911 and bought the property just like we saw on the deed record. He didn't stay here during that time and seems to have gone somewhere out east. He returned around 1913 and hired the Hayward Brothers to build the house on Edgewood. He was teaching medicine at the University. He spent a lot of his time going back and forth to New Jersey," said Anna. "The house was finished in 1915 and after that, he seems to have stayed put. He married Lorna Westhouse. They had four children and Dr. Somner died in 1953." During her show and tell Anna felt certain by the emotion on Libby's face that she had something to share. "I didn't look into Lorna."

"Well, I did!" rushed Libby. "The old doc fell in love with a debutante but her father didn't like the age difference or the fact that he was most likely a Confederate so he refused to allow Edwin to court Lorna. Edwin went off to Thailand for a few years, I think to try and forget about her, but of course, that's not in the records. When he returned Lorna had waited for him! Isn't that wonderful? She refused hundreds of suitors waiting on Eddie to come back," gushed Libby.

"What is the source for your information? Hundreds of suitors?" asked Anna.

"Well, maybe I embellished just a little but whatever. He left the country. She did not marry. He returned and her father couldn't say no. I LOVE a love story, don't you?" asked Libby, bubbling with excitement. "I can only imagine the house- of course, he would have made sure everything was perfect; the structure, the furniture, the fixtures. I guess he didn't think of everything because after living in the house for less than a year, he commissioned the sunroom and the plans were drawn up. I think it must have been Lorna's idea or maybe it was reminiscent of her home back east. It's impossible to know but my guess is that she wanted it and Eddie was quick to acquiesce."

Anna listened with rapt attention wondering where Libby was able to unearth this information. The facts she, herself, had uncovered were the nuts and bolts, dry toast stuff. Libby had somehow unearthed a love story.

"And actually, they had five children. Their third child, a little girl died at age three," added Libby. "Okay, what's next? We know Doc and Lorna were the first homeowners. We need to know who else, if anyone, ever bought it. Once we know the players, we can start to zero in on who our 'lady' may be," ended Libby.

"Do you really think we can figure this out? I mean, the person or whatever it was that I saw? Do you think we can determine who it is or was? asked Anna.

"Maybe. There is one surefire way to know who it is," said Libby.

"How? What do you mean?" asked Anna.

"Lavendar could read the house," said Libby.

"Lavendar? I'm not following," said Anna.

"Lavendar owns SoulShine. He's an amazing psychic. He can go in and read the energy in the house," finished Libby.

"I'm not sure about that. Tony would hate that. He doesn't give any validity to this kind of talk, much less a psychic coming to 'read' the house," said Anna.

"Okay, we'll do it from this plane. With a little luck, maybe we can figure it out," said Libby with her easy smile. "Same time next Sunday?"

When the next Sunday arrived, Anna was waiting at a table for Libby. Before Libby even got in her seat she started talking. "Okay, I've got some more information. According to the records I found, the house was willed to Dr. Somner's oldest son Adam when he died in 1953. Adam lived in Kansas City but Lorna continued to live in the house alone for twelve years after Eddie passed on. She died in 1970," Libby finished in a rush.

"Wow, so it was never sold outside the family? Did it sell after Lorna died?" asked Anna.

"Apparently not! Adam willed it or gave it to his only child, a daughter, Margaret," said Libby.

"Let me guess, is her last name Carmichael?" asked Anna.

"Yes, Margaret Somner married Stan Carmichael. They lived in the house for a few years but they weren't from Columbia. They didn't stay long and moved back to KC and their son, Stan Jr., came to live there. It must not have been his scene either. He put it on the market after a year but took it off, I don't know why. He did that a few more times and even had a contract on it but it fell through. You were super lucky to talk to him when you did-it wasn't even listed with a realtor. It's almost like he was waiting for you and Tony to come along," finished Libby.

"Yeah, when Tony talked to Stan, he seemed reluctant to sell but knew he couldn't hang on to it. A house like that needs a lot of attention. He told Tony he wanted it to go to the right person," said Anna.

"So our lady has to be one of the Somner women. Lorna? Maybe the child that died? One of her other children?" mused Libby.

"How are we going to find out?" worried Anna.

"You said you got a good look at her right?" asked Libby. "If we had a way of comparing the person you saw with some of the old photos on file maybe we could identify her that way," said Libby with an underwhelming sense of confidence.

Anna picked up her bag from the extra chair and thanked Libby for her good scoop of information. She called over her shoulder, "See you next Sunday" and hurried out the door. Libby realized she had never even ordered her coffee. Anna drove straight to the art supply store nearest the downtown district. She hadn't painted in a while but always intended to get back to it. Her easel was in the garage and she knew the perfect place to set it up. At the supply store, she picked up canvases and some oil paints, not sure of the condition of her meager supply. She hurried home and brought in the easel. It was dusty and she was ashamed for having neglected it for so long. She had majored in Elementary Education for her undergrad degree and minored in Art. She had wanted to be an art teacher but her father dissuaded her from that idea saying she needed to be trained for a real job, not arts and crafts. As much as it had stung then, Anna followed her father's advice and it had been a good decision. She'd been a terrific first-grade teacher before becoming an assistant principal for one year. Now, after six years, she was the principal and couldn't imagine doing anything else. Anna dabbed some paint on her palette and closed her eyes for a minute. The weight of the brush in her fingers and the slight smell of the oil paint were both familiar and pleasant. She thought back to the woman on the stairs. She concentrated her memory on what she'd seen and tried to push back what she had felt. Slowly her brush went to the canvas and Anna painted a portrait. She worked quickly and tried not to over-think. She wanted to capture the essence of the person she'd seen if possible.

After several hours, Tony appeared at her elbow drying his hands on a towel. "Painting? It's been an age since you've painted any-thing," he commented. "I thought you'd be at school doing your due diligence."

"Yeah, I need to be. It's almost state testing time. I have a lot to get ready for. I just felt like painting," said Anna.

"It's good. Who is it?" asked Tony.

Anna was worried he would ask so she tilted her head to the side still looking at the painting and said, "I'm not sure." It seemed to sat-isfy Tony and he returned to the kitchen and began seasoning some meat for the grill. He always cooked on Sunday nights as Anna was in the habit of going to school to prepare for a full week of learning for her 30 staff members and 437 students.

Satisfied with the likeness, she wiped her brushes and left the portrait on the easel to rest, and went to gather her 'school bag' for her Sunday night work session. Returning home around 9:30, Anna stood at the counter and ate some of the beef brisket Tony had expertly cooked on the grill. It was delicious, even cold, and she was too tired to heat it. She could hear the tv in the sunroom and popped in to kiss Tony and tell him good night. Climbing the stairs, Anna realized how tired she was. She must have overdone it today researching with Libby, whipping out a painting, and planning for a busy week. She laughed at herself and got ready for bed. She was blessed with the ability to go to sleep right away. She'd heard other people, usually women, complain about how long it took them to fall asleep or how difficult it was to sleep anywhere but at home. She could fall asleep anytime and anywhere if she were tired. It was a standing joke with Tony. He always said if Anna asked him a question, she could be asleep before he could answer. Anna laid down and closed her eyes and sank into oblivion. She never heard Tony come to bed when his movie ended. Sometime in the night, she was roused by the smell of warm cinnamon rolls fresh from the oven. It was such a lovely smell, so comforting. Anna sighed deeply and once again sank into sleep.

In the morning rush to get up and out of the house Anna paused as she applied a swipe of mascara to her warm brown eyes. Would her baby girl have her eyes? She shook her head at the random thought and tried not to panic, she'd be twenty-nine on her next birthday, and still no baby. It was then that she remembered something had disturbed her sleep. She couldn't quite remember if it was Tony coming to bed or a siren outside the bedroom window. Brushing her thick, mahogany hair one last time it came to her. She'd smelled cinnamon. Not just cinnamon but warm cinnamon rolls just out of the oven. She leaned over the bed to kiss Tony goodbye. He was awake and always tried to hold on to her even though he knew she needed to be out the door and on the road by 7:15.

"Good morning, Principal Perry. Any chance you want to play hooky with me today?" he asked.

"Not today, Bad Boy. I've got to run. I'll see you tonight," she said as she kissed his stubbly cheek.

"K, see you tonight," he said sleepily.

Anna turned back at the door and said, "Hey, did you decide to bake something cinnamony last night before you came to bed?"

"Nah, I had some ice cream-which we are now out of," he replied.

"Okay, I'll start a grocery list. See you tonight. I love you," said Anna.

"I love you, Anna," he replied. She hopped down the steps. It still thrilled her when Tony said her name the way he did. It was always more special when he said "I love you Anna' rather than the casual 'love you too'.

Anna climbed in her car with her protein smoothie wishing it was a cinnamon roll and headed to school.

On Tuesday, Anna emailed Libby. She had enjoyed their research time together and decided to ask Libby over for dinner Wednesday evening. She knew the shop closed early and Tony had a seminar in Sedalia and wouldn't be home until Friday. She wasn't sure what Libby would think and hoped she wouldn't think it strange or over-reaching. It wasn't long before she got a message from Libby saying she'd love to. She'd check her pantry and see what she could bring to contribute. Anna loved to entertain but preferred to plan the menu rather than leaving it to chance. Really, she never liked the idea of a potluck or everyone bringing in something random. She liked things to be organized even if it meant she had to do the shopping and cooking herself. Inviting Libby over was spontaneous-the fact that she replied quickly and positively was making Anna feel glad she did. She wasn't going to worry about dinner. They could figure it out together-Anna assumed Libby had some restrictions on what she would eat judging from her general presentation and didn't want to fix something that was off limits.

Wednesday evening, Anna was surprised to hear a quiet knock from the back of the house. She checked the drive but there was no car. She opened the door off the kitchen to find Libby with her woven shopping bag.

"Hi," said Anna. "I was listening for your car, you surprised me."

"I don't live far from here so I rode my bicycle," said Libby. "I parked it back here, I don't want someone borrowing it without permission. I hope that's okay."

"Sure, come on in," said Anna. "Would you like to look at the house?"

"Yes! I was thrilled when I got your message. I've been dying to see exactly where you've seen our lady," said Libby.

"Okay, let's go then," said Anna leading Libby through to the exposed double stairway. The setting sun was slanting its rays through the stained glass at the landing. It made a beautiful sight and Libby stopped and held her breath.

"Oh my! This is spectacular!" she breathed.

"The first time I came in the house before we even bought it, I'm sure I saw her standing on the middle landing, there in front of the stained glass," said Anna.

"The colors coming through that window…" breathed Libby.

"It's quite something. Come on up," said Anna. The two climbed the first flight of stairs and paused on the landing to study the stained-glass panes that were creating a magical light. Libby took a step closer to the window.

"It's so … special!" she breathed as she looked closely at the edge of the pane. "M. Brewer. That must be the artist who created this. It is an art installment. I think we should add M. Brewer to our list of folks to find out about." Anna glanced over her shoulder at Libby. Her face was turned to the beatific light streaming in. She was really glad Libby was here.

"The next time I saw 'her' I was sitting on the lowest step of the upper flight looking at the window and I felt like someone was behind me. She was standing at the top looking at me," said Anna.

Libby had turned away from the window and looked where Anna was describing. The two women climbed the remaining stairs and Anna showed Libby the bedrooms.

"Has anything else happened? Since you've seen 'her'? asked Libby.

"No, well yes," laughed Anna self-consciously. "Tony and I went for coffee one afternoon. When we left it was full daylight so I know I didn't have any lights on up here but when we came back, there was a work light on in the little bedroom on the front. We could see it from the driveway. Tony was sure I'd left it on but truthfully, I didn't even know the work light was in there. I know for sure I didn't turn it on," explained Anna. "And then there were the cinnamon rolls."

"Cinnamon rolls?" asked Libby, her eyes wide.

"It was last Sunday; you and I had talked at The Chez and you mentioned if we could just compare what the 'lady' looked like with some of the social event photographs maybe we could figure out who she is. So, I came home and pulled out my easel, and painted her picture. Well, I tried to paint her picture," said Anna.

"You painted her?" said Libby incredulously.

"I'm a bit out of practice but I thought about what you'd said and I wanted to try and capture her before I forgot anything," said Anna.

"I can't believe you've had a portrait of our lady since Sunday and I haven't seen it yet! Where is she? I can't wait to see her!" Libby's face lit up.

Anna laughed and said, "Okay, come with me. She's in the sunroom." The two walked quickly down the stairs and through the living room never pausing to admire the original fireplace and other features. French doors led from the living room into the sunroom where the easel was standing in the center of the room. Libby walked up to it and stopped. She was completely quiet for a few beats. When Anna, feeling nervous about what Libby may be thinking of her work, began to talk, Libby turned her face to her. Her eyes were glittering with tears.

"She's beautiful!" she said quietly.

Anna was pleased and moved by Libby's reaction. She began to explain about the high-collared blouse. "I got the impression there was a broach or something at her neck. She had long hair which was all put up. I couldn't tell if she was wearing a skirt or slacks but it was high-waisted."

Libby continued to stare at the portrait. "She's absolutely beautiful. I don't know how you did it but this is amazing."

"Thanks, let's just hope it helps us identify her. Do you think it will?" asked Anna.

"There are all kinds of archives for the University. Family picnics, fundraisers, galas. There are bound to be photographs. If she's a Somner, she'll have attended those functions and we'll be able to pick her out just like a police lineup," laughed Libby.

Again, Anna was happy she had invited Libby. "Let's go find something to eat. We could always order in," she suggested.

Libby followed her through the dining room and into the newly done kitchen. "The house is amazing! Thank you for inviting me. I can tell you love it. And if it's all the same to you, I'm sure we can come up with something good to eat. I hate to eat out. You never know what's been done to it before it's on your plate."

Anna found this amusing but turned her smile inside the refrigerator. "Is there anything you don't eat?" she asked.

"No, I'm good," laughed Libby. "As long as it doesn't have a face it's on the menu."

Anna thought about that and then laughed. "So, we're not having tilapia filets, right?"

"Right! I brought patty pan squash and tomatoes I got from the farmer's market," said Libby.

"I've got pasta, mushrooms, and goat cheese," said Anna.

"Perfect! Well have a lovely ragout simmering away in no time," said Libby.

The two set about chopping and sauteing the vegetables. Soon the kitchen was perfumed with the smell of garlic, onion, and the bubbling tomato stew. Anna had wondered if they would run out of things to talk about but their conversation never wavered and they'd both had two longneck beers while they chopped and cooked.

"I can't tell you how much I'm enjoying you being here. Tony would never go for this," said Anna.

"Go for what?" asked Libby.

"Well, first of all, talking about our 'Lady'. He goes beyond being skeptical about anything that is not black and white. I mean, I've never actually experienced anything paranormal but I've always been curious about our soul and how all that works. I'd never met anyone like Tony before and once we got together I felt like I'd known him forever. It just made me wonder, maybe I have known him in a different life. I just feel that there is more than the human realm, even though I have no idea what it may be. I can never talk about things like that with him. We hardly ever fight or disagree and I know he loves me but that is one topic that is off-limits," explained Anna.

Libby's face held no judgment towards Tony. She had a way of accepting people for who they are and being okay with it.

"And this stew? What did you call it, ragout? It's amazing! The flavors are so delicious and complex. I love it! He would not eat it because it doesn't have meat in it. I don't even miss the meat," laughed Anna. "And it's a bonus that you like beer! Tony hates it when I drink more than one. He says it sends the wrong message and wants me to try wine or bourbon."

Libby lifted her long-neck bottle and clinked it with Anna's. "Here's to friends in low places," she said. Anna laughed and drained her bottle. They agreed to meet Sunday at Ellis Library in the heart of the University campus. Now that Libby had a look at 'the lady' she wanted to look at the faculty yearbooks and see if they could identify her once and for all.

Anna was familiar with the library and had spent many a weekend down in the stacks in her study cage as she wrote her thesis for her graduate program. She'd always found the library stately and beautiful. She met Libby near the coffee kiosk and they headed off in search of the faculty archives. Surprisingly, Libby went right to the section of the vast library easily and began running her finger along the spines of the large tomes that were essentially like yearbooks for the faculty and staff that worked for the university.

"Oh! I think we're getting somewhere now." She pulled a heavy volume off the shelf and they both turned to one of the old oak reading tables. They paged through the old book marveling at how the campus looked over 80 years ago. They both agreed that the men looked very handsome in their pinstripe suits. The women were equally decked out in high-necked, long-sleeve blouses and stylish hats.

"We're looking for the period around 1915, that's when Eddie began his tenure here," murmured Libby. "Here he is! Second row, third from the left," she said pointing excitedly at the black-and-white image. The picture was of the faculty and staff of the medical school carefully posed in front of the new Sweitzer Hall. "I guess Eddie didn't believe in smiling," added Libby although most of the faces were somber. They turned the page and found several pictures from the same year's annual fundraiser gala and the family picnic. Edwin was there and easy to pick out from the crowd now that they were getting to know him. He was always turned out in fashionable clothes and always had a serious look on his face. They read all the names carefully and poured over the grainy images looking for Lorna's name or someone who looked like Anna's portrait. Anna gave herself a mental shake when she found herself holding her breath in anticipation.

"Maybe it's too soon. We know Edwin came to Columbia but traveled back and forth to the east coast often. Maybe Lorna's not here yet. Let's try 1917." Libby replaced the yearbook and pulled another from the shelf. Bringing it to the table and leaving the book closed she paused for a second and gave Anna a direct look. "Is she in there? Can you tell?" she asked.

Anna laughed self-consciously. "How would I know? Open it up and let's see."

"Just checking! Making sure you still got your shine," Libby smiled and looked back at the volume. They found the yearly faculty and staff picture and there was Edwin in the front row. There was something different about him and it took Anna a minute to realize what it was.

"He's smiling!" they both said in unison. They quickly turned the pages to find the family pictures. Anna felt a quickening in her stomach as Libby turned the page. There she was! She didn't even have to read the names to recognize her! Lorna was standing on the far right of the picture with all the ladies in orderly rows. Edwin was on the left with the gentleman. Where everyone else was looking directly at the photographer with serious, 'we are doctors and doctor's wives' expressions, Lorna was not. Well not exactly. Her head was facing the photographer but her eyes were canted to her right and the corners of her mouth were definitely up as if she was barely containing a giggle. When Anna and Libby looked at Edwin he too was not as composed as the other men. Although he faced the camera, his eyes were canted left as if trying to catch Lorna's eye. He also had a small smile hovering around his lips.

They quickly turned the intervening pages of directors and associates to find the family picnic and gala pictures. Lorna and Edwin were there! The camera caught the couple a few times at the annual family picnic. In every photo, Lorna is looking at Edwin as if he were a movie star or an action hero. Edwin, too, looked completely different with his face bathed in smiles. In every picture, he was touching

Lorna in some small way, a hand at her elbow, at her back, and even moving a strand of hair from her forehead. Libby and Anna took a second to look at one another but neither spoke.

They turned a few more pages and found the annual fundraiser gala. Both Edwin and Lorna were turned out in magnificent finery. There were several photos of the crowd dancing, and standing in small casual groups. They identified Edwin and Lorna in three photos. The first two were obviously small groups of people talking and caught candidly by the photographer. In both, Edwin had his face turned to Lorna. Lorna was caught full-on in one, and it appeared she had been talking. In the next one, she is looking back at Edwin and they seem to be laughing over something although no one else in the shot seemed amused. The last photograph showed the couple on the dance floor. They made a perfect pair in their beautiful clothes and perfect stance. Even dancing, Lorna was looking at Edwin and he, looking down into her upturned face.

Libby closed the book quietly, unwilling to break the spell they were under. "Wow! They were so beautiful together," she said. Anna agreed by nodding her head. She had a strange feeling, a feeling you get when you've just watched a tremendous film or read an epic novel. The feeling she was getting was big.

"Lorna and Edwin are in your house," said Libby.

"Well, Lorna is for sure but why? What is she there for? Does she mean harm? Does she need help?" wondered Anna.

"Maybe she died in the house and is stuck. I've heard Lavendar talk about that kind of thing. Sometimes they need help moving on," said Libby. "I bet I know a way to find out."

"What? We can't have a seance at the house. Tony would go ballistic," said Anna.

"That's a great idea but I was going to suggest a visit to The Candlelight Nursing Home. I know some ladies over there that would have been around when Lorna was alive, maybe someone knew her," said Libby.

"You know some ladies? Let me guess. You used to work there," said Anna.

Libby laughed as she grabbed her crocheted bag and tossed her blond curls over her shoulder. "It's actually my current full-time job. I have several clients that pay me privately to visit and spend time with their loved ones. Trust me when I say that I know my way around an old folks' home."

Anna met Libby at The Candlelight Lodge Saturday afternoon when Tony had gone golfing. Libby was carrying a basket with a linen towel draped over the edges. Anna wondered about its contents but didn't ask as they went inside. It was surprisingly bright and cheery in the lobby and Libby stopped to sign the guest book. She asked the attendant behind the desk if Ruth was in the gathering room. The attendant thought not so, Libby turned left down the corridor with Anna a few steps behind. Libby knocked on a door that had a wreath of fake lilacs and gently pushed it open. "Ruth, Honey, are you awake? It's Libby and my friend Anna," she said.

Coming into the room from the hallway was like entering a cave. With the drapes drawn the room was dark and Anna got a feeling of too much furniture in too small a space. A small woman sat in a wing-backed chair in the corner by the window. She had a brightly colored afghan on her knees and a small animal in her lap. She appeared to have been dozing but roused as she heard Libby's voice.

"Come in! Come in! Visitors! Oh, my Sonny! I didn't know we'd have visitors today," said Ruth.

"Oh Ruth, what have I told you about keeping these drapes closed? You and Sonny need light. How else can you bloom?" asked Libby as she pulled the heavy drapes aside. Finished with the drapes, Libby dropped to her knees in front of the chair and its occupants and gave Ruth a hug and the cat in her lap a stroke. "I'm so happy to see you and I've brought my friend Anna with me."

"I'm so glad you came Libby, and Anna too. It's so nice to get visitors. Sonny and I don't get too many," said Ruth.

In the light from the window, Anna could see that the cat on Ruth's lap was not a real one but a stuffed animal, although the old woman was stroking it and talking to it as if it was alive. "What did you bring me this time?" asked Ruth.

"Today I have some orange marmalade walnut scones that should satisfy that sweet tooth of Sonny's," said Libby. She pulled back the linen towel and held the basket up directly under Ruth's nose so she could get a whiff of the lovely pastries inside.

"Oh, that sounds decadent! I can hardly wait to taste an orange marmalade walnut scone. Sonny, I don't want you making a mess so I'll eat yours for you," said the old woman. Anna couldn't tell if it was for real or a joke. She watched as Ruth's gnarled hand reached out and how Libby guided it inside the basket so she could select a pastry. "Oh, my! These are scrumpdillyicious!"

While Ruth chewed her treat and stared into space, Libby said, "Ruth, I was telling Anna how you used to live on Edgewood Avenue in that big beautiful house on the corner. You remember that big house, don't you?"

"Does the Pope wear a funny hat? Of course, I remember the house on Edgewood. I may not see so good anymore but I haven't lost all my marbles," said Ruth emphatically. "Yes, she was a grand one. All gingerbread and gables. The porch was so big the four of us kids slept out there on cots in the summer. Mother thought we were heathens but there was nothing better than falling asleep to the night sounds and waking up to the milkman. All those houses were grand, the whole street was just a sight right out of a Hollywood picture."

"Do you remember the Somners? They lived down at the end in the big brick with the wrought iron fence around the front yard," asked Libby as she brushed pastry crumbs off of the cat.

"Lord, Lorna Somner," sighed Ruth. "What a lady she was! She and Mother weren't friendly because Mother thought Lorna was a heathen too. She took care of her own children instead of pushing them off on a nanny or a nurse like most of the doctor's wives did.

She would also have all of us, every last one of us neighborhood kids come to the front yard. She'd make up games for us. My, we had fun over at Ms. Lorna's. She'd always have lemonade and if it were a real special day she'd call us around to the back door and bring out her homemade cinnamon rolls. I don't think I've ever eaten anything as good as those cinnamon rolls." Ruth stopped talking and chewing for a moment and then added, "Except for this orange marmalade walnut scone!"

Libby and Anna laughed with her. Anna had that big feeling again when she thought about waking up to the smell of freshly baked cinnamon. This was getting really weird.

Ruth seemed lost in thought for a few minutes while she quietly chewed, still stroking the cat. "Poor Lorna. She was so sad when she lost that little child. We didn't think we'd ever get to play games in the yard with her or sit under the tree and drink lemonade again. She grieved so hard when that little girl of hers passed. We'd see Adam and Bethany out on the porch but the windows were draped in black and Mother said we were not to intrude. I was surely sorry for Ms. Lorna but I was sorry for us too. We missed playing with Adam and Bethany and we missed Ms. Lorna. We had to make do with entertaining ourselves that fall and we didn't see much of any of them until the next spring."

"Ms. Lorna started sitting out on the step like she used to do and we'd make sure to walk by and wave and call hello. Adam and Bethany started coming down off the porch and into the yard and by early summer we kids were playing again. We made sure we never got too loud or rambunctious so we didn't disturb Ms. Lorna. One day I remember we were playing Capture the Flag but we made sure not to holler and carry on when a team actually captured the other's flag out of respect. Pretty soon, Ms. Lorna came down the porch and asked us what we were doing. Adam told her we were playing Capture the Flag and she said we were doing it all wrong. We were pretty confused by that. There's not much to that silly game and

I'm pretty sure we had the basics. She said the real trick to a good game of Capture the Flag was the strategy your team developed. We weren't too sure what she meant by strategy but before we knew it, she dipped a stick in a puddle and drew us a diagram on the sidewalk so we could understand what she was talking about. We all got really excited about what she was saying and when she said she'd be on the team I was on with the younger kids, we cheered!"

"Of course, Adam didn't think it was fair for her to be on our team but Ms. Lorna always had time to explain and make everyone feel important. She told Adam it wasn't fair to the younger children when Adam, Bethany, and my brother Willy were so much older and able to think up better strategies. By the time she was done explaining, everyone was ready to play. We set up just like she suggested so when the big kids tried to grab our flag, we had our team placed so they couldn't get to it without being tagged. When all of Adam's team had been tagged, Ms. Lorna let out a war-whoop, raced across the yard, and grabbed their flag. We all cheered, even the big kids and they lost! We were so happy to have her back with us."

Again, Ruth paused and seemed to forget to chew or stroke the cat. Anna wondered if she had dozed off. Libby sat patiently and after a few minutes asked Ruth, "Do you know what happened to Ms. Lorna? We know Doc Somner died years before her. Did she stay at the house on Edgewood? Did she die there?"

"Dr. Somner loved Ms. Lorna. She couldn't wait for him to get home and he usually had a clutch of flowers or some chocolates for her. They adored one another! I know our mother and father loved each other but those two were different. Theirs was a big love," said Ruth.

Anna could tell the old woman was getting fatigued. The pauses were coming more often and lasting longer. She raised her eyebrows at Libby as if to say is that it?

"No, Ms. Lorna stayed at the house on her own after Dr. Somner passed on. Her kids were mostly grown or away at boarding school in St. Louis. I used to walk over after school some days and we'd have lemonade on her porch. She appreciated the company. I knew she was lonely in the big house by herself," said Ruth.

The pause this time was so long that it was accompanied by a gentle snore. Libby looked at Anna and they stood up to leave the room quietly and let Ruth have her nap. They had made it halfway to the door when Ruth's voice began again. "Ms. Lorna died in the hospital Dr. Somner worked at all those years. She had heart trouble so the end was pretty clearly coming. All her children were with her those last days and last minutes and Bethany told me at the wake that her mother had thanked each of them for being wonderful children and loving her as much as she loved being their mother.

"Thank you, Ruth. I'll see you next week," said Libby quietly and continued on to the door.

Out in the hall, Anna stopped Libby by touching her arm. "What a wonderful lady! She does know the cat isn't real, right?" asked Anna.

Libby laughed. "Of course, she told me how she missed having a cat in the house and it's strictly against the rules to have a pet so I found the softest stuffed animal I could find. It makes her happy."

Anna was once again taken by surprise by her new friend and her many talents, jobs, and abilities. "I'm just wondering, and I don't know anything about this kind of thing, but if Lorna died in the hospital surrounded by her family, why is she in the house?"

"We could ask her," said Libby.

"We did ask her. She told us Lorna died in the hospital with her loved ones at her side," said Anna.

"Not Ruth. Lorna," said Libby.

Libby turned and continued up the hall they had come down but Anna stayed where she was for a minute or two trying to rationalize what Libby had just said. She didn't say anything more until they were both seated in Anna's car. Before turning the ignition, she turned to face Libby. "How, exactly, do you do that? Ask Lorna."

"Well, you shine pretty brightly. You could ask her and see if you get anything. If not, we could ask Lavendar to come in. And don't be frightened of Lavendar coming over. He doesn't wear funky robes or bring a twisted staff and crystal ball. He just comes in and walks around and sometimes he's able to find stuff out," explained Libby. Anna turned the car on and backed out of the parking spot.

"I'll think about it," said Anna.

Back at home, Anna couldn't help but look at the house through different eyes. Hearing about Lorna firsthand from Ruth and how she adored her husband and loved being a mother made her feel honored, in a way, to live where she had lived. She felt that they had a lot in common except that as yet, Anna and Tony weren't parents. It was something they both wanted with all their hearts. So far it just hadn't happened. Anna walked through the kitchen to her favorite room, the sunroom, and as always enjoyed its warmth and light. If she had to describe the feeling she got from being in the room it was contentment and wellness. Without realizing she was doing it, she spoke the words aloud, "I love this room. It makes me feel good just being here." Before she could say more Tony was at the glass doors.

"Did you say something? I didn't know you were home yet," he said.

"I didn't know you were home either! How was your golf?" she asked him.

"Golf was fine. Dave Wilson is full of shit but I played well. Who were you talking to if you weren't talking to me?" he asked.

Anna laughed, "Talking to myself, I guess. Why don't you light the grill and I'll get some dinner going? We can eat outside on the patio and talk about design plans."

Tony groaned but not wholeheartedly. He had steadily worked through the rooms of the house in the year and a half they had lived there. The next big project was the fabulous back deck he had promised her all those months ago.

Later that evening as they sat at the small glass table on the back patio enjoying grilled tenderloin medallions, Tony told Anna he had to take a few days and go out to Phoenix to help his mom. After Tony's dad passed, Elaine moved to a small villa there, disliking the cold Missouri winters. Now she was ready to move to a retirement community and wanted Tony's help with the move and financial decisions. It had been eight months since she had last visited so Tony felt it was prudent to make the trip and help his mom. "Why don't you play hooky and come with me for a few days?" he asked.

"I'd love to. I miss your mom but I've got summer school hiring and student applications to work through," she said.

"Someday I'd really like it if you had a job that wasn't more important than everything else," said Tony tersely.

"Tony, my job is not more important than everything else. That's not fair. You have times when your work schedule doesn't allow you to plan a trip or time away. I have to hire a staff and fill classes for summer school that starts in three weeks. I can't go to Phoenix right now," she said hoping he'd understand.

"It's always a bad time. State testing, summer school, staff appreciation. Sometimes I think school gets more of you than I do," he grumbled as he picked up his empty plate and headed for the kitchen.

Anna stayed at the table, sad that the conversation had turned south. It wasn't the first time Tony had complained about the demands of her job. She knew he would come around later with a handful of Dove chocolates or a cold beer as a way of saying he was sorry about the conversation. Anna appreciated his peace offerings but wished he wasn't so resentful of the time she spent at school.

Several days later, Anna drove Tony to the Columbia Airport. Things were slightly cool between the two of them. Anna made sure to send along some of Elaine's favorite truffles from The Candy Factory. "Tell your mom hello for me. I hope the move goes well," she said as they stood on the sidewalk outside the small airport.

"I'll see you in a few days. I love you, Anna," said Tony.

"I love you too," she said. She watched him wheel his small case inside the airport and returned to her car. At home, she punched the message button on the answering machine and heard Libby's voice, "So I did something you may or may not be happy about but I hope you will be-happy. Anyway, call me."

Anna smiled at the airy message and punched in Libby's number. "Okay, what is it that may or may not make me happy?" she asked.

"I was so excited after we talked to Ruth that I may have mentioned the whole Lorna situation to Lavendar. He'd really like to help if he could, I know it's an issue with Tony but if you can think of a way for Lavendar to come by, it may be the last bit of information we need," said Libby quickly, trying to get it all out.

Anna laughed at the phone. "Your timing is remarkably perfect. I just dropped Tony at Columbia Airport. He's going out west to visit his mom for a few days. I was going to call you about inviting Lavendar over while he's away. Weird, huh?"

"Of course, it's not weird! It's you. Lavendar's Wednesday night class is over by 7. How about we come around after that?" asked Libby.

"That should work fine. Do I need to have anything special, do anything special to prepare or get ready?" asked Anna hesitantly.

It was Libby's turn to laugh. "Eye of newt, hair from a three-legged cat? No, Silly. Maybe some cold drinks? Something to eat would be nice."

"Sorry, this is all new to me. I'll figure out something to eat and have something cold to drink. See you Wednesday," said Anna.

Anna hung up the phone shaking her head. This whole experience starting with finding out about the Somners and now a psychic coming to the house was almost beyond belief. This was pretty far out there and she hoped she wasn't doing something ill-advised by having Lavendar come in. Libby was lovely and maybe the slightest bit flaky, but so friendly and helpful! Anna realized how much she was enjoying having a friend who wanted to talk about things other than Annual Yearly Progress Goals.

Anna used her evening time alone to look up information on M. Brewer, the name she and Libby found in the corner of the stained glass. Immediate hits began loading on the computer screen; 'Local Artist Received at Governor's Mansion, Glassworker Honored by St. Jude's Hospital'. Anna opened article after article and found out that Micha Brewer was a local artist from southern Missouri. He studied at the University of Missouri and taught there for a brief time. His cutting-edge use of color in glass set him apart from other artists, making his pieces highly respected and in demand. Mr. Brewer's work could be found in the State Capital Building, the Governor's Mansion, and many public buildings. His work was described as magnificent and compelling. One article showed a grainy picture of the artist at work in 1923. The caption below read, 'M. Brewer working on a personal piece, Heaven Window'. Anna made a few notes so she could relay what she had found to Libby.

Wednesday at school was one for the record books. Anna sent three students home for fighting and called an ambulance when the school nurse collapsed with an asthma attack. With everything that was happening at school she never once thought about the evening ahead. She called Tony on her drive home so he didn't call in the middle of whatever was going to happen. They chatted briefly about the beautiful weather in Phoenix, how Elaine loved the truffles and the progress of her move.

"We're going tomorrow morning to sign the lease at the retirement community. Then the moving truck is scheduled around 11. We should be packed up and rolling by early afternoon. I'm going to stay on till Saturday to make sure she is settled in," said Tony.

"Okay, I miss you. This big house gets that much bigger when I'm here alone," said Anna.

"Yeah, we really need to get to work on filling it up with kids or dogs or something," said Tony.

Anna laughed. "No dogs, please. Children would be wonderful."

"I love you, My Anna. I'll be home Saturday," said Tony.

"I love you too," said Anna.

Hanging up the phone Anna kept a smile on her face. Hearing Tony's voice and talking about filling the house with children made her very happy. She unloaded her lunch bag and set her school bag on the stairs. Since she had some time before Libby and Lavendar arrived she decided to make a pizza. Tony loved pizza but only if it was covered in meat. Anna used this opportunity to try something different. She had picked up fresh mozzarella and vine-ripe tomatoes along with a box of long-neck beer. She rolled out the pizza crust nice and thin and popped it in the oven for a few minutes. Going to her window herb garden, she plucked off a handful of fresh basil. She cut generous slabs of cheese and sliced the tomatoes thin. Pulling the crust from the oven she made several loops of olive oil, and added salt and pepper. Then she laid the mozzarella, basil, and tomatoes on the crust. Admiring how fresh her creation looked she left it to bake until closer to time for her guests to arrive.

Kicking off her shoes at the base of the stairs, Anna stooped to pick them up. Glancing up she once again marveled at the beauty of the stained-glass window. As she crossed the middle landing, she found herself talking out loud, "Well done, Lorna." In her room, she changed from her principal skirt and blouse. She wasn't sure how one dressed for a psychic and opted for black yoga pants and a soft t-shirt that covered her hips. Back downstairs, Anna wasn't sure what to do with herself while she waited. She laughed at herself for feeling anxious. She decided the back patio would be a good distraction and grabbed one of the cold beers on her way through the kitchen. She loved the outdoor space Tony had built for her. She had planted many small container gardens with flowers, herbs, and even a few vegetables. She busied herself deadheading the petunias and other flowers while enjoying the late afternoon sunshine. Before she realized what time it was, she heard voices coming up the driveway. Startled, she turned to see Libby and a young man standing at the corner of the house deeply engrossed in conversation. She stood uncertainly for a minute before Libby glanced her way and smiled widely.

"Hey Anna, we're a little early. I hope that's okay," said Libby. "This is Lavendar. Lavender, this is Anna."

Anna walked the ten steps separating them and stuck her hand out to greet the young man. Although she didn't know what a psychic would or should look like this was not what she expected in the least. He was younger than she expected but then she had a hard time deciding how old he might be. His light-colored hair swept across his forehead in a way that could be described as preppy. He was dressed in a pink polo shirt and stovepipe chinos, boat shoes, and no socks. He looked like he had just come from one of the nearby fraternities. The most unusual thing about him was his eyes. As Anna offered him her hand, he looked at her with the most stunning blue eyes she had ever seen. Blue wasn't even the right descriptor. Purple, his eyes were so blue they seemed purple. She found herself staring and embarrassed, tried to pull her hand back. He held on and continued to look at her with an intense, yet warm look. The half-smile on his face made him incredibly good-looking and when he spoke his voice was smooth and modulated. "It's really nice to meet you, Anna. I've been looking forward to it."

"Uh, thanks. I've been looking forward to meeting you as well," she said. Libby just laughed at the two of them.

"Oh, this is going to get good. I may need to wear my sunglasses around you two." At the sound of Libby's voice, Anna was able to release Lavendar's hand and invited them inside. They went into the kitchen and Anna offered them a cold beer which they happily accepted.

Anna was nervous and stammered as she said, "So do you want to look around the house first, or do your, whatever it is you do? Do you want me to tell you the things I've seen and felt?"

Lavender was looking around the kitchen. "This is incredible!" he said.

"What is?" cried Libby and Anna almost together thinking that he had already sensed something supernatural.

"This kitchen! These custom cabinets, quartz countertops, the archway leading into the dining room! Superb job whoever did this," he said.

Anna and Libby burst out laughing at each other. "Are you guys hungry? I can pop this pizza in and it will be ready in 15 minutes," said Anna.

"Sounds perfect," said Lavendar. They filled the time admiring the kitchen and the remarkable job Tony had done. They spent a good ten minutes talking about china Anna had inherited from her grandma. "They are hand-painted so when we moved here and three pieces got broken, I was really upset," explained Anna. "Tony scoured every flea market and antique store from here to St. Louis looking for pieces to replace them. He finally found some in a cute little shop in Washington, Missouri. They are hand-painted but not exactly like Grandma's. If you look closely, you can pick out the different ones. I don't care, though. Tony was so sweet to go to the trouble of finding them. They mean just as much to me as grandma's do." Lavender looked away from the china cabinet and gave Anna a direct look. She felt like he was able to know things that she hadn't told him. Strangely, she didn't feel uncomfortable with him at all. He was terrifically handsome and when he turned those eyes on you it was difficult to remember what you were talking about.

Anna heard the ding of the kitchen timer and went around the corner to remove the pizza from the oven. She put it on a cooling rack and cracked three fresh beers. She sliced the pizza and they all decided to eat outside on the patio. The evening was especially nice and the conversation was flowing easily about dishes and grandmas.

"That was delicious Anna!" said Lavendar.

"Thank you. I've been wanting to try that for some time," she said as she collected the plates and thought briefly about Tony. "Would anyone like another beer?" she asked.

"None for me," said Lavendar as he followed her inside.

Anna stacked the plates on the counter and turned around to find Libby standing alone with her in the kitchen. She raised her eyebrows and Libby indicated with her chin that Lavendar had left the kitchen and gone through the dining room where they had been admiring the china. Libby and Anna turned the corner only to discover he wasn't in the dining room. The French doors were open into the sunroom. Anna realized, with the exception of looking up the stairs first, Lavender was seeing the house in the same order she had first seen it. The ladies watched him through the glass doors. He stood still in the middle of the room with an untroubled look on his face. He seemed to take it all in and after a few minutes came through the French doors into the living room. Without acknowledging Libby and Anna he uttered one impression of the sunroom. "It's perfect," he murmured.

Walking into the living room, Lavender looked like a potential home buyer. He didn't study anything too intently, just surveyed the room and let his eyes sweep from floor to ceiling. He did go up and lay his hand against the mantle. After pausing there a few seconds he moved to the bottom of the stairs. Here he stopped and stood unmoving. The light from the evening streamed through the stained-glass window onto his face giving him an otherworldly look. Anna and Libby stood together a few steps behind. The feeling they were both feeling was that something was happening. Something reverent was happening. Finally, he put his hand on the newel post and started up the half flight of stairs to the landing. Anna and Libby stayed at the bottom. Upon achieving the landing, he faced the second half flight with his back to the colored glass and his head bowed. The window bathed him in a mixture of colors and light. He stood like that for longer than five minutes and when he finally raised his head, Anna saw the saddest expression she had ever seen on a person's face. She touched the newel post as if to follow him but Libby placed a hand on her arm and with a silent shake of her head indicated they should stay where they were. They couldn't hear the soft tread of Lavendar's shoes, but they knew he was going in and out of the small rooms. He was back at the top of the stairs looking at the fading light. He seemed to give a big sigh and then slowly started down the stairs. As he reached the last step where Anna and Libby were waiting, probably without breathing, he silently lifted his arms and embraced both women in a group hug. Anna didn't understand what it was but she felt something big had happened and Lavendar needed their support. They stood in their strange three-way hug for a few seconds and then looked up as one.

"I'm ready for one of those beers now," said Lavendar in a clear voice. Whatever had happened seemed to be over. Anna moved quickly to the door and indicated the cooler she had fixed up outside with ice-cold beer inside. They each took one and had a long pull. As one, they exhaled and looked at the house.

"What a beautiful home you have! It's clear that you and your husband love it in the way you have restored it and cherish it. Lorna loved it too. She and Edwin's prints are everywhere, in every room. Edwin must have stood with his hand on the mantle countless times. Probably in the evenings after the children were in bed or maybe before and they would play for him on the piano that was in front of the window. I could still hear it. Edwin is an echo. I hear him faintly all over the house but Lorna! She's right there, loud and clear. I'm not surprised you've seen her. I think you'd have to be deaf, dumb, and blind not to see her she's so bright." Anna grimaced slightly at that characterization that could be used for Tony. "She was extremely vibrant in the sunroom. It was her happy place. I feel her contentment there and all the love. Edwin built the room for her when she first arrived from the east coast. She was bitterly homesick and pined for her grandmother's solarium where the family used to gather.

Edwin couldn't stand to see her sad so he designed the sunroom to cheer her up. It was such a grand gesture of love. Lorna loved Edwin and she loved that room." Anna and Libby shared a look of understanding but didn't want to break the spell that Lavendar had them under.

"The staircase. Such sadness, profound sadness. Lorna's child died from an illness of the chest. Lorna was devastated. She sat on the top step to listen to the children. She sat there while Edwin tried to save their little girl. She cried there. She cried on the stairs for years looking out the window on the landing. She told the children she sat there so she could see heaven through the window. It made her happy to think her little girl was looking back at her. The children used to color pictures and leave notes on the window sill so their sister would know they were missing her. They called it the 'heaven window.'

Anna shook her head hard and her face was a bit paler than normal. Libby said, "What is it?"

"I didn't get to tell you but I looked up M. Brewer, the name on the stained glass. He was a local artist who did very important work around Missouri. A picture showed him working on a piece and the caption said it was a personal piece entitled, 'Heaven Window'. That has to be the stained glass in the stairway. He made it for Lorna."

Lavender and Libby looked at each other both realizing what a special situation this truly was. "I can hardly believe we know all of this-it's incredible," murmured Anna.

Finally, Libby said, "We understand Lorna lived here with Eddie and the kids. But she didn't die here. She died in the hospital surrounded by her family and loved ones. How is she here?"

Lavendar looked at Libby with his perfect grin that held the subtext 'duh'.

"Love, Lorna was deeply and profoundly in love with her husband and her children. She spread that love into and onto this house.

Her love here has made lasting connections to this house. The more interesting question is why is she here?"

Anna was really confused by Lavendar's musings. "What do you mean why is she here? You said she was here because of her love for the house. That has to be the reason, right?"

Now Lavender and Libby both gave Anna the 'duh' look. "Love is how she got here, not her reason for coming. What purpose does she have that made her come back to this physical place?"

"You couldn't tell that from your reading?" asked Anna.

"No, your ghost is charming but she did play coy with me. She showed me what she wanted me to see and then she shut the door. Speaking of doors, I need to head out. Anna, it was a pleasure meeting you. Thank you for letting me read the house. It's lovely. She's lovely," he said gesturing to the house with his chin as he and Libby stood to go.

"I can't thank you enough. This information is amazing! Can I pay you for your time? I really appreciate you doing this," said Anna.

"This was very special. I appreciate you letting me be a part of it. I think we'll let it go at that," he said, spreading his expressive hands out so far that his thumbs seemed to curl down to his wrists.

"How will I find out why she's here?" asked Anna to their retreating backs.

"Simple," was the reply she heard before they turned the corner of the house. "Ask her."

Anna sat back down at the small table replaying in her mind all she had heard about Lorna. She shook her head in frustration at Lavendar's last comment. She wasn't sure how one goes about asking a ghost why she's in your house and even more frustrating, how do you know the answer? She cleared up the few dishes from their pizza meal and decided to head upstairs and read in bed. She paused on the top step and remembering what Lavendar had described, sat down on the top step looking at the beautiful stained glass window that had surely replaced an ordinary one. She tried to decide how she felt after having the house read by a psychic and learning information that she was willing to accept as truth. Even though it was dark outside, the colored glass was magnificent and made Anna feel something special knowing that Lorna had sat here too and looked at heaven where her sweet little girl had gone. She stood with a smile before moving to her bedroom.

Before she knew it, she was back at the airport retrieving Tony. He was glad to see her and picked her up and twirled her around in a tight embrace. Anna laughed, delighted in this display of affection. When Tony had flown out, things were a bit strained but it was clear he had missed her and was glad to be home. She asked him if he wanted to stop downtown at their favorite burger place but he just reached for her hand and said he was ready to be home even if he had to eat a peanut butter sandwich.

"Anything exciting happen while I was gone?" he asked as they unlocked the back door and flipped on the kitchen light.

"No, pretty quiet. I got summer school squared away so that's good. Libby and her friend came by for dinner one night but that's about it," said Anna.

"No ghost activity?" he asked with a crooked grin.

"No more than usual. How about some cold fried chicken?" asked Anna.

"You know, I'm not all that hungry. I think what I'd like is to take my wife to bed. In my own bed," growled Tony.

Anna laughed and went willingly into his arms. "Sounds perfect," she said.

The two went upstairs and showed each other just how much they had missed one another. Later, lying in bed but not asleep Tony said sleepily, "Whatever your new air freshener is, it's driving me crazy."

Anna turned her face up to look at him. "I don't have an air freshener. You know things like that give me a headache."

"Huh," he said. "I swear I smell baked cinnamon. Like cinnamon rolls. I thought maybe you had a candle burning. Smells nice." Tony's voice trailed away and Anna knew he was asleep.

She hugged him a little tighter and smiled into his chest. "Thanks, Lorna," she whispered. Anna snuggled down and closed her eyes. A feeling of deep contentment washed over her.

Summer started as did summer school. Anna always enjoyed the summer school session as it was less pressure than the regular one hundred seventy-four-day school year. She had time each morning for a brisk walk around the beautiful neighborhood and was home each evening for many hours spent in the backyard. Their back deck had been transformed from a simple patio slab to a two-level deck with a roof complete with ceiling fans and lights. It was like an addition to the house and Anna and Tony both enjoyed spending their evenings staining the wood and putting the finishing touches on the trim. One evening, Anna stood up from where she had been applying stain to the longboards that would be the lower deck. Feeling dizzy she reached for the railing barely catching herself. Tony noticed and quickly came down off the ladder where he was painting the trim work around the new roof. He held Anna by her arms, "What's wrong?"

"I guess I stood up too fast. I'm fine, just dizzy. It's clearing up now. I think I'll clean up my brush and get some tea," she said. Tony looked at her sharply, but let her go and turned back to his ladder. Before he could resume his painting, he heard Anna retching inside the mudroom. He rushed in to see what was happening. Anna was wiping her face with a dish towel and looked as green as a gourd. "Could you clean this brush for me? The fumes are making me nauseous for some reason," Anna said.

"Are you sick?" he asked worriedly.

"I've felt fine all day. Maybe I just got too warm out there. I don't know what's going on with me today," she said.

"You go get a cool shower and I'll clean the brush out. Maybe you should lie down," said Tony.

"I think I will go take a shower but I'm fine. I'll be down in a few minutes and fix us something to eat," she said. Tony watched her hold the railing as she climbed the stairs. He was a bit worried; the heat had never bothered her before. He resumed his edge trimming and was able to complete a few other small areas before he was ready to knock off for the evening and clean up his brush. He wondered about Anna, it had been well over an hour since she went upstairs for a quick shower. As he shook the water out of the brush his stomach rumbled. They hadn't had dinner yet, maybe that was the reason for Anna's shaky behavior. He washed his hands in the sink and went upstairs. He found her asleep on the bed in her summer robe.

Tony sat on the edge of the bed gently. Anna's eyes fluttered open. "Hey," he said softly. "You feeling okay?"

"Sure," said Anna slowly. "The shower felt so good and then I was so sleepy I thought I'd just lay down for 5 minutes. What time is it?"

"Quarter to ten," Tony answered.

Anna's eyes opened wide. "What? I must have slept for an hour! You must be starving," she said as she tried to sit up.

"I'm fine. I'm a little concerned about you though. Dizzy, nauseous, sleepy. You don't think…" said Tony.

Anna at first looked confused and then began shaking her head. They had been hoping for a baby for some time. "I don't know, maybe," she said. Tony gave her his biggest smile and pulled her into his arms.

"I love you, My Anna," he said into her hair. "You come on down and I'll make you a Tony's Deluxe grilled cheese sandwich." Anna smiled up at him as she stood and went to the door. He paused and looked back at her and the love on his face made Anna catch her breath. She put her hand on her belly. Could it be? Really? She was a huge believer in the law of attraction; whatever reality you were most hoping for is the one you should project into the world. "I'm pregnant," she thought to herself. She wrapped her robe around her and went downstairs. She of course stopped on the top step to gaze out the darkened Heaven Window. She couldn't see Lorna but she was sure she was near. Anna couldn't stop herself from saying, "I'm sorry about your little girl. Thanks for being here." She continued down to the kitchen where the smell of toasting bread and melting cheese was waking up her empty stomach.

Anna came back to herself, realizing she had been lost in time and space remembering their early days in the house. She always believed that Lorna had come to help her achieve her greatest accomplishment, her two beautiful daughters. In the years after Ellie was born, either Anna was too busy or Lorna had better things to do because she didn't 'see' her in the house and they never again awoke to the wonderful smell of baked cinnamon. Lorna did make an appearance the year Mia was born. Anna and Tony had always hoped there would be more children but were terribly proud and pleased with Ellie who was precocious and so full of personality there was never a dull moment in the house on Edgewood. They didn't try to prevent anything from happening but had gotten used to the idea that Ellie was their only one.

One night, Anna thought she heard Ellie call out and got up to go across the hall to check on her. At six, Ellie's room was done in magnificent princess style. She was sound asleep in her pink canopy bed. The night light that she insisted on, showed Anna that her sweet girl was deep asleep. Turning back into the hall Anna paused at the other small bedroom. It had been Ellie's nursery until she needed a big girl bed and room for books and stuffed animals. Anna looked at the empty crib and the rocking chair where she had nursed Ellie. It made her smile.

Before going back to bed, she stepped to the top of the stairs and gazed out of Lorna's Heaven Window. Turning around to head to bed, Anna for some reason, once again glanced into the nursery. She was startled and jumped when she saw the figure of a woman sitting in the rocking chair as if she were rocking an infant. Anna held her breath and the woman looked up- Lorna looked up. She smiled and then was simply gone. Anna took a few calming breaths and put her hand on her pounding heart. She wasn't frightened of Lorna but seeing her so suddenly and unexpectedly made her heart feel like it might beat out of her chest. She said quietly to the room, "Good night, Lorna" and went back to her bed.

It was difficult to put her night visit out of her mind and the next day she began to figure out what it was all about. After a long day of school, Anna had to attend a PTA meeting that seemed to go on forever. Her attention was drifting to what Tony and Ellie were doing at home when she realized the meeting had adjourned and people were standing to leave. When she stood up, she had to reach out and clutch the chair in front of her. A wave of dizziness overwhelmed her and she stood still and took some long slow breaths in and out. She wondered if what she was thinking and hoping could be true and decided to stop off at the nearest drug store on her way home.

Eight and a half months later they welcomed Mia home. Tony chose the name after learning the origins can be traced to 'my darling'. He insisted, however, that it be pronounced MY-a instead of the more popular ME-a. Ellie completely doted on Mia and there were times when Anna had to remind her oldest daughter that she, Anna, was Mia's mother. After Mia was born Anna never again saw Lorna on the stairs or in the small room upstairs. She figured the question of 'why' had been answered for her. Twice. Thinking back to when the girls were little and Tony was alive, remembering how the house and their girls had been their pride and joy. So much is different now. Not only was the house different without Tony, Anna was different too. She knew it was time to move on just as Lorna had known. Picking up her handbag, Anna went out the back door onto the fabulous deck Tony had built for her years ago. It was someone else's time here. She hoped they would continue in the tradition Lorna and Edwin had started so long ago.

"What time is it?" asked Mack.

Al sighed. "9:15. She didn't add that it was 4 minutes since the last time he asked.

"9:15? Where's my breakfast? You know I like breakfast before 9."

"You've already had your breakfast," said Al. "It's 9:15 in the evening. You had ham and beans for dinner and apple pie for dessert."

"Where's my breakfast?" bellowed Mack. "By giesh, I've eaten breakfast at 7:00 every day of my goddamn life! Why can't I get any breakfast?"

Al sighed again. The Sundowners on top of the Alzheimer's were brutal. She wished there was a switch she could push and help Mack get past these awful hours where his confusion defied any cajoling or explaining. She would wade through it with him like she did most nights, hating it for him and also for herself.

When Mack first started showing signs that something wasn't right it was easy to explain away. He wasn't sleeping well, he wasn't eating as he should, he was overweight. But when he began to forget normal everyday things like where they kept the checkbook and when to turn on the sprinklers, Al began to take notice. When he began to lose his temper over not knowing where his car keys were or who left the lid off the birdseed allowing the squirrels free access she began to be concerned. When he got lost going to the farm store, a familiar route, she knew for certain what was going on. Al knew how to read the signs Mack was showing. It was the beginning of the end. His dad, Ben, had suffered the same awful fate. Instead of spending the end of his life in his lovely home beside the small lake where he loved to mow the grass, feed the birds, and curse the squirrels, Ben was forced to go to a nursing home. The view from his room was an apartment complex and the place had the distinct smell of old people. He didn't go easily. Ben raged at Mack and Al, refusing to speak to them for months after the move. Even though they were able to visit him regularly, they couldn't go every day. The nursing staff was wonderful but stretched thin. Thank goodness for Libby. When Al mentioned to the charge nurse that she wished there was a way for Ben to have more interaction she told her about Libby Stevenson. Libby was a woman close to Al's age who worked privately for a few of the resident's families. She didn't do nursing or therapy but offered daily companionship and conversation and spent quality time with her clients. Al liked the pretty blond immediately and knew it was money well spent knowing that Ben got time each day to play cards or walk outside with Libby.

She kept Mack home as long as she could. It wasn't easy. His mood swings were unpredictable and his independent nature compelled him to strike out each morning with a purposeful stride. The challenge was that Al was never sure what his purpose was and had to keep a vigilant eye on him. Many times, she had to beg off from the plans she'd made with her friends for lunches, outings, and trips. It was too hard for her son, Nathan, to work and take care of his family and look after Mack. Their daughter, Marie was in Kansas City and would help whenever she could plan ahead and free her busy schedule as owner and manager of her own restaurant. Al stayed at home with Mack and watched as he lost interest in all of the things he was passionate about; golf, baseball, hunting, and fishing. He got to the place where he refused to bathe himself and forgot to eat unless she insisted. The decision to move him to a nursing facility was crushing for Al. There was the guilt she still carried from Ben who never forgave them for taking him away from his home. But also, caring and doing things for the people she loved was what Al did best. She was the one that kept her siblings together after their parents were gone. She enjoyed cooking for loved ones and if they couldn't eat together, she'd deliver a hot meal to their door. She never let a niece's birthday or her sisters' anniversaries go unnoticed. She was the youngest, but she filled the hub vacated by their aged parents. Not being able to care for and do for Mack was a huge source of pain for Al despite the support and insistence from her children that she was doing the right thing.

Nathan and Marie loved their father, but they both enjoyed a more profound relationship with their mother. Mack treasured the children but stood back as if to watch from a distance. Al truly loved being a mom and loved being on the front row of their lives, watching them, cheering them, and supporting them always. She was the one that took up every interest they showed as children and helped them develop the skills, get the lessons, and join the teams of whatever sport or activity they turned their attention to. She helped with school projects, chaperoned dances, and sat at the foot of their beds listening to mashed feelings and nursing hurt hearts. Neither Nathan nor Marie wanted to see their dad in a nursing home, but it killed them to see their mom who was much younger, struggle to care for their dad. Even short trips to visit Marie in Kansas City or the 25-mile drive to Nathan's home were problematic. Mack had gotten to the place where leaving home made him agitated. He was not content to enjoy even a short visit away. Al didn't complain to the kids but they knew she had to be suffering not seeing her family, the goddesses, or being able to leave town.

It had been Mack that first coined the title of 'goddesses' to refer to the group of friends years before. Even though he himself went hunting and fishing and had a huge golf habit, he never understood why girlfriends went on trips or had to see each other multiple times a week. He would get upset and give Al the silent treatment for hours with a few slammed doors thrown in for good measure if she had been off doing something with her friends. During one spat when the ladies had gone to Florida for a short trip, Mack was being a particular ass. After days of not speaking and dark looks, Al had had enough. One morning as they were both in their spacious, airy bathroom ready to start their day, she closed the door on the both of them and stood with her back to it. Mack tried glaring at her but Al simply crossed her arms over her chest and said, "You're going to have to talk to me."

"I got nothing to say," grumbled Mack.

"Well, I do! This silent treatment is for moody thirteen-year-old girls and I'm fed up with it. You knew I had a trip planned with Anna and the girls. I don't understand why you're upset. You go hunting all the time and on golf weekends 4-5 times a year," said Al.

"Knowing about it and being okay with it are two different things. When I go play golf you know exactly what I'm doing-playing god-damn golf! How do I know what you women are up to when you're out? You're always getting dressed up, buying new clothes-hell, I don't trust that Donna Sue or Jackie in the least. I'll bet they're wild as all get out," said Mack. "How do I know they're not out trolling for men? How do I know you're all not out there… looking for men?"

Al hated to fight. She had never been a match for Mack and his temper. Most times, she would tamp down her own anger or hurt feelings and not fight something she couldn't win. This time, however, instead of the anger and frustration of the moment, she felt a giggle in the back of her throat. She tried to stifle it in the face of Mack's seriously mad face. She covered her mouth with her hand but it was just no use. The giggle burst out and became a belly clutching full-on laugh. Mack's face began to turn red but lightened up around the edges as Al continued to bend at the waist and laugh. When she could finally draw in a breath she said, "That's why you're upset? You think we get together so we can look for men? That is the most ridiculously dumb idea I've ever heard," she gasped.

"Why is it so ridiculous? Why else would you all dress up, get all made up, unless you're trying to get attention? From men!" he countered loudly.

"Mack, Mack, Mack! The last thing on our minds is looking for men. I, we, already have a man and trust me, one is enough! We get dressed up because we like to look nice. We put on make-up because we like to feel pretty and when you look good you feel good. We do our hair because, well, we just do! It's a girl thing. Trust me, it's not a man thing. I've told you before if I ever get rid of the man I've got, I'll never have another," said Al.

Somewhat appeased, Mack continued, "You're so good-looking, you wouldn't have any trouble finding a man. It won't be five minutes after I'm gone, you'll have someone new. I think about these things and when you go out looking the way you do I worry. I'm sure a group of goddesses like you all get attention from men wherever you go," he finished.

Al basked in the compliments even though Mack was still obviously mad. At least he was talking. Being an outdoorsy girl all her life, Al was attractive but no great beauty. She had a trim body with strong arms and legs from walking and working outside as much as possible. Her dishwater brown hair was always cut in a chin-length bob as she didn't know what else to do with it. She started to notice a few strands of silver mixed in and decided not to cover it up. Her blue eyes, freckled skin, and her name were the only things she'd gotten from her mother it seemed. She'd been a daddy's girl from the beginning tagging along with him on the tractor before she could walk. He'd been the one that changed the name her mother had given her insisting no little daughter girl should have to write Aunella LeVisa on her big chief tablet so he shortened her name to Al and it stuck much to her mother's dismay. When her older sisters were going shopping and joining Cotillion, Al was mowing the hay-field and planting vegetables and herbs.

Coming back to Mack, she said, "You're sweet to say that and we have gotten some unwanted attention on occasion. But Sweetie, that's not what we're looking for and trust me when I say, with Jackie and Donna Sue around the fellas get the message pretty quick to step off and try elsewhere. You have nothing to worry about. These women, they give me things I need that you can't," said Al.

"Like what?" asked Mack who was considerably less trusting of people than Al.

"Well, sometimes I need help thinking things through. I know I can always talk to you but you have a tendency to want to fix it for me or tell me what I should do. But sometimes I'm not looking for a solution-I just want to talk it out to know what I think or feel about it. I can do that with the girls and it helps me. I know you don't like it that I get so worried about things and can't stop fretting over them. It's easy for you to say, 'just don't worry about it' and I wish I could but I can't. I hate that I get so anxious and I try not to but sometimes I just lose control over it and it swamps me. I can talk to the girls about those things and they sometimes have helpful insights about whatever it is. Sometimes they tell me to shut up and quit whining. If I think we have problems with our kids or," Al didn't want to ruin the conversation by saying 'our marriage' so she said, "You know, home problems, we talk about it and it turns out all of us have those kinds of peaks and valleys. When I get scared that this must only be happening to me or to us or our kids, it turns out that others have been through something similar and it makes me feel better to know I'm not alone. We talk about it and I come away from it with new energy or a different idea on how to cope with whatever it is," finished Al. "I need you! You're my man and I love you. But I need my girls too."

"Well dang, Girl. I had no idea what you all were doing when you stay out late and travel overnight. You know I love the shit out of you," declared Mack. "I really had no idea what you and the 'goddesses' spend your time doing. But now that I know, I'm glad you have them. Just do me a favor and leave our 'at home problems' out of the conversation," said Mack.

Al hugged her husband tightly. It was one of the most productive conversations they'd had in a while. It meant the world to her that Mack saw the validity and need for her female friends. From that day forward the friends were referred to by everyone as the 'goddesses'.

Al snapped back to the here and now. Mack was struggling to get out of bed. "Where are you going? It's bedtime," she said.

"You crazy woman. It's breakfast time. I've been eating my breakfast at 7:00 a.m. my entire life and I'm not about to stop now," said Mack.

Al could tell there was no use fighting to keep him in bed at this point. She quickly snapped on the radio beside the bed. Sometimes solid gold country music could speak to Mack when no other language would. A good old George Strait song, Amarillo By Morning, began to play. Al put her arm over the top of Mack's still broad shoulder. "Hey cowboy, you want to dance?" she asked. Mack's arms immediately assumed a traditional dancer's hold and his feet began to move in a slow but dependable two-step beat.

Al was relieved the music helped soothe the agitation and confusion about breakfast at bedtime and rested her forehead on Mack's shoulder. They'd spent many a night just like this either in a honky-tonk or their own kitchen. Mack loved country music and was insulted by what was played on the country stations in recent times. "That's not country music! Sounds like Michael fucking Jackson if you ask me. No sir, George Strait, Travis Tritt, Alabama. That's REAL country music." Now dancing with his familiar form in her arms listening to him hum along, she was filled up with love for the man she'd married all those years ago.

Her family had a hard time accepting Mack when she first introduced him. Al being the youngest in her family, surprised them all by bringing home a guy who was older than her siblings. Some of them tried to talk her out of getting serious with him but in an uncharacteristic display of will, she continued to date Mack and married him two years after she first brought him home. Al wanted children right away and Nathan was born when Al was twenty-four and Mack was thirty-five. Mack loved the little boy but didn't seem to know how to play with him or later, talk to him. Al would leave the room with the father and son playing checkers on the floor and return to the sound of a wailing Nathan. Mack would have all the red checkers in front of him and say, "What did I do? That's how the game goes. He's got to learn there is no free lunch in life."

Al would scoop up her young son and say, "Maybe he doesn't have to learn all of life's hard lessons before he's five," and take Nathan to the kitchen for some blueberries. Mack's job took him away from home several nights a week, leaving Al and Nathan with lots of time together, just the two of them. They played and read inside but when the weather got halfway decent, Al would bundle the two of them up and they'd spend time outside. Al had always loved nature and would rather do anything outside than just about anything inside. She shared her love for the outdoors with her young son and later with Marie as well as with every class of students she taught. Nature walks, flower collections, and integrative units on living and nonliving were her trademarks and got the attention of the Science Coordinator for the school district. She asked Al to participate in the writing of an entire curriculum based on nature. The Outdoor Classroom was piloted by Al and her class of fourth-graders the following year and continued to grow and evolve into a lighthouse program that was admired and copied in other districts.

Back then, things between Mack and Al were okay but not great. Mack would try to interact with Nathan when he was home and if Nathan gave him any resistance at all Mack would storm off to his man cave in the basement, accusing Al of ruining the boy against him. Al worried about the climate in the house and what it may be doing to their young son. She loved Mack but between his work schedule and his temper bouts, it didn't leave much room for anything else. She wished she had someone to talk to but it was tricky talking to family. They never really approved of Mack so if she confided in them that she was frustrated she was sure of the feedback she'd get from them. Al also knew no matter how much she vented about her husband, she loved him and was always able to forgive and forget and move on. Her sisters and sisters-in-law, on the other hand, were not forgetful or forgiving. She wished for a friend she could confide in. For those few years, she poured her energy into Nathan and made the best of things when Mack was home.

When Nathan turned four, Mack surprised them by planning a trip to the beach. He rented a little house that opened right up to the waves. They brought chairs, umbrellas, toys, and a cooler with snacks and cold beer for Mack and Al. They spent three days in the idyllic setting, catching crabs at dusk, watching the sunset, and enjoying their son as he played in the gentle waves along the shore. It was a very good time for Al and Mack and although they didn't spend any time talking about anything serious, they did enjoy each other's company, and many a slow song danced on the hard-packed sand.

When they returned home, Al discovered she was pregnant. She didn't hesitate to tell Mack the news and he was genuinely pleased. She forgot her fears and worries about the state of their marriage and focused on being pregnant and getting Nathan ready for kindergarten. Marie was born in August. She had a big shock of black hair and lungs that declared her presence in the world. Nathan was pleased and instantly became Marie's best friend and knight in shining armor. He'd do anything to help Al take care of the baby with one major exception.

"You want to help change her diaper?" asked Al.

"No, Momma, that's gross," he said and quickly took himself and his tractor to a different room.

Mack couldn't figure out his tiny girl baby. She was loud and wanted Al for everything-and only Al. "I can't do anything with her. Why is she like this?" he'd say as he would hand the baby back to Al.

"What, you mean because she has a temper? Because she fights for what she wants and doesn't give in or back down?" laughed Al. "She's just like you!" And Al would pull the squalling baby close and croon to her until she had stopped fussing and began waving her tiny fists in the air. Frustrated, Mack would return to the basement and his 52" tv.

After Marie was born the years marched by too fast for Al's liking. Things with Mack were okay but they each had their own things to focus on. Mack would work, golf, hunt, and fish and be on hand for big events with the kids. Al focused on kid activities and kid friends. They were growing up; Nathan was headed to junior high school soon and Al knew graduation would come way too fast. It was at this time that she met Anna Perry and Sylvie Russel.

The three were attending a school board meeting that included an agenda for removing reading intervention services in elementary schools. This was a cause very near and dear to each of them. Anna, an elementary principal, had risen through the ranks of teaching first grade, being the assistant principal, and was now a principal for the last seven years. She took her role as the educational leader of her faculty and staff very seriously. She believed in early literacy and intervention for students, particularly for those from low socio-economic families. The research and Anna's first-hand experiences showed clearly that these students started school at a disadvantage and only with concentrated effort and purposeful intervention would they be able to catch up with their classmates.

Sylvie was a student advocate. She worked with many families that felt their child was not receiving the appropriate level of education they needed and deserved. Sylvie was at this particular meeting representing five families that spoke English as a second language. She knew these families cared greatly for their children and wanted them, desperately, to succeed in school. Many times, these families were overlooked or went unheard in a school board proceeding because of their language or unfamiliarity with the proceedings. Sylvie was there to make sure that didn't happen.

Al, a classroom teacher, attended the meeting to represent teachers. She was also there because of her own little boy. Of course, he wasn't little anymore-twelve years old, and in middle school, Nathan was doing fine. Al remembered how difficult it was for him to learn to read. The two of them spent countless nights pouring over the primers he brought home and that Al checked out of the library. Night after night Nathan would struggle and get frustrated. Al worried and obsessed as to how to help- she knew he was bright but he was working so hard and she didn't know what else to do.

When Nathan got to second grade, he was put in an intervention reading group. The teacher, Miss Morgan, saw right away that Nathan had learned everything in kindergarten and first grade that he needed. He had a wonderful vocabulary and excellent comprehension skills thanks to the millions of books he and Al had read since he was born but something was missing. The text on the page remained a mystery to the bright little boy. In a short time, Miss Morgan figured it out. Nathan was missing the connection between the letters and the sounds they made. She went back to the alphabet chart, which Nathan could correctly identify all 26 letters before he started school, and began making pictures and hand signs for each one. Nathan learned the hand signs quickly and each day they would practice the letter, the sound, and the hand sign. Along about October, it was as if a virtual lightbulb snapped on. Nathan was reciting the chart in Miss Morgan's tiny closet that had been reclaimed as a classroom. "M, man, mmmmmmmm," he said as his hands made the motion of tightening a necktie. He looked at the pretty young teacher who was pointing at the next letter. "M. Marie starts with M. M makes the sound of mmmm," he said.

"That's right. What else do you know that starts with m?" asked Miss Morgan.

Nathan looked excited and began naming everything he could think of. "Mom, music, math, map, Missouri, Miss Morgan, milkshake, monopoly, magic!"

Miss Morgan smiled widely knowing that the missing piece of the puzzle just slipped into place. Nathan would be reading new books by Christmas and be on grade level by the end of the school year.

Thinking back on the story of Nathan learning to read in the small classroom closet with Miss Morgan is what really brought Al to the school board meeting. Not all children learned the same way or in the same time frame. There was a real need for intervention in elementary buildings and she was here to add her voice to the cause. Several people spoke during the open mic portion of the meeting including Anna, Sylvie, and Al who were spread out near the back of the room. The people behind the tables made assurances that they had heard what was said and would consider all points of view before making further decisions. As the meeting broke up, people in the audience stood up and milled about. Sylvie touched Anna's arm and said, "I'm glad an administrator was here too. That really helps when it comes from different positions." Al overheard as she was gathering her purse and said, "Yes, I agree. And your contribution was good too," she said to Sylvie. "School boards are used to hearing from principals and teachers but when the parents speak, they tend to perk up a little more. I'm glad you were here to advocate for the parents."

Anna agreed that they had done well to show up and speak out, even knowing that the way of all school boards is that they will ultimately do what they want and that usually has to do more with the purse strings than student needs.

"Hey, would you all like to go have coffee? We could talk a little more about what else can be done," said Sylvie.

"I'm free," said Al. "My husband was taking the kids to mini golf. He's hoping they'll take up golf and play with him someday."

Anna checked her watch and said, "That sounds great. I just need to check in at home. My oldest is 'babysitting' her sister. I just need to make sure she doesn't have her locked in a closet or something."

"No problem, meet you at The Chez. Take as long as you need," said Sylvie.

And that was how Anna, Sylvie, and Al became friends. One heated topic at a school board meeting brought them together. Their shared passion for education and advocacy gave them something to talk about. In the end, those conversations wove themselves into deep connections and bonds that lasted well past a school board term.

"Hey Al," murmured Mack just above her ear. Al jumped slightly, caught up in her reverie and surprised to hear Mack say her name. More and more these days she was 'hey you'.

Not wanting to break the mood, Al kept her forehead firmly on Mack's shoulder and murmured, "Yeah Mack?"

"I just wanted you to know that I think we did good," he said. At this, Al did pull back slightly so she could look at Mack's face and see if there was a clue as to what he was talking about. "With the kids and all. We did okay. They are both grown and have someone to dance with. That's about the best you can hope for, right?" he asked.

Al felt a huge lump in her throat and didn't want to do anything that would break the spell. Mack was really here with her. His body, mind, and spirit were here. She knew it wouldn't last long.

"Sure, we did!" she exclaimed fervently. "You know we did. Those are two awesome kids who grew into wonderful adults. We did that," she assured him.

"I just want you to know that I know it was mostly you," he said. "I just didn't seem to know how to do the things you did for them. I sure do love them. Thanks for doing all that." Now Al was openly crying. This kind of talk was out of character for Mack before the Alzheimer's, but now it was highly improbable. She could tell he was talking straight from his heart.

"They love you too! They always did, even 'hard-headed' Marie. Look at her now, opening her own restaurant, standing her ground in such a competitive field. I always told you she's just like you," said Al through quiet sniffles.

"And Honey, I know I'm not an easy husband. You should have had someone who sent you flowers and took you to those foreign places you thought were so neat. I just didn't see the need to go somewhere they don't speak English. Just want you to know I love the shit out of you. I always did and always will," said Mack in his gruff voice.

Al couldn't see Mack's pajama top through her tears. She held him tighter and said, "I love you too. Always have and always will." Al heard the last few notes of the George Strait song and relished this moment. As soon as the song ended and a commercial came on the radio Mack stepped back and looked around the room like he didn't recognize it.

"Hey, you. Can you get me some breakfast? I've been eating breakfast at 7:00 a.m. my whole life. How hard would it be to get some cereal and orange juice in here?" he gruffed at Al.

"Okay," she told him. "I'll get you some breakfast if you promise to get back into bed and stay there."

"I reckon I can do that. You know I like the Quaker Oat Squares and some raisins sprinkled on top, and orange juice with lots of pulp," he said.

"I'll see what I can do. You get into bed and I'll get your breakfast," said Al.

Al went to the door of the room and turned back just out of Mack's sight. She watched as he climbed back into bed, pulled the cover up to his chin, and closed his eyes. Nancy, one of the regular attendants that helped in Mack's wing, stood beside Al in the hallway.

"He's a good guy, he just gets so mixed up this time of night. You're awfully good at helping us with him," said Nancy.

"He is a good guy. My guy. He was my one and only. I know I'll never have another." Al turned and walked to the security door of the Alzheimer's wing. Nancy looked after Al, wondering about her remark then checked that Mack was settled for the night and continued her rounds.

Donna Sue

onna Sue turned her chair to the plate glass window and the lovely scene beyond. She'd been thrilled when Ron had surprised her with the large corner office and grateful for his generous offer to have a decorator come in and give her a 'wow space'. She had preferred to decorate it herself and had enjoyed pouring over furniture catalogs with Ron and finding the exact pieces of art that she wanted. The result was a space that was functional and so well thought out aesthetically to be worthy of a spread in Architectural Digest. She thought about the hours she had spent here. With Ron. And without.

Thinking back to the very beginning she had been so young with no real work experience. She'd worked at Zesto's, the local ice cream shop through high school, and gotten on at Dryer's Shoes downtown after graduation. She had applied for the office job with a small but growing property management company just to see what would happen. She'd met the owner, Ron Lake, and even though she had no training or experience in secretarial work he felt like she could pick it up as she went. He liked the looks of the long-legged blond with the easy smile and dimpled chin. She would be the first face customers saw when they came to his business. He liked that she was friendly and outgoing and it didn't hurt a thing that she was gorgeous. Donna Sue loved working with people and learned quickly how to diffuse irate tenants and schmooze iffy renters into signing a lease. Before long Ron was scheduling Donna Sue to show properties more and more which created the problem of no one answering the phone or at the front desk. Over a work lunch at Booches, a favorite burger place downtown, Ron pitched her the idea of going full-time showing properties and developing leads and leaving the desk job for a new hire. Donna Sue was thrilled with the idea of being more involved with the actual property showing and the opportunity to earn more. Ron loved her enthusiasm and knew he'd made the right decision to hire the inexperienced twenty-one-year-old when he did.

Donna Sue did more than catch on. She developed a system for attracting corporate business that was wildly successful and included hosting art shows and restaurant showcase events. Ron was thrilled to have the new business and large accounts and Donna Sue was the one making a lot happen. They shared a mutual respect and admiration for each other and enjoyed a strong team relationship. Ron was a family man with a wife and two young children at home. Donna Sue was always a welcome part of birthday parties and holiday meals at the Lake house. She was always warm and friendly to Jules, Ron's wife, and doted on their kids; Kevin and Pamela. Donna Sue was aware of some veiled jealousy on Jules' part. She and Ron spent more time together working than he did at home. She felt bad for the other woman mainly because she always seemed discontented. She had a fabulous home, a good husband, and two great kids and yet Jules' good nature seemed to come at an effort. Donna Sue wondered if she was happy. At the office, Donna Sue did all she could to encourage Ron to pick up small gifts for Jules or take off early on Friday evenings to spend time with his family.

He confessed to her one evening that he often felt more comfortable at the office than he did at home. Jules had the kids involved in so many activities and camps that they were rarely home on the weekends. Things had become more and more strained between the two of them and he often chose to stay at work into the evening leaving less time for unpleasantness. Donna Sue was sorry to hear about Ron's home life. He was such a great guy and she couldn't understand how Jules didn't seem to appreciate him or the life he provided for his family. Ron was always the life of the party, never knowing a stranger. Early on Jules laughingly told Donna Sue that she had contemplated changing her name to 'Where's Ron'? It was the question she was asked repeatedly wherever she went. Donna Sue harbored a secret hope that someday she'd find a man like Ron to spend her life with.

After closing a particularly spectacular multi-year lease, Donna Sue and Ron were celebrating in the office long after it had closed for the day. Ron kept a bottle of small-batch bourbon on his sideboard and they were enjoying a well-deserved drink in Ron's spacious office. Donna Sue had kicked off her four-inch heels and curled her legs under her in the corner of the comfortable leather settee. Ron had his feet propped on the bottom desk drawer he had opened a few inches and was looking at the lovely artwork Donna Sue had encouraged him to buy. It was a large textile piece, over seven feet long, with a dark background and slender white birch trees. Ron felt such peace when he looked at it. He was once again grateful to Donna Sue for introducing him to the local artist, B. Borduin. After a few minutes of quiet comfortable silence, Donna Sue said, "We did good today boss. This contract will cover some of your bigger property investments. It's great new business and I have a feeling this is going to open the door to other big customers." When Ron didn't respond, Donna Sue put her glass down and came to stand beside his desk. "Ron?" she asked.

Ron had his eyes closed and his hand resting against his brow. He had the look not of a victorious businessman but that of a man with the weight of the world on his shoulders. "What is it?" she asked quietly.

Ron let his hand fall and before the famous Ron Lake smile tilted his lips, she saw a bleak look cross his handsome face. "It's Jules. She's pregnant." Donna Sue sucked in her breath not knowing immediately how to react given Ron's behavior. She was trying to recall exactly how old Kevin and Pamela were. Not long ago she'd been to Pamela's 10th birthday party and Kevin was a few years older. In light of the strained relationship and the age difference of the kids, Donna Sue was unsure of what to make of Ron's news.

"Congratulations!" she said brightly. "I didn't know you guys were thinking about adding to your family."

"Jules always wanted more children. It gives her purpose, I think. The pregnancy, the birth, the newborn, and then the search for the best preschools, best ballet class, best tutors, best camps," said Ron as his voice trailed off. "The thing is, I'm not sure how right it is to bring another baby into our home when I've been thinking maybe it's time for a change." Ron's face was ravaged by the uncertainty of his admission.

"Did you talk to Jules about that?" asked Donna Sue.

"Yeah, six months ago. Things kind of came to head and I mentioned that maybe it would be better for her, the kids, even me if we stopped trying to stay together and entertain the idea of … something different," he said.

"Oh, Ron. I'm so sorry. How did she take it?" asked Donna Sue.

Ron gave a mirthless laugh. "Typical. She locked herself in the bathroom in hysterics. Wouldn't come out for hours. When she came out it was like nothing had happened. She was great with the kids and extra attentive to me. She planned that ridiculous pool party for Pamela, which had fifty people at the house. I had a little too much to drink after the kids had all gone to the basement for the slumber party and the next thing I knew we were screwing on the den sofa. Now she's pregnant." Donna Sue didn't know what to say in light of the picture he had painted so eloquently. She cared for him greatly and felt awful for his predicament. She came around his chair and hugged him.

"It's going to be okay. I believe things are supposed to happen a certain way and I guess this is what's next. Congratulations!" she said and went to the settee to collect her shoes.

At the door, Donna Sue looked back to find Ron watching her. He gave her a half-smile and said, "Thanks, Donna Sue. Thanks for being so good to me."

Work continued and Ron tried to get home in time for dinner every night in the coming months. According to a few comments and the observations Donna Sue made, things seemed to be going well for the Lake Family. Jules was more outgoing and appeared happier, even showing up with cookies from Uprise Bakery for the office staff one day.

Donna Sue returned from showing a property to a prospective renter to find Jules sitting on the settee in Ron's office staring at Borduin's Birches. Donna Sue smiled and greeted Jules with a hug. "You look radiant!" she said, noting the matching lightweight rain jacket and the expensive looking maternity dress Jules was wearing.

"Thank you! It's been a while since I did this. Everything is different now than it was when I carried Kevin and Pamela. The list of what I can't eat, the baby equipment. I feel like a first-time Mommy! Sorry, I realize you wouldn't know anything about maternity things, not having any children," said Jules. Donna Sue took a slight step back feeling the sting of attack.

"No, you're right. I don't know what that's like," she said.

"Well, it's not for lightweights let me tell you. I've had to learn a whole new list of prenatal health precautions and now they even have pregnant yoga. At least the maternity clothes have improved," Jules said. "I was looking for Ron, I thought he'd want to take me to my ultrasound appointment."

"He should be here any minute. He was doing some business at the bank and then was headed back here," explained Donna Sue.

"And while we're out, I may have him stop off at the furniture store. Surely, they'd have something better than this awful thing he has on the wall," said Jules as she looked at the graceful art.

Donna Sue couldn't get away from Jules quick enough. She gave her an air kiss and backed to the door saying, "You look terrific. It was great seeing you." She could feel Jules looking her up and down and it felt entirely different from all the times the two women had been in each other's company previously. Shaking her head slightly as she walked up the hall to her own office, she smoothed her palms on her lime green pencil skirt, noticing they had gotten clammy during her conversation with the other woman. What in the world? That 'you wouldn't know about being pregnant' comment was still lodged in Donna Sue's head. She made herself sit down behind her desk and grab the nearest folder of paperwork that needed her attention. She wrote a note of things she needed to ask Ron about when he returned from his appointment with Jules.

Looking up hours later, Donna Sue realized it was after five, and Ron had not returned. She was surprised but left the note with her questions on his desk. She packed up her Nine West attache case Ron had given her as a gift when she moved from being a desk girl to his number one property broker and headed home. She thought for a minute about her obligatory Chinese takeout for one but decided against it. There had been a guy. He was definitely interesting and a terrific cook. Donna Sue knew it wasn't going to work when he stayed over the first few times. He wanted to rearrange her furniture and then her life. He said she was a fool for not leaving Lake Properties and opening her own company, with his help of course. He was sure she could cherry-pick the best clients and be 'rolling in the dough' in a couple of years. When Donna Sue said she had no intention of leaving Lake Properties he accused her of being in love with Ron. It turned ugly pretty quickly and Donna Sue asked him to leave and take his ergonomic pillow with him. At least he had left a partial case of that good red wine. She'd throw together some veggies and boil some pasta and settle down for an evening of music and paperwork. Being an only child, Donna Sue was used to being on her own. Her dad died at 41-much too young. She remained close to her mother but was so independent they lived very separate lives.

Donna Sue was one glass into the bottle of wine and was just about to lift her pasta when her doorbell rang. Checking the peephole, she was surprised to see Ron on her front step. Surprised, she pulled the door open.

"Hey, sorry to show up like this. I saw your note on my desk and thought it might be easier if I just came by. Am I interrupting anything?" he asked.

"No, not at all. I was just getting ready to eat. Have you had dinner?" Donna Sue realized she was talking a little too rapidly. Ron showing up at her house was highly unusual.

"No, I'm not really hungry. I could use a glass of wine," he said as he came inside her small but immaculate living room. He glanced around and immediately appreciated the simple yet elegant aesthetic of her home. It was lovely and had an easy comfort. He followed her into the small kitchen where she poured him a glass.

"I was just finishing my vegetable saute. Do you mind if I wrap that up? We can talk while I'm doing it," she said as she moved efficiently around the kitchen.

"Sure, yeah. Do what you need to do," said Ron. He leaned his hip on the counter and watched her add mushrooms and tomatoes to the garlic and onions in the small skillet. He talked about the questions she had left him while she drained and rinsed the pasta and stirred the veggies every once in a while. Donna Sue responded with the appropriate comments and took two plates out of the cupboard and plated two steaming piles of pasta and sauteed veggies. The last thing she grabbed from the refrigerator was some aged Parmigiano Reggiano. She looked at Ron as she moved to the second plate and raised an eyebrow as a question of yes or no. Ron gave a nod and continued to explain the plan behind one of their newly acquired properties as Donna Sue grated some of the cheese on top of the veggies. Grabbing both plates she indicated for Ron to open the door to a lovely lanai and followed Donna Sue out carrying both glasses of wine. A small antique dresser next to the house had a wicker caddy for napkins and salt and pepper. Donna Sue directed his attention to it with her chin as he continued to talk. They both sat down and began eating as they discussed the newest plan and the opportunities it presented.

After several minutes, Ron sat back in the comfortable wicker chair and shook his head.

"What?" asked Donna Sue.

"How do you do this? I came here with my gut tied in knots. I haven't been this relaxed in months. How do you do that?" he asked.

"Why is your gut tied in knots?" she asked.

Ron let out a huge sigh. Donna Sue could tell it was big whatever it was that was eating him. "It's the baby," he said. "I went with Jules for the ultrasound and they discovered something irregular about his kidneys. Of course, she is really freaked out and sure of the worst-case scenario. She's insisting I take her to the Mayo Clinic and I just don't know. I think I'm a little old for this."

Donna Sue reached across the small glass-topped table and squeezed Ron's hand. "Oh no, I'm so sorry to hear that," she said with obvious concern.

"The doctor said they'd monitor her closely and decide what to do as the pregnancy progresses. She said it could even correct itself. I want to be optimistic but Jules is really wigged out. She put herself on bed rest and told me I'm going to have to 'step up' and take care of the kids for the next few months. She's going to concentrate on the baby. Exclusively," he finished.

Donna Sue could tell Ron was worried about the baby. She could also tell this was more than that. She could feel his unhappiness that verged on despair.

"Don't worry. I can manage at work so you can get home when you need to. You do what you need to do and I'll take care of the office," reassured Donna Sue.

Once again, Ron looked at her and said out loud, probably what he should have kept as a thought in his head, "Why can't you be my home?" Not knowing what to say, Donna Sue stood up nervously to clear the plates. Ron followed her not knowing how to take back his comment. At the door, he turned to her and did his half-smile. "Thanks for letting me in and the wine and the dinner, that was amazing! I didn't think I was even hungry. I'm sorry for what I-"

Donna Sue cut him off, "Everything happens for a reason. I'm glad you came over. I'm glad I got to fix you dinner. I'll see you Monday," she said as she closed the door. She stood with her back to it for a few beats and realized that she wished the same thing. In fact, she was suddenly aware of feelings she'd had for some time now and had been afraid to acknowledge. She, too, wished this was Ron's home, with every fiber of her being.

As weeks passed, Jules demanded that Ron be on hand and at home more and more. Donna Sue was able to handle the daily business for the most part and when she needed help, she would drive over to their home and they'd go over business. Donna Sue worried about seeing Jules on one of her visits but never did. Ron said her self-imposed bed rest had reached new heights. She'd demanded that Ron hire a nurse to help her bathe in bed, fearing getting up even to take a shower would harm the baby. Donna Sue was quite surprised at this but with no experience of her own, it was difficult to say if this was normal or not. Still, she had loads of girlfriends who had had babies, and nothing remotely like this had happened to any of them. She could tell the isolation from the office and the general climate at home was wearing on Ron.

In May, Donna Sue planned one of her client appreciation events. These were always lovely social gatherings hosted in The Tiger Hotel. Donna Sue had long ago convinced Ron that one had to spend money to make money. She pulled out all the stops, top caterers provided lovely hors d'oeuvres and sweets, and champagne was handed about as current clients were encouraged to talk to potential ones. They were sure to glean a few new accounts after one of her events and the current customers loved the opportunity to get free food and booze from Ron. Donna Sue always looked amazing and totally turned out for the event. Her long trim frame made clothes look spectacular and she'd often go to Kansas City or St. Louis for her evening wear.

For this particular event, she was wearing a black sheath that rested on her exposed collarbones and apparently didn't touch any other part of her body. She swept her hair up in a rhinestone clip and spoke to every person personally. She had a knack for remembering details and introducing people by way of connecting their like interests. Donna Sue was firm with Ron that this was one event she needed him present. Surely Jules would be alright for the evening, tucked safely into bed. The evening was going swimmingly, Donna Sue thought. There were some interesting people from Chicago and she needed to find out more about what they needed in terms of property. She caught Ron's eye across the room and they both moved to the bar. "You look amazing," he said.

"Why thank you, sir! You look good too. It's good to see you in something other than your polo and khakis," she teased him.

"Yeah, it feels good to be out of the house. Who do we need to be talking to?" he asked. As Donna Sue began to fill him in on the Chicago crowd and their needs, his pager beeped. Donna Sue raised a perfectly shaped eyebrow as a question, but Ron indicated for her to continue as he once again hooked the pager to his belt. She continued only to be interrupted by the pager again.

"What is it?" asked Donna Sue.

"Probably nothing. She didn't want me to leave the house tonight so she's paging me. I'm sure it's nothing. I'll go find a phone. Let's pick up right here when I get back," said Ron.

Knowing he meant talking business Donna Sue was still secretly pleased by his comment and walked back to her party with a smile. When next she glanced up, she saw Ron waving at her from across the room. His look said it all. He was leaving. An emergency at home. She worked her way through the crowd as quickly as she could. "What's going on?" she asked.

"Probably nothing. Jules says she's in labor," he said as he dragged his hand through his hair.

"But the baby isn't due for five weeks," she said.

"I know but I have to go. She's hysterical and the nurse has left for the day," he said. "I'll try to come back or touch base with you later tonight." Ron leaned towards Donna Sue as if to kiss her cheek. Instead, she leaned back and touched his arm. Her eyes were warm and she said,

"Good luck. Talk to you soon."

Donna Sue returned to the party and worked the crowd with finesse. As the end of the evening drew near, many of the clients had left except a few hangers-on who were bellied up to the bar. Donna Sue settled the arrangements for payment with the manager and joined the few men at the bar. "Here she is! This kid is a dynamo! Why I bet there's nothing she can't do for you," said Ray Shaw with a smile that verged on a leer. The other three men smiled but didn't join in with Shaw's loud guffaw.

"Ray, I think you've enjoyed quite enough of Mr. Lake's hospitality. How about you walk me to a cab," said Donna Sue with her best smile.

"Why don't you let me take you home," he replied with a definite slur in the last syllable.

Donna Sue reassured the other men with a level look then smiled at Mr. Shaw.

"You've been more than helpful this evening introducing me to your friends from Chicago. Ron and I really appreciate you inviting them tonight. And I know your Mary Ann is waiting for you at home. Be a good boy and walk me out to a cab?" said Donna Sue with so much sweetness her words were literally dripping with it. Shaw stood somewhat unsteadily from his bar stool, basking in her warm words and smile, and offered his arm graciously, never realizing he had been handled. Donna Sue smiled at the remaining clients. "Good night gentlemen. It's been a fabulous evening," she said as she walked with Shaw to the revolving door and out to the street. They watched her go all thinking their own private thoughts.

At home, Donna Sue hung her next-to-nothing dress on the back of the closet door and washed her face. Looking into the mirror she was struck by a feeling of loneliness. Unsure where this was coming from, she went out to the kitchen to pour a glass of wine. Seeing the tequila bottle on the shelf she changed her mind and put a few ice cubes into the silver shaker. She poured in a double shot of Patron and shook it up close to her ear like she'd been taught. Grabbing a lime from the crisper she sliced it into fourths and poured the tequila into a chilled glass. She took her lime wedge and glass and went out to the lanai. It was cool out so she grabbed the soft woolen blanket from the dresser and wrapped it around herself. Looking out into the dark yard she took a steadying drink. Some tequila was for tossing back and getting it over with. Not this. She paid up, and it was the smoothest she had found. She squeezed in her lime and continued to sip her drink. There were times like tonight when she felt lonely or discontented and tequila was the only thing that smoothed off the rough edges.

She tried to do some self-talk and figure out what was bothering her exactly. Shaw and his tipsy innuendos were nothing new and nothing she couldn't handle. She'd had a lot of experience turning away unwelcome attention from men. She could usually do it with quiet grace and a well-timed comment but there were those occasions when that tactic didn't work and she had to resort to shock and awe. Usually in the form of cursing a blue streak that would make a sailor blush and make a guy think twice about trying to go any further with that brand of crazy. Tonight, as she enjoyed her cool tequila and the night sky, she could only pinpoint one feeling. Loneliness. She'd always been independent, even as a little girl. She'd rather do things for herself and have them done right than ask someone for help and have to compromise her own ideas. Donna Sue thought it could be stemming from her age. She was twenty-nine this year. She always thought by now she'd have a steady guy and maybe be thinking about a family. Maybe her biological clock or some such bull shit was messing with her. She drained her glass feeling the fatigue of a long workday and headed for bed. She'd been asleep for some time when the phone beside her bed rang. Looking at the clock, she saw it was 4:20 a.m. Feeling alarmed, she answered the phone. She heard Ron's voice on the other end.

"He's here! The baby is here! Sorry to call in the middle of the night. Just wanted to let you know," he sounded excited.

"What? Oh my gosh! He's early-is he okay? Is Jules okay?" she asked.

"So far everything seems fine. He's little, 4 pounds 6 ounces but he can cry! Jules is fine. A little rattled, things happen quickly with a third baby I guess." Donna Sue could hear how happy Ron was and wanted to feel happy for him but it seemed to come at an effort.

"Congratulations! Wow! A new son! Does he have a name?" she asked with the right amount of enthusiasm.

"Timothy Gerard Lake after Jules' dad. She had it all figured out," he said. "I need to go. I have a few other calls to make. I just wanted you to know. I don't know how long they may keep Timothy here in the hospital. Not sure when I'll get back to the office," he said.

"No worries. I've got it. I can handle most anything that comes up and I'll get with you when I can't," she assured him.

"Thanks, Don. I don't know what I ever did to deserve you," he said and rang off.

Donna Sue hung up her handset and held his voice and his words in her head and her heart. She was starting to get a bead on her loneliness issue and it wasn't looking good for her. She turned out the light and tried in vain to get back to sleep.

There were several weeks following Timothy's birth that Donna Sue never saw Ron in the office at all. Between running Kevin and Pamela to all of their lessons and activities and going back and forth to the hospital to visit the baby in the NICU, there was simply no time. Donna Sue was forced to make decisions without Ron's input and was lucky to get him on the phone for more than a few minutes before he was needed. It seemed like a good thing when the baby was released from the hospital three weeks later. Donna Sue was hopeful Ron would be more present once the baby got home and they were able to establish a routine. Jules was more demanding than ever with Ron's time, insisting he not leave the house at all. Ron was beginning to come unhinged. Kevin and Pamela were being less than understanding as to why they weren't able to accept every invitation and be squired about as they were accustomed. Ron was getting fed up with their sass and entitled attitudes. Jule's behavior was more bizarre than before the baby was born. She hardly slept and was anxious about the baby all the time. Ron hired a daily housekeeper to replace the twice-monthly help they had. He was tired of dirty dishes piled in the sink and the fridge smelling like a zoo exhibit. The baby cried all the time and never slept for longer than an hour at a time. The whole house was coming unglued and Ron felt guilty wishing he could escape to the ordered atmosphere of the office. He knew Donna Sue was handling the business and clients, but he recognized the burden the extra work and extra time were putting on her too.

After the baby had been home for a month, Ron began coming into the office for a few hours every morning. He'd usually arrive around 5:30 a.m. so Donna Sue began her day at that time as well even though she hardly ever left the office in the evening before 7:00 making for an extremely long day. They would sit in his office and work with laser focus on the contracts and deals that needed attention until Jules called him home. Ron was looking haggard and Donna

Sue tried to reassure him that this couldn't last. Ron shook his head and said, "The other kids weren't like this. This baby is never content. He hardly sleeps or eats. I don't understand what's happening."

Donna Sue hated to see him leave the office in such despair. She watched him go wishing there was something she could do or say. Wishing he could stay and work the whole day with her. Turning to her own office she set about another long day on her own. Looking up at the clock, Donna Sue stood from her desk and stretched. She'd been glued to her computer for the last five hours and hated the way it made her feel. She would much rather be out and about in town showing properties, talking to people, and working deals but the paperwork side of things had to be done and Ron was simply not involved enough to complete it. She'd waved good night to Cathy several hours ago and decided 6:30 was quitting time on this lovely June evening. She was looking forward to a nice glass of wine and spending some time outside before once again addressing the never-ending paperwork which had become her nightly routine.

At home, she fixed an omelet and ate it outside listening to the spring peepers from the small creek that ran between the yards. The evening temperature was cooling off so she moved inside, poured another glass of wine, curled up in her favorite overstuffed chair covered in cabbage roses, and began to read over the contracts she'd brought home.

Without realizing it Donna Sue put her glass down and leaned her head back and closed her eyes. She was brought back to reality suddenly by someone knocking heavily on her front door. She jumped up with her heart hammering, scattering papers. Running to the door she peered through the peephole but could already hear Ron's voice calling her name. She unlocked the door and jerked it open before he could pound it again. With wide eyes, she took in his rumpled clothes, wild hair, and red eyes. Ron took one step inside and Donna Sue instinctively put her arms around him. Even without words, she knew what had happened. They stood inside the front door for more than a few minutes until he could lift his head from her shoulder and even then, he couldn't look at her. She kept her eyes on his face but didn't say a word, just kept her hands on his arms as if to steady him.

"The baby. The baby died. He was crying. He was crying but I knew Jules was with him. I didn't go check. I didn't go check and then it got quiet. Jules started screaming. I ran into the nursery and she was holding him and screaming. I didn't know what to do. She wouldn't let me touch him but was screaming for me to do something. I called 911 but I think he was gone before they even got there," Ron's voice was raw. Donna Sue's eyes were filled with tears as she listened to his heart break. "Doctor said he had a weak heart and just wasn't strong enough. He was so little."

Ron started crying again. Donna Sue held him close and cried with him trying to absorb some of the pain. After another few minutes of intense emotion, Donna Sue moved slowly and got him to sit on the sofa. She went to the kitchen and got a healthy pour of tequila and a warm washcloth. She handed him the glass and bathed his tear-splotched face with the cloth. Ron drank the tequila down and looked off into space while Donna Sue gently swabbed his hands. After several minutes he seemed to be aware of her gentle ministrations and brought his gaze to her face. "I'm sorry to bring this here. I didn't know where else to go. What to do. I drove past and your light was on."

"I'm glad. Ron, I'm so sorry about the baby. I can't imagine the pain you're in. I'm glad you came here. What about Jules? Where is she?" asked Donna Sue.

He let out a huge sigh and covered his face with his hands. Donna Sue held the washcloth in her lap and waited. "She's in the hospital. They had to sedate her. She lost her mind. It took three people to get the baby out of her arms. She was like a wild animal. I tried to hold her after they took him away and she attacked me. She was screaming terrible things about how I never wanted him. How I wanted him to die. She was unrecognizable. Like something out of a horror movie," he said. "Hospital staff had to restrain her. When I left they had her arms tied to the bed and had given her a sedative."

"Oh Ron," said Donna Sue, her eyes filling again for the terrible loss and ordeal he was suffering through.

"The kids have sleepovers. I haven't even told them yet. I can't… I don't…"

"It's all right. You can stay here on the sofa tonight. I can't stand for you to drive off alone and stay by yourself," said Donna Sue as she got up to get him a blanket and pillow. She returned with the linens and the bottle of Patron which she placed on the table at the end of the sofa. Placing the linens on the other end of the sofa she stood and made as if to leave the room. Ron looked up at her with a ravaged face and lifted his hand to her. She couldn't leave him like this so she sat down and pulled him over so his head was on her shoulder. She was able to pour another shot of tequila and they talked slowly and quietly but not all the time. They shared the glass and sipped the peppery alcohol until the bottle was empty. Somewhere in the night, Ron's head rested in Donna Sue's lap and she sat and watched over her boss until the room filled with sunlight. Sitting up, he rubbed his face and rotated the shoulder he'd been laying on. Donna Sue sat quietly and watched him wake up, saw the moment when reality revisited him.

"Don, Jesus! I can't believe I barged in here in the middle of the night." He got to his feet and rubbed the back of his neck. "I don't know what I was thinking. I'm sorry," he said.

Donna Sue stood and faced him much like she had done the night before with her hand on his arms. "Hush. Let me know what I can do. I'm so sorry for you and Jules. If you want to close the office for a few days let me know or we can keep it going until you're ready to get back at it. The important thing is that you take care of yourself and your family," she said.

Ron could see the sincerity and compassion in her clear eyes. He wished and wondered again why she wasn't his home. "Who's going to take care of you?" he asked gravely.

She gave him a half smile and pulled him in for a hug. "I can take care of myself. Keep me informed and give me a list of things you need me to do. Let me help with whatever arrangements need to be made. I'm sure Jules and the kids are going to need you."

"I don't deserve you," he murmured as he turned for the door. Donna Sue stood in the same place for several minutes after he had gone. She felt emotionally drained from the night before but knew Ron was going to need her help. She headed for the shower and what was sure to be a very long day.

She didn't hear from Ron for the next two days but on the third day. He called her office and asked if she could help him with the arrangements. His hands were full with Jules and the kids. Jules was still using the sedatives the doctor had prescribed and was either catatonic or inconsolable. She insisted she didn't want her mother and sister in the house and refused to see Kevin and Pamela. Ron tried to explain that the kids were confused and hurt and very sad. They wanted to see their mom and be reassured. These conversations sent Jules into near convulsions of grief. She couldn't bear to see her surviving children when she suffered such guilt for the one that hadn't survived. No amount of consoling or explaining would make her understand that the baby dying wasn't her fault. Ron was overwhelmed between trying to console and soothe the children and trying to manage Jules. He finally locked himself in his home office and called Donna Sue with a list of things that had to be done. He'd spoken to the minister at their church and arranged a small private service but he needed flowers and food for the family and close friends that would be invited back to the house. Donna Sue, in her typical fashion, wrote notes and promised to take care of it right away. She felt like Ron needed to say something else so she waited quietly. Finally, he said, "There's one more thing and I don't know how to ask you this. I've tried and I just don't seem to be able to write his obituary. It needs to go in the newspaper." Ron's voice changed before he got to the end of the sentence.

"I can do it. You take care of yourself and your family. Call me if you think of anything else," she said and hung up.

Donna Sue set right to work arranging the flowers, music, and food. She sat at her computer and stared at the blank screen for quite a while before writing a short but eloquent statement about the life and death of Timothy Gerard Lake. She submitted it to the newspaper and gathered her purse. She waved goodbye to Cathy on her way out catching the surprised look in the secretary's eyes. In the months since Ron had been working from home, Donna Sue had never once gone home before the office closed. If ever there was a day when she needed a little personal time, this would be it.

Donna Sue didn't see Ron until the funeral. He was pale and sad but carried Jules into the sanctuary following the small white casket. Kevin and Pamela trailed behind looking sad and sullen. The immediate family and close personal friends that had gathered listened to the minister's words. There were no words that made this situation less painful. When the service ended the minister invited the guests to adjourn to the Lake house while the family attended the private burial. Donna Sue waited at the chapel door while the guests filed past. The last to leave the room was the Lake family. At the door, clutching Ron for support Jules stopped as she came abreast of Donna Sue. Without looking at her she said, "I don't want you at the gravesite. Go on to the house and make sure things are ready." Donna Sue looked at Ron with confusion.

"Of course, she's coming to the cemetery. She's family," he said quietly but forcefully.

"She's not family. She's not coming," said Jules in a voice stripped of its usual musical tones.

"It's okay," assured Donna Sue. "I'll go to the house and make sure everyone has what they need," she said and quickly ducked her head and went on past the family. She tried not to think about the interaction too much. Jules had suffered a terrible tragedy and was still heavily medicated after all. But her words clung to Donna Sue like an unpleasant smell. At the house, Donna Sue got busy opening wine and making sure the guests found the sandwiches and desserts. It wasn't long before the family arrived and entered the house somberly. Soft voices and gentle words were heard in all the rooms on the lower floor. A late floral arrangement arrived so Donna Sue brought it to Jules who was sitting at the dining room table with the minister and his wife.

"Look Jules, aren't these lovely? The Real Estate Association sent them," she said.

Jules hardly lifted her eyes to the lovely flowers but said to the minister in the same stripped voice, "You know Donna Sue, don't you? She's the woman my husband spent the night with the night our son died." The blood drained from Donna Sue's face and her hands shook so that she almost dropped the heavy vase. The minister made some kind of remark but Donna Sue couldn't understand his words. She set the vase on the table and turned on her heel. She grabbed her purse from the hall closet and walked to the closest door. She got to her car parked out on the street without remembering doing it and drove herself home. Once there, Donna Sue unplugged her phone, pulled the drapes on the front of the house, and laid down on her bed. The last five months came crashing down on her and she closed her eyes and willed herself to float away. At one point she was aware of a hard knocking on her door. She knew who was on the front step but simply turned over and continued her unnatural sleep. The entire office staff had agreed the office would be closed the day of the funeral and the following day out of respect.

When she arose from her bed after sleeping for fourteen hours, Donna Sue grabbed her riding boots and headed to the country. Her friend Mary Jo had a stable and said she could come riding anytime she wanted to. Donna Sue watched the countryside slide by and thought about the fact that for the last five months she had done nothing but work. No time off. No trips. No free evenings. And for what? To keep her boss' business running while he wasn't able to. The injustice of Jules' remark in light of Donna Sue's sacrifice was beginning to burn a hole through her gut. The pavement turned to gravel and Donna Sue took a turn a little too fast, feeling the car fishtail as she came around the turn with too much speed. It reminded her to slow down and take a look out the window. The road was lined with white fences and green paddocks. The large barn appeared and Donna Sue turned into the drive leading up to it. She saw several familiar faces, young girls who spent their time working off their barn tabs. She called hello to Rebecca, who was in charge, and asked who needed a ride.

"Beau has been waiting for you. It's been a long time since you've been to see him," she replied.

"I know. Way too long. Thanks, Rebecca," said Donna Sue and walked down the aisle of stalls to Bittersweet Beau. "Hello Handsome," she said softly as the large paint stuck his nose above the stall door. "I've missed you." Donna Sue continued to talk to the patient horse as she tacked him up in the wide hall of the barn. She gave Rebecca a shout and led Beau out and mounted. They headed out the west paddock at a slow walk as they each got back in tune with the other. Donna Sue knew there was no better place to contemplate big problems than on top of a horse. They spent the majority of the day riding. Donna Sue found her favorite osage orange grove and dismounted. She'd brought along some water and an apple. She ate part of the apple in the shade of the gnarly trees and gave the rest to Beau who was pulling at the sweet grass. She thought about what she should do about Ron and Jules. Every option she thought of made her stomach hurt. After several hours, the horse and rider returned to the barn and Donn Sue went through all the motions of returning Beau to his stall. She promised him and Rebecca she'd try to be back sooner than later and climbed into her car. She still wasn't sure what she was going to do about her situation but decided a day in the country had been a balm for her weary and confused soul.

Back at home, she left the phone unplugged and the lights out. She had no appetite but made some jelly toast and took it out to the lanai. Tomorrow would be here soon enough. She hoped she'd know what to do then. She pulled the soft blanket from the dresser and wrapped up in it and curled up on the wicker settee. Before she knew it, the birds were singing their good morning songs. She stood up and stretched her cramped body. After showering she dressed carefully in a sober suit that fit her well. She put on her Nine West pumps for extra power and headed to the office. The familiar place where she had spent the last eight years seemed somehow alien. She imagined that even Cathy gave her a peculiar look as she walked by her desk. She decided she'd go to her own office first and catch her breath then go see Ron and let him know what she had decided. Before she could put her attache case away Ron was at the door.

"Where have you been? I've been calling, I've been by your place. What in the hell Donna Sue?" he asked in a voice louder than it should have been. "Where did you run off to?"

Donna Sue stood up to her full 5'10" height and looked him in the eye. "I didn't run off. My time is mine to decide where I spend it." Ron took another step into her office to make room to close the door behind him. There was something about the look on her face that he'd never seen before and he knew he didn't like it.

"Okay, what's going on? I looked up at the wake and saw you walking out. I called and couldn't get through. I went by and you weren't there. I've been trying for 24 hours to get a hold of you. What the hell happened? I think I deserve an explanation," he said.

"You want an explanation? Here it is. I resign. I wasn't sure what I was going to say when I came in here but now, I know. I'm leaving," she said with her arms crossed over her chest.

"WHAT?? What are you talking about resigning? What has happened? We are family here, we…"

"WE are not family. You have a family. I have a job. I have two jobs, yours and mine! I have tried to be everything this business needed while you couldn't be here. I've tried to be helpful to your family. But I'm not going to stand around and be accused of sleeping with you and trashed by everyone in town," Donna Sue finished realizing her hands were clenched at her sides and she was leaning towards Ron. He inhaled loudly and said,

"What are you talking about? That's not true. Who said we are sleeping together?"

"Jules told the minister and his wife that we spent the night together the night Timothy died," said Donna Sue, losing some of her steam.

"What? Donna Sue, I don't know what to say." He backed up and sat heavily on the small couch against the wall. "I am so sorry she said that." Donna Sue wanted to go sit beside Ron but she held herself away and slouched against the desk.

"Well, she did. And that's what she thinks. Pretty soon that's what everyone will think," she said. "I don't want that reputation. I don't deserve that reputation. I've lived here my entire life. I'm not going to work for you when everyone thinks we're something we're not."

"You can't resign. I will talk to her. I will make her apologize or whatever you want. You can't leave me-I mean the business. I need you here. I want you here. I want us to be partners, business partners. I should have done this before now. I started this business, but you've built it up, mostly single-handedly. You have to stay. As a full partner, you'll get compensated correctly for all that you do. I'll make it clear to our business contacts that we are equal partners and that will put a damper on any talk about us being… something else. What do you say? I mean it, partners?" he asked. Donna Sue was shocked and amazed by Ron's offer to make her a partner in the business he had started from scratch.

"Seriously? You'd make me a partner?" Donna Sue didn't know how to respond. She'd come in ready to resign and now he was offering her part of the business.

"Hell yes! I should have done it six months ago. You're the reason we have all this new business and these Chicago bids? They're ridiculous. That's all you and that's not even counting you running the whole show while I was out of pocket. I don't know anyone else who would have done that. You did that. You've more than earned the right to own part of this business. And there's no one else I'd want to go into business with," said Ron.

Donna Sue looked at the pointy toes of her expensive shoes. She wanted to say yes, wanted to shout it actually. She felt the need to play it cool and be reserved. "Of course, we'll need Buddy to look over the partnership proposal before I can say for sure," she said.

Ron finally took a breath in and almost smiled. "Certainly, I'll call the law office today and have an agreement drawn up and we can go from there," he said. "A partnership agreement. Not a resignation," he said standing up from where he had been perched on the edge of the sofa. "Partner?" He extended his hand. Donna Sue let him stand for three beats then stuck her hand out and gave a firm shake sans the smile.

"Partner," she said. "Now please get out of here. I have a lot of work to do."

Ron went to the door but stood in the frame looking at his protege, his colleague, his partner before turning and heading down the hall to his own office. He missed the raised eyebrows on Cathy's face as he passed by.

Buddy Wright drew up a partnership agreement that suited everyone involved except for Jules. She sat stone-faced while Ron told her exactly what had happened the night Timothy died. He made it clear to her that where she might be disappointed and angry at him, she had no right to treat Donna Sue poorly or spread false rumors about her. After months of handling Jules with kid gloves,

Ron was firm to the point of being imperious. Jules stared at him dry-eyed and said in her horror film voice, "You do whatever you want with your business and your girlfriend. She is never to come to my house again. And while we're in the mood to issue orders, don't even think of asking me for a divorce. I've invested too much time and too much of myself to let you fuck it up with someone else."

Ron was shocked at the profanity and vehemence in Jule's words. "What are you talking about? This is Donna Sue. She has been a part of our family for eight years. She has been there when you needed her, even when the kids needed her," Ron said in a raised voice.

"Oh, let's not forget! She's there when you need her too!" screamed Jules.

"I don't even know you! Where is this coming from? I have never done anything inappropriate with Donna Sue or anyone else for that matter. You are my wife; I've done nothing to deserve this attitude and neither has Donna Sue." Ron realized he was shouting now.

"If you don't know me, who's fault is that? You'd spend all day and all night in your office if it was up to you. You only come home when I make you. You'd rather spend your time with her than in your own home with your own wife! What am I supposed to think?" said Jules. Her voice cracked and she began to cry in earnest. Ron tried to pull her into his arms but she flung her elbow to push him away.

"Jules, we've just buried our son. We're all torn up. But you need to know I'm going to make Donna Sue a partner in the business and that's that. I'm going to go to work and come home to you and the kids. There is nothing but work between Donna Sue and me and I would appreciate it if you would remember that," said Ron wearily. Jules collapsed back onto the couch.

"Please don't leave me, Ron! Please don't leave me," she cried as she wrapped her arms around herself and rocked back and forth. Ron went to her immediately and again tried to put his arms around her but she didn't fall into him. Instead, she kept herself wrapped up and rocking. Ron looked at his wife for several seconds, realizing from their conversation just how broken she was. He wondered if she would ever return to herself or if she would stay in this tortured anguish for the rest of her life.

"Nobody's leaving Jules," he said. He registered a stone weight in his gut as he said it. He stood and walked to the door, looking back he wondered about the heavy feeling and if it would pass or be a life sentence.

Things changed after that. Ron came home a few weeks later to find all of his personal effects arranged nicely in the guest room. When he questioned Jules about it, she was very sweet and solicitous regarding his comfort. She thought they would both be more comfortable if they had their own space and didn't need to 'intrude' on each other's feelings. "We just need time to heal and I think we can do that better if we're not always barging into each other," she explained. Ron didn't consider the few times they spoke before turning out the bedside light at night as 'barging', but he couldn't think of a good reason to argue for staying in the same room. They hadn't had sex since Timothy had been conceived. He turned around a few times and took in the careful consideration Jules had used to place his things and clothes in a way she knew would please him.

Ron was back at the office full tilt. He and Donna Sue worked side by side and the business continued to grow and do well. Almost six months after signing the partnership agreement the two had worked a particularly grueling week. Ron suggested they go to Murry's for dinner and celebrate. Donna Sue smiled and shook her head. Murry's was her favorite restaurant and she and Ron had eaten there a million times. For lunch. Going to Murry's for dinner would look a certain way and Donna Sue wasn't willing to undergo the scrutiny they would receive. It was impossible to be in the trendy restaurant without running into half a dozen people they both knew. Instead, she suggested Ron come by the house and she could rustle something up for dinner or they could get carry out from House of Chow just down the street. Ron liked the latter idea and said he'd go by and pick up dinner and meet her at the house. Donna Sue was uncertain if Ron realized her reason for wanting to eat in. She was looking forward to spending some time with him outside of the office. They had been working long hours on multiple deals and it was nice to think of having some relaxing downtime.

Donna Sue stopped off at the liquor store and picked up a bottle of Solay from the local Les Bourgeois winery. Its clean fruity flavors were bound to go nicely with the excellent Chinese food. At the last moment, she backtracked and found a bottle of Old Mill Bourbon. She knew this was one of Ron's favorites and it would be nice to have on hand in case they wanted a nightcap. Donna Sue paid for her purchases and tried not to think about the nightcap or her motivation for buying the expensive bourbon. She made it home before Ron was back with the food so she quickly changed into some soft stretchy pants and a comfortable tunic top. She opened the wine and lit the candle in the kitchen and the one on the table on the lanai. In a few moments, she heard Ron's car and went to open the door for him. He had a huge bag in his hand and she helped him into the kitchen and began removing foil containers. "I wasn't sure what to get so I may have gone a little overboard. The owner told me some of your favorites-I'm guessing you go there quite a bit?" he asked.

Donna Sue laughed as she began dishing Mu Shu Pork onto her plate. "I guess I do. It's so convenient and we've been working some crazy hours. It's not much fun to come home and cook for myself and Aimee's restaurant is right there," said Donna Sue. Ron picked up a piece of chicken and popped it into his mouth looking at Donna Sue closely.

"I hate it that you come home to an empty house. Is there… anyone you're interested in? If you don't mind me asking that is," said Ron. Donna Sue leveled her clear-eyed gaze on him.

"Now you know there isn't anyone I'm 'interested' in. When would I have time to do anything about it if I did? We work till

7:30 or after every night and when I do get home I just want to stay home," she said.

Ron looked at his partner standing one step away. He wanted nothing more than to reach out and pull her to him. "I'm sorry I've monopolized your time. You should be going out, having fun, meeting people," he said.

"I get enough going out schmoozing with our clients and maybe I don't want to meet anyone else...," she said. Ron took a half step closer and Donna Sue, for once, didn't move back. Slowly, so she knew what he intended to do, he pulled her to him and bent to kiss her. For Donna Sue, time stood still. She'd thought of kissing Ron a million times. She seemed to be floating above the ground and wasn't entirely sure she was even breathing. Slowly Ron lifted his lips from hers never taking his eyes from hers. Still in an altered state, Donna Sue stumbled forward and Ron steadied her.

"I've wanted to do that for so long," he said softly. Donna Sue nodded her head but as yet hadn't found any words. "I'll say I'm sorry if you want me to but I'm not sorry. Donna Sue, you amaze me. My home life is a wreck and I don't know what to do about that. I know this is horribly unfair to you, but I love you. I've loved you for years. I don't want to mess things up for Lake Properties. We are partners. And I can behave like this never happened if you want, but I couldn't go one more day without telling you that."

After several seconds Donna Sue was able to draw air into her lungs. Ron was still holding her forearms and she stared up into his kind eyes. She opened her mouth, not exactly sure what would come out. "I love you. I've tried really hard not to but I can't change it. I can't change the fact that you are married. I can't change the fact that I hate myself for loving you when you belong to Jules. I don't know how to be the person who loves you and watches you go home to someone else," said Donna Sue, her voice catching on the last syllables. Ron pulled her all the way into him, wrapping his arms around her. He could feel her arms wrapped tightly around him as well. It was surreal. He'd thought of doing this so many times. Wondered what it would feel like. His wildest imagination didn't compare with the feeling that enveloped the two of them standing in the kitchen with the forgotten carry-out.

"You are my home. I may go to the house but that's all it is a house. My wife is someone who lives there but we don't make a life together. I wish it were different but that is our reality. This is ours. I don't know how this will go, but I know I'm not going to give you up. I'm not going to give up this feeling of home," he said into her ear. Donna Sue held Ron tightly as tears coursed silently down her cheeks. This is not something she planned, loving a married man. She also knew there was no going back. "We'll figure it out. Together- if you want to."

Looking up at Ron with her tear-streaked face, Donna Sue pulled him by the hand out of the kitchen and down the hall to her bedroom. "Welcome home Ron," she said.

After that night there was no going back. They continued to throw themselves into work and develop more properties and lucrative bank accounts. At the office and with clients they were the same Ron and Donna Sue they had always been. Professional. Dedicated. Hard-working partners. Outside of the office, they ate dinner together almost every night at Donna Sue's, and many nights he would stay over. They spent weekends at Ron's lake house at the Lake of the Ozarks, a short drive away, a place Jules had never been interested in. If Jules noticed the change in arrangements, she didn't mention it. She had thrown herself into a local support group for parents who have lost children. Ron was relieved to see the positive changes in Jules. She was getting up every morning and dressing. She depended heavily on household help and spent very little time with Kevin and Pamela who were now in high school and becoming more distant from both parents. Ron realized the dysfunction of his marriage and 'home' but didn't want to send Jules sliding back into her bedroom by asking for a divorce. He and Donna Sue decided the status quo would work until it didn't and then they'd figure it out all over again.

Sitting in her lovely office now she felt the last 28 years had gone by in the blink of an eye. Ron was gone. He'd collapsed while they toured a large property last March. While Donna Sue waited for help, she cradled Ron's head in her lap and told him over and over again how much she loved him and loved being his home. Ron lived for two weeks hooked up to machines in the ICU at Boone Hospital. The massive stroke was simply too much and he never fully regained consciousness. Donna Sue visited him every day, although she was quick to leave when Jules arrived in the curtain-lined cubicle. No words were ever exchanged between the two women, but the hostility from Jules was palpable. Kevin came in from Minneapolis where he was attempting to start his own property management business. He and his sister had both copped a haughty, unfriendly attitude toward Donna Sue. As much as she tried to support them in their grief, they were unwilling to extend her the same courtesy. No one in the family called Donna Sue when Ron finally slipped away from the wracked body in the bed. She found out when she came to the hospital early to sit with him before going to the office. She was met by the charge nurse who stopped her before she entered the curtained cubicle that had been Ron's room. "I"m so sorry. I didn't have your number. Mr. Lake died last night around 11:45. I was sure the family would have let you know since you were so close," she said gently. Donna Sue stopped in her tracks as the blood in her veins turned to ice. She forced herself to thank the nurse as she turned back to the hospital corridor, her body seeming to float out of the ward.

Ron was gone. She thought about Kevin, Pamela, and Jules. They had each other. They could lean on each other. Donna Sue wouldn't be welcome there. They'd made that crystal clear in the fact that they didn't have the decency to let her know of Ron's passing.

Suddenly Donna Sue's legs gave out and she found herself slumped against the wall. She was able to dig out her cell phone and somehow was able to press a button. Before she knew it, her friend Jackie was sitting on the floor beside her. The two had met years ago when Jackie's husband decided to upend their happy home and Jackie was forced to find a new one. They met to sign a lease and ended up sucking down martinis at Harpo's Bar. Over the years Jackie introduced Donna Sue to the goddesses. The group of friends understood the level of commitment that Donna Sue had for Ron and the cost attached to it. They never judged but were often sorry for their beautiful friend and the half of a life she was living. Donna Sue was grateful to have such friends in her life. They encouraged her ambition to succeed and accepted her situation for what it was. Before Jackie had Donna Sue in the car, Anna and Al were already at her house. Anna lowered the shades and lit the candles. Al put on a pot of coffee which they ended up pouring down the sink. Sylvie arrived a few minutes later with two fifths of Don Julio and small sandwiches and chips. They wrapped their friend in their goddess love and kept the tequila flowing.

Ron's funeral was an exercise in humiliation and pain for Donna Sue. Jules refused any offer of help and made it clear to everyone that Donna Sue was not to be consulted or involved. The goddesses sat at the back of the church during the service and sandwiched Donna Sue in their midst. The whole day was a blur. Donna Sue remembered being at the cemetery and then very little after that. Jackie had driven her home and the two had sat outside on that cold day sipping tequila and talking very little.

Four months later Donna Sue felt that familiar feeling of being somewhere she didn't belong when she was at the office. She belonged here with Ron. But everything changed. Kevin had a new lawyer and was trying his best to push her out and take over Ron's business entirely on his own. He wanted to change the way they did everything including putting a stop to Donna Sue's business socials which were the most beneficial thing they'd done to grow the business. At first, the idea made Donna Sue furious. She and Ron had worked side by side and built the business deal by deal, client by client. If anyone didn't have a right to be here it was Kevin. But the more she thought about it the more she realized she didn't want to be here. She didn't enjoy the work. She didn't enjoy the client events. She didn't enjoy being here. Not without Ron. She wondered if selling her part was the right course, again wishing Ron was there to discuss it. She went back to her philosophy that everything happens for a reason.

She'd started a job at 21 and here she was a few months from 50. She'd helped build a phenomenal business, met the man of her dreams, and accrued a savings account beyond her imagination. All in all, a good run. She felt surprised that it was all ending. She didn't need to work. With her savings over the last 20 years, she was able to pay off her house and put away a lovely sum, not to mention the amount Kevin would be forced to pay her for her portion of the business. She could certainly do without the hostile glares from Pamela who had summarily dismissed Cathy and taken over the front desk job. The constant attacks from Kevin were exhausting. No, she really didn't need any of this bullshit. Standing, she picked up her attache case and carefully removed the framed Berneche from the wall. Without a word to Pamela, Donna Sue crossed the outer office, stopped at the door, and turned. "Your dad and I made this business. We built it together and it's pretty fantastic. Try not to fuck it up," then she turned on her heel and walked to her car feeling lighter than she had in a while.

Anna didn't know what to do. The party Tony had planned for his fraternity brothers and their wives was a total and complete flop. It wasn't Tony's fault—he'd found the perfect location for the family portion of the reunion. The rental house on the edge of the city limits had five bathrooms, a huge grill, and an in-ground swimming pool.

Anna could tell Tony was frustrated. He was one of the few 'brothers' that had stayed in town after graduating from the University of Missouri and he spent a lot of time helping plan and make arrangements for the annual reunion. Anna got out of the water which she had all to herself even though she had encouraged the others to join her numerous times. She couldn't figure out the women lounging along the pool deck. The pool was absolutely perfect. For Anna, there was no better place than floating on a raft above the cerulean blue of a pool. This one even had a four-foot inflated palm tree feature bobbing out in the middle. It was a cute addition and reminded Anna of a toy her nephew had when he was a tot. No matter how hard you punched the clown he would bounce right back up. But no amount of enticing had worked so far and the palm tree swayed gently with the waves. She shook her head slightly as she walked past the other women paging through magazines and looking pained. Inside the cool dim kitchen, Anna picked up the phone and dialed a number. "Hey, are you busy?" she said into the receiver. "I need a huge favor, I'm at the rental house Tony found for his fraternity reunion and it is a bust. I'm going to die of boredom. I can't even enjoy the pool. Could you come and get me? Tony's here for the duration." Anna listened and then replied, "Great, do what you need to do and I'll see you when you get here. Thanks, bye."

She hung up the phone and went back outside. Diving in the water she came up to see the glare from the nearest lounger. "Oh gee, did I splash you? I'm really sorry. You should get in, the water is great," said Anna.

"No thanks, I just did my hair this morning. We're all going to the Flaming Pit for dinner tonight, I don't want to have to do it again," said the woman. Anna thought her name was Dianne or Dianna. She wasn't sure which but she was sure it mattered.

"Really? The Pit tonight? Tony bought like eight slabs of ribs. I think he is counting on everyone staying around and eating," said Anna as she shielded her eyes from the sun.

"Some of us were talking at brunch and decided we'd rather go to a restaurant than hang out here with the bugs and all. The Flaming Pit was recommended at the hotel so we figured we'd take our chances," said Dianne/Dianna. Anna was starting to get angry thinking about part of the crowd deciding to change the plans Tony and the committee had worked so hard on. Tony would be really disappointed if no one stayed for dinner after he'd spent hours tending the grill. Anna was trying to decide what to say when she heard a "Yoo-hoo!!" from the other side of the privacy fence. Looking across the pool deck she saw a floppy straw hat, corkscrew curls, and the bright blue eyes of her friend Jackie. When Anna had called Jackie to rescue her from the lame party, she had said she had errands to run but would drive out once she was finished. It was clear to Anna that Jackie had left almost immediately after hanging up with her.

"I heard this party was in need of re-vitalization!" she said loudly to the crowd that continued to stare at her head sticking above the fence. "Will one of you heifers be so kind and open the goddamn gate for me?" she said with a face-splitting grin. One of the men walked over and opened the wooden gate. All of the men watched as Jackie turned her megawatt grin on the gatekeeper. Men always paid attention when Jackie was around. She was gorgeous with her upturned nose, dimpled smile, and corkscrew curls. It didn't hurt that she had a killer body-even after two kids. Her most attractive feature was her fun-loving personality. You couldn't meet her without noticing it as she exuded fun. "Thanks, handsome! If you could just get that cooler for me that would be swell. It about killed me getting it here from the car," she said as she turned and waved at Anna in the pool. Her helper struggled to move the heavy cooler inside the fence and wondered what in the world was inside it. Jackie moved along the pool deck making her way over to Tony. "Wow! That smells amazing! I think my hips got bigger just from smelling those ribs!" She gave Tony a peck on the cheek and Tony introduced her to his 'brothers'. Jackie turned on the charm and greeted each of the men surrounding the grill. "How long until we eat? I'm starving," she said as she sauntered away. "Hey, Girl!" she called to Anna. "How come you're the only one in the pool?" Before Anna could reply she said, "Hey, what is that in the middle?"

"A plastic palm tree," said one of the magazine readers in an 'I'm not impressed with you or your smile' tone of voice.

"NO way! That, my friends, is the next best thing to Mickey Gilly's mechanical bull!" said Jackie and with that, she launched herself from the deck attempting to straddle the tree and sit on the inflated island. Her trajectory was accurate but she had too much speed and force. She hit the tree and bounced off and dunked completely, her floppy hat floating to the surface. The palm tree bobbed and rocked crazily before righting itself. The men turned away from the grill and several of the women looked up from their magazines. The surface of the water erupted as Jackie popped up laughing and sputtering.

"Oh! So that's the way it is huh? You're going to be a tough ass," she laughed pointing at the tree and shaking the wet hair out of her eyes. Leave it to Jackie to say she'd come to rescue her and then show up with a full cooler and her string bikini thought Anna. "Anna, you have to ride this bull!" Anna laughed with her friend.

"I'm pretty sure it's just decoration, not an amusement ride!" laughed Anna.

"NO, seriously! I think I can launch from the side and ride that island for 8 seconds or die trying! Besides, decorations are useless things that just sit around collecting dust," she added catching the eye of one of the lounge lizards. "I'm going to try again," she said as she levered herself out of the pool. "Maybe a different angle," she mused. With a 'whoop' she took off and flew through the air but missed the entire structure ending up on the other side of it in the deep end of the pool. She once again came up sputtering water but still laughing and grabbing for her hat. Some of the men had walked over to the side of the pool and were coaching her on how she could conquer the island. After several more attempts, each more splashtastic and hilarious than the last she gave up and lay panting on the pool deck. "I need a drink!" she volunteered. Goose went over to the beat-up orange cooler she'd brought and opened the lid.

"You want a beer or whatever this is in mason jars," he asked.

"I need a beer to quench my thirst and the mason jar to cure what ails me," she said. Goose padded over with a cold can of beer, looking at the mason jar with a puzzled look.

"Oh, thank you, you may have just saved my life." Jackie sat up and opened the beer and tilted it up. She drank the entire can and let out an earth-shaking belch which made the guys laugh and the women tsk. Reaching her hand up for the mason jar she unscrewed the lid and took a small drink.

"So, what's in the jar?" asked Dave.

"Some people call it Moonshine but I call it, 'Tackle a Fucking Palm Tree' said Jackie as she stood up, plopped her sodden hat on her dripping head, and hurtled at the pool toy. "Try it," she tossed out before she once again ricocheted off the tree. Slowly, Goose smelled the liquid inside. "Come on, don't be a wienie! Try it." He tipped the jar up to his lips and pulled it away with an appreciative smile.

"Damn! That's good!" he said and then he waved Jackie away from the float. "Watch out, I'm coming in hot!" He hurled himself at the floating toy and was able to wrap his arms around it briefly before the whole thing sank with him clinging to it with one crooked elbow. As Jackie, Anna and Goose surrounded the elusive float laughing about their failed attempts, Tim and Alan sauntered over to see what all the hoopla was about. "Try that stuff in the mason jar and then see if you can sit on the island. You get 3 points for hooking the tree and 5 if you can sit your ass on the island," said Goose. The other men didn't look all that intrigued but moved over to the cooler and took out the jar. Unscrewing it they smelled it and questioned each other as to its safety before drinking it.

"Oh god damn!" exclaimed Alan before hefting the jar up for another drink. "Blackberry Moonshine!"

"Come on Tim, I bet you can't get your wide ass anywhere near the island. I've got you beat-just like the old days," taunted Goose. Tim handed the jar off to Alan and flung himself at the tree. His tall frame and heavy body completely obliterated the tree. When his redhead popped up there was nothing of the tree showing for a second before it popped up behind him bobbing wildly.

Dave called from the side, "Tim just hold it in place and I bet I can hook it!" Tim held the bobbing tree with one long arm as Dave took a running leap hitting the top fourth of the tree. It bent in half, seemingly with Dave still holding on, and he went face-first into the water clutching the top of the tree with both arms. He came up gasping for air and laughing with the rest of them.

"Okay, this is going to take some planning. Let's convene at the conference table and make a plan of action," said Jackie. They all moved to the shallow end laughing and reenacting their courageous attempts. Goose pulled out the mason jar and took a hit before passing it to Anna. Jackie hunkered down next to her beat-up cooler and dug around the beer cans. Standing up, she triumphantly hoisted another mason jar over her head, the contents a bit lighter in color than the first. "This one's peach," she said. Hearing peach, Tim's wife Mary stood up from her chair and came over to the group around the cooler.

"You guys are crazy. You're never going to be able to sit on that silly inflated toy. You're all insane," she said with a small laugh.

"Sanity is overrated," laughed Jackie. "Sometimes you just have to go off track and say screw it!" offering Mary the jar in her hand. Mary looked at it for a minute before taking it. She smelled it first and pulled it away from her nose with a huge smile.

"This smells just like my grandmother's homemade peach preserves!" she said. Tilting it to her mouth she took a tentative sip and then another longer draught. Pulling it away she wiped her mouth with the back of her hand. "That is the most wonderful thing I've had in a very long time! It makes me feel like summer in Iowa with my Gran."

Jackie turned her 100-watt smile on Mary and said, "Yeah but are there palm trees in Iowa?" Fast as lightning, Jackie grabbed her by the hand and the two went screaming to the edge of the pool at full speed. Leaping into the water simultaneously they tackled the palm tree. Laughing hysterically, they bobbed to the surface pushing hair out of their eyes, knowing they were going to try again. Mary encouraged Renee and Jan to get in on the action. Within an hour of Jackie's arrival, the pool party had gone from a bust to a beast! Everyone with the exception of Diane/Dianna attempted the palm tree rodeo with varying degrees of success and tons of laughter. The ribs finished off nicely and were tender and smoky. The tiki lights were lit as the group enjoyed the darkening sky and friendly conversations. The Flaming Pit was never mentioned again. Around 11:00 the frat brothers loaded up their coolers and towels, slapped each other on the backs, and headed to the hotel. The pool deck got quiet with Tony, Anna, Jackie, and Goose, Tony's best friend, all that remained. Each of them was exhausted and full. The mason jars were empty and a few beer cans were scattered around the deck.

Tony's voice cut through the dark and quiet, "Thanks for coming Jackie. I think this party would have been over if you hadn't shown up."

"Who are you kidding?" asked Goose. "Your party would have never gotten started if she hadn't shown up." There were murmurs of agreement from Tony and Anna.

"Well, you know me, I love to have fun. But, seriously, I think I may have sprained my vagina on that damn palm tree. I'll have my chiropractor send you the bill!"

A while later Jackie was headed to her car to drive home. Anna had wanted her to stay over at the rental house. The kids were at home with their dad but she knew he had an early morning at the hospital so she wanted to be there in the morning when they woke up. Jackie started the car but didn't put it in gear. Sitting in the dark after a long afternoon of sun and fun she realized how very tired she was. And not just because of the beer and pool play. Jackie didn't participate in pity parties and was able to ride the tsunami wave that had become her life for the most part. But then there were nights like tonight when the wave pounded her into the sand. Anna and Tony had become some of her best friends and had been behind her each step over the last ten months. It helped Jackie considerably, them knowing her situation and supporting her, but it also cut a little seeing the wonderful relationship they shared. A year ago, she would have put herself in the same 'happily married with children' category, but that was life before her husband began detonating bombs and blowing holes in their life. She thought back, to her life pre-bomb wondering where it started to go wrong.

She'd met her husband Sebastian at a tennis match on campus. Sebastian was playing, and Jackie was watching from the stands with a friend who thought a tennis match would be a fun form of entertainment. It took two point eight seconds for Jackie to get bored. Her friend began telling her about an obnoxiously rude neighbor and Jackie was full of ideas on how to get even or maybe ahead. The two friends laughed and talked freely while the match continued and before long, Jackie realized the player on one side of the net was giving them a serious stink eye. Once she was aware that their conversation and laughter were affecting him it was game on! Jackie would wait until he was in a full stretch to deliver a hard serve and cut loose with her signature laugh which some called obnoxious but was undeniably memorable. After several well-timed bursts of laughter, the player, a good-looking guy in his tennis whites, put his hands on his hips and stared at Jackie trying to shame her into being quiet. Sadly for him, Jackie didn't take to being shushed and stuck her tongue out and waggled her hands around her ears. She wasn't sure but she thought he might have cracked a smile before switching sides for the next game. After the match, Jackie heard someone call, "Hey." She turned around to see the guy in white leaning over the fence that divided the court from the spectators.

"Hey yourself," she said with a smile that stretched all the way across her face. After the guy informed her of the proper etiquette while watching a tennis match, he invited her to dinner. That was how she met her husband. She thought they made the perfect pair. Where he was introspective and moody, she was outgoing and fun-loving. He was careful and planful and she could be reckless and spontaneous. They were each other's ballast so one didn't get too staid and the other not too outrageous. They were married six months after meeting and Little Sebastian, Seb, was born during Sebastian's last year of residency. Sweet Charlotte came along eighteen months later and Jackie was sure she had everything she could ever want. Her husband was a doctor, she had a lovely home and two perfect children. She worked retail part-time in her sister's boutique even though she didn't have to. She liked the upscale shop and enjoyed helping customers find beautiful things to wear.

But her whole world tilted a few months ago when Sebastian came home and dropped the first bomb. "I'm not happy," were the exact words he had used.

Jackie laughed and said, "You're not happy with what? Our fabric softener? The cost of eggs? The situation in South America?" Her smile died slowly when Sebastian didn't smile back. He just continued to stare at her with a heavy look.

"I'm not happy with us." Jackie was sure this is what it must feel like when a real bomb has detonated. There was a ringing in her ears and a shortage of oxygen in the room.

"Not happy with us? I don't understand what you mean. It's you and me and Seb and Charlotte and we're good. We are family. We are happy," she said all in one breath as she tried desperately to drag another into her lungs.

"I'm not happy. And I've met someone else," he said. Bomb number two took Jackie's legs out and she sat hard on the floor of their bedroom. The ringing in her ears was deafening and the lack of oxygen in the room was making her nauseous. She thought he was saying something else but she couldn't understand the words. It was as if he was talking and she was underwater. When she finally clawed her way to the surface of the altered reality she was drowning in, she heard Sebastian say, "It will be tough for a little while but I'm sure we'll all adjust. I'm going to spend the night at the hospital tonight. We can talk tomorrow." Jackie remembered seeing his expensive brown leather shoe turn on its heel and walk out of the bedroom. She sat on the floor for hours before finally getting up and stumbling out into the hall. She felt like a terrible crime or act of violence had been committed in the bedroom and she was sure she never wanted to go in there again. She walked in a daze down the hall to Seb's room. Her beautiful boy was asleep in his bed amidst his stuffed dinosaurs and his favorite toy, a model airplane Sebastian had brought back from a medical conference. It was Seb's most prized possession and even though it had sharp edges and no soft surfaces he took it to bed with him every night. Jackie went in but was afraid to touch her son. He looked so perfect. She felt another wave of nausea sweep over her. She pulled the door mostly shut and went across the hall to Charlotte's room. At twenty-six months, Charlotte was still in her crib. Jackie knew it was time to move her to a big girl's bed but hadn't gotten around to it. Stepping into her daughter's room and seeing the sweep of her eyelashes laying on her beautiful smooth skin broke the dam that had held back the tears. Jackie once again went to the floor, this time at the foot of her daughter's crib. She stayed there and cried silently for the remainder of the night.

She didn't remember getting Seb ready for preschool the next morning. She was glad when it was time for the carpool and she waved from the front step with Charlotte on her hip. Back inside the house, she couldn't look at Charlotte without tears pouring from her eyes. The little girl traced the tracks of tears on her momma's face. "Momma has an owie?" she asked. Jackie just held her tighter knowing she was going to have to get a grip but had no idea how to do that. She arranged for her sister to come and take the kids for the evening. Seb and Charlotte loved Aunt Sue and she doted on them. If Sue heard something strange in Jackie's voice, she didn't comment on it. She agreed to pick up the kids and feed them dinner and have them home by seven for baths and bedtime stories. That only left ninety minutes for Jackie and Sebastian to talk. Jackie didn't know if it was enough time but then again what was there to say?

Sebastian arrived just as Sue was loading the kids in car seats. He leaned in the back seat and gave each of them a kiss and said something to Sue. Jackie watched from the living room window. It was surreal seeing her husband lean in and kiss their kids like he'd done a million times before, pre-bomb drop. Coming into the living room he moved to the opposite side of the room and perched on the edge of the leather chair in front of the window. Jackie stood in the doorway unsure of where to direct her body. Sebastian looked pained but resigned. She knew him so well. Never wishy-washy. He always knew what he wanted and he never wavered on decisions. The story came out. A young nurse at the hospital, her name is Leah, he didn't plan it, he tried to fight it, he didn't want to feel this way, he does, she does, they want to make a life together, there's no sense pretending or prolonging, he hopes Jackie will accept this. He still loves his children and wants to be their daddy. Just. Doesn't. Want. To. Be. Married. To. You. Jackie didn't ask why or how. She knew it wouldn't matter. She didn't suggest a marriage counselor. She knew it wouldn't work. Once Sebastian said he was going to do something, he did it. He'd paid his way through medical school that way and had a successful practice through determination and an unwavering focus on the end result. She heard her own voice say, "What about the children?"

"What about them? They are still my children. I'm still going to be there for them every day. Their happiness and well-being are my number one priority. I think it's imperative that you and I act as mature adults and handle this turn of events in a way that shows them we are okay so they will be too. I certainly have no interest in trying to divide their affections between us or cause undue drama that they could internalize as trauma," he said. Jackie felt like she was in a laboratory or a morgue, his words were so sterile and clinical. Words like happiness and priority just didn't seem appropriate when her entire world was just obliterated. The laboratory setting seemed real and she was the one on the table being dissected.

"How do you propose we do that?" she asked. She couldn't believe she wasn't crying. In fact, she felt like there wasn't a drop of liquid in her. She felt desiccated. Like that poem about a raisin in the sun.

"Well, it's a simple matter of finding a solution to sharing custody of them. Of course, I want to be with them as much as I can.

We could split the week evenly between your house and mine or alternate weeks to keep more consistency in their schedules." Jackie tried to work up enough spit in her mouth to form words but was finding it difficult. She thought about sweet Charlotte and her separation anxiety issues. Bouncing her back and forth between two houses with two different beds, two separate parents sounded like the worst possible scenario. Going a week without them sounded like a fate worse than death.

"I can't believe you're doing this to me. To us," she said shakily.

"It is unfortunate, but if we stay strong there's no reason this should disrupt Seb and Charlotte unduly," he said in his typical take charge voice.

"You act like we are switching cable companies or selling an old lawnmower! This is our marriage you're talking about! These are our children you are talking about moving around like characters in some sick video game. I don't understand any of this," finished Jackie at top volume.

"I realize this is difficult for you to understand but you're going to have to accept the fact that I have my reasons and accept the fact that this is happening," he said somberly.

"And why? Why do I have to understand and accept any of this bull shit? What if I don't want to understand it? What if I refuse to accept any of it?" she cried running to Sebastian and grabbing his arms as if she could somehow bring back the man she had married.

"Because Jackie." His eyes slid from hers to his feet. "She's pregnant. Leah is pregnant." The loud exchange was completely extinguished with the detonation of the third bomb. The room was devoid of sound. Jackie dropped her hands from Sebastian's arms as if she were touching something repugnant. She backed out of the room seeing his mouth moving but was unable to hear above the white noise that had filled her head. She walked without thinking until she found herself at the neighborhood park several blocks from the house. She found a swing and sat down on it. After a length of time, the numbness started wearing off and she became aware of feelings again. First in her extremities. Then slowly, feeling began to course throughout her body. The pain was white hot like an electrical current moving at a tremendous pace. It burned her gut until she nearly threw up. It singed her heart until she thought she might pass out. It began to burn in her brain and that's when Jackie got up from the swing. Never before had she felt anger this intense. If she had thought about it, she would have been frightened of herself. Seriously, she felt like she could do murder at this moment. Her feet carried her back to the front door she had left an hour before. Sebastian was standing in the living room, maybe he had been watching for her.

"How are you? Are you okay?" he asked inanely.

"No. I'm not okay thanks to you! I'm not okay with you walking out on me. I'm not okay with you destroying our children's childhoods. I'm not okay with you having babies with someone named Leah! I'm not okay having to look at you. I'm not okay with you being in my house! So I'm going to need you to get out!" Jackie roared and actually got behind Sebastian and shoved him towards the door. He had the good grace to move with it and grab his keys from the small table as he went by without trying to say more.

Jackie collapsed on the floor of the living room and that's where Anna found her after an incoherent phone call that had Anna dashing to her car. She got Jackie up to her bedroom and called Tony to bring Ellie and head over to Jackie's. Seb and Char were happy to find Tony and Ellie at their kitchen table when they arrived home. Sue charged up the stairs and Anna stepped out in the hall to let the sisters have a moment. Anna could hear Tony's voice laughing and talking with the children. He was so great with kids and was such a wonderful father to Ellie. Anna offered her gratitude to the universe for him and went back to lay beside her friend who had been retching, then sobbing, and now lay in her bed with silent tears coursing her face. The story had come out in fits and starts but Anna and Sue were able to piece it together. Anna could only imagine the stark pain her friend was suffering and knew the coming weeks and months were going to be extremely difficult.

She and Jackie had first met at Sue's boutique. They discovered they had a lot in common and Anna was able to arrange a preschool screening for Jackie's young son at her school. With Sebastian at the hospital much of the time, Anna and Jackie arranged to get the kids together while they had coffee or wine. Anna invited the whole family for dinner shortly after she and Jackie became friends. The evening was great but Sebastian was aloof and distracted and didn't seem to enjoy the gathering despite Tony's best efforts to find topics of conversation they could both enjoy. After that, they kept it just kids and moms and Tony if he was around. They spent a lot of time at the pool during the summer when Anna's schedule was lighter. Ellie loved trying to keep up with Charlotte while Jackie and Anna talked and laughed and cemented a wonderful friendship. Anna knew this catastrophic event would leave a mark on her fun-loving friend and worried that the damage would be permanent.

Sue and Anna kept close tabs on Jackie those first few weeks, doing everything they could think of to help. They prepared meals, had someone come in and clean the house, and made sure the kids had their normal activities. They were both amazed at the way the children were handling the situation. They hadn't seen any tears or temper tantrums due to the fact that the information they were getting from their mommy was that daddy was okay just somewhere else right now. Jackie made a point to be her cheery, zany self around the children but it was a mask that slipped away as soon as they were out of the room. She stopped eating and was having a terrible time sleeping. Somehow, she was able to find a source of strength, tolerance, and patience when talking to Seb and Charlotte about Sebastian.

It wasn't long before they ran into their first post-bomb skirmish. Sebastian was staying at Leah's condo on the south side of town where property values were high and spaces were small. It had two bedrooms but no beds for the kids. At first, Seb thought it was fun to sleep in a sleeping bag on the floor but couldn't go to sleep and cried for his airplane. Charlotte refused to stay on her pallet and continually tried to crawl into bed with her daddy and Leah. Sebastian brought them back to Jackie after the first night of their two-night visit saying he just couldn't cope with it until they could do something about keeping Charlotte in her own bed and Seb from fretting and crying. Jackie wrapped her arms around her sweet babies and told them to give their daddy a kiss before he went back to work. The vitriolic look she gave him over their tousled heads was enough to make him look embarrassed.

On the next scheduled visit, Sebastian called ahead to tell Jackie not to send any toys with them. The place was just too small and there simply wasn't enough room to have toys strewn about. Jackie asked if he had done anything about beds for the kids. They had a bedroom, so why couldn't they have their toys demanded Jackie. Sebastian reported that he had built a set of bunk beds but sheepishly admitted that Leah was setting up the nursery in the second bedroom leaving no room for anything extra Seb and Charlotte may bring along. With Seb at school and Charlotte down for her nap, Jackie had no problem telling Sebastina exactly what she thought about his living arrangement and the fact that the children he already had, his children, were being displaced by one that wasn't even born yet. She railed against the no toy policy and told him precisely what she thought of Leah. She admitted a certain amount of satisfaction slamming the phone down while her last expletive still rang in the air. But the war was far from over and Sebastian fired back by asking to meet Jackie at the house at a time when he knew the children would be at preschool. She wondered what fresh hell he would bring this time. Sebastian arrived and spent ten minutes walking the yard picking up sticks from a recent wind storm. His first comment when entering the kitchen was a criticism of the way Jackie wasn't keeping up with the lawn care. She let it slide off knowing there must be worse things coming and braced herself for the unknown.

"I've been thinking about the problem we have with the kids at the condo," he started. "There just isn't enough space for my things, Leah's things, all the baby accouterments, and the kids and their stuff." He looked at Jackie and waited for a response but when he saw he wasn't going to get one he continued. "I think it would be a better idea if I came back to the house and you could take the condo." Still, no response from Jackie but the look in her eyes had turned from hard to granite. Sebastian was either too sure he was right or too dumb to see he was pushing her past the breaking point. "Of course, I would still be paying the mortgage here, which I've never stopped doing," his look suggested acknowledgment or gratitude, maybe a brownie point or two. He got nothing from Jackie but the frank, hard stare. The only tell of her seething insides was the flare in her nostrils when she inhaled. "And I would pick up the mortgage on the condo as well- it's overpriced but it is in a nice part of town." When the silence in the kitchen got uncomfortable, he finally said, "What do you think?"

"Get out," she said in a low guttural voice.

"Jackie, we have to figure this out. It's a space issue…" he started.

"Get out of my house!" she screamed at him, feeling like little Charlotte with her fists clenched beside her and her face contorted in rage. "Get out of my house!" Sebastian bit back a comment, ducked his chin and headed for the door. Jackie continued to scream at his back and even at the closed door, "Get out of my house!" Later that night she was able to tell Anna about Sebastian's proposition, barely able to harness her hysteria despite a bottle of tequila and a few long-neck beers. The two friends were able to examine the situation with more objectivity and a considerable amount of profanity. Jackie admitted that the idea of leaving the house didn't really upset her. Between the upkeep and the terrible bitterness she felt, the house certainly didn't feel like home. Anna was able to offer scenarios and 'what ifs' that Jackie would have no way listened to coming from Sebastian. They finally arrived at a solution that Jackie felt she could live with. She would let Sebastian have the house and the big yard, but she would not move to the condo south of town. She wanted something close to Seb's school and the boutique where she worked. Tony suggested a great property management company and gave Jackie a business card for Donna Sue Bryant of Lake Properties.

Jackie called right away and made an appointment with Donna Sue. They met in front of an available rental and introduced themselves. While walking through the small house Jackie explained that she needed a place for her and her children. When Donna Sue asked if she would need to sell her place before doing a deal, Jackie felt comfortable enough to explain that her husband, now ex-husband wanted their existing house for his new wife- soon to be and their baby due to be born in a few months. Donna Sue raised one perfectly arched eyebrow and immediately suggested they go for a cocktail. The two spent the remainder of the afternoon at a lovely bar downtown, sipping martinis and becoming friends.

Within a week, Donna Sue had found the perfect place for Jackie and had the lease drawn up. Sebastian wasn't happy that Jackie didn't go for the easy swap of the two places but had the good grace not to object. He would have to sell the condo south of town but that was his problem. Jackie felt better knowing that Seb and Charlotte would be completely at home now when they spent time with their dad. No more night worries for Seb and climbing out of bed for Charlotte. Jackie wondered briefly what Leah thought about the arrangement but decided she didn't give a rat's ass what the woman who took her husband and now her house, thought or felt about it. The house Donna Sue found was small but cute. Jackie liked the southern exposure and the fact that they could walk to the park. She bought new bedroom furniture for all three of them, charging it to Sebastian, and distracted herself with decorating the children's rooms. She had her first party at the new place the night of Sebastian and Leah's wedding. She invited Sue, Anna, and her new friend Donna Sue to join her for a night of female solidarity and heavy drinking. She established new routines and concentrated all of her energy and efforts on the care and well-being of her precious children.

Between feeling awkward, ashamed, and more than a little afraid of Jackie, Leah tried to avoid contact as much as possible and used post-it notes tucked in Seb's backpack to communicate information between the two houses. Four months of reading crumpled up, cryptic yellow squares took its toll until Jackie was good and pissed off. After a weekend with Dad and Leah, Jackie hugged the kids and waved at Leah parked at the curb. Seb handed her the dreaded post-it note. Without hesitating and not knowing what she was going to say, Jackie charged out the door and ran to the curb where Leah was just ready to pull away. She pecked on the window startling the other woman and motioned for her to unlock the passenger door. It was difficult to tell in the light of the car but Jackie was pretty sure Leah's face went pale. She pulled open the door and sat down in the seat noticing Leah's baby bump. In typical Jackie style, she grinned at the wide-eyed younger woman and said,

"Hey, so look. About these damn post-its. The thing is we're in this together whether we like it or not. I'm sure you'd rather I wasn't here and I know I'd much rather you weren't. But I am and you are, so here's the deal. My kids are the most important and precious things I will ever have. And now they are your kids too. Warts and all. Lock, stock, and barrel. If we're going to survive this, and trust me when I say, I struggle with it daily, I'm going to need you to do something for me. It's big and it may be hard but if you feel anything at all for me, I need you to try your damnedest. I'm going to need you to love them. I'm going to need you to love them the same way I love them. Love them like they are the most precious things in the world to you. I know this is hard for you to imagine, but I need you to love them like you gave birth to them. They need to be hugged and kissed and cuddled at your house just as much as at mine. They need discipline when they do something wrong and praise when they delight you. I need you to encourage them to grow into wonderful, caring individuals who think of others before they think of themselves. I don't want 'mom's expectations' and 'Leah and Dad's expectations'. I want our expectations to be the same. That we are bringing up these two lovely small humans that feel our love and support around them unconditionally. If you do this, if you love my children like they are your own you will have helped me with my most important job on this planet. But you will also have their love in return. You're going to find out soon enough that there is nothing like the feeling when you hold your baby for the first time. It's bigger than you, it's bigger than you and Sebastian."

Jackie's voice broke as she gulped for air. "Seb and Char are going to love your baby! That's their baby brother and I want them to have a wonderfully healthy relationship with him every day for all of their lives, not just holidays and every other weekend." Jackie saw tears flowing from Leah's eyes but she didn't let up. "You think I'm crazy and I am. I'm crazy in love with my babies and I will do anything to ensure their happiness. It's not the way I thought it would be, but we are a family now. It's fucked up but it still counts as a family. These kids, even the one inside you are our kids now. We are a family." Jackie paused as Leah searched the console for a paper napkin to wipe her streaming eyes and nose.

"And families don't communicate with post-it notes so I'm going to need you to be able to call me or talk to me over coffee or something. I don't want to know that Seb had a time out or read about your family reunion on a goddamn yellow piece of paper." Once again, Jackie's huge grin split her face but there was a glistening of tears in her eyes. Leah made a sound that could have been a laugh or a gasp for air and nodded vigorously. Any other two women would have embraced after such an emotional exchange. Instead, Jackie told her to be sure to be rubbing her skin with lanolin to avoid stretch marks and hopped out of the car. She stood on the curb and watched until Leah pulled away then turned back to her door where her children waited inside.

Five weeks later Asher was born, a normal sized albeit a little jaundiced baby boy in a nondescript delivery. Jackie brought Seb and Charlotte to the hospital and was allowed in the maternity unit. After congratulating Leah, Jackie sat on the sofa beside Seb as he held his new brother on a pillow on his lap. She and the children marveled over the tiny baby. Jackie held him so Charlotte could give him butterfly kisses. Throughout the visit, she behaved as if Sebastian wasn't standing at the end of the bed. At the end of the visit, she encouraged hugs and kisses and reassured Leah that she was a phone call away if she needed anything. Without a glance at Sebastian, she left the maternity room and bit down hard on the inside of her cheek. She knew, coming here, was going to be tough but was unprepared for the tidal wave of emotion when she looked down into the sweet face of Sebastain's son that looked almost identical to her own baby boy. She had been instantly transported back to the magical days when her son and daughter had been born. Then she had been overpowered by the amount of love she felt for the new life she and her husband had created. This experience was similar but had a definite Twilight Zone quality to it. Seb and Charlotte were obviously smitten with the new baby and were talking about how cute and little he was. Jackie walked on and wondered how this new little life was going to change them all.

Understandably, Seb and Charlotte's visitation routine went on hiatus while Leah settled in with the baby. Jackie didn't ask if Sebastian was taking any time off from work to help her during the day. She recalled him being on hand for some things but she had done all the heavy lifting when it came to the care of their babies. At the time, Jackie didn't mind or maybe even notice. She was so in love with the tiny person in the bassinet that she made it easy for Sebastian to maintain his normal routine. She wondered if Leah would make it easy for him or demand a more involved partner. Almost two weeks from the day little Asher went home Jackie got a teary call from Leah. At first, she panicked that something had gone terribly wrong, but then she could hear the outraged screams of an infant in the background. Leah wondered if Jackie could tell her over the phone how she could get the baby to stop crying. Jackie assured her she'd be over in five minutes and hung up before Leah could say anything further.

Arriving at the house, Jackie went immediately to the bassinet where Asher was tight-fisted and more than a bit purplish from his exertions. Leah stood in the middle of the room looking shell-shocked. Her hair hadn't been washed in days and her sweat pants were in bad need of laundering. Jackie scooped up the screaming baby and held him to her shoulder immediately beginning to bounce. Over the mega decibel screams, she told Leah to go take a long shower, put on clean everything and climb into bed. Leah may have offered some objection but to no avail. Jackie continued bouncing the irate infant and pointed at the stairs. Leah left the room with her head hanging down and Jackie went about trying to soothe little Asher. After several minutes of walking and bouncing there was very little change in volume. Jackie tried singing, loudly. She tried going outside where the fall air was crisp and chilly. The little guy was really bent out of shape and so far, what she had tried wasn't cutting it. No wonder Leah looked like a zombie. After checking that he had a dry diaper and wasn't hungry Jackie remembered a trick that worked for Charlotte and her colicky tummy. Still bouncing on her feet and murmuring quietly to Asher she went to the hall closet and pulled out the upright vacuum cleaner. She reached behind the sofa and plugged it in and waited. It took a few seconds for the constant screaming and gasping to slow down to just crying then to hiccupping breaths until finally, Asher lay quiet and exhausted on Jackie's shoulder as she stood beside the running vacuum. Leah came hurrying down the stairs, noticeably better looking with clean hair and skin and fresh yoga pants.

"Seriously? Are you cleaning the house?" she asked with wide eyes and an accusatory tone.

Jackie turned to look at her and held her finger up to indicate they should keep their voices down. Leah took in the sleeping baby. The baby that was not screaming. Then she looked at the vacuum that was running yet standing still next to the wall where Jackie had plugged it in.

"I think we can lay him down now. There is a hot water bottle in the bathroom upstairs-it may help. Run and get it," she said as if this were the most natural thing in the world to be directing Leah around a house that had been Jackie's home and was no longer.

Leah looked like she'd just seen a unicorn. She went to the bathroom and got the hot water bottle.

"Where do you want him? In the bassinet or his crib?" asked Jackie quietly.

Leah could only point at the bassinet. Words seemed to have failed her or maybe she was just so exhausted she didn't have the energy for them.

"Wrap the hot water bottle in a towel and put it in the bassinet then I can lay him down." Leah did as she was told and watched as Jackie expertly laid the sleeping baby on his back and curled the hot water bottle around his little form. Both women backed away from the bassinet and the still running vacuum cleaner.

In the kitchen, Leah began with "How? Why?"

"The vacuum?" asked Jackie. "Beats me. All I know is I was about to lose my mind with Charlotte. I'd get her to sleep but I couldn't lay her down. As soon as I made any move to let go of her, she'd start up louder than before. It was a vicious cycle and I thought I was absolutely the world's worst mother! One night she was crying, I was crying. I decided to hell with it. If she was going to cry nonstop I might as well get something done and I hauled the sweeper out. It certainly wasn't going to disturb her so I plugged it in and she and I vacuumed the rugs while we cried. For some strange reason, that droning noise soothed her and she gave up and went to sleep. I laid her down and kept that Kirby running! I don't understand it, but I remembered it worked with her so I tried it with Asher.

Leah looked at Jackie with a look that said 'you saved my life' and then she reached out and hugged her. Jackie hugged her back and said, "I've got two hours before Charlotte is finished at pre-school. Run upstairs and grab a nap. I'll be here if he wakes up." Leah backed away and whispered thank you before slipping upstairs. Jackie looked around the kitchen. It was a mess. She checked to make sure the baby was still sleeping and went to work unloading and loading the dishwasher. The fridge was full of food past its prime and was beginning to have an odor. After she finished cleaning out the fridge and wiping down all the counters, she thought she heard little noises coming from the living room. Going in she could see a little fist waving around and peeked over the bassinet to see Asher awake and not pissed off. Shutting off the vacuum she picked him up and immediately changed his diaper. She could tell by the way he was rooting around that he was looking for something to eat. She knew Leah had breast milk in the fridge so bouncing and talking, the two went to the kitchen where Jackie warmed the bottle. Returning from work, Sebastian found his ex-wife feeding his newborn son a bottle in a sparkling clean kitchen while his new wife was nowhere to be seen.

Standing, Jackie handed him the hungry baby who was actively going after the bottle. "Leah is taking a much-needed nap. They were both at the breaking point when I got here. I would suggest you take some time off from work. She needs help and you need to give it to her. Oh, and he has colic in case you haven't noticed." With that, she kissed Asher on the top of his head and walked out.

Two days later Jackie had another panicky call from Leah. Asher wouldn't stop crying and the vacuum trick wasn't working. Jackie was at the boutique and couldn't leave so she told Leah to undress the baby and put his naked skin against hers. If that didn't help, she should stand in a warm shower with him, skin to skin. Leah thanked her for the ideas, apologized for bothering her, and promised she'd call to let Jackie know if things improved. Jackie went back to work but had a hard time concentrating on her tasks. She recognized the convolutedness of worrying over her ex-husband's new baby and wife but she couldn't help it. She worried about the little guy knowing he had the same intestinal malady Charlotte had suffered as a baby. She also worried about the baby's momma, she didn't seem to be taking to mothering as seamlessly as one could. Jackie was also coming to the realization that not only was Sebastian not being on hand and helpful for Leah but that he hadn't been on hand for her when Seb and Charlotte were born either. It was a bit of an 'ah ha' moment when she realized just how little he had been home and how little he did to help her. For the first time since he began blowing holes in their lives, Jackie experienced a moment of relief that he was no longer hers to worry about. She promised herself she would check in on Leah and the baby tomorrow.

Leah greeted Jackie at the door the following day and once again she was crying. Jackie put her hands on the other woman's arms and guided her into the kitchen all the while listening for Asher's cries. "Where's the baby? Is he alright?" she asked urgently.

Leah nodded her head and murmured that yes, he was alright. He was sleeping in his crib.

"Then why are you upset? Asher's taking a nap, you should be laying down now. What's wrong?" asked Jackie.

"I feel awful telling you this but Sebastian is being so awful. He's stressed out about the southside condo not selling and when I ask him to take time off of work to help with the baby, he says he can't afford it." She began to cry harder but felt the need to explain the way things were to Jackie. "I know I have no right to look for sympathy from you but honestly, I didn't think it would be this way. He loves Asher but he wants me to do everything for the baby. If I ask him to hold him in the evening so I can do the tiniest thing he gives me that look. When I complain about not getting enough sleep, he's quick to explain that we are all capable of more than we think we are. I thought we were going to do this together but it turns out I get more help and support from you than from him and that is way messed up." With that, Leah took a few gulps of air and tried to stabilize her breathing. Jackie sat back and studied the young woman.

"You know, he was exactly the same way with me. I was just too dumb to know it. I was so into it all that I didn't even see it until you showed me through your eyes," said Jackie. "Why is he so stressed about the condo? It will sell, this just isn't a good time."

"He moved some stocks into a high-risk bracket to pay down the last of his student loans and things didn't go according to his plan. With paying the mortgage here and the condo as well as your place, he says we're in a pinch. It's really stressing him out," said Leah.

"I can see how that would stress Mr. Five-Year-Plan," said Jackie thoughtfully. She felt for Leah and again had the feeling of relief and release that this was someone else's husband they were discussing.

Jackie found Sebastian at the door the following Saturday as she was dropping the kids at the house. Leah must have been taking a nap, Jackie hoped. After eighty-four kisses from Char, she had turned and was walking back to her car when she swung around and went back. The kids had taken their backpacks to their rooms and she found Sebastian standing at the kitchen counter. Without preamble, Jackie started, "Hey, you need to step up the new parent program with Leah. She's really struggling and she needs your help. I know you and I have been through all this before but she's not as sturdy as I was. She needs you to help her, support her, and reassure her that she's doing okay. She's exhausted too. You need to take the baby every once in a while, so she can sleep or rest or bathe. Last I checked, it takes two to make a baby so it goes to reason there should be two taking care of it. Your work will still be there and your bank account will be too. Your wife and baby need you on hand and present so you need to work that into your five-year plan!" Jackie realized that was the most words she'd said to her ex-husband in several months. She stood waiting to see what he would do.

"Believe me, I'd like to be here more to help. But thanks to you, we are in some deep financial trouble," he said.

"Me?! I've put us in deep financial trouble?" spluttered Jackie. "How do you figure I did that? I didn't break up our family. That was all you!"

"Yes, but you could have easily moved into the condo saving us the hassle of selling it and the cost of your place," he explained as if this was the most logical thing in the world. "I've gone from one mortgage to three and now there's the child support you demanded. I took a significant hit in the stock market. Thanks to you, we are stretched beyond thin. If I'm stressed it's because I have to provide for all of us and I'm not getting any help from you."

"You are out of your mind!" she wanted to scream but instead hissed through clenched teeth. "You're the one who had an affair and decimated our family and now you're telling me if I had moved into that crappy condo and not held you accountable for your own children everything would be hunky-dory? I call bullshit! Rank, hot stinking bull shit! You are so full of yourself you can't tell your ass from a hole in the ground. You didn't have to play hard and fast with your investments, you could have kept them right where they were but no! It's coming up on ten years since you finished residency and your little plan was to have all your debt gone by then. But you screwed around and got another wife and another kid! That certainly wasn't in your original plan, was it Mr. Planful? Your money problems are a direct result of your choices and I won't stand here and listen to you tell ME that it's my fault. You better get yourself together and start showing up for your wife and baby. Figure out what to do about your money 'pinch' and pull your head out of your ass." With that, Jackie turned on her heel and stormed out the door.

In the coming weeks, things seemed to get tighter. So much so that Jackie began stopping in at the house every day when Charlotte was at preschool just to check on Leah and the baby. Most days she took the baby who invariably was crying and sent Leah to take a shower or to bed for an hour's reprieve from the colicky baby. On the few occasions, little Asher was actually asleep, Jackie would fix two cups of tea and the two women would sit at the kitchen table chatting as friends would do. Jackie hated to bring up the topic of Sebastian but felt like avoiding it was a little like avoiding the dinosaur in the park. Naturally, Leah began to cry.

"It's worse now than before! His quarterly taxes are due and he had to dip into an annuity in order to cover the costs. Of course, he went crazy over the penalties for pulling the money out. I don't know what to do. When he's not here I wish he was and when he is here, he acts like this crazed person who can only think about money and I wish he'd go back to work," she finished as tears and snot ran down her face. Jackie handed a paper towel to Leah and sat thinking. As much as she'd like to tell Sebastian to go lie in the bed of roses he made for himself she knew it was affecting them all. Seb had come home from their two-day stay at Dad's and gone right to his room. Noticing that he'd left his airplane by the front door, Jackie carried it down the hall. Seeing her sweet boy sitting on the floor with an army jeep he hadn't played with in ages was her first clue something was wrong. His forlorn look was a dead giveaway.

"Hey, Doc, how are you doing? You left this in the other room," she said as she sat cross-legged opposite her son.

Seb glanced at the plane and shrugged, continuing to roll the jeep back and forth.

"What's wrong? Remember, we're on the same team here," she encouraged.

Seb looked up again and Jackie's heart did a little trip at the pain coming from his eyes behind the long lashes he'd inherited from his dad. "I don't think Daddy likes me anymore," he said.

"Oh, I think you're wrong. Daddy may be busy but he loves you and Charlotte and Asher all the way to the moon and back," she said.

"He wasn't busy. He was just sitting there. I asked him to play airplane with me but he wouldn't. He told me to play with Char but she's not good at airplane. Daddy can lift me up and swing me around and he makes all the cool noises. So I tried to do the noises myself and daddy yelled and threw my plane on the ground. Now the landing gear is broken."

Jackie held the airplane in her lap while trying to think of what to say to comfort her son even as her brain was plotting the murder of her ex-husband. "I'm sorry about the landing gear, but I bet we can fix it with some gorilla glue. And Daddy loves you! He loves you so much that sometimes he goes a little nuts trying to figure out all the ways he's going to show you how much he loves you. I think that's what happened today. Daddy was worrying over the best ways he can show you and Charlotte and Asher how much he loves you that he forgot you were right there. I bet the next time you see Daddy he'll have figured it all out and be ready to play airplane with you," she said with as much conviction as she could muster. The hopeful look in her little boy's eyes told her he bought it. She hoped desperately she hadn't just told a whopper of a lie and was already preparing her remarks for Sebastian.

Jackie didn't want to have a showdown anywhere near the children so she showed up at Sebastian's office at the end of the following day. She made cheery small talk with the receptionist and waited until Sebastian's last patient was gone. She knew the office staff would log off their computers and clear out pretty quickly. Walking down the short hall to his office she could feel the steam building in her head. She rounded the corner ready to start shooting from the hip but was drawn up short by the dejected man who sat at the desk with his head in his hands. The self-assuredness and the calm capability that were his trademarks were stripped away completely.

He looked up when he heard her inhale and wasn't able to hide the fear in his eyes before looking away.

"Sebastian? What's happening here?" she said, hesitancy replacing the ire she came in with. Instead of straightening his shoulders and cocking his head in the confrontational angle he typically resorted to, he sighed deeply.

"I've lost it and I don't know how to get it back," he said. For a nanosecond, Jackie wondered if he was talking about their life together.

"What is it that you've lost, exactly?" she asked not sure how she would react if it was what she thought.

"My way. My plan. I never wanted to be the guy that laid awake at night worrying about how he was going to pay for his house, his kids, everything. I never wanted to live on margin just hoping that things didn't come due at the same time. I planned carefully. I worked hard to make sure that wouldn't happen. But here I am. I've ransacked my tax annuity that was supposed to help when the kids were college-age. I've borrowed money to pay my quarterly taxes and even after all of that I don't know how I'm going to pay insurance and mortgages next month. On top of all of that, my wife is threatening to take the baby and leave if I can't be more supportive," he finished with a sound between a sigh and a groan.

Jackie sat down in the chair opposite the big desk. "Well then, we better figure this out," she said matter of factly. Sebastian gave her a wide-eyed look.

"What?" Jackie felt a sense of deja vu after her discussion with Leah regarding the children but continued anyway. "Whether we like it or not, our wagons are hitched together. If you go down, we all go down, so let's get to work. What's the most immediate crisis situation? We can start there and work out to the more long-range issues." Sebastian took a breath and she wondered what was going through his head before he began systematically laying out the money crunch.

"So we know you need to unload the condo," she mused, thinking her friend Donna Sue could be helpful with that.

"And your lease, it's really expensive since we took it year to year. Is there any way you can see your way clear to pick up the rent?" he asked sheepishly. "I know that if I had those two monthly payments off my list I could save enough for the insurance and taxes. Three mortgages are killing me." Jackie stared hard at him for a full two minutes. Sebasian was fully aware of her passionate nature and waited for the worst.

"No, Charlotte is only in daycare for half days and I won't pawn her off on a sitter. What if there was another solution? One that would relieve you of my lease and the daycare issue too?" she asked.

"And what would that be? I've racked my brain trying to figure this out and other than getting a second job I'm fresh out of ideas."

"What if I moved back into the house?" Sebastian's expression was unreadable. "What if we all lived in one house?" She didn't pause or allow him time to interrupt. She sat forward in her chair and laid out the idea. "The lease on my place would be gone, we'll get my friend involved to sell the condo. The kids already have rooms in the house and I'll take the guest room in the basement. It wouldn't take much to expand the wet bar area into a small kitchen. I can continue working at the boutique but will be on hand to help Leah with the baby when you're not there and vice versa when I have plans. We need to work out some kind of system so I can be saving up for my own place when you're on firmer ground."

Sebastian was completely taken aback at the audacious idea and studied the woman he knew so well sitting across from him. "You'd do that? You'd move back into the house and live with me and my wife and baby?" he asked incredulously.

"I didn't say I'd like it. Hitched wagons remember? Now it's time to circle those wagons to make sure we all live to tell about it," Jackie said as she stood. "I'll get in touch with Donna Sue. She can help with both properties we want to let go of. You do what you need to do to make this okay with Leah. I'll be in touch."

Jackie made it to the door before she heard him say, "Thank you. I don't know if I deserve this."

"Oh trust me! I'm way more than you deserve," she said and couldn't quite pull off her trademark grin thinking about the plan she had just laid out.

Coming up with the plan set things in motion and once rolling, they seemed to move right along. Once Donna Sue got a hold of the reins things began to happen. Jackie packed up her cute little house and prepared to move back into the home she and Sebastian had purchased as excited newlyweds. The situation was bizarre and Jackie didn't tell many people about the arrangement. Of course, Sue knew and didn't approve after the terrible way Sebastian had behaved. Jackie agreed with her sister that he was the lowest form of pond scum but tried to explain that it was temporary and would be mutually beneficial and most importantly beneficial for Seb and Charlotte. Her friends knew as well and after the move had been made and the dust had time to settle, they planned an evening together at Anna's.

When Jackie arrived, she didn't bother going to the front door. The back deck was where the party always happened. Anna had candles burning and Tony had laid a small crackling fire for them in the fire bowl in the center of the deck. Anna unfolded herself out of a cushioned wicker chair as Jackie rounded the house. The two friends didn't say anything, just clung to each other. One trying to soothe and restore, the other trying to breathe and balance. Arm in arm they climbed the five steps to the deck and curled up in chairs. They had their first shot of tequila before they even spoke a word. Sylvie emerged from the kitchen with a plate of hot stuffed banana peppers. Before Jackie knew what she was doing she'd gobbled three of the delicious appetizers. Her stomach appreciated the sustenance and grumbled loudly for more. Soon they heard the clip-clop of high heels and Donna Sue's signature greeting, 'Hey Gal.' Slowly the six chairs filled up and food and drinks were passed around and enjoyed. Al added more wood to the small fire and they enjoyed the crackling and flickering light it provided. After some time, Libby's voice cut through the dark, "So, how are you doing, really?"

Jackie gulped but wasn't afraid to answer. She knew she was completely safe in her circle of friends. "It's like living in one of those fun houses at the carnival. From the outside, everything looks perfectly normal. But on the inside, it's all topsy-turvy. I don't know if she's living in my house or if I'm living in hers. I had to open every kitchen cupboard to find where she moved the tea bags. Makes sense to me you keep them by the mugs but no they are somewhere else. A few nights ago, I came home and she and the baby were sitting in the dark. She'd blown a breaker but didn't know where the breaker box was. I mean, you can relocate every single item in the kitchen cabinets but you don't know where the breaker box is? She lets Seb and Char have the run of the pantry no matter what time of day or night. Then, of course, I come in and tell them to put the handfuls of cookies back as dinner is in an hour and I'm the bad guy! And she has a message board in the kitchen so we can all stay up to date and informed about who's doing what and when. She wants me to let her know if I'm going out. I swear it feels like I'm living with my mother, but then I get completely grossed out when I remember it's Sebastian's wife! It's crazy and if I think about it too much, I start to get vertigo."

"Are you sure you want to be faced with her all of the time?" asked Al. "Is this what you really want to do?"

"Hell no, it's not what I want to do! It's the last thing in the world I want to do, live with my ex-husband and his new wife and child. It's revolting! It's disgusting!" Jackie took a few beats to breathe hard. Her friends listened to the outpouring of pain. "Some days I think, I can't do it. It's too hard. But then I see Seb and Char being natural and happy and I know this is what I have to do. Their happiness is what I want more than anything! I want my babies to grow up knowing they are loved by their mommy and their daddy. If that means Leah, then Leah too. Now that they have a little brother, I want them to live as siblings every day, not just every other week and on holidays."

Jackie continued with a firm voice and glistening eyes. "My marriage may have failed but I will not fail my babies. They are going to be loved like they deserve to be loved and I will make sure of that."

It was almost like a church service with words of support and encouragement coming from the circle. The tequila went around again. To outsiders, Jackie's acceptance of Leah and the living arrangement they had seemed bizarre but many figured it made sense in an amicable situation. The goddesses knew at what cost her decision came. They also knew her motivation behind it. Jackie would always be civil and supportive of Leah for Seb and Charlotte. They had no doubt she loved little Asher too and would treat any other babies that came along, with love and affection for Seb and Charlotte. She would treat Sebastian with respect, never letting on how his betrayal had nearly obliterated her. She would bury her devastating heartbreak in a place never to be seen by her children. She would gladly sacrifice this part of her heart and spirit until they were a little older and had time to develop and flourish into the wonderful persons they would become. The friends finished the evening strong with lots of good food, good drink, and a rousing rendition of Gloria Gainer's 'I Will Survive'. As they began to collect their things and head home each was thinking their own thoughts about their beautiful friend and her unique situation. No matter how crazy or bizarre life was, each of them was thankful for the friendship they shared and the support they knew they could count on no matter what.

Libby

Growing up in a small town seemed to set certain limits on a young person's imagination and mind. Libby had known every kid she went to school with from kindergarten all the way to their senior trip to the St. Louis Zoo. Things didn't change much after high school. The pairs that had naturally evolved as high school sweethearts became husbands and wives and then parents. Libby never thought too much about it-it seemed like she and Roddy had been together since they were children. They had grown up together- everything they did for the first time they had done together. It was like they were on an auto-mated track where they could see where they were going but couldn't change directions, their course was predetermined. Libby felt like she was floating on air the day she married Rodney Craigmile. Her dress was store-bought in Columbia but the bridesmaids' dresses, the cake, and even the flowers were made by Libby and her posse of girlfriends, many of whom were already married to their high school sweethearts. She'd said 'I do' to the familiar dark-eyed boy she'd first kissed when they were in the third grade. They bought a small farmhouse a short distance from both sets of parents and Libby thought she was happy. Roddy got hired at the local plant where they made bricks and had done so since the early 1900s. He wasn't really a brickmaker. He was really a farmer who needed a steady income until he could afford to farm full-time like his dad. Libby took a job at a local daycare. She thought she'd love it, but within six months she was moody and discontented. Roddy didn't know what to tell his young wife when she told him she just wasn't happy at her job, and that it didn't fulfill her. He was pretty sure he wasn't feeling fulfilled working in the brick plant all day, but he knew it was honest work and a steady paycheck and benefits they needed. His concept of adulting was that you got a job, you worked. Feelings of fulfillment had never been explained to him as something that was important.

Just after Thanksgiving, Roddy came home from work to find Libby curled up on their bed crying.

"Baby, what is it? Are you sick? Do you have a migraine?" he asked as he sat on the side of the bed. Libby suffered from migraines regularly and he hated to see her in pain. "Can I get you a wet cloth or some Excedrin?" Libby didn't reply, just burrowed her head deeper into the pillow and continued to snuffle and sob. "Did something happen at work today? Libby, talk to me. What's wrong?" he demanded.

"I can't do this anymore!" she blurted out.

"Do what?" asked Roddy.

"That awful job! I can't go there. Not one more day. I hate it! I feel like I've been sentenced for something and this is my punishment. I can't do it. I can't stay there," she said.

"Did something happen? Was someone mean to you?" asked Roddy trying to understand the motive for this emotional tirade.

"No Roddy! No one was 'mean' to me." Libby sat up in the bed almost yelling at him. "I hate the fucking job!"

Taken aback by the volume and vehemence of her words, Roddy said, "Okay, calm down. I'm just trying to figure out why you are so up…"

Libby didn't let him finish. She leaped from the bed and began pacing around the room. Her hands were clenched at ear level and the snot and makeup were making a mess of her pretty face. "Of course, you don't understand! You're content to fall right in line with every other guy around here. You go to work, you come home, you never want anything different, you never want to do or go anywhere new! I'm not like that! I need something else! I need more!" she finished. Roddy stood up and faced her. His compassion and concern for her were getting displaced by a wave of slow-burning anger.

"What are you saying? You want what to be different, exactly? The job or me?" he asked in a steely tone. The edge in his voice cut through the hysteria in Libby's brain and she ran to him and clutched his arms.

"No, no, no! I'm not saying I want you to be different! I just need something different for me. I can't work in this small town where everyone has such small minds. I want to make a difference. I want to meet new people and find out new things about myself. I just want something …different." She searched Roddy's familiar face for a sign that she hadn't completely pissed him off. He gave her a hard look for another two beats before he pulled her into his tight embrace. Their bodies fit together perfectly and were so familiar to each other it was difficult to know where she stopped and he started. He held her close for a minute and without pulling away said,

"If you want to work somewhere else then do it. I don't care where you work just as long as you come home every night. To me. I love you Lib." He could feel Libby's tense body relax into his.

"Oh Roddy, thank you! I'm sorry I'm such a basket case. I just got so worked up and I wasn't sure you'd understand," she said. "I'll go make dinner. Can I get you a beer?" she asked as she reached up and kissed him before leaving the bedroom.

"Sure," he said, watching her go. Two things from their 'fight' were hanging in the air and he didn't like the stench they left. One was the comment about him having no life ambition. She'd known who he was when she married him. Hell, she'd known him since they were ten years old! Her comment about his lack of interest in doing other things was out of left field. Of course, in the heat of any argument there are always careless words that cause hurt but the other thing, the way worse thing wasn't what she said, it's what she didn't say. When Roddy told her he loved her there was no reassuring 'I love you' in return. For the first time since they were children, he felt like he didn't know what was in Libby's head or heart and it worried him.

Before Christmas Libby had a job in Columbia, thirty miles away. She was going to work as an office assistant for Barbara Hinshaw, an event planner who worked out of the Hilton Hotel and Convention Center. She was thrilled about the job and much to Roddy's relief, life at home rebounded to the easy comfortable relationship they had always enjoyed. Libby loved the work and had a natural ability for organizing events and planning parties. She decided none of her clothes were suitable for the new job, a fact that made Roddy nervous as they were on a tight budget after having to buy a new car that would be reliable transportation for her out on the highway. Luckily, she had a good eye for quality clothes and was able to find several gently used things in thrift stores and consignment shops. She always looked impeccably dressed in her newly adopted boho style that was very different from the basic fashions she and her friends back home had always worn. Her girlfriends commented on her chic apparel and how she didn't even look like herself anymore. Libby would laugh at their comments which sounded a smidge like a critique and began spending less and less time with them.

More and more frequently Libby's boss would ask her to attend the events she was helping to plan at the convention center. Libby's natural good looks and easy smile made her a real hit with visitors and convention goers. When Roddy began to grumble about how much time she spent at work she would remind him that when she worked a convention all weekend she got paid overtime. Roddy wasn't entirely sure that the extra income was making up for the time they were apart. Libby looked and acted so differently. She showed little interest in weekend cookouts with their friends and would tell him to go without her. It annoyed him that she wanted to talk exclusively about the exciting people she was meeting in Columbia. Libby had said she wanted to make a difference. Roddy was sure of one thing, Libby's job was making her different.

On their third wedding anniversary, Roddy surprised Libby by taking off an hour early and showing up in her office. He was dressed up in his khakis and newest button-up Wrangler shirt and held a small bouquet of flowers in his hand. When Libby looked up from her computer screen she was shocked.

"Oh my gosh! What are you doing here?" she said as she came around the desk. Roddy leaned in for a kiss but Libby held him away looking over her shoulder at Barbara's office door.

"I came to take you to dinner. You're always telling me how great Columbia is so I thought I'd take off a little early and we'd celebrate our anniversary," said Roddy. Libby took the flowers from Roddy and was shaking her head slowly.

"Roddy, we have a huge convention starting tomorrow. I wish you'd called first. I don't think I can get away now," she said. Hearing voices, Barbara came out of her office.

"What's this? Flowers? A gentleman?" she asked. Roddy thought Libby acted flustered as she introduced him to Barbara and she left off saying anything about it being their anniversary.

"I thought I'd sweep her off her feet beings it's our anniversary but she says she has a lot of work left to do," he said with a smile that didn't make it all the way to his eyes.

"That's ridiculous!" said Barbara. "Of course you'll go celebrate! I insist!"

"But I haven't finished printing all the name badges or the table assignments," rushed Libby.

"Name badges and table assignments are not important when your handsome prince rides into town. You two lovebirds get out of here. I can finish all the little details. I'll see you tomorrow. It was lovely meeting you Rodney. Happy Anniversary to you both!" she said before turning back to her office.

Libby watched her leave the room and looked back at Roddy with an expression that was difficult to read. He couldn't help feeling like she didn't want to go with him and was almost sorry he'd come. Just as quickly, she buried her nose in the flowers and when she looked up he recognized the beautiful smile he'd been missing. "Okay, Handsome Prince! Where shall we go?" she asked.

He gave her his best redneck drawl and said, "Somewhere they got good grub!" After deciding to take Libby's car and leaving his big truck in the parking lot they headed for the downtown district. Libby was talking excitedly about the new Indian restaurant or there was the Formosa. Roddy shook his head, "Isn't there any real American food around here? I'd like a nice steak." Libby felt bad for not being more excited when Roddy had surprised her at the office. She wanted to make it up to him so she turned the car around and headed for Alexanders, a locally owned steakhouse. Once seated in a deep red leather booth they perused the menu. When the server came to take their orders, Roddy ordered the prime rib, kings cut medium-rare. When it was Libby's turn, she ordered a salad.

"What? You're not hungry?" Roddy asked.

"Oh no, I am! I'm starving- I just don't want a big piece of meat," she explained.

Roddy snorted, "Since when? I've seen you eat a steak so rare it did all but moo. Get a steak," he encouraged.

Libby sat up a little straighter in the booth. "I don't want a steak," she said. Roddy signaled the server back to the table. "I think my wife made a mistake," he said.

Libby's face turned a deep purply red, "No I most certainly did not make a mistake!" she exclaimed.

Roddy smiled at the server who shrugged and went on his way. "Sorry. I thought you were just being careful because of the money or something. You love steak, I was just trying to help," he said.

Libby was trying to get her emotions under control with some deep breaths. "I don't need help ordering what I want. I simply can't stomach the thought of a piece of red meat on my plate." It was clear to Roddy that meat wasn't the only thing she couldn't stomach. The injured look in his eyes made Libby look down at the table. They forced their way through dinner and the next two years of marriage before throwing in the towel. They both cried the day she loaded the little car with her clothes and coaxed the golden retriever mix they had adopted together into the front seat. She would stay with Barbara's daughter until she could find something she could afford. She backed out of the driveway crying so hard she couldn't see the dust her tires kicked up on the gravel road, feeling like she was leaving part of her physical body behind. She remembered a horrible story Roddy's buddy Charlie told about a fox that chewed off her leg in order to escape a trap. As painful as leaving was, she knew she would surely suffocate if she stayed in the little house in the little town for one more minute.

She found a cute rental with a small, fenced yard for Carmello near the heart of downtown. Her landlord, a man named Lavendar, owned a Spiritual Shop and was 'out there' according to anyone from her hometown. The two became immediate friends and Libby helped out at the shop on Wednesdays when Lavendar taught classes for people interested in everything from reincarnation to paranormal activity. She also discovered running and biking, things people on gravel roads don't do much of-and met like-minded people who loved spending weekends biking the Katy Trail.

Although she hadn't planned on changing jobs, she fell into an opportunity to apply at a law firm. She thought she'd be answering phones and filing but at least she'd have her weekends free to bike or run. She was surprised when she got the job that it was mainly doing research and helping the lawyers gather information they needed. Libby found the work fascinating and felt important helping to build cases. It was close to the first anniversary of her new life in a new town when one of the lawyers, Tom Huff, invited her to join him for dinner with a client. He offered to pick her up but when he told her the meeting place was Boone Tavern she volunteered to meet him there as it wasn't far from where she lived. Upon arriving, Libby found Tom sitting at a corner booth on his own.

"I guess your client is more fashionably late than I am," she said with her bright smile.

"Actually, there is no client," he said. "I was afraid you wouldn't come out with me any other way. I hope you're not mad."

Libby ducked her chin, letting her blond curls cover her face for an instant. A small thrill shivered through her and she knew she wasn't upset by the subterfuge but allowed him to think she was.

"So, this is a date huh?" she asked, her smile reappearing.

"I've wanted to ask you out since you started at the firm, I just didn't have the opportunity," he said excitedly. "Gary keeps you pretty busy and it's hard to find a time when he doesn't have an eye on you." Libby felt another shiver run through her. This experience was exciting and she sat back ready to enjoy the evening.

After that first date, Tom and Libby began spending a lot of time together. At the office they maintained a professional distance, especially around the senior partner Gary Banks. From an observer's point of view, Tom and Libby were co-workers, friendly but not overly so. But nearly every night he'd show up at her little house and she would fix them a late dinner, roasted vegetables for her, and a steak for him and he would spend the night. Libby was excited about the new relationship but didn't understand why it had to be kept under wraps from the other people in the office. Discovering everything about this new person was exhilarating and the sex was exciting but there were times when she wished Tom would go to his own condo and she could do things without his constant input which often came with criticism. He had a need to know where she was and what time she'd return that was beginning to rub. She wished she could enjoy a long bike ride or run without worrying about him having an attitude when she returned. She wore herself out trying to placate him into a better mood, always hating it when he was upset with her.

She loved the office job and she thought she may love Tom too. She had a knack for tracking down and organizing information. She got very familiar with the archives and public records in the City Building as well as the law books housed in the office and the library on the University campus. Everyone in the office was pleased with her work and Libby found it extremely rewarding. She was starting to feel like she was making a difference, doing important work and meeting lots of interesting people. Including Tom. Four months flew by with Tom and Libby practically living in each other's pockets.

In September the senior partner, Gary Banks, asked Libby to start assimilating the background and history of a local company he was building a case against. The information needed would go back more than a decade and would take time digging out. Libby headed downtown and made her way through security and down into the archives in the lower level. She set to work and could hardly believe it when the security guard told her they'd be closing up in ten minutes. She'd been working for hours reading the information, taking notes, and making photocopies. Straightening up she realized she was stiff from pouring over the large ledgers for so long. A lovely long run on the trail was just what she and Carmello needed to get the kinks worked out. She hoped Tom wasn't planning on coming over tonight. He didn't run and his pouty resentment of the time she took to get in a few miles before they had dinner or went out was annoying. She wished he was more interested in being active or at least a bit more accepting of her use of her time. She gathered up her bag and decided to take the information she had found back to the office before going home. She knew Gary would need it first thing tomorrow. She keyed into the outer door knowing the receptionist would be long gone this late in the day. She was just leaving the information on the conference table when a heavy hand landed on her shoulder and spun her around. Her heart froze and she sucked in her breath at the rough treatment. Seeing Tom's angry face made her sag with relief until he pushed her too roughly against the wall.

"Where have you been?" he demanded in a harsh voice.

"What are you talking about? I've been at the City Building all day," she said struggling to make sense of this strange behavior.

"You left hours ago. I don't think you were there all this time. Where were you? Who were you with?" he demanded.

Libby didn't know if she should be more afraid or angry. Tom's hands were clamped painfully at the tops of her arms and his demeanor was definitely threatening.

"I don't care what you think, I was working at the City Building for Gary. Let go of me," she said as forcefully as she could.

"I think you were out with someone else. Who is it? Were you out with Gary? Did he meet up with you somewhere?" he snarled.

Anger won out and Libby pushed back against him. "I wasn't out with anyone. I was doing my job, working for Gary. You need to let go of me and back up," she said inches from his face. Tom's arms dropped to his sides and Libby quickly scooted around him and closer to the door. "What's wrong? You're scaring me," she said.

Tom looked down at the floor for a few beats. When he looked up, he tried to laugh off the whole situation. "You make me a little crazy is all," he said. "I can't stand the idea of you being with someone else. Don't be scared. How about I take you out for dinner?" he offered with his most charming smile.

Libby rubbed the tops of her arms and looked at Tom long and hard. "I've had a long day and need a long run. I hope it's okay with you if I just go home," she said. Tom's look said it really wasn't okay with him but nodded his head silently and left the conference room. Libby watched him walk back to his office before grabbing her purse and hurrying out. The whole episode was bizarre. She couldn't wait to strap on her running shoes and put this whole day into perspective with some sweat and distance.

At home, she quickly changed and grabbed Carmello's leash. The two loaded into her small car and looked forward to the trail. After a hard sixty-minute run the two winded friends climbed the two steps to the back door. Libby was alarmed to see the door was unlatched, her alarm grew when she found it was unlocked as well. Keeping the dog close to her side she went into the house slowly looking for signs of an intruder. The small dining room and living room looked exactly as she had left them and she began to breathe a bit easier. In her hurry to get to the trail before complete darkness she must have forgotten to lock the door. Climbing the stairs to shower and change into comfy clothes she was drawn up short when she came eye to eye with the bathroom mirror. Red lipstick letters. Words written on the mirror in red lipstick, the ruined lipstick thrown in the sink. Libby backed up as quickly as she could, getting tangled up in Carmello. She raced down the stairs, grabbing the cordless phone and not stopping until she was in the driveway. She dialed 911 and waited for the police cruiser to pull up.

A thorough search of the house only relieved Libby a little bit. The fact remained that someone had come into her house and written 'I'm watching you' on the bathroom mirror. When questioned about anyone she knew who would do such a thing she answered truthfully. She couldn't think of anyone who would do something like that. The officer suggested she stay with a friend if she were feeling uneasy. Not wanting to go home to her parents and admit that she was scared, Libby and Carmello spent the night in the sunroom on an uncomfortable wicker sofa. Libby took comfort in the fact that the big fluffy dog had no trouble curling up and falling asleep. She hoped it was a sign that there was nothing to be afraid of. Nonetheless, it was an uncomfortable, sleepless night and she wasn't looking like her normal polished self when she stumbled into the office. As Libby was explaining to Dorothy, the receptionist, what had happened, Gary came out of his office and listened as well. He was alarmed about the situation and concerned for her.

He offered to let her have the day off to rest but Libby assured him she was more comfortable at the office than at home. As she went down the hall, she was surprised to see Tom working at his desk. Obviously, he had heard part or all of her conversation and yet hadn't shown any interest of concern. She walked on to the break room to stow her lunch, her mind already a jumbled mess from her sleepless night and now Tom acting so distant. He must be upset at the way she had pushed him away yesterday and refused dinner. Libby knew she worried too much about what others thought of her. She obsessed after an evening with Tom or friends wondering if she had said anything to offend. As hard as she tried to concentrate on her work, she couldn't help but fixate on his attitude and what she should do to make up with him. By mid-afternoon, Libby was tied in knots. She picked up a file and knocked on Tom's door.

"Sorry to bother you. I found a file on my desk that you asked for," she said with her brightest smile.

"Thanks," he said without looking up.

Coming further into the room and lowering her voice she said, "Is everything okay? Would you like to come over for dinner tonight? I can pick up a steak and…" Before she could finish her sentence, Tom interrupted her.

"I've got a lot of work to do. Maybe some other time." Libby backed out of the room blinking back tears. This behavior was just as unexpected as yesterday's. Although Tom was obviously unhappy with her, Libby wasn't sure what she had done to deserve it. She finished up in the afternoon and drove home feeling as small as she had ever felt. Carmello's happy greeting did very little to cheer her up. Not feeling like cooking, she poured some wine and curled up in front of the tv. She must have dozed off as it had grown dark outside and she hadn't turned on any lights. She woke to a scraping sound. She sat straight up and held her breath, her heart in her throat. Carmello ran to the kitchen barking loudly. Before Libby could decide what to do, she heard a heavy footstep and then a man's voice talking as Carmello's barking turned into the sound of her prancing feet, something she did when a treat was being offered. Standing up on shaky legs she walked a few steps to the kitchen door. In the light from outside, Libby saw Tom standing in the kitchen giving her dog a treat and patting her on the head.

"What are you doing here?" she asked tremulously reaching for the light switch.

"What do you mean? You invited me over for dinner, didn't you?" he asked with his rakish grin. Libby wanted to feel reassured but there was something so not right with the way Tom had responded to her today and entered her house without knocking or turning on the lights.

"I did but I didn't think you could make it. You said you had a lot of work," she said.

"Well I finished up and I'm hungry. Let's have that steak."

"I didn't go to the store. I didn't think you were coming over. I could fix you something else or we could go out if you want," she added quickly.

Tom gave a mirthless snort. "No thanks, tofu burgers may be your thing but they're certainly not mine. I'll just have to drink my dinner and maybe snack on you," he snarled. Libby smiled but rather than feeling the rush of warm excitement when Tom reached for her, she felt a cold blast through her center like someone had just walked on her grave. After a short but intense bout in the bedroom, Libby lay with her head on Tom's shoulder.

"You scared me when you came in tonight. You know someone broke into my house while I was out running yesterday. I was afraid whoever it was had come back," she said into the darkened room.

"Oh that. It was probably some kids daring each other to go into someone's house while they were gone. I don't think they'll be back," he said.

"Really? How can you be so sure? They left a threatening message. Why would kids bother leaving a message?" she asked.

"I think you're being dramatic. No one is watching you. Kids watch those dumb thriller movies. You know the ones where they trace the call and it's coming from inside the house. It was probably their idea of a joke," he said. "Now I'm about ready for my dessert course," he said, moving over her again.

Afterward, Libby lay facing the wall listening to Tom's snores. She kept turning the conversation over in her mind. Something was out of place and her fatigued brain couldn't quite put her finger on it. Tom thought it was kids looking for a thrill who had come into her house. But the door was locked, she was almost positive she made Carmello wait while she turned back to lock up. There was something else too. But what? Suddenly, Libby's eyes narrowed as she replayed her conversation with Dorothy and Gary at the office. She told them someone had broken in, but hadn't said anything about the lipstick message. Tonight, in bed, Tom had said 'no one is watching you'. He knew there was a message and what the message said. There was only one way he could have known either. Libby got up quickly without rousing the sleeping man beside her. She grabbed her clothes off the chair and tiptoed downstairs.

Sitting at the dinette table with nothing but the soft street light streaming in she pieced it all together. Tom accused her of having been with someone, a man, while she had been working away from the office. He'd reacted quasi violently when he grabbed her. When she refused to let him buy her dinner she knew she'd upset him. He must have come over while she was on her run. She'd used the hide-a-key enough times for him to know which clay pot it was under. He was the one who left the message on the mirror. She wasn't sure if it was to scare her or if he really believed she was seeing someone else. Either way, Libby was completely freaked out. She waited for dawn to break before she and Carmello headed out for a long run through town. She left a note on the table next to a plate of oatmeal muffins, 'Couldn't sleep, went for a run. Help yourself to coffee and muffins. See you at work. L' She didn't know how he would take waking up with her gone, but knew she couldn't hide her fear and worry sufficiently. She had a lot of thinking to do and running was the best place to do it.

It wasn't long before she was at the office, knocking on Gary's door. He kindly asked her how she was feeling after the break-in and if the police had any leads. She pitched him the theory of kids looking for a thrill but he seemed unconvinced. She went through his schedule with him and made certain that for the next few weeks, her time would be monopolized by research and assistance he needed. This would keep her away from Tom, at least at work. Once she was home, she called the one person she always went to with her worries, problems, basically anything that happened to her. Roddy. If he thought it was weird that his ex-wife called him when she was crazy happy or deeply sad, he didn't let on. They'd been friends for so long it seemed more unnatural not to talk to each other even though they weren't married anymore. She didn't want to tell him about the break-in, but when she asked if he'd come to town and check her locks and windows he figured it out. They agreed to meet Friday night and he'd give the little house a going over. He let her know, once again, his opinion of where she lived and a few suggestions as well. Libby smiled at them as she hung up the phone, never realizing how strange it was that the person she trusted most in the world was the man she'd left at the end of a dusty road.

When Friday night rolled around, Libby had the fridge stocked with Busch Light and some lovely roasting ears for the grill. She'd picked up a buffalo steak for Roddy and was confident he'd grill the meat and corn for the both of them. She and Carmello met him in the driveway as he parked his big truck. The dog jumped happily around Roddy as he and Libby exchanged a quick hug. "This is a busy road. I hope you don't let her out without a leash," he observed.

"I'm careful. This road is never quiet," she said.

"So, someone broke in?" he asked. "Maybe if you weren't right downtown, you'd be safer?"

"I think I'll be fine here. I really like living here- it's close to my job and SoulShine. If you could just check the house, I'd feel perfectly safe," she said.

"Are you going to tell me what happened or do I have to guess?" he asked as they walked along the sunporch.

"It was really nothing. Carmello and I had gone for a run after work. When I came home the back door was not latched and I could tell someone had been inside. I called the police and they came and checked it out. Nothing was taken and they think it was kids just looking for a thrill," she said. Omitting the part about the lipstick on the mirror was hard for Libby, but she knew Roddy would go ballistic and refuse to leave her here if he knew about the threat. She told him enough of the truth to sound convincing.

"Kids, huh? Did you lock the back door? Was it latched when you left?" he asked as he attempted to push in or raise the windows on the backside of the house.

"I thought I did but maybe in my rush to get to the trail I didn't lock it or maybe I locked it but it didn't latch," she said. They'd worked their way to the back door that faced the driveway and Roddy once again looked at the busy road.

"With this kind of traffic, it's hard to imagine someone breaking in during daylight hours. Surely someone would have seen something," he mused. Libby nodded her head understandably but didn't meet his eyes. "Please tell me you don't have a hide-a-key back here somewhere."

Her sheepish grin made him groan. "Lib, you don't live in small town, USA anymore. You can't go around leaving your doors unlocked or a key in a flowerpot and think you're not asking for trouble," he admonished. He went right to the third clay pot and picked it up. The bronze key lay underneath and he snatched it up and turned on her. "No more hide-a-key! Do you hear me? Someone could just let themselves in anytime whether you're home or not. I can't stand to think of what could have happened if you'd been home when these 'kids' were out looking for a thrill." Roddy's color was high and his voice full of concern and conviction.

Libby hung her head until he threw an arm around her shoulders. "If I can't be here to keep you safe, you have to do it. Okay?" he demanded.

She nodded her head as fat tears splashed her shirt. She tucked the key in her jeans and they went inside to check the front door which she rarely used and the windows on the front side. Roddy made her a list of things to get at the hardware store to secure the lower windows. He lit the grill and carried the platter of corn in the husks and meat outside while Libby made a salad at the kitchen counter.

Coming in to get a fresh beer Roddy said, "I don't know about this place. I swear I've seen the same black Lexus go by at least three times."

Libby's eyes jumped to the window that looked out at the street. "It's a busy road," she said and hoped she sounded casual. After a few more trips in and out the back door, they sat down to eat at the dinette table. Roddy caught Libby up with the gossip and news 'back home'. Mid-sentence he jumped up and ran to the back door and down the two steps to the driveway. Libby caught up with him as he was looking up the road at a set of tail lights.

"It was that black Lexus again. I think we should call the police. It actually slowed down as it went by and that has to be at least six passes since I've been here," he said. "Do you know who that is?"

Libby shook her head looking up the street. She hated lying to him but if he knew the black Lexus belonged to the man she worked with and had been sleeping with he'd lose his mind. "I don't think we need to call the police. I'll keep an eye out and if I see it again, I'll report it," she said.

"I don't like this, Lib. Not one bit. I don't know why you couldn't stay somewhere else or come home…"

"Roddy, let's not fight. I appreciate all of your help and I'm going to get the window bars tomorrow. I'm fine, really," she said. "Come on, let's finish dinner before it's cold. I know you have to help your dad feed in the morning and it's getting late."

Before leaving, Roddy made sure Libby was locked in good and tight. She promised she'd call if she had any trouble or saw the black car again. After clearing up their dinner dishes, Libby headed for bed. She hadn't had much sleep all week and realized she felt so much better having Roddy go over the house as she tucked Carmello and herself into bed early.

Libby was deep asleep when she was awakened by the sound of glass breaking. Carmello charged downstairs and barked frantically at the back door. She grabbed the cordless phone and called 911 while her heart was pounding a mile a minute. She gasped out loud when she heard another loud crash. The emergency operator told her to stay in her room. A unit had been dispatched. Within a few minutes, police officers were at the backdoor knocking loudly and announcing themselves. Libby opened the door with wide frightened eyes. After checking the house and yard, the police assured her there was no damage or sign of anyone except for some broken clay pots on the back steps. Several of them had been smashed on the sidewalk. Libby knew that was what had awakened her and she also knew who had been there and why.

On Saturday, she waited until a decent hour before calling Gary Banks at home. His wife Susan answered and Libby apologized for disturbing their weekend. Susan assured Libby it was not a problem. Gary had an early tee time and was already at the golf course, he'd finish around noon. Susan wondered if she could pass on a message or have Gary call when he got in. Libby's voice caught a little as she explained that she really needed to see him in person if only for a few minutes. Susan sensed the gravity in Libby's voice and suggested she drive out and have lunch with them. Libby had always appreciated Susan's lovely manners and considerate nature. The two always had plenty to talk about at holiday parties and family events.

She accepted the offer of lunch only after Susan assured her it was no trouble.

Libby stayed busy going to the hardware store for the items on Roddy's list. She picked up new deadbolt locks and wondered if she could replace them herself. New locks would take some explaining if she asked Roddy to do it. Back at home, she shut Carmello in the bathroom with her as she took a shower and applied a bit of makeup. She hated leaving the dog at home. She hated feeling afraid. She locked up and headed to the country. Gary and Susan had a lovely home built on rolling pasture land. The view was lovely and Libby had always appreciated Susan's understated taste and decor. Susan greeted her warmly and offered to bring the iced tea to the sun-porch. Libby looked around appreciatively. Gary and Susan were so good together, their house reflecting their commitment and stability. Libby could sense their contentment and experienced a wave of sadness as it washed over her.

Susan carried in a tray with fresh tea and lemons and the two made themselves comfortable. "Gary isn't home yet but I'm sure he'll be here soon. That will give us time to catch up," said the older woman.

They enjoyed talking about Gary and Susan's grown children and Susan's horses before there was a lull in the conversation. Libby tipped her tea glass a little too far and tea drippled on her white blouse. Embarrassed, she dabbed at it with her napkin and before she could stop herself, she was crying. Susan immediately moved over to share the love seat with her and wrapped an arm around her. "Something's up. I know it, I was just waiting for it to pop out," she said, smoothing Libby's hair.

Libby pulled in air as best she could and willed her tears to stop. Seeing nothing but concern and interest in the other woman's face she haltingly told how she had been dating a guy for a while. She felt like it was pretty serious, she certainly wasn't seeing anyone else. But lately, things had been happening that not only made her question the relationship, but made her feel unsafe. Susan pulled her hand away from Libby's hair and said, "Unsafe? What do you mean, unsafe?" Libby explained about someone breaking into her house and writing the threatening message on the mirror, then the attempted break-in after she removed the hide-a-key. She was positive the man she was seeing was responsible for both.

Susan seemed to breathe a sigh of relief. "Well fortunately, you work in an office full of lawyers. We'll get Gary or Tom to draw up any number of legal documents, restraining orders, etc. and we'll put a stop to this nonsense. I'll not have some masochist asshole harassing you…" Susan's voice trailed off as fresh tears coursed down Libby's face.

Libby stood up and walked to the window with her back to Susan, her shoulders heaving with sobs. "Okay, what am I missing here?" she asked. "If you're worried about this guy getting to you, I can assure you once he starts getting registered mail from the law firm promising all kinds of legal actions, he'll wish he had never thought about bothering you. There are all kinds of new 'stalking' legislation. He won't know what hit him," she said.

Libby shook her head, her beautiful face contorted and red from crying, not able to get any words to come out. "Oh no, he's a lawyer. Is he a lawyer?" asked Susan. Libby nodded her head looking at the floor and then she raised her eyes to Susan and everything became clear. "He's a lawyer in the firm, isn't he?" she asked. Libby's acquiesce was a sob that shook her entire body. Susan grabbed Libby's arms and pulled her close. At the same time, she heard the garage door go up. She pushed Libby to the bathroom in the hall and told her to stay there until she had a chance to talk to Gary for a few minutes. Libby stumbled into the bathroom and bathed her face in cold water. She perched on the edge of the tub and sank her face into the lilac-scented hand towel. She could hear Gary and Susan's voices but couldn't make out distinct words. After a few minutes, there was a soft knock on the door and Libby opened it to find Gary standing there with two snifters of amber-colored liquid. He offered her one and they each took a small sip. He motioned with his chin for her to follow him to the porch. Susan was out of sight and Libby could hear noises coming from the kitchen.

"I'm so sorry this happened. Susan told me the gist but I'd like to hear it from you," he said. Libby was thankful for the distance between their seats, the small glass of courage in her hand, and the concern in the senior partner's eyes. She reminded him of the break-in and now added the information about the lipstick message. She went on to tell how Roddy had come to check the windows and door locks and how a certain car had gone by too many times to be a coincidence. Gary winced as she got to the last bit about the broken clay pots on the same night she had removed the hide-a-key.

"Okay, so you haven't said but I think I know who we're talking about here," he said.

"Of course she's talking about Tom," inserted Susan from the door. She was holding a platter of sandwiches. Gary gave Libby a direct look and she confirmed in a small voice that yes, it was Tom. "We knew we'd be here someday and here we are. I'm just sick that he set his sights on Libby," said Susan as she set the platter down on the glass coffee table.

Libby looked from Susan to Gary. Gary looked like he had just eaten a bite of rotten meat. "Unfortunately, this isn't the first time this has happened. Tom came to us with a history but he assured us it was a big misunderstanding. He's a brilliant guy and we took him at his word but several years ago there was a young woman who worked for the courier's service that filed a stalking complaint against him. I was able to work it out with the young lady so it never went further. I thought after all of that he was straightened out, but apparently not. I can't fire him but I can make sure he stays far away from you. The question remains, do you want to continue working at the firm? We can make it work if you are okay with it but I understand completely if you need a severance package and a good reference."

Libby was moved by the consideration from the senior partner and loved working at the law practice, but knew she wouldn't be able to cope with Tom even if they didn't work together. Fresh tears formed as she said she thought she better look for something else. Gary and Susan reassured her that they would make certain she wouldn't hear from Tom again in any way. She could pick up her severance package and a letter of recommendation from the office any day the following week. Libby left the lovely home in the country feeling better for having told her boss, but feeling uncertain about her future.

Libby picked up some hours working for Lavendar at SoulShine while she looked around for a job. While helping a customer in the shop she heard about an unusual job at a nursing home. It was an intriguing position as a private caregiver for patients whose families wanted more attention for their loved ones than the overtaxed nursing staff could provide. The job entailed giving assistance, comfort, and companionship above and beyond the scope of the nursing staff. Libby had always been good with people and the nursing home setting gave her a sense of safety. The pay was good and she could arrange her schedule to suit her own activities. Once she met the patients and families she would be working with she felt that she was exactly where she was supposed to be.

Her patients, or clients as she called them, three lovely ladies and one grumbly, grouchy man were as precious as they were difficult. Libby learned their stories, their interests and the little tricks that helped soothe them when they got confused. Two ladies, Viola and Winnie, had families that visited often. The third lady, Eloise, was her oldest client and had no family in the area, and never had a single visitor. Her last client was Ben, a decidedly difficult case and Libby understood why the Schmitt family hired her. They lived in the area and visited regularly but the Alzheimers made Ben cantankerous and difficult. He was royally pissed off at being forced to leave his home and was easily agitated. He didn't make it easy on any of the staff and was particularly hard on his family.

Libby adapted to her new job easily and fell in love with her clients and many of the other residents. Her easy smile and charm made her a welcome face during meals and in the halls where many of the residents spent time during the day. She became friends with Al Schmitt, Ben's daughter-in-law, and the two often made time for coffee together after Al had been to visit Ben. Before long, Libby was coming for dinner at the Schmitt's house and the two ladies enjoyed wine strolls and signed up for a gardening class together.

After several months at the nursing home, Eloise's health began to fail. She no longer wanted to join the others in the dining room and only with Libby's urging did she take any food at all. With some difficulty, Libby was able to get the phone number for Eloise's great-nephew in Florida. It took several calls before she finally was able to speak to him in person. Apparently, Mr. Frank Martin was very busy and almost always out of the office. Even though the nursing staff had been in touch, Libby tried to fill in the gaps about Eloise's condition. Hanging up she thought Mr. Martin to be distracted at best, disinterested most likely. She was surprised when she came into Eloise's suite a few days later to find a handsome, middle-aged man sitting on the side of the bed holding her hand. He stood as she entered and extended his hand.

"Frank Martin. You must be Libby," he said. Libby smiled automatically and couldn't help but be captivated by the piercing gray eyes and commanding look he gave her.

"Hi, yes. I'm Libby. We spoke on the phone," she stammered wondering where her pique was from their phone conversation. "How is she today?" Libby went over to Eloise and leaned down close so the woman in the bed could see her clearly. "Hello, my sweet friend. I hope you had a restful night. It's so nice that your nephew came to visit with you. I think we should get up and comb your hair so you can enjoy a proper visit. Would you like that?" Libby took whatever sign from the old woman as assent and turned to the visitor. Eloise's words were mostly gone and she and Libby communicated in a combination of gestures and expressions. "Mr. Martin, why don't you go enjoy a cup of coffee in the gathering room while we ladies get ourselves presentable."

"Oh, sure. And it's Frank," he said.

"Great," said Libby with her easy smile. "We need fifteen minutes or so." She closed the door behind him and began the process of helping Eloise get out of bed. She was grateful for Frank's visit as Eloise seemed to be sinking into depression as her health declined. Libby hardly ever got her out of her room and even though it was a lovely suite with a large bay window she knew it would do the lady good to move about and get a different view from time to time. After washing her hands and face and helping her into a fresh house dress, Libby stood behind Eloise with a pearl-handled hairbrush. At ninety-one, Eloise still had hair midway down her back. Libby couldn't tell what color it had been but it still held a lovely natural wave and Libby knew Eloise was proud of it. She seemed to enjoy the feeling of having it brushed and Libby always took her time doing it.

With her hair done, Libby reached for the blush and handed the soft brush to Eloise. She was pleased when she took it with a trembling hand and began brushing it on her cheeks. Meanwhile, Libby opened the Rose Kiss lipstick and applied it to Eloise's lips. "Well my, my! You look like you're ready for the theater. You look lovely!" she said. "How about we surprise Frank and meet him in the gathering room?" Once again, she took a non-verbal sign as agreement and helped her to the wheelchair parked near the door. Going down the hall, Libby said hello to patients and staff and was always good to lean down and remind Eloise who they were greeting. They found Frank Martin in the corner of the gathering room talking on the courtesy phone. He wrapped up an apparent business call as Libby locked the brakes on the wheelchair. "I'll leave you two to visit…" Libby started before Frank interrupted her.

"Please stay and talk with us," he said. Libby knew there wasn't a lot of talking with Eloise and she could sense that her nephew didn't have any idea how to fill any amount of time with her.

"Sure, I have an appointment with another client at 1:30. He's scheduled for a haircut but he was so awful the last time he went, the salon said he couldn't come back unless I went with him," she laughed. She felt the weight of Frank's eyes on her.

"You like doing this?" he asked.

"I love it," said Libby. "They are all precious, even grumpy Ben. Eloise is the sweetest lady! You're so lucky to have her as your aunt."

"Great aunt actually. Yes, she's a treasure. My grandmother's sister and the only decent woman in the entire family. She taught me to fish and sail a boat when I was a kid. I wanted to name my daughter after her but my wife had other ideas. She said she'd never shackle a child with such a name and turned around and named her Eden like some soap opera."

"Oh Eden is a lovely name," said Libby. "Where are your wife and daughter? Did they come with you?"

"I have no idea where my ex-wife is and I don't care. She left when Eden was three. Eden is at home in Florida," he said.

"How old is she now?" asked Libby wondering about a woman who would leave a three year old daughter.

"She's six. Full of piss and vinegar. Too strong-willed for her own good," he said.

"I'm sure she's wonderful!" said Libby. "Who's keeping her while you're here?"

"I have a whole team of au pairs, nannies, etc. I'm gone to work a lot. She's in good hands," he assured.

"That must be hard for both of you, being gone so much," said Libby.

"It's all she's ever known. My job has me out of town two hundred, seventy days a year. We're used to it," he added. Libby was appalled at the fact that the little girl's father was gone more than twice as many days as he was home. She wondered about the little girl being raised by au pairs and nannies. They continued to talk about various topics and Libby tried to steer the conversation to Eloise in the hopes that talking about the past would resonate with her somehow.

When it was nearly time for Ben's appointment, she stood and shook hands with Eloise's nephew. He was a strange man, a hard man for sure. "You two enjoy visiting, it was nice meeting you," she said.

Frank's eyes were oddly piercing as he held Libby's hand in his. "Actually, I was hoping you could help me get her back to her room. I'm ready to head out as well," he said.

"Of course," said Libby, trying hard not to judge him for leaving so soon. They walked back to Eloise's suite together. It was clear to Frank how well-liked Libby was by the constant greetings she exchanged in the hallways. Once in the suite, Libby got Eloise situated in her easy chair that was directed out the bay window. She had always enjoyed watching the birds on the numerous feeders Libby kept filled for her.

As Libby turned to go, Frank stopped her at the door. "I'd like to have dinner with you this evening," he said. Libby tried to think of a reason to decline but her brain was sputtering under his direct gaze.

"I was supposed to meet a girlfriend for coffee later," she offered.

"You can do that some other time I'm sure," he said as he continued to block the door. "I really think you should come out with me tonight." Libby didn't know how she felt about the high-handedness of the invitation, especially after her last dating disaster.

She found herself saying, "I guess I can do that," hesitantly.

"Marvelous, give me your address and I'll come by and pick you up around 7," he said.

"That's okay I'll just meet you at Murry's. Do you know it? Good food, good jazz on the south side of town," she said.

"We'll see about the food and the jazz," he said doubtfully. "Fine, we'll meet at Murry's at 7." It wasn't until Libby gave a verbal affirmative that Frank moved out of the door and Libby walked down the hall wondering if she had made a mistake accepting the invitation.

She finished her day and remembered to call her friend Al to tell her about Ben's haircut. Libby had gone to the salon armed with miniature candy bars. She'd bribe Ben into being nice if need be. It would be unfortunate if he got banned from visiting the salon housed in the nursing home but such things had been known to happen. Fortunately or unfortunately, a memory wire connected when Libby asked Ben what he'd had for lunch. Sitting in the raised chair with the apron around his chest he said he'd had 'flied lice for runch' in a falsetto voice. The stylist, a young Asian woman, held up her comb and laughed which just set Ben off on a whole spiel. Libby tried to change the subject and get Ben to stop, but he was egged on by the other two gentlemen cracking up while waiting for their turn in the chair. She apologized to the stylist who chuckled along with the gents while she quickly cut Ben's hair. His comments weren't horrible but neither were they appropriate. By the end of it all, Ben had a good haircut and a quick clean-up with the electric razor. Stepping out of the chair he bowed deeply at the waist to the stylist before leaving with Libby who once again apologized for her client's humor. The stylist smiled and shrugged. Funny Ben was better than grumpy Ben any day.

Al and Libby had a laugh before Libby remembered to cancel their coffee date for later. They agreed to talk in a week and rang off. At home, Libby went for a run with Carmello. She realized it was later than she thought as she began to get ready for her dinner date with Frank Martin. She pulled out her long black skirt and a previously owned caftan-like sweater she'd found at one of her favorite thrift shops. It was a given that she would be late.

Having finally arrived at Murry's, Libby noted the packed parking lot realizing they might not get a table for some time. Making her way to the hostess stand through the crowd at the front door, Libby saw Frank seated at one of the best tables. He stood as she approached and the small smile on his face did little to cover up the fact that he wasn't pleased that she was late. Making her way through the crowd, she tried to calm her fluttery stomach as she sat down.

"Wow! I didn't think they'd seat you until your whole party arrived. And you got the best table in the house," she said a little too brightly.

"Getting a table wasn't a problem. You're being late, on the other hand," he said. "What kept you?"

Libby laughed and tossed out, "Life! I'm always running behind or double booking myself."

"Sounds like a problem," he said. "Interesting outfit."

"Thanks, I found this wrap in my favorite little shop. I love the colors in it," she said looking down at the blues and greens swirled together in a crazy pattern.

"Yes, well that gives us two things to work on, your sense of time and your wardrobe," he said dryly.

Libby took a gulp of wine to cover her reaction and wondered if there was any way possible to cut the dinner date short. She had driven herself, after all, there was nothing to stop her from getting up right now and walking out. It's not like she was ever going to run into this man again, but she chose to stay, not wanting to make things unpleasant. She'd make the best of the evening and have a wonderful meal and get him to talk about Eloise who was the only thing they had in common. She ordered her favorite salad and an order of Brock's Rings. She typically stayed away from fried foods but the delicate batter on the green pepper rings dusted with powdered sugar made a wonderful appetizer. Of course, her date lifted an eyebrow and curled a lip when the bowl was set on the table between them.

"I know it sounds bizarre! Two things that shouldn't go together, fried pepper rings and powdered sugar, and yet they are so perfect together. They just work," exclaimed Libby. It always mattered to her that people liked her and she felt like she was trying a little too hard with this man but she couldn't help herself. When Frank tried a green pepper ring, he agreed it was odd. Libby smiled to herself when he went back for more until the small bowl was empty and they both had traces of powdered sugar on their mouths.

After that, the conversation seemed to flow easier. Frank shared about his upbringing, a wealthy family on the east coast. His father died when he was young and his mother simply had no interest in him. She tolerated him as best she could until he was old enough to attend boarding school. Even then she couldn't be bothered and sent her seven-year-old son off with her driver to his new school 'home'. Unable to handle time home for holidays let alone the long summer, his mother looked around for things to keep him occupied and supervised. As a last resort, she contacted her Aunt Eloise, a wealthy matron who lived in South Carolina. Eloise was more than happy to provide a vacation destination for a ten-year-old boy and so began the tradition of Frank going to Hilton Head anytime there was a school holiday or vacation. Aunt Eloise had never had children of her own and loved showing the boy all the interesting things to do along the coast. She showed interest in him and his hobbies but being the age of a grandparent, she wasn't able to participate in all the activities. Instead, she paid for private lessons, booked excursion trips, and enabled the boy to experience life as best she could.

Libby couldn't help but notice the parallels to Frank's daughter who was being raised by a nanny and a troop of au pairs. She couldn't imagine having a child, a daughter, and not being with her every possible moment. The music started around 10:00 making it difficult to talk. Libby was enjoying the three-piece combo and was surprised to hear Frank's voice in her ear, "Let's get out of here." Standing, she picked up her purse and led him to the door. She assumed this was the end of their evening together and was prepared to thank him and say goodnight. As she turned back before heading to her car she was surprised to find Frank so close behind her that they bumped one another. He reached for her arms to steady them both and Libby had the feeling he was going to kiss her. "I need a nightcap. We'll leave my car here in the lot and take yours. Surely there's somewhere respectable around here," he said.

Libby only nodded, being a little discombobulated at their very close proximity but feeling a thrill of electricity and excitement. "I'm parked over here," she said, jerking her gaze from his. Climbing into her compact she felt self-conscious. She headed down Providence Road to Broadway. There were several nice places she could think of in the downtown district. She found parking on Tenth Street, half a block from the Harvest Moon. They made their way through the crowd in the lounge area, Libby looking around for seats at the bar. She felt a little tug on her elbow and turned to see the back of Frank's head as he followed a hostess to a small two-top against the wall.

"You are the luckiest guy to get the best tables everywhere you go," she said.

"Luck has nothing to do with it, I assure you," he said. "I know what I want and I make sure I get it." Libby was both alarmed and attracted to the decisive way Frank handled things. He reminded her of a lion-so self-possessed and more than a little dangerous. She was definitely intrigued by him but also wary. It was clear from the comments he made, that he did not mess around and furthermore, that he was interested in her. She wondered what she would do at the end of their evening. Frank talked more about his business developing shopping malls, housing tracts, and so on. He traveled all over the country and Libby asked about places that she'd always wanted to visit; Telluride, Jackson Hole, Nashville. He thought it was quaint she'd never been anywhere but Chicago and suggested that she join him on an upcoming trip. The thought of going to any of the locations he mentioned excited Libby and she assured him she'd love to experience the cities and the travel itself. She could almost visualize what a trip with Frank would be like; top accommodations, exciting people, beautiful places.

They talked more over another drink and Libby could feel an incessant pull toward this enigmatic man who both interested and unnerved her. Eventually, they found themselves at her backdoor. Libby knew if he came inside what it would mean. She knew she should slow this freight train down but her brain didn't seem to be in command of her mouth when she offered to fix them a drink or a cup of tea. Nervously, she led the way up the back steps and placed her keys on the counter and tried to calm the excited Carmello who needed some time in the yard. Frank looked all around the small craftsman with an appreciative eye. When his gaze came back to hers, she knew he didn't want tea. Crushing her against the sink he wrapped her in a hard embrace. Libby struggled to breath but kissed him back with everything she had. She felt him pushing her towards the stairs without ever breaking the kiss. She heard poor Carmello whining to come inside but was powerless to stop the wave pushing her along.

That was the way their relationship worked for the next twenty years. Frank was a force of nature that Libby simply couldn't control or resist. When he called, she abandoned all her plans and bought a plane ticket to whatever city he was working in. She would return to work on Monday exhausted and broke but euphoric from the experience and Frank's attention. Although she questioned the relationship in her mind, she was incapable of resisting him. At times she'd wait weeks for a call or an email each time thinking she must have done something wrong. When the call came, she happily forgot her worry and fear and went to be with him. The goddesses questioned her, trying to ascertain what it was about the man they had never met in person that had their young friend so firmly invested. Libby talked about how exciting it was to travel, seeing all the sites, dining at the best restaurants, and staying at the finest hotels. Of course, Frank picked up the tab once Libby was with him but her travel expenses and wardrobe were costs she could scarcely afford. She promised herself and her friends that she would have a long hard talk with him about their relationship and establish exactly where she fit into his world but it never happened. Frank never had time for relationship talk and Libby was ever fearful of pushing him further away so it hung in the air like an invisible lead balloon when they were together, both ignoring it but for different reasons.

The one good thing the goddesses agreed on was Eden, Frank's daughter. Libby loved her from the moment the two met when Eden was a young child with long red, wavy hair. After meeting once, the two talked on the phone long distance and sent email messages daily. Libby loved sending her postcards and small gifts in the mail. Even when she didn't hear from Frank she was constantly in touch with Eden.

Libby was thrilled when Frank allowed his daughter to spend a week in Missouri during the summers. The two had a ball going to the pool, walking Carmello on the trail, and visiting Zestos for tall ice cream cones at the end of a hot day. Libby felt like she'd found something she didn't know she was looking for. The bright girl was headstrong to be sure but filled Libby with a feeling she'd never experienced before. She found out just how strong-willed the little girl was one night when they had planned to visit the Sky High Drive-In. They had made the plans earlier in the week and had everything down to the snacks and pillows. An hour before movie time Libby got a call from the Nursing Home. Winnie's health had been declining steadily and she had finally given up her fight against the sickness and advanced age that had wreaked havoc on her body. The family would need Libby. She explained the situation to Eden expecting her to be disappointed but was totally unprepared for the giant fit she threw. It started with her yelling and crying and saying awful things about Libby and then Winnie. Libby was shocked when Eden ran to the spare room she had decorated for her and slammed the door. No amount of pleading or insisting did any good. Eden remained behind the locked door still ranting about Libby and her dumb job. Not knowing what to do and unable to get Eden to open the door, Libby called Al. As Libby climbed into her car, Al could tell she was visibly shaken by Eden's behavior.

"Don't worry. I'll be here when she comes out of her room. I've seen these pre-teen tsunamis before. You go and help your family-and I'm so sorry about Winnie," said Al. Libby looked back at the house wondering how something so small as a change in plans could bring on such a huge reaction. She thanked Al again and backed out of the drive.

Returning home sooner than she probably should have, Libby found Al reading a magazine while Eden sat in front of the tv. Al asked about Winnie and Libby told her about the end. She'd been there to help the family but left as soon as they notified the funeral home. Al raised her eyebrows and then her hands in a shrug as she looked into the living room. Libby thanked her for coming over but assured her the two of them would be fine. Libby promised she'd call if she needed any further help. Sitting down on the edge of the damask chair, she reached out and touched Eden's wavy hair.

"What are you watching?" she asked.

"Dumb reruns. Can we get sushi?" asked Eden as if their last exchange had never happened.

"It's kind of late for sushi. I think we need to talk about what happened earlier," said Libby.

"Why? I was upset. I'm allowed to express myself when I'm upset," said Eden. The words sounded strange coming from a child and Libby wondered if she had heard a therapist say something similar in an effort to explain adult behavior.

"Yes, sure but you were rude to me. I couldn't help it that I had to go to work. Poor Winnie. Her family was really sad…"

"Whatever. I don't know Winnie and I don't care. I was expressing my disappointment. I can't help it if your feelings were hurt by that," she said again incorrectly parroting constructive advice.

"Actually, that's not right, Sweetie. We are responsible for how we make others feel. You were disrespectful to me and my friend Winnie. Using your disappointment as an excuse to be rude isn't okay," explained Libby calmly.

"Whatever," said Eden. "Can I call my dad?"

"You know you can call him anytime you want to. But I would hate it if you worried him because you and I are having a difficult conversation," said Libby. "Don't you think we can talk about it like two big girls?"

"No, I'm done talking about it," said Eden, turning back to the tv. Libby felt like she should say more but didn't know how Eden would respond. She thought the apple surely didn't fall far from the tree when it came to topics Frank and Eden didn't want to talk about.

The visits got further apart as the power struggles and blowups got bigger. The advantage of a long-distance mother/daughter relationship was that the time and distance apart allowed them to forget the drama and harsh words. As Eden got older the blow-ups were over bigger issues; slinky clothes, piercings, smoking. Libby was in a difficult spot not having any real relation to Eden. She loved the girl desperately and wanted to provide the mothering she thought she needed. Her relationship with Frank was tricky, to say the least. Frank made it clear from the beginning that he was calling all the shots. Libby didn't like the fact that she could go weeks without hearing from him and then he'd call and want her in Minneapolis Friday evening.

Every time she went, she vowed she was going to finally have that talk with him and find out just exactly what he thought their relationship was. But each time she arrived, he would be attentive and generous and she would allow herself to hope again that this was real. Her fear of losing Frank was larger than her resolve to hash it out with him. If there was no Frank, what would that mean to her relationship with Eden? She knew neither relationship was perfect but she wondered what she'd be without them in her life.

Over the years the goddesses had tried to point out that Frank was not good for Libby and that Eden was using her as leverage with her dad. She couldn't help but agree with them. He wasn't good for her and Eden did use her to get things she wanted. But then he would call and she'd forget her resolve. It went that way for years, far longer than any of the goddesses would have hoped. The relationship started to unravel the first time Eden was arrested for possession. When Libby got Eden's hysterical call from the county jail in Jackson, she could hardly understand her. She wound up on an expensive flight out of St. Louis and arrived at the jail nine hours later. She asked the desk officer about the proper procedure for getting Eden released. The officer on duty informed her that Eden had already been released. Libby had a difficult time assimilating this information and was about to ask another question when he abruptly slid the partition shut. She turned to go, trying to estimate how much a cab would cost to Frank's house. She had to know if Eden was okay. She arrived fifty-eight dollars poorer and knocked on the door calling Eden's name repeatedly. She was beginning to think she wasn't there when the door finally opened to reveal a scantily clad Eden who had clearly been asleep.

"Jeez, Libby. I was sleeping," she snarled.

"Eden, are you alright? I got to the jail as soon as I could. How did you get here? Tell me what happened!" Libby demanded.

"Calm down. I'm hungover and you are way too much to handle like this. I couldn't wait in that smelly jail all night. I called one of dad's people and they bailed me out," Eden said, sinking into a chair and covering her eyes with her hand. Libby could see the remains of a stamp from whatever club she'd been to the night before. At sixteen, she had no business in a club. Anything could have happened.

Libby's mouth opened and closed a few times but no words came out. "You called me," she gritted out. "You called me and said you couldn't get your dad and needed my help. I stayed up all night getting here and spent money I don't have so if I'm too much for you, I'm sorry. Why didn't you call me back if you had someone to get you out?" sputtered Libby.

"I guess I didn't think about it. I just had to get out of there," said Eden, still not grasping the magnitude of the situation.

"Where did you go last night? That's a club stamp on your hand! And possession? What did you have? Eden, you are sixteen years old!" said Libby.

"So what if I go to a stupid club! Everyone does! I can't help it if you live in the back of beyond!" said Eden. "I had less than an ounce, it's no big deal."

"No big deal?!" sputtered Libby. She wanted to grab the girl and shake her. Her nonchalant attitude was tearing Libby up. "It is a big deal! You had illicit drugs; you were underage in a club! I don't know what is going on with you anymore!"

Eden stood up swaying slightly, "Nothing is going on with me. And you're not my mother so it's really none of your business," she said evenly and walked to the door of her room. Libby stayed rooted in the middle of the floor, unable to accept the conversation that had just happened. She turned numbly for the door. Somehow, she got herself to the airport and home. It has been less than twenty-four hours since Eden's call as she pulled her car into her own driveway and shut off the ignition. She was exhausted and emotionally spent. Uncharacteristically, she called in sick and climbed the steps to her bedroom. She wanted to call Frank and let him know how frightened she was for Eden. They really had a situation on their hands, clubbing, and possession? And the way she had treated Libby? They were going to have to talk about that as well. Within seconds of her head hitting the pillow, Libby was lost in a world free of ungrateful teenage girls.

She awoke much later to find it was no longer Thursday. She'd lost a whole day. She quickly let Carmello out in the yard and was headed for the shower when a familiar car pulled into her drive. She waited at the door for Al to come the short distance.

"What brings you here this time of the morning?" she asked her friend.

"I was worried about you. We had the Gala at the Missouri Theater Wednesday night and you didn't show up. We called and called. Donna Sue even drove over here but all we could see was that your dog was home but your car wasn't. Then you weren't at the nursing home so I decided I needed to see for myself. Is everything okay?" asked Al.

"Oh god! Al, I'm sorry! I had a situation and I completely forgot about the Gala. Would you like to come in?" said Libby, hating herself for worrying her friends. Over coffee, Libby relayed her story to Al starting with the panicked phone call, her mad dash to the St. Louis airport, and finally catching up with Eden. Al's face mirrored all the emotions Libby had experienced.

"Oh my gosh! That poor kid. And where was Frank in all of this? I can't believe you were able to get to her so quickly. She must have been so relieved," Al's voice trailed away when she saw a tear gathering in the corner of Libby's green eyes. "She was relieved to see you, right? She was grateful for your herculean effort to get hundreds of miles with no hesitation or concern for your time or expense?" By now, Libby had ducked her head and grabbed a napkin from the table to wipe her eyes.

Al's eyes narrowed into slits as she listened to Libby explain how Eden wasn't at the police station when she arrived and her reaction to Libby when she did catch up with her. "That spoiled little brat!" she said.

"Libby, you know I love you, but I've got to remind you about boundaries. You need some! You need some boundaries to protect yourself from people that take advantage of you, namely Eden and her father!" Libby nodded her head in agreement but was unable to talk. "Please, honey. It's so hard to watch you give and give and give and get nothing in return. Nothing but hurt and lame excuses. Would you do me a favor? Hmm, please?" Al waited until Libby's glistening eyes met hers. "The next time either of them call you and say they need you to drop everything in your life to fulfill their needs or whims or god damn impulses, I want you to stop. Stop and ask yourself; 'Is this what I want? Will being there bring me joy or am I going to be broke and heartsick at the end of it? Again! Will you please do that for me?" implored Al.

Libby nodded through her tears and said she would try. For a good long while, after the Florida trip, Libby did say no when Frank called and 'invited' her to join him somewhere. He never seemed overly concerned and Libby thought for sure the relationship was over. Months passed without a word from Eden or Frank. She wanted more than anything to call either of them and ask what she had done wrong or failed to do right but some thin strand of self-preservation kept her from doing it.

She was surprised one Monday when she picked up the phone to hear Frank sounding just the same as he always did. The sexy talk, the endearments, and then the invitation. This time he was traveling to Tennessee and wanted her to meet him in Gatlinburg on Friday. Libby tried to tease apart her feelings while she listened to Frank's voice over the phone. The fluttering in her stomach was the familiar excitement and anticipation of seeing him, being with him, and then there was the sheer relief that he had called.

As she thought about the boundary talk she and Al had, she heard herself explaining that she didn't have money for a plane ticket. Without skipping a beat, Frank suggested she drive it, after all, it was only a nine to ten hour drive. If she left Thursday after work and came through the night she would be in early Friday and they'd have the whole weekend together. Libby shut her eyes as she held the phone to her ear. Even she could hear the ridiculousness of the suggestion but apparently, it made perfect sense to Frank. It took everything she had inside of her not to capitulate but she told Frank she couldn't drive all night after work, spend the weekend with him and then drive home and be ready to go to work on Monday.

He didn't try to persuade her further and ended the call with terse responses to Libby's inquiries about Eden, all tenderness gone.

Libby felt worse every day for the rest of the week. Her stomach was sick, she couldn't sleep for thinking about the invitation. After spending all night pacing, she called in sick to work and went next door. The teenager that lived there liked to earn a few dollars taking care of Carmello and bringing in the mail. She gassed up her car and pulled out the folded road map in her glove box. Her mood lightened as she headed east away from town. Frank would be surprised, and she hoped pleased when she called him from the state line. She made good time, only stopping for gas and restroom breaks. To save money, she had packed lots of fruit, trail mix and water. When she arrived on the outskirts of Gatlinburg, she was tired but self-satisfied. She'd made the trip easily and was looking forward to seeing Frank. She called his office number knowing they always knew where to find him. The address she got was outside of town and she gaped at the beauty of the surroundings. The low, blue mountains were spectacular. The pastures and fields were lush and green.

She stopped once to ask for directions at a small gas station and convenience store and marveled again at the rugged beauty of the landscape. Finally, she found a gate with a brand that matched the nearest mountain peaks. Mountain Home Ranch was stamped in a banner of metal. She drove up a sweeping drive dividing beautiful green paddocks enclosed by white fences to a long low ranch house. The front was covered in mountain stone and the porch went the entire length of the house. She got a little thrill when she pulled her small car up next to Frank's large SUV. She noticed another car parked next to his as she stepped out onto the driveway. Entering the open garage, she found her way inside. The door to the interior was open and she paused, not wanting to interrupt if he was doing business with a client. She heard Frank's voice and then all talking subsided, Libby kept going and suddenly he was there in front of her in a huge kitchen. His back was to her so he was unaware of Libby standing there staring at him. Libby didn't make a sound as she watched as a pair of female hands twined around Frank's neck and burrowed into his hair. She was obviously interrupting and as much as she wanted to turn on her heel and leave, she couldn't take her eyes off of the spectacle in front of her. Some small noise or maybe intuition made the woman's hands freeze and lift from Frank's neck. Libby saw a face peek around his left shoulder and heard a gasp. Frank turned and saw Libby, never letting go of the beautiful young woman he still held in his arms.

"Libby, what are you doing here?" he asked.

Libby's mouth opened and closed but no words came out. The young woman had the decency to excuse herself and disappeared deeper into the house.

"I…I changed my mind about making the trip. I drove all day to get here," she stammered. "Who is that? What's going on Frank?"

"I made other arrangements when you said you couldn't be bothered," he said without any sign or remorse or embarrassment.

"It's the money," started Libby dully. "I'm still paying off my credit card from flying to Florida for Eden. And Colorado with you before that. I don't have extra money for these trips." She heard herself speaking in a monotone and it was difficult to breathe.

"I'll give you some money for your trip back. It's a little awkward since I asked Vivian to join me for this weekend," he said.

"Vivian?" Libby was beginning to find her voice. "Vivian, your intern? How old is she? I hope she's older than Eden," said Libby in a volume approaching yelling.

Frank's eyes narrowed in a way Libby had seen when he was conducting business over the phone with a tough client. He was intense on a good day and formidable when crossed. "Who I invite on a weekend is none of your business," he said with a steely tone.

"It is my business when she's wrapped around you like a pole dancer at a strip club," screamed Libby. She didn't know when she had begun to cry.

"Here's a couple hundred bucks. I think you need to get back in your car and go home, Libby," he said, reaching into his pocket for his money clip.

"I don't want your stupid money," she scream cried. "I want to know what's going on! I thought we were something! Are something! I'm not leaving until I know!"

"This is really unattractive Libby. Let's go outside," he said.

Libby actually jumped up and down like a little kid throwing a temper tantrum. "I'm not going anywhere until you tell me what. Is. Going. On!" Liby gasped for breath and held her ground as Frank came and stood inches from her face.

"Here's what's going on. I came out here to close the deal on the ranch. I asked you to join me but you declined so I asked someone else. That's it. That's what's going on," he said through gritted teeth.

Libby huffed air through her sobs. "I thought you loved me!" Frank's expression hardened.

"Grow up, Libby! We're all adults here. I enjoy spending time with you but you'd be wrong if you think I don't see other people. You've made this uncomfortable for all of us. Why don't you take the money and find a nice five-star hotel and enjoy the area before you head back?" he said, extending the folded bills. His face was devoid of emotion other than irritation. Libby stood staring at him through her tears. She had never felt so stupid or so small.

She turned on her heel and fled the house the way she had come. She heard Frank call out to her but she put her chin on her chest and forced her feet to take her to her car. She jammed the key in the ignition and slammed the gear shift into reverse. Straightening the wheel, she slammed her foot on the gas, spraying gravel as her small car sped out of the drive. She looked in the rear-view mirror hoping against hope to see Frank standing there, feeling something. She found her way back to the highway and joined the interstate headed north. After an hour the shock began to wear off and she began to cry again. Hard racking sobs made it difficult to see the road. She found an exit and pulled off. Somehow, she was able to guide the car to a parking lot of a grocery store. She shut the engine off and sat staring out the window, unseeing. She was unsure how long she sat there but the light was soft like evening when she was roused by a ringing that just wouldn't stop. Like a person in slow motion, she looked around for the source of the sound, finally resting on her crocheted shoulder bag that had slid to the floorboard. She reached for the bag, pulling her small new flip phone out of the inside pocket. She couldn't afford such a luxury but after the last fiasco with Eden, she wanted to be able to get in touch no matter where she was. So far, she'd only used it a handful of times deciding it was only to be used for emergencies. She opened the phone and pressed it to her ear, not saying anything. She could hear a voice on the other end calling her name and tears once again drenched her face.

"Libby?! Libby! Can you hear me? Are you there? Libby? Say something!" yelled Anna through the phone.

"I'm…here. I'm here Anna," she said faintly.

"Libby? Where are you? What happened?" implored Anna.

"I'm in… I'm in Tennessee. I think. I'm not sure where I am," said Libby in her slowed-down speech. Her brain wasn't firing on all pistons so her words came out like thick molasses.

"You're in Tennessee? Where in Tennessee? Libby, what happened? Are you hurt? Do you need medical attention?" continued Anna in her capable take-charge voice.

"Not sure, some small town with a Piggly-Wiggly. It's off the interstate," Libby said.

"Okay, can you drive?" asked Anna.

"How do you think I got here?" asked Libby.

She couldn't see Anna's expression, but Anna was relieved to hear a little of Libby's natural spunk rather than the somnolent voice she had been using.

"Great, see if there's a Howard Johnson's or a Hilton. Go check yourself in and then you have to call me with the address of where you are. This is important Libby. You have to call me back with your location. Can you do that?" asked Anna.

"I think so. Could you stay on the phone with me though? I don't know how much longer this phone will last before I have to charge it but I don't want to hang up. I don't want to be alone," said Libby. Anna could hear the tears flowing over the phone.

"Of course, I'm right here. Right in your ear. Just be careful driving," said Anna calmly. She wanted to ask Libby all sorts of questions but knew it would have to wait until Libby was off the road and safe.

After a few minutes of not talking, just being connected, Libby said, "I see Dolly Parton."

"Really? Like Dolly is actually there or is it a billboard?" asked Anna trying to keep the panic from her voice.

"No, she's made of stone. It's a statue of her and her guitar," said Libby. "There's a Super 8 up ahead. I don't think I can go any further."

"Perfect," said Anna.

"I don't want to hang up," said Libby.

"It's okay. You're okay. Hang up and get checked in. Once you're in your room you can call me from there. Okay, Libby?" asked Anna.

"Okay," said Libby and disconnected the call. Anna paced wildly back and forth waiting for the phone to ring. She had been calm and reassuring for Libby but her heart was pounding and she was worried Libby wouldn't call back and other than Tennessee and Dolly Parton she had no idea where she was. Anna's extra sense had been jangling all day. When she saw the paper moth battering itself on the window screen, she knew someone she loved was in trouble. Somehow, she knew it was Libby. Her phone rang and Anna leaped on it.

"Libby?" she asked.

"I'm in room 212," said Libby. "I'm just so tired," she said in that weird sleepwalker voice.

"Wait, Libby! I need to know what town you're in!" rushed Anna.

"Dolly Parton town I guess," said Libby, and Anna heard the clear click of the phone being closed.

Anna knew Mack Schmitt was the one to ask about Dolly Parton and Tennessee. He was the reigning authority on all things country music. The problem would be if he was having a good day or not. Anna got Al on the phone and briefly described the conversation with Libby. She heard Al turn to Mack and ask him where in Tennessee was there a statue of Dolly. Anna had no trouble hearing Mack's booming voice over the phone, "Sevierville, Tennessee! Hometown of Dolly Parton!" Anna thanked Al for the intel and assured her she'd get back to her as soon as she knew anything. She disconnected the call on her end and punched in the number for Donna Sue.

"Hey, Gal! What's cooking?" asked Donna Sue after the first ring.

"It's Libby. We've got to get to her. Are you still in touch with that pilot friend of Ron's? Do you think he would fly us to Knoxville?" asked Anna making a list on the pad of paper as she spoke.

Donna Sue didn't miss a beat. "I'll call him right now," she said, hanging up and immediately thinking of Ron and wishing he were there. She looked up Troy Dyer's number and punched it in remembering all the times he'd flown her and Ron places to look at properties. After a brief discussion catching Troy up on the demise of Lake Properties, at least the one he knew, she asked about an emergency trip to Knoxville. He agreed immediately and told Donna Sue to be at the Boonville Airport in three hours. She redialed Anna and agreed to swing by and pick her up.

Anna redialed Al and relayed the plan to fly to Knoxville and get a car and drive to Sevierville, thirty minutes away. They both knew Al wouldn't be able to leave Mack so unexpectedly.

"Damn it, Libby, we talked about boundaries! I thought it was over this time for sure. He hasn't been in touch in quite some time. I guess he called and she just couldn't resist," said Al imagining all kinds of situations Libby may have found herself in. "When you run into that butt munch, I've got a few ideas on what you can tell him.

Tell Lib I love her. You girls be safe," said Al wishing she could go, knowing she couldn't leave.

"I'll call you when we have her," said Anna. Next, she punched in Jackie's number and went through the whole story again.

"Oh, I'm coming with you!" she said. "I'll be at your house in an hour." And that was how three goddesses were able to stand outside room 212 of the Motel 8 in Sevierville, Tennessee banging on the door until a sleepy Libby opened up. The three piled into the room kicking off shoes and dropping shoulder bags. All four women ended up in the bed Libby had just climbed out of. Despite the millions of tears she'd already shed, fresh ones appeared as her best friends held her, stroked her hair, and waited for the story to come out. They cried for her and with her. When the story was over and they'd discussed one hundred and one ways to dispose of a body, they sat back and were quiet.

Libby looked at the faces of her dear friends. They found a way to get to her. Through the night. In another state. This was real love. She was sure now, what she had felt for Frank wasn't anything like real love at all. She started to cry again in the face of her epiphany. Lucky for all of them that Jackie pulled a bottle of Patron from her bag near the door.

"Enough tears! Times like this, we need tequila!" she declared.

"Breakfast-we need food!" said Donna Sue.

"Okay fine, tequila then pancakes!" said Jackie grinning wildly. She hoisted the squatty bottle and toasted, "To god damned boundaries!"

Mia

(Goddess in Training)

Mia sat against the bathtub staring at the broken bathroom door. The room was a sad reminder of the depths she had sunken to. The sink, pulled away from the wall, hung tenuously by a pipe. The countertop was chipped and dirty. All nature of trash, food wrappers, and the like were strewn about the small space as if someone actually lived in this dismal space. The floor she sat on was filthy and the window barely allowed light through the dingy film.

She hugged her knees listening for sounds from the rest of the trailer. How did she even get here she wondered for the millionth time? Her of all people. Here. She winced as she heard something break behind the closed door. Could be glass. She checked that the lock button was pressed in on the flimsy door.

Her relationship with Darren didn't start out like this. He was super attractive and different from the other boys she had gone out with. Her dad called him edgy and not in a good way. Mia hated that her folks didn't like Darren but he was so interesting and different, she couldn't help but fall for him. He liked weird music and read crazy books and talked constantly about alternative energy, universes, and personalities. Mia felt he was somehow liberating compared to her safe and sheltered childhood. Tony and Anna, and even her big sister, Ellie kept close tabs on her-something Mia had never minded until she met Darren. He never said anything negative when he was in her parents' home but would offer cutting remarks about how they wouldn't allow Mia to do anything without their approval. She recalled a conversation after they had dated for a few months when they stopped by the house or 'the manor' as Darren called it. After a brief and strained conversation with Anna and Tony, they headed for Darren's old car parked out on the road.

"Man! You amaze me," he said. Mia turned a smile to him basking in his compliment. "I don't know how you can even breathe in that house," said Darren.

"What are you talking about?" Mia laughed uneasily as her smile slid away from her beautiful face.

"Are you kidding?" scoffed Darren. "They're like puppet masters and you're their precious little puppet. Look how cute and perfect she is," he teased in a falsetto voice.

Mia stopped on the way to the car. "You're wrong. They're not like that. They just like to know where I'm going and who I'm with. It's sweet."

"Sweet like saccharin. You know saccharin kills lab rats, right? You can't go anywhere without them knowing. Do you even know a single person that they haven't been introduced to or signed off on?" Darren didn't give Mia time to answer. "I bet you don't have a single thought in your head that they didn't stick there."

Mia, stung by Darren's words, rose to her own defense. "I do so have original thoughts and I can go places without them knowing about it."

"Oh yeah," Darren sneered. "Prove it. What's an original thought not brought to you today by the amazing Anna and Tony propaganda train?"

"Well," Mia said slowly. "I like it when you undress me and hold my hands down while you make love to me. I'm pretty sure they didn't stick that idea in my head," offered Mia slyly. Darren crooked his elbow around Mia's neck pulling her in for a deep, over the top kiss.

"Then let's cut those puppet strings for real. Move in with me," he said.

That was eleven months ago when Mia moved into the beat-up trailer on a wooded lot. Less than a year and Mia's world was completely upside down. Tony was gone, taken by a massive heart attack suffered on the golf course. He and Mia had had little to say to each other after she moved in with Darren. Mia always assumed she'd have plenty of time to repair her relationship with her dad. As it turned out, she didn't and now her life had turned to complete and utter shit. She tried to be there for her mom and Ellie but they were hurting so from Tony's death, they didn't hold back on their views of Mia's living arrangement.

Losing her dad, seemed to peel a layer from Mia's eyes and she started seeing things she hadn't seen before. The interesting music that Darren had turned her onto was dark and full of negative images and messages. What she thought was New Age, turned out to be an old story of glorified death and abuse. The interesting books that he was constantly quoting and touting as a message for the future all had the same theme- the end of times and the pointlessness of life. When Mia would try and talk to him about her take on the literature, Darren would rant and rave about her naivete and sheltered life.

"Of course, you don't get it. How could you? You know nothing of life. You know nothing because you only started to live when you moved out of the manor and came here," Darren shouted. Seeing her hurt look, Darren was always so smooth with cajoling words and deep kisses and Mia would forget for a time.

The interesting friends Darren introduced her to never seemed to have a place to be during the day and showed up at all times. She always believed Darren when he explained that someone was going through a rough patch and needed the couch for a few nights.

At first, she thought it was cool having a place where friends could come and relax, hang out or stay over but that soon wore off. It was always Darren's friends, never their friends. Mia first threw a fit when the groceries she shopped and paid for were annihilated overnight while she was sleeping and Darren and a few friends were partying. She waited until the friends stumbled out of the trailer and lit into Darren.

"This is ridiculous! I spent $70 on food yesterday and there's nothing to eat for breakfast! Your friends can't just help themselves to anything that is in this house just because they are staying over," Mia yelled.

Darren looked rough and felt shitty from the all night party. He started down the hall for the bathroom but Mia tugged at his arm. Suddenly Darren spun around quickly and the look on his face was darkly dangerous. He grabbed Mia by the tops of both arms and pulled her into his face.

"It was a few lousy groceries. It was nothing. The store is full of food. Go get something if you're hungry," he growled.

Mia stood very still in the face of this unfamiliar Darren. Her arms were sore where he was squeezing too tightly. Just as quickly, he let go of her, turned back to the hallway and threw out, "I'm going to get a few hours sleep."

Mia rubbed her arms and watched him go, shocked and confused by his behavior. She wondered if he had called into work but the bedroom door was already shutting so she left it unsaid. Still thinking about the rough treatment, hurtful words, and her empty stomach she loaded her backpack and headed to her car for a full day at the plant nursery where she was doing a yearlong internship.

Once at work, Mia threw herself into the pruning, watering, and documentation work in the greenhouse. The work was very exciting and Mia was learning so much about sustainability, crop management, and cost-effective ways to provide wholesome food to the public. She hoped to use this year of training and learning to start her own natural-grown garden business that would eventually expand to her very own farm to table bistro. She worked through the morning; her mind caught up with the work of her hands. A small tension headache had settled between her eyes and she knew it was leftover from the unpleasant start to her day, something she was going to bring up with Darren but didn't want to think about at the moment. Midafternoon she was shocked to see Darren talking to one of the other botanists at the door of the greenhouse. The other man turned towards Mia and nodded his head as if showing Darren the way. Mia watched as he made his way around the tables of vegetables. He was grinning and looked nothing like the strange person from the morning. He stopped two steps from her and dropped his chin to his chest. When he looked up, his hair had fallen over his forehead and he gave it a toss, perfectly timed with his chipped tooth grin.

"I was worried about you and your empty tummy so I brought you something," he said as he extended a reused brown paper lunch bag.

Mia slowly reached her hand for the bag. Before she could get it completely unrolled, the smell of freshly baked peanut butter cookies wafted up to her nose. She looked at Darren with surprised eyes then quickly opened the bag all the way. Fresh, still warm from the oven, homemade peanut butter cookies were nestled inside the bag.

"Where did you get these?" she asked as she reached in and took out a cookie taking a big bite.

"I made them. I felt bad about our morning and the guys wiping out the kitchen. I wanted to make it up to you so I made you your favorite," he smiled. "Forgiven?"

Mia chewed on her cookie. It was really delicious and they were her all time favorite. The fact that he had made them himself and brought them all the way out to the nursery meant a lot.

"Forgiven. But seriously, there needs to be some rules or at least some guidelines about your friends and our house," she said.

"They are your friends too and I'll talk to them about contributing if you'll stop being so uptight," he said.

Mia wasn't sure how to take either part of his remark. They weren't her friends. In fact, there were hardly any girls that came by or stayed. It was always guys and she hardly knew them. She didn't know what he meant about 'contributing' and as for being uptight, the ache in her head began to throb again.

"Come on, you said forgiven so eat your cookies and I'll see you after work," Darren ducked his head down to look up into Mia's face. She wasn't completely over the upset but knew they were in the wrong place to hash it out.

"Okay, I'll see you after work," she said a big grudgingly. "And thanks for the cookies." Darren smiled the crooked smile she fell in love with and turned around and wove his way back out of the greenhouse. Back at work, Mia had quite the conversation in her head. While her hands worked, her head planned out all the points of the conversation that needed to happen. She fervently hoped it would go as well as it did in her head and this morning's unpleasantness was a one time only. The pulse that continued to beat between her eyes reminded her of Darren. He felt bad, he made cookies but he never said he was sorry.

After work, Mia found the kitchen cleaned and some burgers ready for the grill. She told herself it would be the perfect time for a needed discussion but as she washed her hands in the sink, Darren came in the backdoor followed by his friends, Kyan and Jerome. They were laughing and drinking beer and stopped short when they caught sight of Mia at the sink.

"There's my sweet Babe!" Inwardly, Mia cringed. She hated being called 'babe'. "You're just in time for dinner al fresco. We've got the grill going and a cooler full of beer," said Darren. Jerome and Kyan had the grace to look embarrassed about the situation from the night before and looked anywhere but at Mia.

"That sounds good but I was hoping we could talk tonight," she said.

"We can talk anytime you want Babe but Jerome just got canned from his job and needed a little pick me up. I called a few of his buddies and they'll be here in an hour," said Darren. "If you want, we can talk now. What do you want to talk about?"

Knowing that Darren had no intention of talking about anything meaningful, Mia grabbed a water bottle from the fridge and turned away from the men.

"No, it can wait. I'm not very hungry anyway. I'll just go do some reading in my room," she said.

"Okay, Babe but you're missing out," Darren said but he was already turning away. Mia wasn't sure she heard correctly but it sounded like one of the guys said something about uptight and pussy. She was sure she heard all of them laugh loudly before the door closed completely.

Several weeks passed without any meaningful discussion or major upsets. There never seemed to be a time when Darren wasn't too tired or surrounded by friends. He went to work most days but Jerome had moved in more permanently than semi-permanently. The two would stay up late every night and get high usually on weed but Mia suspected they were dabbling in something worse. There were signs that their partying was more than just a couple of guys getting loose after a day of work. Jerome said he was looking for a job but Mia was doubting that too. Every time she tried to bring up a serious conversation about Jerome or the other friends that were hanging around more and more, Darren would put her off. Mia couldn't keep food in the pantry or the place picked up. There was always other people's stuff strewn about-a fact that really bothered her. She liked her place to be neat, it helped her stay focused and in a good mental place.

She thought about the lovely home she had grown up in. Her mom and dad enjoyed the grand home they had slowly and lovingly restored to its original beauty. They took great pride in the fact that it was ready for guests at any given moment. Tony had friends in six counties and if he saw a friend or acquaintance in the grocery store, he was very likely to invite them over on the spot. This was a regular occurrence and generally worked out well as Anna was always ready for company.

Mia looked at the disgusting hall bathroom. Darren's friends used it but they didn't have any interest in tidying up. Dirty towels were piled on the floor, the trash can was overflowing and the sink was a mosaic of toothpaste, soap scum, hair and whatever else Mia didn't want to contemplate too carefully. Her inclination was to clean the mess but she decided if they made it like this, they could keep it like this. She had her own bathroom attached to the bedroom she and Darren shared.

Just as she was leaving the hovel of the bathroom, she saw a crumpled brown paper bag sticking out of a drawer that someone had closed crookedly. She was going to tuck the bag in and shut the drawer completely but decided to look inside. She was shocked and appalled to see syringes, rubber tourniquets, and white powder in a tiny zipped top bag. Her hands began to shake with fury. Someone had brought drugs, real drugs, bad drugs into their house and left them there for anyone to find. Not knowing what to do but knowing this was not something she would allow in the place where she lived, Mia took action. She shook the powder in the moldy ringed toilet and carried the remainder of the bag out to the fire pit. She started a fire and threw the bag and its contents into the flames. The rubber smoked and made a terrible smell. Mia added more wood and let it all burn. A new item just went to the top of the conversation list. She contemplated leaving without saying anything at all to Darren. He seemed so different now from the guy she first met and fell in love with.

Going home wouldn't be easy. She felt terrible guilt about the strained relationship with her dad and the fact that it was too late to do anything about it. She wasn't used to the new distance that seemed to exist between her and her mom. The loss of Tony had left them all unsure how to talk to or comfort each other. Mia decided she had made this difficult stand to be an adult and move in with Darren so she owed it to herself and to him to at least talk about the things that had gone wrong. She sat by the fire until it burned out and all traces of the items in the paper bag were destroyed. She got up stiffly and went inside to go to bed wondering where Darren was, it was late and he was supposed to work in the morning.

Around 3:00 a.m. Mia woke up to someone thumping the side of the trailer. At first, she was afraid that someone was trying to break in. She jumped out of bed and grabbed her cell phone. Then she identified Darren's voice. He apparently couldn't find his key and so was banging on the trailer to wake her up. Her initial fear was replaced by hot anger. With her heart pounding and ready to do battle she opened the trailer door to a wild Darren. He was laughing loudly and could barely stand. He was so wasted. Kyan was there and a girl that Mia had never seen before.

"Babe!" Darren roared with a huge, unnatural smile on his face.

"Darren, what are you doing? It's the middle of the night! I have to work in the morning! You have to work in the morning!" said Mia.

"Babe, Babe, don't be so uptight! My friends and I are having a good time but we've run out of party so we came for reinforcements," he said in slurred speech.

"NO! You guys aren't coming in here and you're certainly not going to keep your party going," asserted Mia.

"Babe! What are you talking about? Of course, we're going to keep our party going. Be a good Babe and get out of the door," Darren lurched as he talked.

"Stop calling me babe and your friends need to leave," said Mia as firmly as she could.

"Babe, sorry. Hon, no one is leaving." With that, Darren achieved the last step into the trailer and pushed Mia aside with his shoulder as he turned to the others. "Y'all come on in. Don't mind her, she's cute but too uptight," said Darren. "I've got reinforcements in here."

Angry tears jutted from Mia's eyes. She couldn't believe Darren was so messed up. He was completely beyond reason. The terrible things he said about her made her mad enough she wanted to hit him. Suddenly she realized Darren was walking unevenly to the hall bathroom and a terrible thought jumped into her head. The bag. Reinforcements. The stuff was Darren's. How did this happen? How was this the same person she moved in with a few months ago? Mia caught up with Darren as he was pulling open the drawers in the bathroom. As he didn't find what he was looking for in the first he pulled open the next until all three drawers were open and crooked in their tracks. He looked up at Mia with a confused look on his face.

"It's not there Darren. I found that vile stuff and I got rid of it," she said.

Darren continued to look confused, swaying slightly as he stood in the dirty bathroom.

"Babe, I don't know what you mean but I need my stuff. I need you to get it for me right now," he said.

"Darren, listen to me, you don't need that stuff. You need to come to bed. You need to sleep this off and we'll talk about it tomorrow," entreated Mia.

Darren's confusion was starting to clear up and a hard look replaced the confusion. "Babe, I'm trying to be nice. I'ma say it one more time. Where is my stuff?"

Starting to feel a prick of real fear, Mia squared her shoulders and said, "Outside."

"Outside? Babe, why would my stuff be outside?" he puzzled.

"Because I burned it! It should never have been in our house. I can't believe you had that stuff here. That you use that stuff!" cried Mia.

The confused look was completely gone. In addition to the hard look from before, Mia also saw another look. Crazed. Like an animal. Darren shoved Mia out of the bathroom door and ran to the backdoor of the trailer. She heard it slam and then heard his shriek as he saw what was left of her fire. When the door slammed again, Mia was terrified. She didn't have time to get to the bedroom so she slammed the bathroom door shut and pushed in the lock button.

Darren beat on the door with both fists, yelling unintelligible things, unspeakable things. Mia looked around for anything she could use as a weapon to protect herself. She was crying for real now. Afraid for her life from the man she thought she was in love with. How did I get here? She continued to think over and over. Mia searched the room and found very little that would serve her in any way if Darren made it through the door. The window was not an option being too small for her to fit through. The situation was so completely out of control-that Mia wondered what crazy wave in the cosmos had brought her here. She suddenly thought of her mom. She remembered her phone clutched in her hand. If the door held against Darren's abuse, if she could wait him out and hope that the trip he was on would peter out she knew. Knew with clarity and certainty that she did not want to be here. Now or ever. No matter how sorry Darren was, no matter what grand gesture he offered, this is not the place where Mia belonged or wanted to be.

Without hesitation, Mia punched her mom's name on her contact list. She didn't even wonder what she would say at this darkest hour of the night. She just knew she wanted her mom. Anna picked up after the first ring. Before Mia could begin to speak Anna started in,

"Mia! What's wrong? Are you okay?"

"Mom, I need help. Can you get someone to help you and come get me? I don't know what happened but …"

Anna cut Mia off without waiting to hear more. "Are you safe?" she asked in a calm, self-assured tone.

"For now. But I need help," with the last syllable, Mia's voice cracked.

"Give me 20 minutes. Help is on the way. Hang on my love, Mommy's coming," said Anna and disconnected the line.

Mia tried not to think about what Darren was doing, it was strangely quiet on the other side of the door.She wondered what had happened to Kyan and the girl. She tried to distract herself by reciting the phylum, genus, species of plants she was working with at the greenhouse. After several minutes she heard a motor running. She cocked her head and listened carefully. Her heart leaped into her throat when she thought of the power drill she had brought home from her dad's workshop. Suddenly, the bit of the drill appeared through the flimsy door. Mia screamed out loud. With some difficulty, Darren pulled the drill out of the door roughly, not knowing to switch the mode to reverse. Amidst more strong cursing and struggling to pull the heavy drill out of the door, Darren's eye appeared in the half-inch circle he had drilled in the door.

"I'm going to drill the door full of holes and then I'm going to start on you," he snarled.

Trying to distract him and his clumsy efforts, Mia began to talk to him.

"Darren! Listen to me! You don't want to do that. Remember, how we like to listen to music together? We like a little weed and we like a little music. We have fun together. I'd love to be able to do that with you, smoke a little weed and put on some really radical music, and just float. You'd like that too. I know you would." Mia was straining to listen for activity as Darren had lost interest in the drill after his third attempt. The holes gave Mia a way to see a tiny glimpse of the other side of the door. The front door was standing open and there was no sign of Kyan.

As Mia stood half a step from the door, she saw a blur of motion and suddenly the door and even the wall shook. She jumped back, screaming involuntarily. Unable to work the drill easily, Darren had given it up and instead was backing up the two steps the hall allowed and was running at the door with all of his force. The state he was in didn't allow for good coordination and he fell hard after hitting the door. It was clear to Mia that even in his condition , the bathroom door wouldn't hold up to too many of his full-body impact blows. She looked around wildly for anything at all she could throw at Darren once he was through the door. Under the sink, there was half a bottle of rubbing alcohol that Mia snatched up and held ready. She couldn't think how long it had been since she hung up with her mom but hoped help was close. The door and the wall shook again violently as Darren hit the door and slid to the floor cussing anew when his face hit the door frame.

"I'm going to fucking kill you, bitch!" he screamed.

Mia knew she needed to aim carefully for Darren's eyes with the alcohol. She'd only get one chance to get past him once he was in the door. She grabbed the hand soap from the broken sink and quickly unscrewed the top. She dumped the contents on the floor. Darren's rant was subsiding some and Mia could tell he was gathering himself for another ram of the door. She knew it wouldn't hold up a third time.

Mia heard Darren scream out a crazed battle cry as he launched himself at the door. A second before impact, she yanked the door open and Darren's momentum combined with the slippery soap on the floor had him skidding and trying to catch his balance. She threw the alcohol in his face and tried to dart out into the hall. Darren was frantically clawing at his eyes and slip sliding on the floor. Mia knew she only had an instant to get out of the bathroom they were both occupying. She got one foot in the hall when Darren's hand shot out blindly and he grabbed her arm.

"You entitled little bitch!" he roared. "You are dead!"

Mia tried to wrench out of Darren's hold but the drug high he was on had given him super strength and she was unable to break free. Just then a big car roared up to within a foot of the open front door. Three doors and the trunk opened at once and Anna, Jackie,

Al, and Libby were out and up the steps in short order. Mia called out, "Mom!"

Darren squinted in the direction of the front door, still unable to open his eyes all the way. He could make out the figures standing there and when he realized it was Mia's mom and her friends, he began to laugh hysterically.

"Perfect, the Oats bus came to save the little princess!" he laughed wildly but retained his hold on Mia's arm. "You bitches can damn well leave. Me and the princess are going to square some things up. She owes me for some valuable resources," Darren sneered.

"We'll certainly be leaving," said Anna crisply. "And my daughter will be coming with us."

"You ugly old biddies take one more step and I'll break her arm," shouted Darren. He swung Mia around in front of him taking her arm up behind her back. She winced as the pain shot up her arm. "Now what? She's staying and you witches need to get out of my house," said Darren firmly even though he couldn't keep both eyes open at the same time and his nose was trickling blood from hitting his face on the door.

Anna stood still not knowing the right thing to do with Mia in the position she was in. From one step to her right, Al said in a steely voice, "You're wrong you snot-nosed piece of shit. She is coming with us. Right now," with her last two words, Al raised a sawed-off shotgun that she had carried in unseen at her side.

Libby blanched seeing the weapon. Jackie's mouth opened but no sound came out. Anna covered her surprise by addressing Darren directly, "We just want to go now and Mia WILL be coming with us. We don't want you to get hurt but this is a case that any jury would find in our favor. You are holding my daughter against her will. You are threatening her and ourselves. We have justification to shoot you right here, right now. "

"Darren, you're a smart enough guy. Even with one eye closed, she's going to spray you with buckshot," said Jackie.

Darren gave a humorless laugh as he continued squinting and rubbing at his eye with his one free hand. "You don't know how to shoot that gun! You're so fucking stupid! You think you can scare me?"

Al took another half step in his direction. "My husband was a big hunter and loved all kinds of guns. I spent many weekends with him at the duck blind, loading shells, cleaning guns and yes, Darren, shooting them. One thing he taught me right from the start was you never point a gun at anything or anyone unless you are prepared to shoot. Now I am prepared to shoot and maybe I'm full of shit and don't know a bolt action from a semi-automatic. But maybe I do. You don't seem to be having such a great day or night as it were. Are you sure you want to go with your gut on this one?" she asked.

Darren was definitely wavering in light of the gun barrel a few feet away. Mia's face was stark white. She felt like she was living in the twilight zone. First the bizarre scene with Darren and now her mom and the goddesses were toting guns and talking like heavy action movie stars.

Anna took another step towards Mia and Darren. He clutched her arm and drew in his breath like he was about to say something. "Let go of her arm," said Anna in an authoritative voice. "We'll leave and you can return to your depraved, pathetic life." At her final word, Anna was holding Mia's free arm. Al stood with the gun four feet away. Jackie and Libby had their eyes locked on the three figures.

Suddenly, Darren released Mia's arm and pushed her at Anna with savage force. The two stumbled back and continued to the open door. Jackie and Libby went out behind Anna and Mia, never taking their eyes from Darren. Slowly, Al began backing to the door, never breaking eye contact and keeping the gun leveled at his chest. At the door, Al could hear Donna Sue behind the wheel freaking out, saying something about the gun. She revved the motor of the big Cadillac and Al slowly and carefully backed down the steps. Darren followed her but left space between them, still not sure if the old broad knew her way around the weapon. Even in his drug-sodden brain, the risk of the shotgun outweighed any ideas of charging the old lady. Once Al made it to the open rear door of the car she said,

"You are as worthless as tits on a boar hog as my husband used to say. You aren't good enough to wipe dog shit from Mia's shoes." With that, she swung the gun around to Darren's battered, beaten up car and pulled the trigger. A loud bang and then a thud sounded before a large splat of bright orange paint bloomed on the driver's side door. She quickly climbed into the backseat as Donna Sue dropped the pedal to the floor and the big car fishtailed out of the yard. When Darren saw the paintball, he charged the car at full tilt, screaming obscenities and threats. Byt the time he got to the grass, the big caddy was only tail lights.

Darren continued to scream in rage and rub his eyes while look-ing at his paint-splattered car. In his drug fogged brain even he could see how ludicrous it was to be bested by a bunch of old ladies with a paintball gun.

The Plan

Damn, damn, damn! Sometimes it was just too much thought Anna! She thought about what Tony would say to her when she was trying to solve big problems at school or with their girls as they were growing into adults. 'It's not your job to have the solution to everything. Give the world a little credit and share the responsibility with the rest of us, huh?' Well Tony was gone. Along with Chip Russell, Mack Schmitt, Ron Lake and Logan Algorotti, Jackie's second husband. Even Frank Martin was no longer in the picture. Anna had always been strong and independent as were all of the goddesses in their own ways. But she missed more than ever the sweet sense of security of being able to sit on the back deck with Tony and lay out ideas until a solution was clear.

The friends had all struggled at evolving from being part of a couple to a person alone with varying degrees of success. And now things seemed to be going in a direction that Anna couldn't control and was finding hard to accept. Sylvie was going to have to move into a nursing home, Al was having to sell her home in the country and Libby was still working a full-time job to get through each month. Anna chopped the vegetable for the soup with a vengeance. The goddesses were coming over tonight, a last hoo-ray, before some big changes. She looked at the lovely vegetable stew she had simmering on the stove and said, "Screw it," under her breath. Going to the phone she dialed a number she wasn't sure she would remember. Placing an order to be delivered later she went downstairs and got the blue cooler she kept by the deep freeze. She had to knock some cobwebs off as it hadn't been used in some time. She gave it a quick rinse and set it out on the deck to dry. Hopping into her Four Runner she went the few blocks to the small liquor store. She and Tony had been regular customers over the years and the owner, Sevuk, recognized her right away.

"Hello, Mrs. Are you here for some nice wine? I have some lovely white in the cooler and some nice Rose'. You like Rose', yes?" he asked. Although they'd been on friendly terms for many years they'd done business together, Anna always felt Sevuk was a bit, or a lot, judgmental of her alcohol purchases.

"Oh, no thanks," she said and smiled as she walked to the beer cooler. Reaching in she took out two cold eighteen packs of Miller Lite and lugged them to the front.

"This is all you want?" asked Sevuk with an openly disdainful look.

"No actually, it's not," said Anna. "I need the tequila on the shelf behind you." Sevuk turned slowly to the shelves behind him.

"A small bottle, like this?" he asked without smiling.

"No, I'm going to need the biggest one you have but not that cheap stuff. I want the most expensive bottle you have," she said. Anna thought it ridiculous that at 71 she still found it difficult to buy the liquor she wanted from the disapproving shop owner. She wondered why she and Tony had continued coming here. She and Tony. She was hoping that her nostalgia and strong feelings meant he was nearby. After all these years, she still wasn't used to it. She signed the slip and shoved her wallet into her purse. Grabbing a box of beer and the tequila, a lovely bottle of Don Julio, she noticed that Sevuk had picked up the other beer box and was following her to the car. After placing the boxes of beer in her back seat he stood and watched as she backed the big car out of the space and angled to the road. One thing Sevuk and Tony had in common, was that they both hated it when she drank beer. Well too bad. Desperate times require desperate measures.

Back at home she had plenty of time to fill the cooler with the long neck bottles and pack it with ice. She had just finished putting the tequila in the freezer and cutting some lime wedges when she heard Al and Sylvie coming up the drive. Sylvie wasn't able to traverse the five steps to the deck so Anna had moved the party down to the ground level. The three friends embraced before two helped one get settled in a cushioned chair with a comfortable foot rest. Sylvie was scheduled for knee replacement in a week. Since she would need help with basic needs, doctor visits and intensive physical therapy her sons had decided she would need to go to a nursing home for convalescence. Sylvie was appalled at the idea of living in Lenoir Senior Home even if it was temporary. She'd always been incredibly private and the idea of living in a room that had a curtain for a door was almost more than she could bear. She was embarrassed and frightened about the whole thing. The goddesses gathered around, all present except for Libby who was often late, and expressed interest and concern for Sylvie.

"You got anything to drink around here?" asked Jackie. Her feistiness always peaked when someone she cared about was struggling. Anna opened the cooler and the group let out a sigh of relief at the sight of the cold long necks inside.

"Old school! I love it!" said Donna Sue tilting one back.

"Seriously, the best Alex could come up with was a nursing home?" asked Al. "Doesn't that fancy wife of his have connections in the health-related field?"

Sylvie blew out a word none of them understood. "Are you kidding? If it was up to her, she'd have me euthanized," she said. This made the group throw their heads back and laugh.

"You know you could come and stay here with me," said Anna. "We could make you a bedroom in the sunroom. Getting up these five steps would be the only problem and there isn't a shower on the first floor. We could figure out something."

"Surely between all of us we could get you to therapy," said Donna Sue.

"If I could get my house sold, I could come live with you and be your taxi driver," added Al.

"And you can't go live with Danny?" asked Jackie, digging another cold beer from the ice.

"They're busy," said Sylvie. "Of course, they have time to go on a cruise with her mother but there's no time in their schedules to bring me to therapy and doctor appointments." The circle of friends could hear the level of pain in Sylvie's voice. "I love you all for being willing to help but the truth is it's more than we can handle. The nursing home is the best solution-now there is a sad commentary. If Chip was here…"

"If Chip was here," finished Al. "He'd kick those boys in the throat for putting their mother in a nursing home." There were murmurs of agreement in the dark before they heard another person approaching from the driveway.

"Hey, I have a delivery here. Five gyros with fries and a Greek salad," a male voice said. Anna jumped up and met the delivery man at the edge of the circle.

"Yes, thanks!" she said as she handed him the money she had folded in her pocket.

"Gyros? You know we can't eat that anymore. We'll never sleep tonight eating this late as it is," said Sylvie.

"Are you trying to kill us? We haven't eaten gyros in years?" asked Al.

"Oh take a Prilosec with your beer. And if she were trying to kill us, we'd be drinking tequila," said Jackie.

"Fine, there's some vegetable ragout on the stove if you want. I just thought if Sylvie has to go to a nursing home and eat nursing home food, we should eat something good tonight. And as I recall there is nothing better than gyros and fries from Tony's Pizza Palace," said Anna. All talking ceased while the friends enjoyed the tender spiced meat, pita bread and tzatziki sauce. When they had eaten all they could hold and opened another beer to wash it all down they sat in silence. It was Sylvie who spoke first.

"So, no luck with the house?" she asked.

"Nothing too promising yet," said Al. The timber in her voice was heavy and resigned. After Mack retired and before he got sick, he'd found the perfect place in the county. They moved into their dream house complete with a barn. Al loved being in the country. She had a huge garden, flowers everywhere and a couple of goats and a donkey she loved to mess with. Unfortunately, when Mack got bad and had to move to a care facility it took everything they had. Now Al was faced with having to sell the place and move to something smaller and in town. Her friends knew what it meant to her to be in a place free of privacy fences and sirens. She hardly ever watched tv but rarely missed the evening sunset from her back porch. The idea of moving back into the confines of a neighborhood with unwelcome sights and sounds was a lot like the feeling Sylvie was having about moving to a nursing home.

"Like Sylvie said, it's the only solution to a sucky problem," said Al.

The quiet was interrupted by the sudden appearance of Libby at the edge of the circle. Everyone except Sylvie stood to greet her. She found the empty seat in the circle and sat down with a white box on her lap. Anna offered her a cold beer which got a raised eyebrow from Libby but a nod of agreement too.

"What's in the box?" asked Jackie.

"Oh, it's baklava from International Cafe. I brought it to share," said Libby.

Anna suspected there was something not okay about their friend and her quiet entrance but the baklava sealed it. "What's wrong?" she asked.

"Yeah, you haven't eaten sugar since 1991. What's going on?" asked Al.

In a tremulous voice Libby blurted out, "I'm bankrupt!" and began to cry.

"What? How? I mean, how many gauze skirts do you own?" asked Donna Sue.

Al stood behind Libby stroking her hair while Anna went to look for a tissue. Jackie held her hand in both of hers.

"It's so dumb. I can't believe I am so dumb," repeated Libby. The friends murmured reassurances but waited for Libby to say more. Libby was the most optimistic person any of them had ever known. She refused to give in to defeat or depression. Even during some of the hardest things the friends had experienced together, Libby always pointed out a positive sign or the lesson to take away. She acknowledged evil in the world, but looked for the best in everyone. She was the absolute best friend to call if you were having a bad day. You simply couldn't stay down when she was around to point out the beauty in the world and within your own heart.

Donna Sue pulled her chair so it was touching Libby's. "Tell me what is so dumb. How are you bankrupt?"

"Credit cards. I've been trying but it's impossible," she said.

"What are you charging on credit cards? You buy your clothes at thrift stores and you don't eat meat," sputtered Jackie.

"Frank stuff. I stopped dating him ten years ago and I feel like he's still dragging me down. Airline tickets, shopping trips I couldn't afford, Eden's school stuff, her legal trouble," her voice trailed away. Life without Frank had been an adjustment. It was bizarre to Libby how she had allowed him to take up so much room in her life when he hadn't really been there at all. She missed him or rather she missed what she wanted him to be. She admitted to herself and the goddesses that she missed the thrill of travel and experiencing new places and things. She relished being with someone who understood money and handled it easily. Of course, with Frank out of her life, so was Eden. Libby tried to maintain her connection with the young woman but it was clear Eden had as much interest in Libby as her father did. One of her last communications with Libby she casually revealed that her dad and Vivan were living at the ranch in Tennessee and were planning a wedding. Eden thought the idea was hilarious and had no idea the news was like an ice pick to Libby's heart.

"It's been a while since you've mentioned anything about Frank. Are you hearing from him-are you over him?" asked Anna.

"Over? That's funny in a sick sort of way. I don't think it ever started with him. He never loved me," said Libby.

"What about you, Chicca? Did you love him?" asked Al.

"I thought I did but looking back it was more like an addiction. Anytime I'd fly somewhere to see him or drive hundreds of miles to meet him, I always knew he wasn't good for me. Every trip ended up hurting me but I kept going back for more," she said.

"But without Frank you'd have never met Eden," added Jackie.

"Without Eden maybe you wouldn't be bankrupt," added Al from the corner of her mouth.

"Easy, Gal," put in Donna Sue quietly but firmly. "We've all made choices. Choices that other people questioned and certainly judged. But those choices are what made us who we are and what we are. They brought us together and forged this friendship into something that rarely exists. Eden was supposed to be in Libby's life just like Ron was supposed to be in mine. Doesn't mean it was easy but sometimes that's the way the universe tumbles. Sometimes we're the windshield, sometimes we're the bug."

Libby let out a small gasp, "And I co-signed for Eden's car several years ago and she defaulted on the loan," she said.

"You did what?!" shrieked Donna Sue.

"Why would you do something like that?" demanded Jackie, standing up from her chair suddenly.

"Why did she need a loan? Her dad could have bought her any car she wanted. And if she did need a loan-that's her parent's job- not yours!" added Sylvie.

Anna moved next to Libby. "I'm just dumb. That's all," she said again.

"You are a lot of things Chicca, but dumb is not one of them," said Al.

"Why did you co-sign for Eden? I know you and Frank aren't together anymore but where is he in all of this mess?" asked Anna.

Libby was cry talking, "Frank cut Eden off after that last time she got in trouble for possession. He refused to bail her out so I did. He told me then not to complain to him if she left me holding the bag. He was done throwing good money after bad and he was done with me too for helping her. I can't call him. I won't call him. He's probably too busy moving into his Tennessee ranch with his new wife." Libby completely broke and sobbed openly. Anna excused herself from the circle and walked quickly to the house. In a universe so immense she returned to find her five closest friends standing in a space no larger than a hula hoop. Anna popped the top of the Don Julio and began filling shot glasses.

"Oh my god! She really is trying to kill us," said Sylvie as a brimming shot glass was handed to her.

"Just drink," said Anna. As one, they threw the tequila back and took a collective breath. "We have to get our bearings here. The world is definitely tipping and our universe is atilt." Anna filled the glasses again and Donna Sue began questioning Libby about the legal notifications, timelines and court dates she'd received. Al went to the house and came back with a pad and pen and jotted notes as Libby answered all of their questions. The situation was dire. The chairs came a little closer and the tequila bottle less full.

"Well, this is some fine kettle of fish!" declared Sylvie. "I'm going to a nursing home; Al is selling out and Libby is bankrupt. Some final chapter for women who call themselves goddesses. Is that tequila all gone? At this point I think death by tequila sounds like a humane solution." Anna got up to bring the bottle around again. The small fire crackled and flickered and revealed a small smile playing around the corners of her mouth.

"What are you thinking? Or are you drunk? Lord, I haven't been drunk in years," said Sylvie.

"No, I'm not drunk," said Anna as she found her seat in the circle again. "But what if we write a different chapter?"

"Like what?" asked Jackie. "Gas up Donna Sue's Cadillac and do a Thelma and Louise off the Grand Canyon?"

"No, what if we could help each other?" she asked. "Our kids have their own lives and families. I love my girls but, truthfully, I don't want to go live with them. We are all fairly healthy and of stable minds. What if we lived together?"

The outburst came from several directions at once. "All of us live here?" asked Jackie in a too loud, incredulous voice.

"You have three bedrooms and a fold out couch. I love you gals but I'm not about to learn how to sleep with one of you," added Donna Sue.

"Mack always said company was like fish, after three days it starts to stink," added Al.

"No, no, no. We wouldn't stay here. I've been thinking for years now that the house is just too much for me. I already have to pay someone to do the lawn, the leaves and the driveway. And there's so much of it I just don't use anymore. The girls are rarely here and I rattle around in there without even my ghost to talk to. I've been thinking it may be time to sell it and find something smaller," said Anna.

"Now I've heard it all!" said Sylvie. "You're going to sell this grand house on Edgewood? It really is the end of times."

"What are you thinking, that we could somehow find a neighborhood with six houses for sale?" asked Al.

"Five, I'm afraid, I'll have to live in a shed out back of one of you," threw in Libby.

"You'll never find anything like that in this market," added Donna Sue.

"Think about it. We each live alone so we don't need all the bedrooms and extra space. What do we really need?" probed Anna.

"Our own bedroom," said Donna Sue.

"Our own bathroom," said Sylvie.

"A small living area and a kitchen," said Jackie.

"Are you suggesting apartments?" asked Al. "I don't think I could live in a house that is stuck to lots of other houses."

"No. Not apartments or condos. What about tiny houses?" asked Anna hesitantly.

"Tiny who?" asked Jackie, who had a closet the size of some houses.

"I read an article about seniors buying tiny houses so they could live in their son or daughters' backyards. That way they have their own space but are close for safety and comfort purposes.

"How tiny is tiny?" asked Jackie.

"And where would you propose we put our tiny houses?" asked Donna Sue.

"They come in different dimensions and sizes. It really depends on what you want. I've been researching them and they seem pretty nice," said Anna. "And as to the location, we could look into buying a few acres or …"

"I'm afraid to ask. Or what?" asked Sylvie.

"We could ask Mia if she would let us build on her eighty acres. Her garden business is going great and she's going to open the Bistro soon but she has plenty of land," finished Anna quickly.

"You think Mia would want us underfoot?" asked Jackie.

"Well, she does owe us for saving her life that time," mused Al.

"And we could help her out with the garden and bistro," said Libby.

"Speak for yourself! I'm not going to be an indentured servant who has to work off rent every month," said Sylvie.

"No one would have to work if they didn't want to and she has a lot of land. I'm sure, if she agreed, there would be plenty of distance between us and her," said Anna, beginning to doubt the idea she had sprung on her friends. The circle got quiet as they mulled over such a radical and unexpected idea.

"You know what?" said Donna Sue slowly. "This really could work."

"What? You'd move to the country to live in a shoebox and pick tomato worms off plants in the scorching sun all day?" squeaked Sylvie.

"I'm just saying, this idea has merit. If we sold our houses, which some of us are already doing," she cut a kind look to Al. "We could use some of the money to buy our tiny homes and lease some land from Mia. Anna, what are the costs of the houses you've been researching?"

Anna's smile had returned. "Anywhere from $25,000 to $50,000 depending on the design and size.

"Four walls? My house has 2800 square feet. Where am I going to put all that stuff?" groused Sylvie. Libby leaned over and squeezed her hand.

"Don't worry, we'll have a garage sale," she said, smiling for the first time since she arrived.

"If we're going to sell our houses and live in cardboard boxes, I'm going to need some more tequila. I thought tonight might be a little depressing, but I didn't know it would be downright whack-a-doo crazy!" said Sylvie.

"I'd love it if we could live out in the country," said Al, taking a drink directly from the bottle. "I could be content with a lot less house as long as we had great outdoor spaces."

"Yes! Pass me that tequila and a page out of that note book," said Jackie. Using her styrofoam box as a desk she quickly drew six pentagons scattered in an uneven circle. Then as her friends watched she drew a large bean shape in the middle of the shapes.

"What's that?" asked Libby.

"The POOL!" said Jackie and Anna in unison both grinning from ear to ear.

"And here's the great part, we can save money on it because it only needs to be four feet deep!" declared Anna. They all looked at Sylvie and laughed. It felt so good to laugh together after the start of their evening had been so bleak. Sylvie wanted to keep a straight face but found that she couldn't. Her deep belly laugh joined in with the rest.

"If there's a pool there has to be a hot tub," added Donna Sue.

"And a fire pit," added Jackie enthusiastically.

"Let me have it," said Libby. She grabbed the box desk and began adding to the drawing.

"Now what? A massage and yoga center?" asked Sylvie. Craning her neck to watch Libby's pen, Al began to nod her head.

"Yes, and be sure you add…mm-hmm. Good!" The two turned the plan around for the others to see.

"It's Tony's deck-you know without the house. We'll need a place to cook together and have room to hang out like we do here no matter the weather. We need outdoor furniture, a mini fridge, the works," said Libby, warming to the idea. "I mean you all can. It's not like I can contribute anything."

"Don't you worry, Gal. You'll contribute plenty," assured Donna Sue. "This is going to take a village if we really do pull it off."

"Oh, I love that! We'll bring Tony's lovely deck with us to our… village," said Jackie.

"And I know what we'll call it," declared Al. "Edgewood Village!"

"Our own assisted living community!" added Donna Sue.

"Goddess Style!" laughed Jackie.

Anna looked at her friends sitting so close to one another that their knees touched. She thought about how grateful she was for each of them.She listened as they laughed and talked about their crazy plan. A crazy plan that would keep them from being alone. She whispered a quiet 'thank you' to the universe. She was pretty sure she felt Tony at her elbow and there was a faint whiff of cinnamon in the air.

The Village

Fait accompli. Six small houses brought in on trailers were now anchored to their cement pads amidst lots of dust and turmoil, both the physical and metaphysical types. It seemed that everyone had an opinion about the tiny house village. As if selling homes that were too large and very empty in exchange for small houses next door to your best friends was the same as running a Mustang convertible over the Grand Canyon.

Sylvie's boys put up a particularly loud squawk. At first, they thought they could harangue their mother into seeing the lunacy of her decision to sell the tri-level on the edge of town that she and Chip had molded into the perfect family home. The large shop that sat out back held all of Chip's woodworking tools and kept the mess of his many hobbies contained and out of Sylvie's sight. When they first saw the property years before, Sylvie knew the house hunt was over as soon as she saw the outbuilding. He'd finally be able to have projects going that didn't take up the entire garage or worse, the dining room table, the family room and occasionally the spare bed. When Sylvie pointed out the outdated kitchen and the family room that was dark and small, Chip vowed he would work until he had a kitchen she would be proud to make her mother's homemade con le sarde in and a family room that would be both inviting and cozy.

And indeed, he had. He had all the right skills and tools. He was downright giddy about having a proper workshop. He happily set to work and produced a high-end custom kitchen, doing most of the work himself. Downstairs, he was able to open up the space by removing a wall that allowed light from the sliding French door to brighten up the entire room. Once the outdated dark paneling was gone and he laid a nice bamboo floor, the whole room took on a different feel. When the boys were growing up the family spent their evenings watching movies or playing scrabble while the fireplace crackled. Chip had delivered on every promise he had ever made to Sylvie. All but the one about growing old together.

She thought her friends were out of their ever-loving minds when the idea of the tiny houses came up. She was the biggest and loudest critic. But being here alone didn't give her the same sense of home that it used to. She found herself talking to herself or to Chip and worried she might have not so early onset dementia. And the stairs. The tri-level design required her to traverse stairs to the bedroom and to the laundry and family room. Both knees were a wreck and the stairs really made them bark even though she'd had the left one, the bad one, replaced. Time wasn't going to go backward and she knew it wasn't going to get easier.

She hadn't intended to include the boys in her decision to sell the house and move but Danny and Beth Anne dropped in one Sunday afternoon when she was clearing out some childhood things of the boys. Now in their thirties and forties, they'd had plenty of time to take anything they valued to their own homes. What was left was the usual childhood detritus that they didn't want to deal with. When she told Danny she was planning on moving he was immediately against it.

Sylvie stood back with her hands on her hips while her grown son told her she couldn't sell 'Dad's house'. Her sons were very familiar with her passionate nature and Danny was going pretty good before he recognized the tells that Sylive was heating up, realizing her nostrils were beginning to flare. He tried to placate her while maintaining the idea that she couldn't sell the house. Where would she go? What about all of Dad's tools? Where would they stay if they all got together? He wondered how much she had seriously thought about it?

Sylvie gathered herself with an effort. "Have you thought about what it's like for me to be here? By myself? I'm alone in a four bedroom home. I have a half acre to mow and a shed full of tools that I don't use. I have a gourmet five burner stove but the last time you were here for a meal was last Christmas. I have to go up and down the stairs several times a day. What difference does it make where I am when you make your 'check in on mom calls'? I've seen Alex once since Dad died and that was at the Holiday Inn. So I'd say, I've thought about it quite a bit. More than you have thought about what it's like for me. I know you boys don't want things to change, but they already have changed! If I want to sell the house that your dad and I loved, maybe you ought to consider that I have valid reasons." Sylvie finished slightly out of breath. Beth Anne was making hand motions indicating it was time to go. Typical, she thought. She'd been with Danny for years but had never gotten comfortable when Sylvie got heated or voiced her strong opinions regarding politics, education, or any topic for that matter. Sylvie thought the reason was that Beth Anne didn't seem to have any strong feelings about anything. She never wanted to see the documentaries that Sylvie and Danny used to love to watch and discuss for hours. She didn't like to discuss the news if it was upsetting. Sylvie always felt like she had to walk on eggshells around her and that was a talent she distinctly lacked.

Acknowledging that it was time to go, Danny ducked his head and moved in to hug his mom. Sylvie held him tightly and heard him whisper, 'I love you'. Her sons were definitely at the top of the list of things she was passionate about. She loved them desperately. But where Chip had had a tendency to shelter them from hurts and disappointments, Sylvie was always the one to encourage them to push on, push through, and find ways to achieve their goals despite obstacles. The three boys all agreed that their mom was unstoppable. Once when Alex was 15 he invited a girl from the neighborhood to come over to watch a movie long after Sylvie and Chip had gone to bed and certainly without their permission. Sylvie, awakened by the sound of a girl's laugh, first called to the boys from the top of the steps and then went to investigate. The boys assured her there was no girl in the house. They promised her, they chided her for not believing them and finally called her crazy. But Sylvie being Sylvie wouldn't be stopped and refused to return to bed. She continued searching the family room while her two oldest sons laughed at her, telling her she was nuts. Finally, she pulled open the game closet to find a girl squeezed between the shelves and the door.

The boys knew their mom was a force to be reckoned with, but they also knew she, above anyone else, was their greatest advocate. She wanted them to succeed in whatever they put their mind to, but she wanted that success to be from their own initiative, desire, and drive. She would encourage any interest they showed and never allowed them to quit in the middle. Sylvie watched Danny back out of the drive and resumed dragging boxes out of the garage headed for the Salvation Army. She knew it wouldn't be long before Alex would call and she knew she'd have to go through the whole thing again.

She didn't have to wait long. She'd just finished loading her car when she could hear the phone in the kitchen. She closed up the garage and moved steadily towards the phone, wiping her hands on a towel as she moved past the sink. She took a deep breath and let it out before she picked up the receiver.

"Hello?" she said.

"Mom? What's going on? Dan said you're selling the house? Is there a problem? If so, we should talk about it. I don't think you should be making such an enormous decision on your own. Why didn't you talk to me about it?" asked Alex from hundreds of miles away.

Sylvie let Alex come to the end of his tirade. Of the three boys, he was wired most like her. He was highly intelligent and extremely passionate about anything he threw himself into. In high school, it was debate and political clubs, in college, it was protesting and social media education, and eventually law. His job in Washington D.C. was high powered and made good use of his gifts and talents. Although it kept him busy and away from his home state, this wasn't always a bad thing. They'd learned since college that there were fewer blowups and loud words exchanged when Alex was away. Sylvie and Chip were so proud of him and his accomplishments. But Sylvie and Alex in the same house for more than 48 hours was like sitting on a keg of gunpowder knowing it was a matter of time before one of them would blow.

"I'm well. How are you?" asked Sylvie sarcastically.

"Mom, don't give me that attitude crap. Do you have a realtor? Have you signed a contract? Where are you going?" Alex demanded.

"Donna Sue is helping me. She was in the property management business for a long time. We haven't gotten to the realtor stage yet but I assure you when we do, I'll go over it carefully and make sure everything is kosher. How's Meredith?"

"We're fine. Stop trying to change the subject. I'm not sure Donna Sue is the right person to be advising you. And you know there is a lot involved with a real estate contract. I don't want to think of someone trying to take advantage of you. I'll give you my fax number at the office. Send me any documents you are looking at—before you sign them—and I'll make sure they are appropriate. If Dad was here…" said Alex.

"Alex, dear," broke in Sylvie. "I know you are concerned as was your brother, but if I want to sell my house I will. Sell my house. I also wish with all my heart and soul that Dad was here. But he's not. And believe it or not, I'm not completely senile and can still smell a rip-off a mile away. Thanks for calling, give my love to Meredith," said Sylvie as she reconnected the phone at the base, cutting off anything further Alex had to say. She was certain it wasn't over with him- knowing he was tenacious just like herself. She fixed a cup of tea and went to the spare room to see if there was anything in there she wanted to keep. She was interrupted an hour later by a voice calling hello from the foyer. When it rains it pours, thought Sylvie straightening up to greet her youngest son, David.

"Hey, what are you doing?" he asked, holding a cannoli in his hand.

"As if you don't know," snarked Sylvie.

"No, I don't know. What's going on here? It looks so empty. Are you spring cleaning again?" he asked.

Sylvie felt a little bad for her less than warm greeting. Obviously, David was marked off the phone tree or maybe he was unavailable to his big brothers' calls. "Yeah, you could say that. You want some coffee with that cannoli?" she asked.

"Sounds great. You got anything else to eat?" he asked, following her down the stairs into the spacious kitchen. David worked several part-time jobs and was independent-ish. He did get a lot of his meals from Sylvie's fridge. Partly from necessity, partly because Sylvie was an amazing cook. As she pulled leftover pasta from the fridge, David started the coffee.

"I've talked with both of your brothers today and they both let me know exactly what they think about my decision. I might as well go three for three and make this a monumentally sucky day. I've decided to sell the house. The stairs up to bed and down to the laundry are a challenge, I have three empty bedrooms that are just warehouses for stuff I don't need. I have a dining room table for eight but I eat on a tv tray downstairs. The lot is more than I can deal with and I have a 30'x40' outbuilding full of every kind of woodworking tool known to man, none of which do me any good. I've made up my mind I'm going to sell the house," Sylvie finished quickly and jammed her hands on her hips bracing herself for opposition.

David looked up from his plate of pasta chewing. "What?" he managed around a big bite.

"I'm just waiting for you to tell me I can't sell the house, or ask what would Dad say? What about our home and all of our childhood leftovers that nobody cares enough about to move to their own house?" said Sylvie with narrowed eyes.

"You're going to sell the house? I can see that it's a lot to deal with," he said and went back in for another heaping fork of pasta.

Sylvie's eyes narrowed a little more. She couldn't tell if he was playing her by being so amenable or if he was sincerely sincere. David saw the look and put his fork down and came around the big island. He put his hands on his mom's shoulders.

"I can understand. You and dad poured a lot of time, money and thought into this house. Together. It's great, but you don't have anyone to enjoy it with. I worry about you here alone," David pulled back and laughed a little. "Not from a security standpoint. A guy would have to be full-on crazy to storm Sylvie's castle with her in it. I just mean, we grew up in this house. Now it just seems so empty," he said.

Sylvie felt tears welling in her eyes. Leave it to David, the one most like Chip, to not only listen, but to hear her.

"Besides, you always told us that if we don't like something you can stand on the sideline and cry about it or get your ass in the game and do something about it. Sounds like you got your ass in gear. How can I help?" he asked with a crooked grin that was so like his father's.

Sylvie's smile was like a sunbeam breaking through a cloud. She pulled David to her and hugged him hard. She may have to spar more with Alex and Danny but it felt good to have an ally. And she was pleased that some of the wisdom she tried to impart to her sons, apparently, had sunk in to at least one of them.

◇◇◇

Al had a similar response from her son. When she explained the tiny house village plan to him, he started by laughing it off like it was a joke. When he saw she was serious he became earnest and explained why Al couldn't move to a tiny house community or at least the one she described. Out of frustration he resorted to anger and went so far as to insist Al move in with his family. Al loved the sentiment even if it was slightly misguided, but couldn't see herself in their modest home that seemed to get smaller as her grandsons got bigger. It bothered Al that Nathan was so against her plan, feeling like he was so against her. Her children were her pride and joy and she knew she was blessed to have such strong relationships with them and their spouses. She let a few days pass without making an effort to communicate. She knew Nathan would call Marie. That was another of her most cherished blessings. Her children not only liked each other but counted on each other in their daily lives. She knew the two of them talked regularly and hoped that the conversation would help her situation. She was committed to the goddesses and the plan they had hammered out, but would feel so much better if she didn't have to worry about the kids being unhappy or overly concerned to the point that it would affect their normal interactions.

She was right about Nathan not wasting any time calling his sister, not even waiting for the end of the workday. Luckily, Marie wasn't swamped and was able to take the call. She let him rant and rave for a few minutes thinking he sounded a lot like their dad. When he finally unloaded all that he had built up he said, "What do you think about it?"

"Well, I admit it sounds a little crazy. But I keep coming back to the fact that this is mom. The same mom that has always done what she's supposed to do. Think about it. She learned how to roller skate when I wanted to do roller hockey and needed to practice. She was faithful about visiting grandpa in the nursing home even though he thought she was someone who worked there. And dad? Look at how she stood beside him that whole time he was sick."

"So, you're saying she should buy a house the size of your closet and move out to the sticks because she took care of dad and grandpa and taught you how to roller skate?" Nathan asked not yet ready to be reasonable.

Marie laughed. "No, I'm saying she's always done what any of us needed her to do. No matter what it was. She did it freely and happily because she knew it was what we needed or wanted. Have you forgotten how you got your wings?" she asked.

Nathan was quiet on the other end of the line for a few beats. He was only seventeen when he finished high school and the recruiters were hot and heavy for him to sign on the dotted line. Nathan needed a parent's signature and Al refused. Not because she thought the armed forces weren't a noble calling or a righteous endeavor. She worried that without the full use of his frontal lobe at seventeen, Nathan was being swayed by the recruiter's talk and wasn't making the choice freely. They made a deal, he would go to community college for two years and then if he wanted to join up, Al and Mack would be proud for him to do so. Al sweetened the pot a little by also giving him the money he needed for flying lessons. Since he was a little boy, Nathan had wanted to fly. He'd worked diligently every summer mowing yards and had saved most of his earnings for a pilot's class. He was short by a couple hundred dollars which Al said she would provide if he took the deal. This was huge as Al was terrified of flying and had a terrible time with the idea of Nathan putting his life in danger in the small aircraft he was training in. She did her best to stifle her anxiety during Nathan's lessons for fear that it would affect his confidence. She always made sure she stayed busy with a task at home until he returned from the small airport in Boonville, twenty-four miles away. Nathan was a natural and aced the course earning his pilot's license and Al's grout had never been cleaner.

Now he cleared his throat, "Yeah, she hated the idea of me flying. She still does."

"Right," agreed his sister. "But she was the one who helped that happen even though she was terrified for you. She made sure you got to do that even though it went against every fiber of her body."

"So you're saying, I need to give mom her wings?" he asked.

"Exactly. Or in this case, keys to her tiny house," laughed Marie.

As much as Al hated it, things were somewhat strained between her and Nathan in the following months. Marie, sounding like the parent, encouraged her to be patient and wait him out. She was confident her brother just needed time to wrap his male brain around the plan and reassured Al everything was going to be fine. It turned out she was exactly right. The day after the tiny homes were moved in and anchored, a work truck and trailer rumbled up the newly graveled lane that ran along the orchard on Mia's farm. Nathan and his two sons plus a friend piled out. Al came out of her house where she was busy putting things into their designated spaces.

"This is a nice surprise," she said as she got some big hugs from her grandsons. "What are you burly men doing out here?"

"Well, I figured you all would need a good-sized fire ring to dance around and howl at the moon, which of course I assume you do. I've got leftover materials and three indentured servants who are ready to work," said Nathan with a small smile. Al knew it was his way of saying he was sorry for giving her such a hard time about moving and that he was okay with it and with her. She smiled back at her son, seeing the dark-eyed boy she had played catch with so long ago.

"A fire ring is mandatory in a situation like this!" she exclaimed. "We've already got a spot picked out for it, I'll see about getting some worker dude lunches rustled up."

Chase, her youngest grandson, requested Sylvie's delicious spiedini and Al laughed as she assured him she'd find something good to eat. She watched her son give clear directions for the boys to unload the stones and bags of cement from the trailer. It was going to be alright-everything was going to be alright.

◇◇◇

Anna's girls had accepted her decision to sell the Edgewood house easily but it wasn't without some drama. They both knew how much their mom loved the house, but with Tony gone, they knew she wasn't happy there. The three of them walked through the beautiful rooms tagging furniture they wanted and deciding what should go to auction.

"You don't think I'm doing the wrong thing, do you?" she asked Ellie as they went through the breakfront hutch in the dining room. "I mean, this house has been your and Mia's home for your entire lives. What about holidays? Visits? Will you hate it that we're not all together in this big old house?"

"Mia and I have homes, Mom. This was our childhood home and it is grand because you and dad made it grand for us. You did everything for us. Now it's time for you to do something for you. You always told us your biggest aspiration for us was that we are happy. Happy with who we are, happy with who we spend our life with, happy with what we do and where we are. I am! I love my husband and my practice. Mia has her farm and her business is growing every year. We want you to be happy and, in a place, where you are happy. This is going to be fine. You'll see," finished Ellie, squeezing her mom's arm gently as she went upstairs to clear out more things. Anna watched her go, marveling at her daughter's beautiful and generous spirit. She continued sorting dishes for some time before she noticed Ellie standing at the door to the dining room.

"Mom, who is this?" she asked, holding up an 11" x 14" canvas that had the portrait of a woman's head and torso. Anna recognized the painting she had done so long ago when she and Libby were learning about Lorna and the history of the house.

"Oh that old thing?" said Anna. "It's just a painting I did shortly after dad and I moved in here. I forgot all about it."

"Weird, she looks so familiar. I swear I dreamed of a lady that looked just like this. It seems so strange that I would remember my dreams from when I was little but I distinctly remember her sitting at the foot of my bed. Those dreams always made me feel so…" Anna held her breath in anticipation of what Ellie would say. "I just felt safe. Like I knew you and dad were downstairs. But the lady was upstairs with me so I could go to sleep and not worry. Really weird," she finished. Anna wondered if she should tell Ellie what she knew of Lorna and her own experiences with her, but at that moment Mia came in the kitchen door calling for them.

"We're here, darling," called Anna from the dining room.

Mia rounded the door from the kitchen and took in her mom and sister. "What's that?" she asked Ellie. Ellie turned the portrait around so she could see it. "Oh yeah, the lady. I forgot all about her."

Ellie and Anna looked at each other then back at Mia. "The lady?" asked Ellie. "You know who this is?"

"Sure. She's the lady on the stairs that used to sit on the end of our beds when we were going to sleep," said Mia easily.

Anna wasn't sure what to say. "You saw her? On the stairs? In your room? Were you afraid? Why didn't you ever tell me about it?"

Mia shrugged her lovely shoulder. At thirty-one she was still slight like a young girl with her mother's warm eyes and sun-kissed skin from being outdoors all day. "She was just part of the house. I never felt afraid. In fact, there were lots of times when she'd come to sit on the end of my bed if I was having bad thoughts or dreams, and the next thing I'd know it was morning and I was waking up. I never thought to tell you because I never thought of her in the daytime. She had to have visited you too, Ellie."

Ellie's eyes got wide as she thought about what her sister had described. "I guess I did see her. I thought I dreamed her. But how could you paint a picture of someone I dreamed of?" she asked her mom.

Anna took a breath and explained how she saw Lorna the first time she stepped foot in the house. She explained, briefly, how Libby had helped her learn the history of the house and described the family that lived and loved in it. She told them about Lavendar and the

Heaven Window. By the time she was done, they were all staring at Lorna's portrait with their own private thoughts.

"That's incredible," started Ellie. "I had no idea we were sharing the house with a ghost. Is she still here, do you think?"

"I haven't seen or felt Lorna for thirty years and I guess I'm not surprised she was there for you both. From what I learned about her, she adored her children and loved being a mother. I think she was watching over you in your rooms. Who knows, maybe the new buyer will be visited by her as well," said Anna. She watched her two grown daughters put their dark mahogany heads together as they walked through the emptying rooms. She smiled at the sight of them and whispered a prayer of gratitude to Lorna for keeping her precious babies safe and secure.

It turned out one of the goddesses herself posed the biggest hurdle in pulling off their ingenious plan. After they all researched tiny houses, they decided they really needed to see one to have a clear idea of what they were getting. Each of them had their own idea for a floor plan but they needed to see the features and floor plan options in person. They discovered there was a manufacturer 150 miles away in Illinois. They set up a time for a tour, found a lovely Inn to spend the night, and made a road trip out of it. They were all intrigued as they entered the large warehouse, listening to the representative explain the building materials, etc. They took turns going into the first model home, marveling at its small size but also, its efficiency.

As they moved to the next house on display, Jackie looked around noticing that Sylvie wasn't with them. They told the rep they'd be right back and retraced their steps out the huge double doors to the parking lot. Sylvie was sitting in the front seat of Donna Sue's Cadillac. If the stony look on her face wasn't enough of a tell about her frame of mind, her arms crossed tightly over her chest sealed it.

Anna pecked on the window even though they all knew Sylvie was aware they were gathered around the car.

"Sylvie, what's wrong? What are you doing in the car?" Anna asked. At first, Sylvie didn't respond. Knowing her well, they knew that if she was upset, she would feel the need to tell them precisely why she was upset. It was a helpful trait with their passionate friend. One never had to guess what she was feeling because she couldn't keep it to herself. The ladies looked to each other, not knowing what to do when the door to the big car opened and their friend climbed out.

"If you think I'm going to live in one of those death traps you are seriously delusional!" she started.

"What's the trouble, Gal? You knew the houses were going to be small-I mean they are called 'tiny houses'," explained Donna Sue.

"They have all kinds of floor plans. We barely got started on the tour," added Jackie.

"I read the brochure. There are lots of different designs and dimensions," said Al. They all backed up half a step when Sylvie began to shake her head back and forth spiritedly.

"It's not the floor plan or the number of rooms. I saw what that was made of. For crying out loud I watched Chip build a doghouse out of the same plywood. You want me to live in a doghouse?" said an agitated Sylvie. Anna, always the maternal one, touched Sylvie on the arm gently.

"Honey, what's bothering you about the houses? Of course, you're not going to live in a dog house. What is it?" she asked in her soothing voice.

"Well, I'll tell you! Chip built a doghouse out of the very same wood I saw in there. We put it in the backyard when the boys wanted a beagle puppy. They cried and clamored because they didn't want the poor dog outside in the weather. So Chip built a spectacular doghouse. Not some cheap little thing. He wanted to make the boys happy so he made it extra roomy with a roof that stuck out like an awning for shade. It was deluxe, shingles, siding, the whole shebang. The puppy never spent a single night in that doghouse."

"Do you know why?" Sylvie's voice was raised and strident. "Because before the beagle was big enough to be in the outdoor pen and doghouse, the wind blew it away!" Sylvie's eyes snapped as she looked at her friends standing around her in the dusty parking lot. "That's right! A house not that much different from the one you're showing me in there got picked up and carried away. It landed in a field across the road and the only way we were able to identify the pile of rubble was the hand-painted sign the boys did with the dog's name on it." She was working up to her crescendo. "If you think I'm going to move into, basically, a doghouse, and get picked up and carried away the first time the wind blows well then, you are all crazier than I gave you credit for." Sylvie turned to get back into the car. "You all do what you want to do but I'm not going to get blown away in my own house. If that's what you want, more power to you. It was nice knowing you." Her last sentence was punctuated by the slamming of the car door. Donna Sue looked back and waved at the representative who stood waiting from them to return and finish the tour.

"You all get in. I'll go explain," said Donna Sue. The others piled into the big car. Taking two cars would have made sense but they had all been riding around in Donna Sue's vintage Caddy for so long it seemed silly to split up. They drove back to the small Inn in silence. Once the big car was in the parking spot the doors opened and the ladies climbed out looking at each other, unsure of what to do next.

Al suggested, "How about a little lie-down time before dinner. I noticed a cute little tavern as we were driving in. Let's meet here at the car at 5:30."

They agreed and dispersed to their different rooms. Al and Libby decided to change into their walking shoes and get a little bit of exercise while the others relaxed in their rooms. They headed down the sidewalk ready to explore a bit of the town. They passed a small college with beautiful grounds and had to wait at the intersection as a cement truck turned out of the drive just as another one turned in. Letting the sidewalk lead them, they stopped when they turned a corner to find the cement truck that had just turned in getting ready to download into preset forms. They had to wait before crossing the street and Al watched as the wet cement came down the chute into a grid of rebar. Libby noticed Al was much quieter on the walk back to the Inn but assumed she was worrying over this new wrinkle in the plan.

At 5:30 the goddesses assembled by the car and debated if they should walk the few blocks or drive. It was March and even though the day had been mild, the evenings were still cool. They loaded up in the car and Donna Sue turned left out of the lot. The atmosphere in the car was weighted. Sylvie's outburst and walkout earlier had taken them all by surprise. No one was exactly sure how to clear the air. It took less than five minutes to get to the Tavern on the Green and Donna Sue slid the gear shift to park.

Sylvie started, "I know you are all mad at me. I'm sorry about that. I'll find somewhere else to live and you can go ahead with the plan. I would never be able to relax thinking about what those houses are made of and how a good stiff wind could pick it up and carry it off with me in it." There were a couple of beats of silence before Al said from the backseat.

"What if it couldn't?"

"Couldn't what?" asked Jackie.

"What if we made it so the tiny houses were attached to the ground and couldn't be picked up and carried off?" said Al.

Sylvie, Libby, and Donna Sue all turned from the front seat to look at Al. "How would you do that?" asked Sylvie.

"Anchors!" said Al.

"Yeah! Anchors," agreed Donna Sue.

Sylvie and Libby looked at each other with raised eyebrows.

"The houses will be sitting on cement pads. What if there were anchors in the cement attached to the house?" asked Al.

"I get it," said Libby. "An anchor! It will hold the house to the cement pad."

Jackie's face split in her huge grin. "Hot damn! Buy me a drink! We've got a village to build!"

After that, their plan born out of frustration, confusion, and loss started to become a reality. As the homes where they had lived as wives, mothers, and partners emptied, the village site began to take shape. Excavators leveled the area and cleared trees and brush. Electricity and water lines were laid and a newly graveled lane curved around the south orchard of Mia's farm. The 16' x 32' saltwater pool was installed in the midst of a large pool deck with the pavilion at one end and the six tiny houses placed around the sides and opposite end. Sylvie's was closest to the driveway and pavilion, next door to her was Anna. Jackie and Donna Sue's homes were at the end of the pool opposite the pavilion and Libby and Al were opposite Anna and Sylvie. The deck Tony had built for Anna at the Edgewood house was visualized and recreated in the village. The covered pavilion opened at one end of the pool deck and was closed in on the north side. It was equipped with an outdoor kitchen, storage, room for a grill, and picnic tables. It was a wonderful shared space.

Charlotte came to help Jackie with the move. She presented the goddesses with a gift for the pavilion where they would cook, eat and gather together under a common roof. It was a beautiful laser-cut banner made from reclaimed steel. The age and patina of the metal along with the beautiful quote from Helen Keller was the perfect touch to the community space they so lovingly created. The words, 'I would rather walk with a friend in the dark than alone in the light', were an affirmation that their decisions, though difficult, were sound ones and their plan the right one. As Nathan finished mounting the beautiful banner to the back wall, he stepped back to admire it along with his mom and her friends.

After a few beats of silent reverie on their part, he cracked, "I remember the day when your banner said 'Tequila is like duct tape, it fixes everything'." The comment broke the solemn mood and they all laughed.

"We may not be vaulting onto floating palm trees anymore but we still have some tequila shots left in us!" smirked Jackie. Sylvie snorted and turned away. Al hugged her son and thanked him for hanging the banner and for the magnificent fire pit he had constructed for them. Hugging his mom, Nathan thought how she had given him wings in more ways than one. He could sense the rightness in the plan now. He hoped he would be as brave and generous with own children.

Following the move, Charlotte went back to New York, delivery trucks no longer rolled up the lane and the friends began to settle into new routines. They each had their own way to start the day, but when the sun was warmest, they would appear around their lovely pool and float on rafts or sit on the side with tall glasses of iced tea minus the tequila. Dinner was usually a combined effort. Sometimes it was planned but most often it just happened organically. Libby would bring out cheese and fruit that would get everyone's appetite whetted. Al always had red wine and a baguette or a box of Cheez-Its to share. Before long Sylvie would come out with some lovely variety of pasta tossed with veggies or meat and the friends would sit in the twilight enjoying the country night sounds and quiet conversation. Anna loved to bake and always had some delicious homemade treats for dessert. Many nights the friends wished each other good night and finished the last of their day in their own home reading or watching tv. Some nights they would find themselves talking long into the night. Occasionally the bottle of Patron was brought out and they sipped the quality tequila and laughed or cried depending on the topic and of course, the amount of tequila.

It was one of those nights when they had stayed out long together near the end of their first summer in their tiny house village. One by one the goddesses said goodnight and drifted to their own door. Anna had always been a night owl and was usually the last to leave the pool or pavilion. Libby hung back as Donna Sue wished them a good night with a yawn. Anna waited a few minutes until Donna Sue's front light went out and then turned her face in the dark to where Libby sat quietly.

"What is it?" she asked. She heard rather than saw the smile that spread across Libby's face.

"You still shine," said Libby. "You knew I needed to talk to you without the others."

"So, what's up?" asked Anna.

Libby was quiet for a few beats then started in. "I don't know where to start. I'm a mess. This whole bankrupt thing has really made me stare long and hard at myself and it's not a pretty picture. I'll never be able to show Donna Sue how much I appreciate the payment plan she devised for me. I feel like I'll never be able to get out of the hole I dug for myself, although I know that any one of you, every one of you would help me. Being I'm almost 70 now I just thought that I'd have this figured out, that I'd be able to stand on my own and not have to lean for help. It seems like I've been leaning my whole life and I just didn't think it would be this way."

Anna stayed quiet, listening and hearing the words that sounded rehearsed and knowing something big was coming. Knowing she probably wouldn't like it. Libby continued, "I wanted to come here with you all. I wanted to belong here but it's not where I'm supposed to be." Libby's voice began to wobble more and the practiced ease of words was gone. This was from the heart now. "The voice in my head is like a stuck record and just keeps repeating all the things I've fucked up over and over."

Anna leaned over her chaise and held Libby's hand in her own with a firm grip. "You know not one of us thinks you are or have fucked up." Libby tried to interrupt but Anna refused to let her. "That being said, what is it that you want? I want you here with us, but more than that I want you to be happy. What do you need to be happy Libby? What will kill that sick in your stomach and quiet that voice in your head?" In the dark, Libby knew Anna was looking directly into her. Into her eyes, into her heart. Into her soul.

"Roddy!" she squeaked out. "I want Roddy."

Anna sat back in her chair but didn't release her friend's hand. Libby's response was unexpected and Anna was trying to see the logic or lunacy in the statement before she said anything. Libby was also silent except for some deep sucking breaths that may have been sobs. When Anna did speak it was one word that stretched through the darkness with the weight of the world hanging on it, "Why?"

"I know you think I'm taking the easy way out, going back to my ex-husband but it's actually the hardest thing I've ever done. I love you all so much and I dreamed of this vision with you. Moving here was the absolute best thing I've done for myself in a very long while. Leaving here seems absurd. But I turned my back on Roddy a long time ago and what I've come to realize is that I left a big part of myself there with him. I know it sounds crazy. I wasted years with Frank and I blamed that failure on him but I was more of a failure than he was. I told him he had my heart. That I loved him but it was a lie. I left my heart at the end of a gravel road years ago. I thought if I was fool enough to leave a good man, I must be happy with the life I left him for. I lied to myself every day."

"If it weren't for you, Donna Sue, and Jackie I would still be fooling myself and believing in something that never was. Roddy knows all of me. The best and the worst and I'm the first to say there is more of the latter. But the crazy thing is he still wants me." Libby's voice faded. Anna heard her take a deep, shuddering breath before she said, "I may have missed my chance at a great love. But what if I haven't? What if I met him when I was ten years old and was too stupid to know it?"

"And Roddy is the place you want to be? You're certain?" asked Anna quietly.

"Yes," breathed Libby. Her exhale carried every ounce of the tension and angst she'd been carrying around for weeks. Anna felt the weight of the breath and leaned into her friend.

"Then that's what we'll do," said Anna as she wrapped her arms around Libby. The two held on to each other, not talking for some time each feeling the relief experienced by the other. When they pulled apart inches from each other's faces their smiles were pure and their hearts lighter. Anna knew there would be more words, more tears when the others heard the news but for now things were right with the universe.

They broke the news to the group the next morning. It had taken years and several rough patches for the six friends to realize that although their relationships were constant, they were also fluid. Jackie and Donna Sue loved shopping and would sometimes disappear for days on a trip the others weren't included in. Al and Libby loved being outdoors and spent a great deal of time helping Mia in the garden or walking the trails together. Nevertheless, at times there were hurt feelings when pairs split off and someone felt left out. Over the years they had learned to trust their love for one another and not give in to petty feelings of pique.

Since Libby's news would affect them all, Anna knew it needed to be discussed and right away. She stayed up after she and Libby spoke and prepared her specialty overnight coffee cake and an egg casserole- a favorite among them all. Setting the hot dishes out on the picnic table she clanged the triangle hanging in the pavilion. It was a gift from David and the group was split between those that loved it and those that despised it. Al and Jackie popped their doors open immediately on hearing the triangle ring. They were both early risers and often enjoyed coffee outside together before any of the others emerged. Libby was up and looked like she hadn't had much sleep. Telling Anna had been a huge relief, but she still had to tell the others and worried about what they would think.

Finally, Donna Sue and Sylvie appeared. Sylvie grumbled as she opened her door to the morning sunshine,

"What is happening that can't wait until a decent hour?" she demanded.

Anna laughed and tilted up the coffee cake drizzled with white icing.

"It's worth it, there's coffee cake. And extra icing," she said. Sylvie had a terrible sweet tooth and had a special penchant for the warm cinnamony danish that oozed with sticky, white icing. As they all gathered around filling their coffee mugs and scooping up the warm egg bake, Libby looked pale and antsy.

After putting a large bite in her mouth, Jackie said, "So what's going on? With a breakfast this good the news must be monumentally bad." Anna gave Libby a long look that said go on, they'll hear you.

"Well, you know I love you all so much," started Libby.

"Come on, Gal. Cut to the chase. We're too old to beat around the bush and by this time we've heard every kind of bad news there is to hear. Out with it," said Donna Sue.

Libby, ever aware of Donna Sue's censure, used an old trick her grandmother taught her. If you feel overwhelmed by emotions and you don't want to cry, open your mouth a little and breathe deep from the diaphragm. Libby did this now and, on the exhale, she breathed out,

"I'm leaving the village. I'm going home. I'm going home to Roddy." There. She'd said it.

"Huh, that's it?" quipped Jackie. " I thought it would be something… different."

"My money was on cancer," threw in Al.

"Alzheimer's. That's what I thought. I'd take cancer over Alzheimer's," added Sylvie.

"My friend Peggy has Parkinson's so bad it's got her bent over at the waist. She can't see anyone's face, she has to look at their shoes," added Jackie. Libby looked from one friend to the other and finally rested her hands on her hips.

"I just told you I'm leaving the village and all you can do is name the top three ailments of senior citizens? Don't you care?" she sputtered.

Al stood up from her place at the table. "Of course, we care, Chicca," she said as she put her hands on both of Libby's. "But in the scheme of things, your news doesn't rank with some of the tough sentences handed down to too many people we know."

Jackie stood too and came close, "And it's not really a surprise. You've been carrying a torch for that man as long as we've known you." Sylvie struggled to her feet and joined the circle, after having both knees replaced it took a little time to work out the nighttime stiffness. "If you can have a day, a week, a year of what I had with Chip I say go for it. Hang on to him as long as you can."

Anna stood nodding and smiling her own affirmation. Libby looked at the beautiful faces of her friends and once again counted herself lucky to have these women in her life. Donna Sue was the only one who remained at the table while the others clustered around Libby. After a minute, she got up from the table and walked back to her tiny home, and shut the door. Anna gave Libby a small smile and shake of her head to let her know it was still okay. Donna Sue liked things to run according to plan. This was definitely not the plan.

Things went quickly after Libby made her decision known and in a few days her things were packed and she was waiting for Roddy to take her home. She was thinking the words, 'Irony kicked her butt' should be written on her tombstone someday. She shook her head and turned when she heard a small sound, surprised to see Donna Sue leaning against the open door. Of all the relationships, theirs was the most tenuous. There was never an open grudge or specific event that strained their relationship. Rather it had to do with each woman and how they viewed the world and themselves in it.

Donna Sue, if asked, would voice impatience when Libby didn't show up for something. She thought it was terrifically irresponsible to have friends buy a ticket or save a chair in a crowded bar for it to go unclaimed. If Libby's worst attribute was flaking out and not being present, her best asset was the flip side of that coin. Libby had an uncanny ability to connect with people on a deep level. It could be the first time you met and she could make you feel like she'd always known you. Donna Sue thought it had to do with the way Libby really paid attention to whoever she was with. She seemed to listen and attend with every fiber of her body and mind. She could make you feel like you were the only person in a crowded room. Donna Sue marveled at this trait and recognized her own tendency to hold people at arm's length. Being a more private person herself, she admired the way Libby could immerse herself in another's joy or troubles. Truth be told, she wondered if her life would have been different if she had been a little more like Libby.

Libby was always aware when she annoyed Donna Sue. She hated it when anyone, especially the goddesses, were unhappy with her and vowed to check her calendar each time she fluffed off an event. But secretly, she chafed under Donna Sue's need for organization and planning. She hated letting her friends down but Donna Sue insisted on planning things months out. Where Donna Sue seemed to be in such careful control of her life, Libby couldn't quite get the hang of that.

Where Libby didn't appreciate Donna Sue's planful nature, she did love and highly respect her confidence. In Libby's eyes, Donna Sue's ability to speak her mind with conviction, disagree courteously and leave a party if she weren't having fun were traits she wished for herself. Where Libby was afraid of saying the wrong thing, Donna Sue was able to say what she thought even if it was diametrically opposite of another's opinion. She never put anyone down for disagreeing with her, she simply knew her mind and spoke it eloquently. Where Libby worried people wouldn't like who she was or what she said, Donna Sue simply didn't. She was courteous and kind, intelligent and verbal and if you didn't like that, well, that was okay. In that way, Libby wished she were more like her statuesque friend. Now here they stood in the tiny house looking at each other.

"Listen, Gal. Are you sure this is what you want to do? If it's the money, we've got plenty. I don't want you leaving here feeling like you have to. I don't want you winding up somewhere you don't want to be," said Donna Sue.

"Oh, Donna Sue! I know it sounds crazy and IS crazy, but this is my choice. This is what I want to do. I've always been so unsure of where I belong and worried that I'm missing something by being somewhere else. You are all amazing! And this thing you're doing! It makes me so happy to think about you all being together, looking out for each other, being each other's family," said Libby.

"Now look, you're a part of this family, just the same as the rest of us," interrupted Donna Sue.

"Oh, I know! I know! But the thing is, I ran from home because I felt like if I didn't I would never know what else was out there," rushed Libby. "I mean, I had a wonderful childhood, minus the meat and gravy at every meal. My parents loved my sister and me unconditionally. They just couldn't encourage us to be anything beyond their imagination. If I'd stayed, everything would have been decided for me. So, I ran from the small town and small way of thinking. When I got to Columbia I grew up and learned a few things about this big old world. I met some amazing people and some real douchebags along the way. But then I met Anna, and Al, then you and Jackie and Sylvie."

"Our friendships have taught me everything I needed to know. I learned I could be myself, my real self when we're together. I've never felt that way with anyone else-except, it turns out, Roddy.

I'm always going to worry if I said the wrong thing or if you're mad at me because I was late but nonetheless, I can be me and that is a rare and precious gift. I know I can trust and depend on each of you with my life. You showed me through your love and support that I am valued, validated, and appreciated. I like myself thanks to you all. I just know that I missed something when I fast forwarded over Roddy. He has never given up on me and no matter what happens, he's always the first person I want to tell it to. I want to…I need to do this for me. And for Roddy."

Donna Sue looked deep into the eyes of her friend trying to detect any of her characteristic wishy washiness. All she saw was unwavering, pure light coming from within. "Okay, Gal! But you know the Goddess Rule," she said with a small smile.

"What? Nobody shushes a goddess?" asked Libby with an answering smile.

"Goddess friends are like the stars. You can't always see them but you know they are always there," said Donna Sue. The two friends fell together in a tight embrace when they heard a man's voice at the door.

"Am I interrupting something?" asked Roddy with his slow grin. At 69, he had lost the tautness of a young man's body but had the weathered edges of a real man. Working with his hands his whole life gave him strength and a confident aura. His hair was thinner and had more silver than salt. He stood with easy confidence but his eyes and brow held a question. "Am I taking you home?" he asked looking past Donna Sue to Libby.

Libby's face immediately bloomed into her beautiful smile and she said, "Yes, I'm going home." She went to him and they wrapped each other up in an embrace full of promise, commitment, and love. Before the embrace ended, Al, Sylvie, Anna and Jackie appeared. They stopped and were quiet, noticing Donna Sue wiping tears from her eyes.

"Well, dang, maybe you guys should borrow a tiny house," hooted Al.

"Yeah, you know she's going with you right? You're not saying goodbye here. This is really hello," said Sylvie.

"Mmm, I remember hellos," murmured Jackie. "No one has said hello to me like that in a really long time."

Roddy backed a half a step from Libby but didn't let her go. He ducked his head slightly. "I'd like to thank you ladies for taking care of my sweetheart all this time. I didn't worry so much about her when I knew she had all of you on her side. Lord knows you're a force to be reckoned with."

"You got that right," added Sylvie. "I pity the fool that thinks they can take us on and not have hell to pay."

Libby looked at her beautiful friends. Each of them had stood beside her, they'd held her hand or her hair. They had laughed, cried, and experienced all facets of life with her. She knew she would always be a part of these special women and she thought about their individual gifts. Jackie and her fun-loving spirit, Sylvie and her passion, Donna Sue for her certainty, Al for being their defender, and Anna, the mother who always seemed to know them best. These amazing women, her friends, now stood around her, and taking a step she joined their circle for a hug that had no clear beginning or ending, it just went on and on. Roddy stood back and marveled at the beauty of the six friends in one embrace. He was fairly certain this didn't happen every time some ladies got together for Chardonnay. There was something special about these particular women and their love for each other. Goddesses. Goddess love.

"Oh, I almost forgot," snuffled Libby. She reached to Roddy who handed her a small gift bag. "Thank you, Darling. I know this isn't goodbye but I wanted to give you all something." She reached into the small bag and pulled out a small white box for each of the goddesses. "It's just something silly I made when I was working at the Artist Guild." They each opened the box to find a ring. A ring made of six strands of fine metal, each of a different burnished hue, wound together in an artless knot. The effect was simple yet stunning. There was no way to follow one strand as it bent and melded with the others. The goddess knot. Beautiful individuals made stronger by being wound together.

Without any more words, Libby backed away until she felt Roddy's hand reaching for her. Slipping the rings onto their no longer young hands they waved goodbye as the big truck backed slowly out of the drive and away from the village.

They had barely arrived and now a tiny house sat dark and empty. The event of Libby leaving left them all with different feelings. Of course, they were happy for their friend who had always seemed in search of something. It was the fervent hope and prayer from her friends that going back where she started was the place she'd been missing all along.

After some weeks passed the conversation turned to what to do about the empty house. They all owned a fifth of it as Libby had been unable to purchase it in light of her financial problems. The possibilities ranged as they nominated candidates to fill the house, not unlike naming a new judge to the supreme court. Any new resident would be subject to intense scrutiny as to their ability to live in the peace and harmony that the goddesses enjoyed for the most part. Another suggestion was to leave it empty as a guest room for visiting family members. But it was Al who suggested the empty house be temporary housing for Christian Winslow, Mia's only full-time employee.

He'd been working with Mia off and on for years and had become indispensable to her as he was very knowledgeable about growing things and could keep all of the equipment up and running. Al, who spent a lot of time helping out at the garden, had come to see how closely and how well the two worked together. She'd made the mistake once of teasing Mia that she and Christian were like an old married couple the way they argued and toiled day in and day out. Apparently, the comment touched a nerve and Al was delegated to the farm stand for days after, her least favorite place to work.

Mia hadn't dated a lot since the fiasco in grad school. There was one guy, Bradley, who stuck around for a while. The goddesses, of course, knew he was all wrong. His sports car, preppy way of dressing, and condescending attitude towards Mia's mother and her friends were enough evidence for their conviction. Anna would always insist Mia was fully capable of knowing her own mind and heart and she'd know when she met the right one. She must have been right. Shortly after Christian started working full time, Bradley stopped coming around. In sharp contrast to Bradley's clean cut, coiffed looks, Christian looked more like a lost boy with his unruly brown curls and bushy beard. His wire-framed glasses gave him a look similar to a wizened hippie or woodsman. The ladies in the village tried to guess how old he was but had trouble deciding if he was twenty or forty. His lean physique was from eating only when he was hungry and his hands were permanently stained from axle grease and good honest dirt. His quiet friendly personality combined with the fact that he was never too busy to help a goddess with any kind of task, made him beloved in the village.

Mia would often find him sitting beside the fire or alongside the pool in the late evenings of summer when she came to enjoy some time in the village. The ladies wondered if Christian didn't come to visit them in hope he'd run into Mia. The two would enjoy a beer while listening to the goddesses tell stories although they never seemed to have a lot to say to each other. The older ladies became very fond of Christian and each of them encouraged Mia to see his attributes.

One night in particular after Christian and Mia had enjoyed a late-night dinner around the fire ring and said good night, the god-desses who may have had more than a few long necks, entertained the idea that if they were thirty years younger, they would make a play for Christian themselves.

As summer faded into fall, Al was helping Christian get the beds ready for overwintering. As she walked up the lane that wound through Mia's orchard in the crisp fall morning, she saw him climb out of his old Ford truck. Unnoticed, she watched as he stretched and then pulled the shirt off his back and reached into the cab and pulled on a different one. Coming alongside the truck she jokingly asked if he had pulled an all-nighter. Never one to draw attention to himself but honest to a fault he admitted that indeed he had. His place, more or less a shack, on a buddy's farm was barely habitable at best. With temperatures dipping below freezing at night the water in his cabin wasn't working so he slept in the truck and cleaned up in the building they processed produce in.

Al was aghast at the idea of him sleeping in the cramped cab of the truck and immediately brought Christian's plight to the attention of the goddesses. It was agreed that he could, temporarily, use the empty house until he located more suitable housing. Before he could move in, Mia arrived at the village in a tizzy. Her flannel shirt was flapping in the stiff autumn breeze as she expounded all the reasons why it was totally inappropriate for Christian to stay in the village. Sylvie and Donna Sue gave up after a bit and went to their homes, out of the wind. Jackie tried to convince Mia by telling her all the helpful things he had done around the village. Finally, Mia, Al and Anna were left to hash it out. Slowly, Al kept backing up until all three of them were in the lee of the pavilion. She kept her eyes on Mia but went about pouring three shots of their favorite tequila. She simply couldn't understand why Mia, who was the most level-headed intelligent woman, was so dead set against this idea. It was Anna who finally got to the bottom of it. They'd been standing holding their full shots when she said, "Mia, why do you not want Christian to live here with us?"

Mia looked away, took a breath, and blew it out. "Because, if he comes here, he will never want to leave. I mean, look at this place! It's perfect. He'd have dinner waiting for him every night, the pool, the hot tub, the fire, and all of you doting on him." Anna looked at her daughter and tried to see what she wasn't saying.

"And that's a problem because you want Christian to …"

"Fine! I want Christian to want to live with me! If he's here with you all I don't stand a chance," she blurted.

"Well, if that don't beat all," said Al. Anna smiled and raised her shot for the others to clink against.

"I knew you'd know it when the right one came along," she said while their glasses touched.

"Here's to you my Darling. I wish you and Christian every happiness." They all tipped back their glasses and let the lovely liquor warm their cores.

"Don't get ahead of yourself. So far, he doesn't have a clue that I've been thinking about this," warned Mia.

"Oh, I think he does," smiled Anna. "And if he doesn't, he will soon!" They all finished their drink and Mia gave Al and Anna a hug before climbing into her SUV.

The sixth house remained vacant.

Vita di Villaggio
(Life in the Village)

Twelve years. Twelve good years together in the village they dreamed up in the dark, wrestling with the reality of growing old alone. They dreamed it and thus, they created it. When the six of them first arrived, they had been a little scared but ready to embrace the future on their own terms and together. Although they loved each other there had been a real learning curve when it came to living together day in and day out. They could bend without breaking and they did when times required. There had been bumps along the way, mashed feelings, silent treatments and screaming matches-mostly done by Sylvie. But there was never a time when the relationships cracked or the plan to live together and support one another broke. Libby leaving so soon after they arrived had been a surprise but, in the end, it was clear that had been the plan all along.

Sitting in the dark listening to the quiet night sounds, Al thought back to what felt like a short time ago when the idea to sell their homes and build their own assisted living community was born on Anna's driveway. It was strange thinking of the 'birth' of their idea. With all things living, death is a natural and inevitable part. The friends looked at the end of their lives much as they had looked at every other aspect. They made their end-of-life plans, made their wishes known, and got their houses in order, so to speak. It was their intention and sincere hope to avoid the chaos associated with one's dying. They talked openly about the afterlife and shared their philosophies on soul life. Sylvie, who had always been steady in her belief in God and Heaven, was imagining a day when she and Chip would be together forever. Anna knew that Heaven was real but had a feeling it wasn't the end. She firmly believed that death in the physical world couldn't break the soul bonds she felt for the special people in her life. She wasn't exactly sure how it worked but she was confident she'd meet Tony again and most likely Al, Sylvie, Jackie, Donna Sue and Libby.

Try as she might, Al couldn't help but worry about the end and how it would affect Nathan and Marie as well as her friends. She worried about losing them as well. Worry had always been her cross to bear. She'd been offered medication by doctors years before to help her with general anxiety but she resisted taking pharmaceuticals and instead looked for more homeopathic remedies. She had tried CBD oil, the occasional gummies, and prayer, meditation, and yoga over the years. She smiled in the dark thinking of the goddesses around the pool deck with their yoga mats. In their seventies and eighties, it was a sight to be sure. They were never able to finish a session without someone letting out a big fart and the rest dissolving into giggles like so many junior high school girls. Al worried and prayed and tried to trust that there was a bigger plan.

It was true, what they say, the older one gets the faster life goes. The days and weeks seemed to flash by leaving a technicolored stream of light in its wake. Libby's empty house was never filled even though the topic came up several times over the years. Individuals were suggested, discussed, and lobbied for but no one new ever came to live in the village. Truthfully, they never found anyone they could all stand and who in turn could tolerate them.

'When I am old, I shall wear purple' was an adage with a lot of truth in it. They each had their share of eccentricities and had all along, but where they had once been filtered and inhibited, they now flourished. Certainly, the loss of filters is an advantage that should be granted to anyone over the age of seventy-five and it was safe to say any and all filters they may have had were long gone. It started with where they sat when they were together. It was never discussed, but the occasional comment of 'you're in my chair' was bandied about more than a few times. Around the fire ring, Jackie sat closest to the wood rack as she insisted on messing with the fire. Sylvie had to sit next to Anna-always. Al sat where she could keep track of everyone. Around the pool deck, they were like a bunch of Baptists, always sitting in the same lounge or chaise. Even the picnic table in their pavilion might as well have had names stenciled on the benches. They had individual strangenesses as well and they ranged from mild to pretty far out.

Donna Sue had always taken great pride in her looks and slender physique and went to great effort to maintain a certain physical standard. As she got older, she realized she would need a little more help and so began her interest in supplements. She started with Vitamin D and peptides. By the time her seventy-eighth birthday rolled around her yogurt looked more like a chemistry project than breakfast. She added dandelion oil for cholesterol, kelp for anit-oxidants, and slippery elm for inflammation. Her list of supplements was extensive and came by FedEx in huge cardboard boxes. She refused to eat anything that wasn't organic and so roasted hotdogs, one of their favorite late summer night treats, became a hard no for her. She hadn't been able to find organic wine and that along with Anna's baked goods were the only exceptions she made to her stringent eating rules.

Sylvie had always loved holidays and in years past had an extensive holiday wardrobe. She went all out with sweaters, socks and shoes for every special day, right down to her handbag. Living in a tiny house didn't allow for such a wardrobe so her holiday fetish was relegated to her small front porch and yard area. She had tchotchkes and gimcracks for every day of the year. It started innocently enough with a ceramic goose that had a different outfit for each holiday and season. But with time the goose was upstaged and was barely noticeable as more and more items were added to her holiday collections. Of course, living in a 300 square foot house she couldn't store her 'holiday collection' and enlisted her son David to be her holiday helper. She'd fix him a meal that would provide leftovers for days in exchange for him hauling in a huge tote stuffed with everything she'd need to decorate for the next special season. They'd spend the afternoon together gathering up one holiday and putting out the next. At the end of the day, David left with his foil-wrapped dinner and full tote for his garage.

In the beginning, they all enjoyed Sylvie's decorating as it was festive and got them all in the mood for whatever season was upon them. However, with the ever-increasing collection, it became a thing. Whereas they all agreed that Sylvie had every right to decorate her porch and yard as she wanted, it really started to wear on some nerves. It bothered Donna Sue the most as she had always subscribed to the less is more philosophy. Once the National Egg Day and Flag Day decor were cleared away in late June, out came the Fourth of July tote. As the friends stood admiring the red, white, and blue buntings she'd hung on her porch rail, Donna Sue suggested that perhaps the four foot Uncle Sam along with the twenty wooden rockets and umpteen small American flags was a bit much. That night Sylvie ate her dinner inside, refusing to participate in a lovely day by the pool followed by seafood salad and watermelon from the farm stand.

Although the topic was never brought up, the empty lounge chair and vacant spot at the picnic table forced Donna Sue to look at the others with a question on her face. "Come on, Gals. I can't be the only one who doesn't want to look out and see a Hallmark flea market scattered all over her yard. It's bad enough when it's the Fourth of July or Christmas but now she makes up holidays. Whoever heard of Fruitcake Toss Day or National Strawberry Shortcake Day?"

The others chuckled but Donna Sue knew she'd have to make it up to her friend. She got her chance as September rolled into October. Sylvie was anxiously awaiting a delivery and was thrilled to see the FedEx truck roll up their narrow lane. The others gathered around as she unpacked her newest and largest decoration to date-an eight foot inflated spider that clung to a web suspended from her roof. They all marveled at the picture but wondered how in the world she could get it where it was supposed to be. They all smiled appreciatively when Donna Sue volunteered to get the ladder from the pavilion and helped install the monstrosity.

Since learning about Lorna, Anna had long been fascinated with spiritual and paranormal phenomena. She spent a great deal of time researching different topics related to the spiritual realm. The latest topic to catch her attention was past life regression and she delved into it with intensity. With the help of a psychic named Beverly, Anna was able to trace numerous lives in her past. In one she lived as a servant girl in the fifteen hundreds and suffered deplorably. She went hungry often and died at the age of fifteen. In another, she was the matron of a boarding school and was responsible for nearly one hundred girls, some of whom were very small. In yet another life she was a man with a boat. The boat was home and the water provided all that he needed. Beverly's theory was that the past lives give us wisdom and guide us in our current life journey. Anna's strong maternal instinct may have come from her lives serving others and watching over them. Her comfort and ease in water were connections to her life on the boat.

Anna was so enthralled by the information she and Beverly were able to garner that she insisted Mia and the goddesses explore their own pasts. Some were hesitant and Sylvie refused outright saying it was an abomination. Al participated in several sessions and discovered she had died in Pompeii, sleeping close to her children when the molten lava from Vesuvius rushed into the city. Beverly suggested the experience could explain Al's difficulty with anxiety and sleeping. Donna Sue and Jackie discovered they had been married to one another-a discovery that neither shocked nor amazed any of them. Mia reluctantly agreed to a session just to get her mom to stop pestering her. She refused to continue after hearing that she had been Anna's mother in a previous life. Anna was fascinated by the concept and took great comfort in knowing that she and the goddesses would meet again.

Twelve years together. Nearly two years since Sylvie left them. Al's eyes filled with tears when she thought about Sylvie. She knew it was unreasonable to think she could have kept her safe or somehow known about the large blood clot forming inside her. It had been a lovely, unseasonably warm day at the end of November. They had all come out to help Sylvie and David string hundreds of Christmas lights that literally wrapped around her tiny house several times. They had laughed and worked enjoying the wintery sunshine and when darkness fell, they stood back as Sylvie did the honors and plugged in the lights. They had gasped collectively at the beauty of the hundreds of twinkling lights and proclaimed it was her best Christmas display ever. They wished one another good night and headed to the warmth of their individual homes, the twinkling lights visible from each of their windows.

Sometime in the night, Sylvie slipped away. When she didn't appear at her usual time, Al went to check on her and found her in bed in her candy cane nightgown with a small smile on her face. She'd seen the face of her Savior and with any luck at all, Chip was three steps behind. Even though they had talked at length about this event it was a harsh blow. The friends returned from the funeral home in the late winter afternoon. The thought of going into their own homes to be alone with their loss was repugnant so Jackie and Al set about laying a fire. They got blankets from the chest in the pavilion and gathered around the warmth of the blaze. At first, there was no talking. No crying. Just the crackle and pop of the fire. "If Sylvie was here, she'd say it's colder than a witches' brass brassier," said Donna Sue.

"Sylvie is here," said Anna wistfully.

"Well if she's here I'd like to tell her she left one hard act to follow. I mean dying in her sleep? Wearing her candy cane nightie? How are we supposed to top that?" said Jackie with a stab at her trademark smirk. Their weak humor was an attempt to find some familiar ground on which they could stand. No amount of preparation could ready them for the sense of loss they were feeling.

"It's times like this when we need tequila!" said Al trying to invoke the days of old when they rallied around bitter things with the help of Don Julio or Patron. The halfhearted response she got from the others didn't deter her. She went to the bar in the pavilion and brought out a beautifully wrapped foil box.

"What the hell is that?" asked Jackie.

"It's Nathan's Christmas present to us. I was saving it for a big occasion. I guess it doesn't get any bigger than this," said Al as she unwrapped the box and pulled the heavy round cork from the bottle.

"I'll get the glasses," said Anna. She returned with the special shot glasses Ellie had gifted them years earlier. The six heavy glasses, each with a name embossed in beautiful script, sat in the tray made perfectly to fit. Al handed the bottle to Donna Sue who poured all six shots. They lifted their glass and looked into the faces of their beloved friends in the flickering firelight. Before any words could be spoken Donna Sue set her glass down without any explanation. She hurried from the group as they raised their brows in question and watched her retreating form. Quickly rounding the pool deck, Donna Sue headed for the porch of Sylvie's house. In a few seconds, the whole deck was lit with hundreds of tiny Christmas lights. Returning to the circle, she reclaimed her glass. She lifted it and said, "To Sylvie, our passionate, trick playing, card sharking, holiday decorating friend. Beviamo alla nostra." They sipped from their glasses and the tearing in their eyes had nothing to do with the cold air or smooth tequila.

"Dear Sylvie, I'm happy for you in your transition home even though my heart is breaking. We will miss your beautiful smile and your enormous heart. Give our love to Chip," said Anna, taking a sip.

"To Sylvie, I love you and miss you. Thank you for being my friend," said Al as her voice broke.

"Hey Sylvie, I hope they have twinkle lights and tchotchkes in Heaven," said Jackie.

"No need-I'm confident the kilowatts from that tiny house are enough to shine all the way up there," added Donna Sue. For the first time since Al walked into Sylvie's house and discovered her, the friends threw their heads back and laughed. They drank the remainder of their shot leaving the two glasses brimful and untouched on the tray. Donna Sue put the cork back in the lovely bottle. "We better save this, we may need it again," she said. Her remark was the punctuation to a very long day. The four friends reached in and hugged each other hard before they said good night.

Life in the village was more than a little diminished without their vibrant Sicilian friend. It was by tacit agreement to continue Sylvie's holiday decorating-but only the big holidays and on a much smaller scale. They missed Sylvie dearly but continued to talk of her, to her, and live their lives as fully as they were able. Time slipped by and a year passed quickly. In the early spring, Jackie received grave news that her dear sister Sue in Florida had gotten a terrible diagnosis. After many long talks and rivers of tears, she made the decision to go and be with her until the end came. The friends gathered in the pavilion and raised their embossed glasses once again. The first toast was to Sue. The next was for Jackie.

"Jackie, I just want to say," started Al. "I love you and will be praying for you and Sweet Sue. And thank you for being- you. I can't imagine what my life would be without your joy, your laugh, your light in it." Jackie threw her curly head back and laughed.

"I'm not dead! I'm going to Florida," she said, but the smile dimmed on her dimpled face when they all thought of the reason for her journey.

"Al's right. I want you to know I love you and I'm so thankful we met all those years ago when our babies were babies and we were young and hot," said Anna. That made Jackie laugh again.

"We were, weren't we?" she said. Not knowing how long she would be away she had packed down her tiny house and had her suitcase loaded in the back of the old Cadillac ready to go to the airport. Being old apparently makes one inherently brave and the old friends didn't hesitate to say the things that needed saying. They were all aware that any given hello or a goodbye could be the last opportunity.

There was a marked change in the atmosphere with Jackie gone. Now three houses stood dark and empty. The three remaining friends spent more time together than apart. Their weeks were spent sitting in the shade of umbrellas on their pool deck or going to doctor visits for one or the other. Summer drifted into fall and the temperatures began to dip into the thirties and forties at night. It was a shock to them all when Anna slipped on the rain-slicked walkway and broke her hip and two ribs. Donna Sue and Al knew better than to try and help her up but kept her warm and as comfortable as possible until Mia and EMT workers arrived. They watched as Anna was loaded into the back of the ambulance. They heard her telling them not to worry. They saw and heard and they knew. This was a game changer. Anna would definitely recover, but it would be long and slow and with winter coming on, the village was not the place for her convalescence.

They each had some hard thinking to do but one thing was clear, a new plan was needed. A plan that most likely wouldn't be drawn on the carry-out box from Tony's Pizza Palace or involve a swimming pool or the occasional long neck beer.

After surgery to repair Anna's hip she did a short stint in Rusk Rehabilitation Center. While there, Al, Donna Sue, and Mia discussed the best place for Anna to come 'home' to when she was released from her intensive physical and occupational therapy. The remaining goddesses were loath to declare defeat but knew the village wasn't practical or safe for Anna who would be on a walker for some time. Mia cleared her office on the first floor and made a room for her mother in the farmhouse where she and Christian lived. Although the work never stopped on the farm, the cold season did give her more time at home which she used for planning for the coming season. They worked out an arrangement where Al and Donna Sue would take turns staying with Anna during the day allowing Mia to work. When Mia was finished with her day the two friends returned to the village. Mia could see how the recent events were affecting her mom and her two dear friends. They made an effort to stay chipper when talking to her and one another but the reality of the changes in their situation was stamped visibly on each of their faces. Mia knew that Al especially was concerned about their situation and the village itself. The fact that it took up space on Mia's farm, and that it was mostly vacant with the probability of getting more vacant in the near future was a worry. She and Mia spent many an afternoon over mugs of tea discussing the village, the garden, and the future.

Of course, they stayed in touch with Jackie daily, keeping her in the loop of Anna's recovery and Sue's condition. They were heartened to learn that she was responding to treatments and was fairly pain-free. Jackie wished there was a way they could all come to Florida where the winter weather was warm and sunny and the salty air was restorative. They talked about it wistfully but knew there was a snowball's chance in Florida of that happening.

As it happened more times than not, both Donna Sue and Al were sitting with Anna on a particularly bleak winter day in Mia's kitchen. The heavy clouds hung just above the trees and by midafternoon there was so little light it was as if dusk had fallen early. Too cold to snow, the barren landscape offered nothing but monochromatic shapes. Anna was well aware of the winter doldrums they were all suffering from due to the grim weather, among other things. She kept looking at Donna Sue as Al was telling her about one of the newest youths helping Mia at the bistro.

For years, Mia had been hiring young people who were challenged by the mores of society. Some of them had been in trouble with the law, some of them had terrible family histories or no support system at all. Mia had a connection at an outreach organization and tried to employ these young people. Al, who had always been active and involved with the farm, took a huge interest in these young people and got to know them. She admired Mia for giving them a chance to work and more importantly, a vote of confidence. When it was clear that neither Donna Sue nor Anna was listening to her story Al's voice trailed off.

She looked at Anna who was studying Donna Sue as she stood staring out the window. "And then he lit his hair on fire," finished Al in the same tone of voice she had been telling her original story in. Donna Sue didn't stir, obviously a thousand miles away. Anna turned her look to Al and apologized.

"I'm sorry, Al. I was trying to listen to both of you. I'm afraid I didn't get all of that," she said. Al looked from one friend to the other. Donna Sue had yet to turn from the window and hadn't uttered more than three words since they sat down with their tea. "What is it, Donna Sue?" At the sound of her name, Donna Sue did turn her head from the window. At eighty she was still strikingly beautiful. The lines and wrinkles on her face drew attention to her eyes and mouth. Her platinum hair still framed her face much as it did forty years ago and her slender frame belied the fact that she was an octogenarian.

"Hmm? Oh, nothing. I was just thinking," she said.

"About what?" pressed Anna. "I can tell there's something, what is it?"

"Oh, you know it's just this awful winter weather. I'm missing the sunshine and feeling warm. Seems the older I get, the cold gets inside me no matter how many layers of Cuddle Duds I wear," mused Donna Sue.

"What else?" continued Anna.

"Nothing else. I'm fine. I was just thinking about Jackie and Florida…"

"You need to go to Florida!" said Anna with certainty when Donna Sue began shaking her head. "Yes, that's what it is. You're cold and sad. Go to Florida. Be with Jackie and help her with Sue. She'll be there alone when Sue's battle is over and she'll need help. She'll need you. I have Mia and Christian and Al."

Donna Sue tried to interrupt but Anna, ever the maternal goddess, wouldn't let her. "Who knows what comes next. There was a time in our lives when we needed the village. That time may or may not be over. We'll just have to wait and see. You've always believed that things happen for a reason. We built the village, the place, to help each other live to the fullest but really, we are the village. Whether it's in a tiny house or a sandy beach, it's our love for each other that has sustained us. Jackie needs you. Sue needs you. Go to Florida. Warm up and find your smile," said Anna with a warm smile and glittering eyes. Donna Sue's and Al's eyes were brimming with tears as well and it was decided.

Anna and Mia tried to convince Al to stay with them in the farmhouse instead of returning to the village where only one porch light shone. She loved them for the concern, but felt strongly that someone should be in the village and make sure everything there was as it should be.

"I just don't like the idea of you being there all alone," said Mia one night as Al was gathering her things to leave. "Don't you know someone who would want to come and stay with you until Mom can come back?"

Al paused as she shrugged into her warm coat. "Maybe I do," she said. Mia raised her eyebrows and waited. "I was thinking about Masie and Marquita. They've worked for you for almost a year now. They are good kids who got a crap deal from their families, school, and life. What if they moved into the village? They could work more hours and finish their community service stuff without ever having to leave the farm. I'd be there to chaperone."

Mia crossed her arms over her chest and narrowed her eyes at Al. Giving work and allowing community service kids to work off their hours was one thing. Housing them, being responsible for them 24/7 was something else altogether. "You think on it. I'll be back in the morning," said Al without a trace of the worry lines that were usually stamped on her forehead. Mia felt a little like she had all those years ago when Al, the protector, had held off her drug-crazed boyfriend with a paintball gun and spouted lines straight out of a Dirty Harry movie. She hadn't flinched and had been so sure that everything was going to turn out alright that night. Maybe this new idea could turn out right too. With some carefully drawn-up guidelines, she could see how the tiny house village could be an ideal situation for the right young people who were looking for a little help getting their lives on track. They just needed a place to do it and some support. Mia couldn't help but see the strong parallels to the original village and the genius of this new idea. She felt a certain sense of right-ness that this was what was supposed to happen next. How many times as she was growing up did she go to one goddess or another with her broken heart, fears, and worries? She asked for advice and looked for affirmation from them all. She could hear Donna Sue's voice in her head, "I know you're hurting Gal, just remember that everything happens for a reason." Mia went to find Christian and get his thoughts on this new plan for the village.

Final Chapter

Anna leaned on her walking stick and walked carefully around the edge of the pool. At eighty-three there were certain words she refrained from using; cane was one of them along with elderly and senior citizen. "We're experienced," she'd say to Al.

"Seasoned," Al would reply. "Really, really well seasoned." Anna delighted in the warm temperature of the late spring afternoon and was anticipating the day when the pool would be warm enough to float in. She was happy to be spending the afternoon in the village and watched as the two young women carried their things into their new home. There was no heavy lifting and very little to carry. They had few possessions, making it seem as if the tiny house village had been built with them in mind when the opposite had been true. When the goddesses arrived, they had forty-plus years of beautiful furnishings and happy memories they had been forced to let go of. Anna was struck by the contrast between the two women moving in today and wondered what unseen things they may be letting go of. Hearing one of them, she thought it was Masie, let out a string of expletives when she forgot to duck under the staircase for the third or fourth time made Anna chuckle.

She thought about Jackie and her potty mouth. Sylvie was always after her to clean up her language. Even though she was the most passionate of them all, Sylvie rarely cussed and depended on sheer volume, a few choice Sicilian epitaphs, and lots of hand gestures to let them know she was upset. The only time Anna could recall Sylvie cutting loose with her language was that awful day in the cemetery. Anna was swept away in a reverie where she could hear Sylvie shouting and Jackie's ringing laugh. Her attention was drawn back to the present as Masie came stumbling out rubbing her forehead. She caught Anna's gaze and cut her eyes to the ground. The two young women were appreciative of their new living arrangement to be sure but were uncertain about the two old ladies, one of which was their bosses' mother, and how they were to act around them. Anna gave her a small smile. "It took us a while to get used to the houses too. Donna Sue was 5'10" when we moved in and cracked her head more times than we could count. She spent the majority of the time bent over just for that reason. I bet if we measured her now, she'd only be 5'8"". Masie rubbed the red spot on her forehead and came closer to where Anna's chair was in the sun.

"So, there were six of you when you moved here?" she asked hesitantly not wanting to do or say anything that could potentially mess up their arrangement with Mia.

Marquita had finished moving her few bags and ambled over near the conversation. She was more hesitant to talk to the older women fearing she had nothing in common with them. She and Masie had made unlikely friends working at the bistro. Their backgrounds couldn't have been more different. The only thing they had in common was finding Mia and the village.

"Yes," answered Anna, warming to the conversation. "Six beautiful friends."

"Why did y'all come all the way out here? You come out here to die?" blurted Marquita.

Masie was embarrassed at Marquita's blunt remark and added, "Yeah, it's a little ways out here. I would have thought ladies like you would move to the Country Club or some fancy senior community." Her unruly blond mane and delft blue eyes were a sharp contrast to the tattoos on her neck and the sleeves up both arms. Anna understood from Al that Masie came from money. She could also see the hurt the young woman tried to cover with tattoos and skimpy clothing. If Mia and Al's plan worked, it would be vastly beneficial to all involved. Mia offered work and housing for young women seeking a way out of their current situation. Although Mia had talked to several applicants from the outreach center, there were three that passed her personal screening and were offered the chance to come to Edgewood Village to live. A tiny house was theirs to live in. They could use the pool and pavilion as long as they were respectful of the two old women who lived there, one of them being Mia's mother. The pay was small as living on the property and getting one meal a day provided by the bistro was part of the deal. Anna wondered what made these young women 'right' and thought again that surely Mia had inherited her 'shine' as Libby had called it.

"Did we come here to die?" mused Anna nonplussed by the question.

"We came here because we wanted to be independent but not alone. We wanted to decide what we did all day and all night without rules. We wanted to choose what food we ate without restrictions. We wanted to keep on living and this was the best thing we could come up with."

"And we wanted a pool," added Al as she joined them on the deck.

"Exactly right! We wanted a pool and a party deck and that beautiful fire pit. We found out our need for lots of things got replaced with wanting to be surrounded by friends. I think as you get older the idea of simplifying becomes more attractive. No, my dear. The answer to your question is that we came here to live," finished Anna.

Al knew a little of Marquita's story too. "Besides, you and I both know there are things worse than dying." Marquita's eyes never dropped but her chin lifted slightly to acknowledge Al's remark. "We had lots of good times here. And yes, this is where our dear friend Sylvie breathed her last but we were here for her and we were here for each other."

"Sylvie wasn't afraid. Death is natural. And I have it on good authority that she is happy across the veil," added Anna. Marquita and Masie shared a look over the old woman's head. They'd heard that one of the old ladies talked to the dead or something of that nature.

"Anyway, the point is that we knew the road we were on and where it would end for us all eventually. We knew we couldn't do it on our own so we figured out a way to make it work but in our own style," explained Al.

"Goddess style," added Anna.

Anna stood slowly and got her walking stick positioned in her hand. She loved spending time in the village but the early spring sun was waning and the temperature was dropping. Al would drive her back to Mia and Christian's. As she began her slow progress toward the driveway she turned and looked steadily at the two young women. "I sincerely hope you two will support each other during whatever time you have here in the village. There is no love like goddess love." She turned back to Al who helped her over the gravel. Masie and Marquita watched as one old lady helped another old lady into the car. They heard them both laugh out loud before the doors closed and the car pulled away.

"Goddess love? What the hell is that?" asked Marquita.

"No idea," said Masie. "But if they want to let us live here, I'll give it a try. Whatever it is."

"Yeah, okay. Whatever," repeated Marquita as the two turned into their own tiny house. For Marquita, the tiny house was the most luxurious living arrangement she'd ever experienced. Growing up in the projects, there were always too many people crammed into too small a space. Sharing a clean place with one tatooed white girl was a step up from her most recent living situation.

Yesenia moved into her tiny house a few days before Jackie and Donna Sue came for the summer. They timed their visit purposefully to skip the unreliable spring weather and waited until the pool was open and the summer nights were perfect for sitting out under the stars. Sweet Sue left the beach condo to Jackie and she and Donna Sue had forsaken the Missouri winters and taken up semi-permanent residence, returning to the village for June, July, August, and September. The new tenants didn't know what to expect when the old Caddy came up the gravel lane a little too fast with the horn blaring. The young women came out of their houses slowly, watching as two old women climbed out of the Cadillac. The driver was tall, dressed in a turquoise sundress that held on at her collarbone and fell away effortlessly in soft folds to just above her knees. Her skin was tanned to a honey glow and although wrinkled, was supple and soft looking. She was long and lean and had no trace of extra anywhere. The cleft in her chin and her steely blue eyes made her striking to look at. The laugh lines around her eyes were well worn, something she had decided not to have worked on. The passenger was shorter and dressed in black cigarette pants and a zebra print top. Her hair was shoulder-length corkscrew curls that were mostly gray with a bit of tawny brown mixed in. Upon spying the three young women standing awkwardly by the pool, her face split into a huge grin creating deep dimples in her cheeks. She immediately raised her hand to wave, setting the forty to fifty bangles on her wrist to jangling.

"Hey ladies! How about helping a couple of old broads with these bags?" she called. "And where's the rest of the gang?" The door to Al's house opened and she came out carrying a tray with a glass pitcher that looked like iced tea.

"Welcome home!" she called as she set the tray down and went to hug the new arrivals. "Oh, my word you look amazing Donna Sue! You'll have to show me where the cut marks are," she said as she laughed. "And Jackie! Welcome home! I can't believe you're here! I didn't sleep a wink last night thinking about you. Where did you find those pants? They're to die for!" By the time the three had had two-way hugs of all combinations and then a three-way hug, Anna had made it all the way to meet them. She'd graduated from a wheelchair to a walker to a cane and as long as she paid close attention to where her feet were, she did a fine job getting around. She and Jackie grabbed each other's arms and didn't say any words for a bit. They just held on and breathed in the other. Finally, they slid back a bit and the smile that lit their faces was brighter than Sylvie's Christmas lights.

"It's been a long, long winter. I can't tell you how glad I am to see you," she said. Then she turned her attention to Donna Sue who had waited quietly for her turn to greet Anna. When they'd last seen each other, Anna had limited mobility and was receiving physical therapy following hip surgery. To see her standing in the middle of their pool deck, in their village with her warm brown eyes that had always been able to see more than most wanted to show, moved Donna Sue to tears. She stepped close and wrapped her arms around her dear friend. The young women carrying the enormous bags stood awkwardly to the side. This wasn't just some old ladies saying hello. This was more than that. There was definitely joy in seeing each other and it was clear that they loved one another but there was something else that was even bigger. They seemed so grateful, so relieved to be together. It was as if the universe was able to exhale a sigh of relief over this small feat.

"Good grief, we've buried people and lost kingdoms without this many waterworks. We're getting hysterical in our latter years," Al grumbled good-naturedly as she moved over to the tray and pitcher she'd brought out. "Ladies, refreshments are served." Marquita and Yesinia were rolling the big cases to the houses they knew belonged to the newcomers but stopped in their tracks when they heard Al. "Ladies! That includes you. Come over and get properly introduced." Al proceeded to pour drinks and the young women shuffled over. Jackie moved over on the chaise lounge that had always been her spot and patted the cushion beside her for Masie. The young woman sat beside her and marveled at the stylish woman and her outright friendliness. "I want to raise a glass to welcome home our friends Donna Sue and Jackie and welcome our new friends, Masie, Marquita, and Yesenia to Edgewood Village," said Al. They all tipped their iced drinks up and took an appreciative sip. Marquita pulled her glass away looking at the contents.

"What is this?" she asked.

"Tequila," said Yesenia. Being the newest person to work for Mia and move into a tiny house she hadn't said much at all to anyone. She ducked her head and said, "I mean it tastes like tequila."

"Tea-quila," replied Jackie. "We invented it about one hundred fifty years ago. Iced tea, tequila, and fresh lime juice. Great on a hot summer day," she said with a laugh showing her dimples again.

"We used to drink it on any day that ended with 'y'," mused Donna Sue.

"I tamed it down a bit in light of the number of pharmaceuticals some of us are on, but I thought it wouldn't be a rightful homecoming without it," said Al. The young women exchanged some raised eyebrows as they enjoyed their cocktail. These old women were not what they had expected. In fact, they were a huge mystery and a surprise to them. The conversation swirled around as they caught up on all the events they'd missed out on in the intervening months. News of children, grandchildren, illnesses, and deaths was shared. When the pitcher was empty, the old ladies needed a 'lie down' before dinner. Kisses and hugs were once again exchanged and an 8:00 dinner time was agreed on. They made their way to their respective homes. Masie helped wheel the big case to Jackie's door. As she turned to leave, Jackie stopped her.

"Tonight I want to hear all about what you beauties think of our village and what kind of hopes and dreams you have. Lord knows, this is the place where they can grow," she said as she closed the door leaving the young woman thinking about her hopes and dreams and wondering if she still had any.

At 7:30 the sun had gentled and the little kabuki lights were turned on around the pool. Al had the big grill lit and the smell of burning charcoal was like a heady perfume for the young summer night. Masie had spent the day floating on a raft while Marquita sat waist-deep on the steps. Not knowing how to swim, she didn't own a swimming suit so made do with her sports bra and shorts. They hadn't seen Yesenia since cocktails but she was still getting used to everyone and seemed shy. When Anna opened her door, she called to Marquita. The young woman wrapped a towel around her hips and went to the door where Anna handed her a huge tray of fresh vegetables sliced in slabs and drizzled with olive oil and seasonings. Marquita carried it carefully over to the pavilion and noticed that Al had changed from her garden uniform of a button up cotton blouse and utility shorts for a soft t-shirt dress in sage green. She had on earrings and possibly even some make-up. She'd taken her hair out of its usual knot and used a colorful scarf as a headband.

"Thank you Chicca," she said as she scraped the grill with the wire brush. "Set them there on the table. I hope you're hungry! We're eating well tonight." Marquita set the vegetables next to a platter of the strangest looking steaks she'd ever seen. It wasn't like she could be choosy if they wanted to cook steak for everyone far be it for her to complain about what they looked like. She could count the times she'd had steak on one hand so really, she was no expert.

She passed Anna as she settled in her favorite chair and continued on to her house. She didn't have any dressy clothes but at least she could put on a clean shirt and maybe do something with her hair which she had let go natural. Rejoining the group, she noticed that even Masie had 'dressed' for dinner in something a bit more covered than she usually preferred. As far as Marquita could tell the girl loved tattoos and loved showing all of them to everyone. Tonight, she was wearing short shorts but her top covered her mid-section and Marquita wondered if it was out of respect for the old ladies. Donna Sue emerged in a white jumpsuit looking like a movie star. Her looks weren't fussy or overdone but had an ease and an elegance that Marquita guessed cost a whole lot of money. Jackie appeared in linen slacks and a silk t-shirt, bangles still jangling on her wrist. Finally, Yesenia emerged from her house wearing a simple jersey skirt and blouse. She looked very different with her hair down around her shoulders. She carried a dish to the pavilion and said shyly, "It's only rice but my mother always say you don't go to a party empty-handed."

"That is so sweet of you and rice will go perfectly with dinner," said Anna warmly. She'd been trying to engage Yesenia in conversation in the few days she'd been in the village but hadn't had much luck. A good old goddess cookout may be just the thing to help the young woman feel more comfortable and at ease.

"It's actually more like dessert," said Yesenia looking down. "When I was little we didn't have much but we always had rice and beans. I learned to fix the rice for my brothers and sisters as a treat for after dinner. If you don't like it, I can take it back…"

"That sounds perfect," said Donna Sue. "This will be just what we need to complete this amazing meal Al is cooking!"

"Al IS cooking so who is in charge of the cooler?" asked Al wielding a pair of tongs.

"The cooler?" asked Jackie with the beginning of a huge grin. "Don't tell me you loaded the cooler!"

"We could all be dead before morning and I wasn't taking any chances so YES I loaded the cooler," explained Al. Anna clapped her hands and laughed. Donna Sue threw the lid up on the old blue cooler loaded to the top with ice.

"That is a beautiful sight!" she said as she reached down into the ice and pulled up a long-neck bottle of beer. Masie and Marquita didn't know what they were expecting but the beer wasn't even close. And it wasn't some fancy import or froo-froo craft beer. No, straight up Miller Lite. By the cheers and clapping from the old ladies you'd thought it was Cristal 2008. They each took one and continued to watch the old ladies salute in unison and say, 'Beviamo Alla Nostra.'

The young women didn't know what it meant but they all tipped their bottles up and took a long pull.

"To Sylvie," said Al and they all repeated her toast and drank.

"To Libby," said Jackie and the process was repeated.

"To goddesses everywhere," said Anna. "May their crowns hold many jewels and their hearts be full of love and light." Masie gave Yesenia a smile at her confused look and Al went back to the grill as the others found their places around the picnic table.

"Okay, come and get it before I throw it to the hogs," said Al bringing the platters to the picnic table. They all began reaching across for the serving utensils. In addition to the grilled zucchini, tomatoes, onions and mushroom there was a fresh lettuce salad dressed in a bright lemon vinaigrette to go alongside the steaks. Everyone put food on their plates and began eating although the conversations never stopped. Marquita was hesitant about the vegetables having never tried zucchini and never had heard of cooking them on a grill. She started with the steak. Putting the first bite into her mouth she chewed slowly with a strange look on her face. If she hadn't been sitting with the old ladies, she would have spit it out on her plate.

"Marquita, do you like the tuna steak?" asked Al.

"Tuna? That's a fish. This ain't no fish," she said.

"It is fish. We brought some fresh tuna steaks from Florida," said Jackie. "Miss Thing," she nodded at Donna Sue, "won't eat red meat and I'm a carnivore so tuna steaks, salmon filets, and grouper are our meat group." Marquita looked dumbfounded at the thick piece of medium-rare meat on her plate. Her brain was having a difficult time processing the fact that this wasn't red meat but fish instead. Who knew it could taste like that? She took another small bite and began to nod her head. It was really very delicious. She smiled for the first time at the ladies around the table and that got another cheer from everyone. When they had all cleaned their plates, Jackie brought Yesenia's rice dish to the table. Yesenia looked at her hands in her lap. Small bowls were passed around and everyone took small experimental bites.

"Oh my! This is wonderful," said Donna Sue.

"What is in this?" asked Anna as she ate another bite.

All around the table everyone was scraping the sides of their bowls and exclaiming about the dessert.

Yesenia smiled and explained it was rice, dulce leche, pineapple, and strawberries. She was pleased that they liked it and felt happy to be sitting at the table. As the amazing meal finished; dishes were stacked on the table. Jackie helped Anna stand and continued to hold her arm as they found more comfortable seats around the pool deck. The soft glow of the kabuki lights and the evening sounds of the country cast a spell around the small village. Masie had an eerie feeling she was in a dream yet fully awake. Marquita began to gather the silverware when Donna Sue stepped close to her. She leaned her head close to one shoulder and looked at Marquita out of the side of her clear eyes.

"Those can wait, Gal. The night is young like you. Let's go enjoy life while we can." Marquita's eyes got wide but she couldn't resist the stately woman with the white-blond hair and followed her silently out to the circle of chairs.

Masie had once again curled up at the end of Jackie's chaise. Yesenia, feeling a bit braver after her success at dinner, sat next to Al. The seat next to Anna remained empty and throughout the evening, she would turn her attention to it from time to time as though listening for a comment. Donna Sue and Marquita found their places and listened while Al explained about the new specialty garlic she and Christian were planning for the fall. It was clear Mia's business was a growing success. They were all so proud of her and her vision and a little bit proud of the fact that they had helped in small ways. Soon the conversations turned to other topics including the story of two businessmen who tried to pick Jackie up in the airport.

"I swear, I was away for five minutes and she's got one bozo pulling her case and the other one trying to figure out what gate she needed," said Donna Sue dryly. Jackie's resounding laugh was full of mirth.

"I can't help it if they thought I looked helpless. I was going to convince them I needed help right up to the martini bar before you blasted them with your full on Donna Sue stare down," she laughed. "A girl's got to have a little fun."

"Woo-wee! We did have some fun didn't we?" agreed Anna.

"I'll say. I almost got divorced because Mack thought we were all out 'trolling for men.' Hell, we spent as much time beating the guys away as we did on our hair and makeup. When I finally explained to him that we had absolutely no interest in looking for or finding men he started to understand us. That's when he called us a bunch of goddamn goddesses getting gussied up for each other," said Al.

"Do you remember the time we danced on the dry bar at Deja Vu?" laughed Jackie. Masie had heard of the old dance club in the heart of downtown. It was known for having multiple dance floors and a comedy club upstairs. It was the most happening place on or off campus and in a college town that's quite a title.

Al laughed, "Do I? That was Anna's 50th. We got dressed to the nines, had drinks at The Heidelberg, dinner at Murry's and no one was ready to go home. The only thing Anna said she wanted for her birthday was to go dancing so we hit the doors of Deja Vu like Charlie's Angels."

"More like Hell's Angels," murmured Donna Sue. "We were cool until that crazy song came on and the next thing I knew I was hoisting Jackie onto the dry bar. I couldn't believe it when Anna wanted up too. After that it was all or nothing. We were all up there shaking our classy asses to Mustang Sally and having the time of our lives." They were all laughing, the old women at their own ridiculousness, and the young women for thinking of women older than their mothers, dressed up and dancing on the bar in the biggest club in town.

"It might have ended differently if we hadn't seen the kids staring at us like they'd seen some unholy ghost," said Al.

"Wait, what? Whose kids?" asked Masie, still trying to picture her mother dancing, let alone on the dry bar of a dance club.

"Anna's Ellie, Jackie's son Seb, and my Nathan were out with friends. They were on the upper dance floor when they noticed us," said Al sheepishly.

"Noticed us? They made a scene trying to pull us down and almost caused a riot. Turns out some of the crowd had an appreciation for 'classic women' and didn't want to see our number cut short," explained Donna Sue.

Jackie was laughing so hard she snorted, "By the time the bouncers came over Nathan was chest to chest with some big football player who was making some very specific comments as to our accouterments."

"Luckily, we all got out of there and Nathan didn't have to defend my honor. It's a good thing too, that big boy would have pounded him into dust. It took weeks before he would look at me and he refused to talk about it. He's a little more like his dad than he realizes. I guess he never considered I could be anything else besides his mom," mused Al.

"That's the secret," said Anna with a knowing smile. "You young beauties will discover that the important people in your life all need things from you. Mia needs you to be a good employee; hardworking and responsible to keep your job and her business going. Your families require other things from you. And as you get older those requirements evolve and change too." Masie couldn't maintain eye contact and looked away. "If you are lucky to find a mate and I hope you are, you will constantly need to compromise to keep that relationship alive. It's wonderful to share your life with someone but it takes a lot of effort and a willingness to alter your own idea of what happiness is. But when you find friends, true friends, you can be the real you without having to filter yourself or compromise the real you. As long as you love your friends and they love you, you can be your true self with no filter, no mask."

The circle was quiet after Anna's words. The goddesses thinking about the reverence and the rightness of the words, the younger women wondering at the very possibility of such a thing. The hilarity of the earlier conversation was replaced with a solemn feeling that was soft and warm without being heavy. Jackie struggled to get out of the chaise while singing an old Willy Nelson tune, 'Turn out the lights, the party's over'. Masie helped her up and was surprised when the old woman pulled her in for a tight hug. It has been a long time since anyone had held her and she stood still and concentrated on not melting into Jackie. Other hugs were shared and Donna Sue noticed how Marquita stood behind her chair placing a barrier between herself and the others.

"Good night my goddesses and beauties," said Anna as Donna Sue took her arm to help her to her tiny house. "It's another day tomorrow, God willing and the creek don't rise."

The goddesses fell into a familiar and gentle rhythm, emerging from their homes mid morning to enjoy the sunshine and the pool. With the help of the handrail, Anna was able to go down the four steps to her float. Mia had found one that was more like a recliner and easier to get off and on than the old cheapies they used to buy at the dollar store. After her fall, the thing Anna fretted the most over the long dark winter was if she'd be able to maneuver herself into the pool. Her doctor was surprised when she began asking how soon she could start using her pool. He was completely supportive when he heard that she swam at least a mile in laps every day and thought it would be wonderful therapy for strengthening her hip.

While Anna did laps, Jackie and Donna Sue soaked in the sun on the deck. Jackie's red bikini from earlier days was replaced by a one-piece that appeared to wrap around her making her waist look tiny and her boobs look big. Even in the pool, she was never without her jewelry, bracelets, toe rings and pendants made her even more glamorous. Her only acknowledgement of being an octogenarian was a wide floppy hat made of straw to keep the sun off her face. Donna Sue was still a show stopper in her two-piece. Of course, it wasn't the two-piece of days gone by or even twenty years ago. The white shorts came to her belly button leaving only two inches of midriff exposed between the top and the bottom. Her long lean legs looked amazing for a woman her age and she kept them coated in sunscreen, something she wouldn't have dreamed of doing thirty years ago.

They talked lugubriously watching Anna do her slow but perfect crawl back and forth. Eventually she joined them on her own float. When the early afternoon sun got too hot they'd climb out, dry off, and head to their own sanctuaries for some quiet time. Al worked in the garden each morning. There were a lot of things she didn't feel like doing anymore but she still preferred to be outside rather than work in the roadside market or bistro. She hitched a ride with the beauties every morning and often walked the half-mile home if Christian was too busy to give her a ride on the ATV. All the sunshine and physical work had kept her body lean and strong. Her honey brown hair was mostly gray but her face was still freckled and her nose was perpetually red from the sun. She'd always hated the short bob she'd worn for years and had let her hair grow until it was past her shoulder blades, the longest it had been in her entire life. Most always she had it twisted up in a small knot that left little tendrils around her face and neck. Back at the village, she'd get a cool shower and have a rest. The four goddesses would meet up in pool attire around 4:00 and enjoy floating, sunning, and drinking iced tea minus the tequila.

Dinner was usually around 7:30 and although casual, the goddesses always 'dressed'. The young women were always included in the evening meal if they weren't working a shift at the Bistro. They too had gotten in the habit of dolling up just a little before joining the old friends in the pavilion. The evening meal always consisted of whatever was fresh from the garden. Their dinner plates were always heaped with fresh greens and vegetables leaving a little room for a piece of fish or some grilled seafood. Marquita had to admit, she'd never enjoyed eating vegetables so much in her life. Hell, she'd never enjoyed eating this much. Everything tasted so good! She didn't know if it was the freshness of what they ate, the fact that she was doing physical work in the garden, or the way the old ladies cooked. She began helping whoever was preparing dinner and the goddesses noticed her attentiveness and willingness to learn. They delighted in sharing their secrets for salad dressings and marinades and felt sorry there had been no one in Marquita's history to show her how to prepare food. After all, food was love. Where had Marquita known love?

Yesenia was a talented cook and although still reserved around all of them, she contributed side dishes and made suggestions when the goddesses were discussing meals. Al mentioned Yesenia's talent to Mia thinking she may be better in the kitchen at the Bistro instead of working as a server. Of all the goddesses, Al spent the most time working for Mia and refused to take anything but fresh produce for her efforts. They had a solid relationship and had come up with the concept of bringing the young women to live in the village together. As much as Mia appreciated the time Al spent working, her ideas and insights were even more appreciated.

Occasionally, Mia joined the group at the village for a late afternoon swim and dinner. On one particular night, Marquita was working but Masie, Yesenia, and the goddesses had once again enjoyed a delicious dinner of fresh tomato and mozzarella salads along with some white fish cooked with lemon pepper and capers. Mia had brought a couple of bottles of a lovely pinot grigio and everyone was enjoying the twilight and the crisp white wine. The mozzarella salad reminded Al of The Pasta Factory and they all enjoyed reminiscing about the lovely brick courtyard where they used to enjoy wine and bread dipped in olive oil before their meals. Jackie brought up a particular evening they had stayed longer and enjoyed the lovely fare at the restaurant when it occurred to one of them to visit the catacombs.

"Catacombs? What's that? Was it a club?" asked Masie.

"Don't tell me you all went to the catacombs," said Mia with raised eyebrows.

"Not all of us. Sylvie opted out," said Donna Sue.

"Boy was she mad at us too," said Al. "She didn't speak to us for a week."

"When did you all go to the catacombs? How old was I?" asked Mia.

"Oh, you were home with dad and Ellie. You were probably eight or nine," explained Anna.

"So you went to this place too?" asked Masie to Mia.

"No! I never went there. I only heard about it and I can't believe my mother went there," said Mia, sounding like a little girl instead of a woman in her fifties.

"Was it like male strippers or something? It sounds pretty crazy," laughed Masie.

"No nothing like that. We didn't have any interest in male strippers. It was just a place downtown," began Anna.

"Where people smoked pot and did all kinds of drugs," finished Mia.

"It wasn't that bad," said Anna. "It was a bunch of musicians and artists under an old textile manufacturer next to the city bus station. People went there to play music or read original poetry. Just hang out."

"And buy and use drugs," continued Mia in disbelief.

"You don't know because you were never there," said Anna gently.

"Right! Because Dad and Ellie both warned me never to go there. You had to know the secret knock and all kinds of craziness," said Mia.

"There was something about the knock," said Jackie thoughtfully. "Seems like we had some trouble getting in and had to call Tony."

"Yes, I remember. He told us the way to get in was a certain knock and a particular name. Once we were in, the door person just waved us on and we didn't know where to go. The building was huge and full of old sewing machines. We found a door but it was a bathroom. We had Tony on the phone trying to figure out where to go. I know he thought we were ridiculous and kept telling Anna to get out of there. While she was reassuring Tony that we were okay I noticed another door in the bathroom. That door led to the stairs and down we went. We didn't bring anything to drink and there was no bar. Some guy offered to let us ride along with him on a beer run. Tony overheard him through the phone and went crazy! He was screaming at us not to go with anyone," laughed Donna Sue.

"I was scared to death," said Al. "I'd never smoked pot or been in a place like that. It was so…illicit. I just remember being fascinated and excited by the whole thing."

"It didn't take long before Donna Sue and Jackie had attracted the attention of some friendly young men. They offered to share their marijuana cigarette with us," mused Anna.

"And here was dumb me," laughed Al. "I had no idea what I was doing with this weird metal cigarette and when it came to me, I put the wrong end in my mouth." This got big laughs from everyone and even Yesenia ducked her head and covered her mouth. "Thank goodness for Libby. She just took it and passed it on and said 'you're too cool for that.'

"So, what happened?" asked Masie once again, amazed at these old women who seemed to have lived a much different life than the one she assumed.

"Nothing. We listened to the music and chatted a while then we left," said Anna.

"I can't believe you guys! I can't picture my mom going to Hooters much less an illegal drug den," said Masie.

"It wasn't a terrible place. No one got hurt there that I know of," said Anna.

"You could have been hurt if anyone would have caught you there," said Mia forcefully. "Principal of an elementary school, Al, a teacher! You could have lost your jobs!"

"That's just it Gal," said Donna Sue. "By ourselves, we would never have gone to the catacombs but together we were safe and we had the freedom to experience it without fear of judgment. Going there was like letting go of all of our titles and responsibilities as wives, mothers, professionals. And it was only a few hours. We were glad we went and we were glad when it was time to go back to our real world," said Donna Sue evenly.

"Oh my gosh! I still can't believe you'd go to a place like that!" said Mia, still worked up about it.

"Well, there's really no limit to the places we can and will go when we're together. Our combined heart and courage gives us the strength we lack on our own. Sometimes it's to explore things we'd never do otherwise and sometimes it's because someone we love needs us," said Jackie. The look that passed between Anna and Mia was not missed by the two young women. The tension in the air crackled.

Thinking back to the night they roared up to a trailer house in the wee hours of the morning to rescue Mia had all the goddesses quiet for a moment. This wasn't the night for that story and it was Mia's story to tell if she so wanted. Anna said, "We only did what we had to do that night."

"What night? What happened?" pressed Masie.

Anna was not going to tell the story of saving Mia so instead she said, "Well sometimes you have to go places you hoped you'd never be to help someone get out." Masie watched the laden glances all around the circle. Mia looked down, her previous upset at her mom forgotten. Masie didn't know what happened but was definitely picking up that something big had happened that involved Mia and the old ladies.

Suddenly, Yesenia was crying. Al made her way over to stand beside the young woman who was racked with sobs as they all looked on. "What is it?" asked Al as she tenderly pushed the long black hair behind Yesenia's ear.

"It's…my…baby" she gasped between sobs. All eyes swept the circle trying to see if anyone understood what she was crying about.

"Yesenia, you are safe. Take a deep breath. Breath with me. Tell us what you are upset about," said Al using her teacher's voice. The young woman tried to calm her breathing as Al continued to hold her hair and Jackie stroked her hand.

"My…baby. I have a baby girl. Jasmine," said Yesenia in jerky breaths. "She was with my brother and his girlfriend since I couldn't work and keep her. It was only going to be for a couple of weeks-I had no choice. Now my brother has gone down south on a work crew and his girlfriend is not in the apartment they rented. I went there. It was somebody else. They say she has gone to live with some-one in a trailer park in Moberly. I don't know where this Moberly is but I have to go there. My baby is there," finished Yesenia collapsing into Al's arms. Mia stood in alarm at the young woman's declaration. "I'm so sorry for telling you this. But I am listening to you tell of how you are brave to go places together. I have no one to go with me but I need to be brave. I need to go places and find my baby," cried Yesenia. Jackie had filled a glass with sweet lemonade and pressed it into Yesenia's hands. They all wiped tears from their cheeks as they gathered closer to her.

"Donna Sue, you better get the car started," at the sound of Anna's voice Yesenia looked up through her tear drenched lashes. The look on Anna's face was sheer determination.

"Mom, you can't go barging in places at your age. You're still recovering from hip surgery. This is not your fight," said Mia.

Anna looked at her daughter and said, "I know it's risky and scary and crazy and it may not be my fight but I can't sit here, safe and sound, knowing there's a baby who isn't. A baby that needs her mother. A baby that needs our help."

"Yeah, I don't think you guys should go busting in some barrio. You could get shot or something," added Masie with real concern.

"If not us, who?" demanded Anna.

Mia raised her chin to reply but instead let out a big sigh. "Okay, I'll go. You guys have no business getting mixed up in something like this." She looked from Anna to Donna Sue to Jackie and Al. She remembered how they had burst into that trailer and threatened to shoot Darren with a paintball gun. There had been no backing down that day and Mia could see the same steely determination in their faces now. "Okay, fine. But I'll drive. Yesenia, Donna Sue, and mom will come with me but the rest of you are staying here," said Mia. "I can't believe I'm doing this. I must be as crazy as the rest of you."

In a few short minutes, Mia's SUV was out of sight and Al, Jackie and Masie were left standing on the pool deck. Al immediately got busy building a stick fire in the big fire pit. She brought out small pieces of wood and stacked them alongside walking back and forth from the woodpile to the fire ring. Jackie went to her house and emerged with pillows and throw blankets for the lounge chairs. Around 11:00 Marquita was dropped off by a co-worker and was surprised to see half the group up and around the fire. It wasn't unusual to find Anna and Jackie up when she closed the Bistro but this was different. The fire was just getting going. She walked into the soft kabuki lighting wondering what was happening. After some of the stories she'd heard, she wouldn't be surprised if the old ladies were throwing a rave or holding a seance. Al greeted her with a smile and asked about her evening. Marquita gave her typical few details while she looked around at the pillows and blankets on the lounge chairs.

"You all doing some kind of girl scout thing?" she asked.

"Marquita! You're not going to believe it. The goddesses were telling us about going to some wild underground drug den and

Yesenia started bawling and said she had a baby that her brother basically kidnapped and she needed help rescuing so Mia, Donna Sue, and Miss Anna took off to find her," blurted out Masie.

Marquita looked at the two old ladies, one busy rearranging the woodpile and the other sanding on a block of wood. They defied everything she knew and understood about rich white women so she didn't know why she was surprised to hear that they'd gone off into the night to get a baby that none of them even knew existed, but she was. She settled herself on one of the lounges and kicked up her feet.

Hours later, Mia's SUV finally rolled up. Marquita helped Al stand up from her lounge and Masie roused Jackie from the chair where she'd been snoring for the last hour. They walked to the edge of the drive and waited as the car doors opened and out came Mia looking like she'd been to hell and back. Donna Sue went around and helped Anna out of the back seat and finally, Yesenia came cradling a sleeping dark-haired baby in her arms. Masie and Marquita went to her immediately and she smiled at them radiantly. Donna Sue told them there were some bags in the back they would need carried in. Masie and Marquita carried in shopping bags filled with baby stuff and diapers to Yesenia's house with her trailing behind them, never taking her eyes off the sleeping child. Mia helped her mom to her house and stayed inside until she was safely tucked in bed before getting back into her car and going home without a word to any of them. The pool lights were turned off but the remains of the fire in the pit burned away as the occupants of the village each closed their door.

It was late morning before any of them roused. Marquita lifted her nose and followed the tantalizing smell of bacon frying in the pavilion. Al was there with what looked like three pounds of bacon draining on paper towels. A large griddle was warming up and there was an enormous bowl of batter sitting nearby. Jackie stumbled out with an empty mug and went to the industrial sized coffee urn. She filled it to the top and drank a few sips before tuning and greeting Al and Marquita. Donna Sue came out looking impeccable as always although her eyes looked tired and she too headed for the coffee urn. Anna opened her door and called to Marquita for some help carrying. There were no visible signs that the activities the night before had had any ill effect on her. Marquita grabbed the hot pads from the counter and picked up a large casserole that smelled of cinnamon, nutmeg and pecans.

"Great minds think alike!" said Anna as she joined her friends at the picnic table. "I figured we would need some love after a night like that. Looks like Al had the same idea."

"Who wants pancakes?" asked Al. "And if you say you want yours without blueberries, I will kick you in the throat." Masie's eyes widened at the comment but Jackie assured her it was just a figure of speech. Well, sort of. Al's stacks of pancakes and bacon went around the table along with Anna's delicious cinnamon pecan coffee cake. Finally, Yesenia and the baby emerged from her tiny house. She seemed shy joining the group around the picnic table but a place was made for her and Al quickly filled a plate.

"This is Jasmine," she said with so much love in her voice it caused a lump in many of their throats.

"Hello, Sweet Girl," said Jackie. The baby peeked out under long dark lashes. She gave Jackie a smile and they all delighted in her tiny white teeth. Jackie tore up a pancake into small bites and Al put some fresh blueberries in a cup. They all watched as Jasmine reached out a little hand and grabbed a bite of pancake and poked it in her mouth.

"She's so beautiful," marveled Masie. "How old is she?"

"Fourteen months," answered Yesenia. "I can't believe I ever let her go," she said, starting to cry.

Anna handed Jasmine another blueberry which she was happily chomping. "You did what you had to do," she said. "That's what being a mother is. Mothers do incredible things for their children. Impossible things. Some that aren't pleasant or easy or popular. Having a baby is like having your own heart walking around outside your body. You did what you had to do at the time." Yesenia's eyes weren't the only wet ones.

"So, are you going to tell us what happened last night? You didn't take my paintball gun so I'm assuming you didn't have to shoot your way out this time," said Al. Marquita looked from one old lady to the next wondering again about them.

"It was no hill for a climber," said Donna Sue. "We drove around the trailer park until Yesenia recognized her brother's truck and we went in and got the baby."

Jackie looked from Anna to Donna Sue and back again opening and closing her mouth like a fish out of water. "If you think that is going to satisfy us heifers, you are sorely mistaken. We want every sordid detail."

"Well, Yesenia, Mia, and I went to the door. Four or five women were sitting around and lots of kids and a big dog. The girlfriend, Lez, was about as friendly as a rattlesnake. Yesenia told her she was there to get the baby and Lez said the baby wasn't there. They discussed it loudly in Spanish and had lots of help from the other ladies in the room. It was clear to us that there was some resistance. I didn't know if the girlfriend understood English but I think I got my message across. I explained to her that we weren't leaving without the baby," said Anna.

What Anna didn't say and what Yesenia witnessed was in the midst of the chaos inside the house trailer, Anna stepped around Yesenia and squared her shoulders to Lez and her friends. She stood with her cane in front of her and both hands resting on it. Mia stood at her elbow. The ringing authority in her voice and the granite set of her face made several of the women back up as she explained who she was going to call and what would happen if the correct paperwork couldn't be provided.

A couple of the women left the trailer at that point, grabbing their kids and scuttling out the door. The others understood enough to know the old lady may be crazy but if she was brave enough to come up in their house, she may very well deliver on what she was promising. They backed off leaving Lez and the big dog blocking the narrow hallway to the bedrooms. Lez, who understood English fine, had been unwilling to back down. Without breaking eye contact with her, Anna instructed Yesenia to call for her daughter. Yesenia shouldered around Lez but was unable to get past the dog that continued barking loudly. After calling her baby's name a few times, a tiny form came tottering out of a bedroom crying and reaching up her arms for Yesenia. Anna continued to stare at Lez as Yesenia scooped up the baby and ran for the door. Yesenia didn't know if any more words were exchanged. She was finally able to exhale when all of the doors shut and Mia drove them out of the trailer park.

The baby was dirty but otherwise seemed well. They stopped at an all night Wal Mart and Mia ran in and grabbed diapers and other necessities. Sitting across from Anna now and hearing her describe in a few sentences what had happened the night before was unreal. The look on Anna's face as she'd faced Lez and her friends, the power she had exuded seemed alien to the lovely, white-haired woman with the warm brown eyes eating pancakes. Yesenia didn't know the word 'formidable' but if she had she would have used it to describe the woman she saw last night. A formidable mother warrior who would have done anything at all to get to her child. Yesenia knew she would owe Anna a debt for the rest of her life. She also hoped she would be as formidable as the old lady when it came to caring for and protecting Jasmine.

Maybe, like wine that improves with age or memories that get sweeter with time, that summer turned out to be one of the most perfect summers in goddess history. Donna Sue's belief that things happen for a reason was proven out again. Yesenia's problem of child care was solved with the best built in babysitters; Anna and Jackie. They figured between the two of them they could keep up with the tot. They delighted in the tiny girl with the huge dark eyes and captivating smile who was equally smitten with her Tias. Yesenia was a transformed woman now that she was reunited with her baby. She held a job on the line in the kitchen and was part of Chef's team that planned weekly menus. Where she had been shy and reserved, she was now engaged, interested and involved.

Al and Anna continued to show Marquita how they prepared their favorite foods and were excited when she asked if they could show her how to grill pork chops and fry catfish. She was slowly losing the hard outer shell that made her slide away from their hugs and open affection. For a girl from the projects, she was adjusting to a different life, a life in the country. She was a hard worker and surprisingly had become Christian's right hand in the garden, a bizarre fact as he was the first man she'd ever met that she had begun to trust.

Masie continued to hold out despite Jackie's efforts to get her to open up to her pain. It seemed the more the older women tried to build a relationship with her, the more she held back. They were sure there was a thorn buried deep in the young woman's heart and they hoped that someday she'd be ready to do something about it. It was clearly a good thing that the three young women, known in the village as the beauties, had formed a bond that the older women hoped fervently would grow and flourish.

As for the goddesses, Anna regained her strength and mobility swimming laps and keeping up with Jasmine. She took great pride and delight in introducing the little girl to the water and teaching her to float and paddle at less than two years old. She hardly ever used her walking stick and the goddesses were relieved to see their Anna, strong and sure return to them. Al continued to work the garden and tend the potted plants and hanging baskets at the village. As long as she had people and plants to tend to, she was perfectly content. Jackie and Donna Sue talked a little about Sweet Sue's last days. It had left a mark on them both to watch a strong, vibrant woman wither and expire. As a kind of therapy, Jackie had taken up woodworking and created beautiful wooden boats out of Russian Mahogany and rich cherry wood. She loved sanding the wood to reveal the inner beauty and fitting the pieces together. Donna Sue continued to practice her diet and health regime. Her old friends were relieved to see she wasn't as strict with herself as she once was and even enjoyed a hotdog roasted over the fire one night. She was content but Anna often caught her statuesque friends with a faraway look in her eye that was full of longing and she wondered if she was thinking of Ron Lake all these years later. They'd heard from Libby several times over the summer. She and Roddy were foster grandparents and absolutely loved having kids around their place. The goddesses were heartened to hear the true happiness in their friend's voice and knew that even though Libby didn't live in the village for long, it was what had brought her to her real home.

Halcyon. It was a word that described the climate, the air, the aura around the tiny house village between June and September that year. It was a tranquil time for old friends that loved being together. That loved each other. That understood there were no guarantees of tomorrow or next summer. They never spoke of it and it never troubled their hearts or minds. They were rich beyond measure and appreciated every day and every minute. It was a time of new beginnings for the young women as well and they grew in ways they never expected to. The fact that the three had become friends, accepting each other, encouraging each other was a wonder in itself. Their backgrounds were so different and if it weren't for the village, they would most likely have never met. Even more wild than their unlikely friendship was the fact that they met four old ladies in their eighties. Not just met them, but learned from them, laughed with them, and grew to love them. The tiny house village with the pavilion, pool, and fire pit was the place where the magic of acceptance, healing and love happened.

But the real magic was the goddesses themselves, they were the village. God willing and if the creek don't rise, they'd pass their special brand of magic on to the next group of women who could no doubt muddle along on their own but would find life more abundant, fuller, richer, if they could do it, Goddess Style.

www.ingramcontent.com/pod-product-compliance
Lightning Source LLC
Chambersburg PA
CBHW070444300726
48975CB00007B/2035